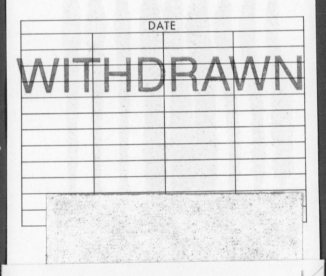

WITHDRAWN

This Self is not realizable by study nor even by intelligence and learning. The Self reveals its essence only to him who applies himself to the Self. He who has not given up the ways of vice, who cannot control himself, who is not at peace within, whose mind is distracted, can never realize the Self, though full of all the learning in the world.

Katha Upanishad

See all things, not in process of becoming, but in Being, and see themselves in the other. Each being contains in itself the whole intelligible world. Therefore All is everywhere. Each is there All, and All is each. Man as he now is has ceased to be the All. But when he ceases to be an individual, he raises himself again and penetrates the whole world.

Plotinus

You have the same faculty as I...only you do not trust or cultivate it. You can see what I see, if you choose....

William Blake

I am he who comes forth advancing, whose name is unknown · I am Yesterday · "Seer of Millions of Years" is my name · I pass along, I pass along the paths of the divine celestial judges ·

I open the door in heaven · I rule my throne · I open the way for the births which take place on this day · I am the child who traverseth the road of Yesterday ·

I am "He who cannot be known". The Red Fiends have their faces directed against me ·

Hail, O my Creator, I am he who hath no power to walk, the Great Knot who dwelleth in Yesterday. The might of my strength is within my hand, I am not known [by thee], but I am he who knoweth thee I cannot be held in the hand, but I am he who can hold thee in his hand.

Hail, O Egg! Hail, O Egg! I am Horus who liveth for millions of years, whose flame shineth upon you and bringeth your hearts unto me. I am master of my throne. I advance at this season. I have opened a path. I have delivered myself from all evil things.

The Book of the Dead, 15th Dynasty, circa 3700 BC *Translated from the Medici Society version, 1913 by E.A. Wallis Budge, late keeper of Egyptian and Assyrian Antiquities, British Museum.*

Copyright (c) 1977 Gerry Goldberg
All rights reserved. For information write:
St. Martin's Press, Inc., 175 Fifth Avenue, New York, N.Y. 10010.
Library of Congress Catalog Card Number: PN6071.S412S7.

Library of Congress Cataloging in Publication Data

        Goldberg, Gerry.
        Strange Glory.

1) Self-realization — Literary Collections.
2) Self-realization — Quotations, maxims, etc.

PN6071.S412S7   1977   820'.8   77-76635

First published 1975 by McClelland & Stewart, Ltd., Canada.

Produced by James-Christen Associates, Toronto, Canada.

ISBN Hard cover   0-312-76.387-5

       Soft cover   0-312-76.388-3

STRANGE GLORY

edited by Gerry Goldberg

Mara rabbi allardi dini endavour esa couns alim.

transmission picked up from the moon surface by
Alfred M. Worden the pilot of the command lunar
module the *Endeavour* on August 1, 1971 at 11:15 a.m.
during the flight of Apollo 15.

ST. MARTIN'S PRESS   NEW YORK

INTRODUCTION

Compared with what we ought to be, we are only half awake. Our fires are damped, our drafts are checked. We are making use of only a small part of our possible mental and physical resources.

William James: *The Energies of Man* (1936)

Our 'everyday' awareness of life is so limiting that we are as sleepwalkers and our culture, rather than shaking us awake, serves to perpetuate this state of somnambulism. Our ethics, morality and value systems are based on the idea that it is more desirable to spend our lives enslaved by material possessions than to struggle up through levels of "being."

We are defeated not only by the narrowness of our perspective and fear of the darkness, but by our excuses. We believe that without habits, social conventions, routines we could not exist and so we hide behind them, but what we think protects, in fact, oppresses us. Circumstances become our prisons, other people our jailers. We live in silence and squander our birthright. Even our brain betrays us in the name of security. It becomes a "reducing valve," shutting out stimuli that, in our pursuit of everyday goals, we have decided are unimportant and extraneous, and so we are denied the full richness, meaning and wonder of the world. Being less than we are, we fail to touch life. Insulated by our segregated and attenuated senses, we feel, we see, we listen, we taste within predetermined limits. Never do we experience the intensity of real awakening, except for the sudden crisis or pleasure that changes our reality, allowing our true nature to break through for an instant. Yet like the magician Houdini, who drew on his latent powers of control, will and perception to free himself from wordly restraint, we can draw on our latent powers to become aware of a potential "knowing" within us beyond the ordinary, *a source of power, a glory.*

The limitations of our biological equipment may condemn us to the role of Peeping Toms at the keyhole of eternity. But at least let us take the stuffing out of the keyhole.

Arthur Koestler: *The Roots of Coincidence* (1972)

Grasping our potential is an individual quest, a type of "cosmic heroism." Through this quest all mankind will ascend to the next stage of evolution, where all our faculties and abilities are working in harmony; where the outer world and the inner world are one. Our hope lies in mind, body and spirit being rejoined, but first we must realize that our present way of doing and being is not good enough and cannot last.

The world conceals a tremendous reality that we can "see" if we know how to "look." The ancient Hindu Scriptures, the Vedic hymns, the "Upanishads," and the "Bhagavad-Gita" teach that the human soul, the Atman, is identical with the Godhead, Brahman. Thus if one could penetrate through the outer layers to the depths of being, one would find Brahman, and the deeper one penetrates the closer one approaches the strange powers that all men can possess. Zen teaches that the mind is like a pond, and we must quiet the surface so that it becomes a mirror reflecting the moon, our basic divinity, showing us our inner self.

Each chapter of *Strange Glory* depicts a step in the

inward journey, and opens and closes with one of the Zen Buddhist "Oxherding Pictures." The pattern of Jesus's life is similar to that of the sage seen in these pictures. The Oxherder has lost his ox, symbolizing the self. The ox is found, made to change its direction, tamed and gradually transformed from black to white. For a time the ox disappears and nothing remains but the full moon, symbolizing the Mind, the Dream and the Earth. But this is not the final stage. The Oxherder returns riding on his ox. And now he loves. He reflects what is about him, and what is about him reflects what is in him. He is in harmony within himself and with the outer world. He is now prepared to perform acts of significance with faith, love and courage. The Oxherder's journey of self-regeneration is the journey of self-awareness that we all must take.

In Chapter One the Oxherder is lost and alone, alienated from himself and the natural world. In Chapter Two he finds the power of the senses, but he must liberate them from the tyranny of his ego and the fears and miseries of the world. Chapter Three is the union of acquired knowledge and imagination. Within this union he will find creativity and commitment to himself and the world about him. From this Chapter Four emerges. Only in dreams will we ever build a "New Jerusalem," and in building, we see and experience glimpses of our potential. Seeing what he could be, the Oxherder enters the fifth and final stage, Chapter Five. Stripping away his false beliefs and worldly possessions, he hears the voices of the gods and sees their faces. In touching their hands, he becomes a reflection of all that surrounds him — *he becomes a god.*

As a man grows and gains new freedoms, insights, he becomes aware that at each point...he must risk himself anew....He confronts new aspects of himself, which, though wonderful, may also be terrible.

Zarkon: *The Zarkon Principle* (1975)

Our normal state of consciousness shuts off the awareness of our affinity with creation, our union with the divine. If we are capable of modifying or editing our sensory processes then we are capable of enhancing them to child-like or animal-like sensitivity. This ecstatic state has been referred to as: "cosmic consciousness," "peak-experience," "satori." All our senses are functioning to their fullest potential. We see an upward spiraling of evolution in which we will find our true purpose and significance. All of us have had the power and the glory of the heavens, yet we have lost them and they are strange to us. When we regain our primitive condition of awareness, *we will walk in eternity with the gods.*

There is nothing new except what has been forgotten.

Attributed to Marie Antoinette's milliner while remodeling a hat for the queen in 1789.

gerry goldberg: october 11, 1976.

DEATH.

THE STAR.

CONTENTS

1. Despair

Around and within him, he sees only the lifeless, the despairing, the monstrous. There is no refuge, no solace no escape.

2. Liberation

The sunrise, the dew on a flower, the silence between heartbeats — these are not answers, but questions. He listens — and hears a music beyond sounds; he looks — and sees a vision beyond light; he waits....These are a prelude to order.

3. Creativity

The order disclosed, he longs to be folded in it. But he must not only accept the world — that would be half a life. His imagination and the world are two hands clapping.

4. New Jerusalem

The sail and the wind that become motion, the sea and the sand that become shore, the universe and the imagination that become man. He is home.

5. Godhead

Seeing himself, his shape vanishes; dreaming himself, he is real; being most human, he is God.

Dedicated to Virgil Finlay, Hannes Bok and Lynd Ward, who gave us their personal glories.

moments, people and places that gave the book a worth, many thanks to: harlan ellison, who taught me to yell against the darkness with hope; colin wilson, who taught me to see and believe; gareth colman, who drew it; the who, who sang it; jerry title and peter maher, who forced me; david allen and ronnie hoffman, who listened and spoke softly; richard harris, who gave me "mac arthur's park"; rollo may, george b. leonard and r.d. laing, who helped me to grow with strength; 11:43 p.m.; trips to miami, new york, cleveland and buffalo, which gave my family precious and unforgettable moments; annette cohen, barbara jacobsen, joan laird, marilyn lightstone, virginia and *the toad*, who taught me kindness; marvin hamlish, who gave my wife "the way we were"; especially barrie reynolds, who not only began this journey but was always either beside me or infront of me; h.p. lovecraft, george wright, richard matheson, eric slavens, ray bradbury, and harvey goodman, who live within me; leonard gasparini, ivan t. sanderson and allen spraggett, who understood; tom dunne, who had the faith; rita ellen burns and frank touby, who said "hello"; the late jim croce, who gave me "time in a bottle"; may 12 and september 24; robert bloch, who became my friend and cared; my mother, who taught me to touch life; my brothers, who give and give; my father, who taught me to grasp beyond my reach; my wife marion, who put up with a lot and taught me about things that really matter; my daughters sari and shalyn, who taught me to be....

to sari and shalyn with envy, dreams and joy
8·8·   october 14, 1976

STRANGE GLORY

There are things in the psyche which I do not produce,
but which produce themselves and have their own life.

C.G. Jung

DESPAIR

"The beast has never gone astray, and what is the use of searching for him? The reason why the oxherd is not on intimate terms with him is because the oxherd himself has violated his own inmost nature. The beast is lost, for the oxherd has himself been led out of the way through his deluding senses. Desire for gain and fear of loss burn like fire; ideas of right and wrong shoot up like a phalanx. Alone in the wilderness, lost in the jungle, the boy is searching, searching! Exhausted and in despair, he knows not where to go."

SEARCHING FOR THE OX

First of the Ten Oxherding Pictures, by Kaku-an Shi-en. Chinese. Sung Dynasty, 960—1279.

The Theogony

Hesiod,
Translated by C.A. Elton

Embraced by Saturn, Rhea gave to light
A glorious race ...
But then, as issuing from the sacred womb
They touch'd the mother's knees, did Saturn huge
Devour, revolving in his troubled thought
Lest other of celestials should possess
Amidst th'immortals kingly sway, for he
Had heard from Earth and from the starry Heaven
That it was doom'd by Fate, strong though he were,
To his own son he should bow down his strength.
Jove's wisdom this fulfill'd. No blind design
He therefore cherish'd and in crooked craft
Devour'd his children. But on Rhea prey'd
Never-forgotten anguish ...

We are betrayed by what is false within.

George Meredith

**The outer divorced from any illumination from the inner
is a state of darkness. We are in an age of darkness.**

R.D. Laing, *The Politics of Experience* (1967)

Midnight

Archibald Lampman

From where I sit, I see the stars,
    And down the chilly floor
The moon between the frozen bars
    Is glimmering dim and hoar.

Without in many a peaked mound
    The glinting snowdrifts lie;
There is no voice or living sound;
    The embers slowly die.

Yet some wild thing is in mine ear;
    I hold my breath and hark;
Out of the depth I seem to hear
    A crying in the dark;

No sound of man or wife or child,
    No sound of beast that groans,
Or of the wind that whistles wild,
    Or of the tree that moans:

I know not what it is I hear;
    I bend my head and hark:
I cannot drive it from mine ear,
    That crying in the dark.

When the Waters Were Changed
Idries Shah

Once upon a time Khidr, the Teacher of Moses, called upon mankind with a warning. At a certain date, he said, all the water in the world which had not been specially hoarded, would disappear. It would then be renewed, with different water, which would drive men mad.

Only one man listened to the meaning of this advice. He collected water and went to a secure place where he stored it, and waited for the water to change its character.

On the appointed date the streams stopped running, the wells went dry, and the man who had listened, seeing this happening, went to his retreat and drank his preserved water.

When he saw, from his security, the waterfalls again beginning to flow, this man descended among the other sons of men. He found that they were thinking and talking in an entirely different way from before; yet they had no memory of what had happened, nor of having been warned. When he tried to talk to them, he realized that they thought that he was mad, and they showed hostility or compassion, not understanding.

At first he drank none of the new water, but went back to his concealment, to draw on his supplies, every day. Finally, however, he took the decision to drink the new water because he could not bear the loneliness of living, behaving and thinking in a different way from everyone else. He drank the new water, and became like the rest. Then he forgot all about his own store of special water, and his fellows began to look upon him as a madman who had miraculously been restored to sanity.

It would be the final error of reason...to deny that the furies exist, or to strive to manipulate them out of existence...We may, of course, be able to buy off the furies for a while; being of the earth and ancient, they have been around much longer than the rational consciousness that would entirely supplant them, and so they can afford to wait...

William Barret, *Irrational Man* (1958)

The Whimper of Whipped Dogs

Harlan Ellison

On the night after the day she had stained the louvered window shutters of her new apartment on East 52nd Street, Beth saw a woman slowly and hideously knifed to death in the courtyard of her building. She was one of twenty-six witnesses to the ghoulish scene, and, like them, she did nothing to stop it.

She saw it all, every moment of it, without break and with no impediment to her view. Quite madly, the thought crossed her mind as she watched in horrified fascination, that she had the sort of marvelous line of observation Napoleon had sought when he caused to have constructed at the *Comédie-Française* theaters, a curtained box at the rear, so he could watch the audience as well as the stage. The night was clear, the moon was full, she had just turned off the 11:30 movie on channel 2 after the second commercial break, realizing she had already seen Robert Taylor in *Westward the Women,* and had disliked it the first time; and the apartment was quite dark.

She went to the window, to raise it six inches for the night's sleep, and she saw the woman stumble into the courtyard. She was sliding along the wall, clutching her left arm with her right hand. Con Ed had installed mercury-vapor lamps on the poles; there had been sixteen assaults in seven months; the courtyard was illuminated with a chill purple glow that made the blood streaming down the woman's left arm look black and shiny. Beth saw every detail with utter clarity, as though magnified a thousand power under a microscope, solarized as if it had been a television commercial.

The woman threw back her head, as if she were trying to scream, but there was no sound. Only the traffic on First Avenue, late cabs foraging for singles paired for the night at Maxwell's Plum and Friday's and Adam's Apple. But that was over there, beyond. Where *she* was, down there seven floors below, in the courtyard, everything seemed silently suspended in an invisible force-field.

Beth stood in the darkness of her apartment, and realized she had raised the window completely. A tiny balcony lay just over the low sill; now not even glass separated her from the sight; just the wrought-iron balcony railing and seven floors to the courtyard below.

The woman staggered away from the wall, her head still thrown back, and Beth could see she was in her mid-thirties, with dark hair cut in a shag; it was impossible to tell if she was pretty: terror had contorted her features and her mouth was a twisted black slash, opened but emitting no sound. Cords stood out in her neck. She had lost one shoe, and her steps were uneven, threatening to dump her to the pavement.

The man came around the corner of the building, into the courtyard. The knife he held was enormous — or perhaps it only seemed so: Beth remembered a bone-handled fish knife her father had used one summer at the

lake in Maine: it folded back on itself and locked, revealing eight inches of serrated blade. The knife in the hand of the dark man in the courtyard seemed to be similar.

The woman saw him and tried to run, but he leaped across the distance between them and grabbed her by the hair and pulled her head back as though he would slash her throat in the next reaper-motion.

Then the woman screamed.

The sound skirled up into the courtyard like bats trapped in an echo chamber, unable to find a way out, driven mad. It went on and on....

The man struggled with her and she drove her elbows into his sides and he tried to protect himself, spinning her around by her hair, the terrible scream going up and up and never stopping. She came loose and he was left with a fistful of hair torn out by the roots. As she spun out, he slashed straight across and opened her up just below the breasts. Blood sprayed through her clothing and the man was soaked; it seemed to drive him even more berserk. He went at her again, as she tried to hold herself together, the blood pouring down over her arms.

She tried to run, teetered against the wall, slid sidewise, and the man struck the brick surface. She was away, stumbling over a flower bed, falling, getting to her knees as he threw himself on her again. The knife came up in a flashing arc that illuminated the blade strangely with purple light. And still she screamed.

Lights came on in dozens of apartments and people appeared at windows.

He drove the knife to the hilt into her back, high on the right shoulder. He used both hands.

Beth caught it all in jagged flashes — the man, the woman, the knife, the blood, the expressions on the faces of those watching from the windows. Then lights clicked off in the windows, but they still stood there, watching.

She wanted to yell, to scream, "What are you doing to that woman?" But her throat was frozen, two iron hands that had been immersed in dry ice for ten thousand years clamped around her neck. She could feel the blade sliding into her own body.

Somehow — it seemed impossible but there it was down there, happening somehow — the woman struggled erect and *pulled* herself off the knife. Three steps, she took three steps and fell into the flower bed again. The man was howling now, like a great beast, the sounds inarticulate, bubbling up from his stomach. He fell on her and the knife went up and came down, then again, and again, and finally it was all a blur of motion, and her scream of lunatic bats went on till it faded off and was gone.

Beth stood in the darkness, trembling and crying, the sight filling her eyes with horror. And when she could no longer bear to look at what he was doing down there to the unmoving piece of meat over which he worked, she looked up and around at the windows of darkness where the others still stood — even as she stood — and somehow she could see their faces, bruise-purple with the dim light from the mercury lamps, and there was a universal sameness to their expressions. The women stood with their nails biting into the upper arms of their men, their tongues edging from the corners of their mouths; the men were wild-eyed and smiling. They all looked as though they were at cock fights. Breathing deeply. Drawing some sustenance from the grisly scene below. An exhalation of sound, deep, deep, as though from caverns beneath the earth. Flesh pale and moist.

...the experience of evil, and to some extent this experience alone, produces maturity, real life, real command of the powers and tasks of life.

Heinrich Zimmer, *The King and the Corpse* (1960)

And it was then that she realized the courtyard had grown foggy, as though mist off the East River had rolled up 52nd Street in a veil that would obscure the details of what the knife and the man were still doing...endlessly doing it...long after there was any joy in it...still doing it ...again and again....

But the fog was unnatural, thick and gray and filled with tiny scintillas of light. She stared at it, rising up in the empty space of the courtyard. Bach in the cathedral, stardust in a vacuum chamber.

Beth saw eyes.

There, up there, at the ninth floor and higher, two great eyes, as surely as night and the moon, there were *eyes*.

And — a face? Was that a face, could she be sure, was she imagining it...a face? In the roiling vapors of chill fog something lived, something brooding and patient and utterly malevolent had been summoned up to witness what was happening down there in the flower bed. Beth tried to look away, but could not. The eyes, those primal burning eyes, filled with an abysmal antiquity yet frighteningly bright and anxious like the eyes of a child; eyes filled with tomb depths, ancient and new, chasm-filled, burning, gigantic and deep as an abyss, holding her, compelling her. The shadow play was being staged not only for the tenants in their windows, watching and drinking of the scene, but for some *other*. Not on frigid tundra or waste moors, not in subterranean caverns or on some faraway world circling a dying sun, but here, in the city, here the eyes of that *other* watched.

Shaking with the effort, Beth wrenched her eyes from those burning depths up there beyond the ninth floor, only to see again the horror that had brought that *other*. And she was struck for the first time by the awfulness of what she was witnessing, she was released from the immobility that had held her like a coelacanth in shale, she was filled with the blood thunder pounding against the membranes of her mind: she had *stood* there! She had done nothing, nothing! A woman had been butchered and she had said nothing, done nothing. Tears had been useless, tremblings had been pointless, she *had done nothing!*

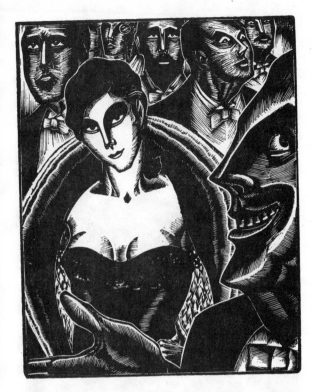

Then she heard hysterical sounds midway between laughter and giggling, and as she stared up into that great face rising in the fog and chimneysmoke of the night, she heard *herself* making those deranged gibbon noises and from the man below a pathetic, trapped sound, like the whimper of whipped dogs.

She was staring up into that face again. She hadn't wanted to see it again — ever. But she was locked with those smoldering eyes, overcome with the feeling that they were childlike, though she *knew* they were incalculably ancient.

Then the butcher below did an unspeakable thing and Beth reeled with dizziness and caught the edge of the window before she could tumble out onto the balcony; she steadied herself and fought for breath.

She felt herself being looked at, and for a long moment of frozen terror she feared she might have caught the attention of that face up there in the fog. She clung to the window, feeling everything growing faraway and dim, and stared straight across the court. She *was* being watched. Intently. By the young man in the seventh-floor window across from her own apartment. Steadily, he was looking at her. Through the strange fog with its burning eyes feasting on the sight below, he was staring at her.

As she felt herself blacking out, in the moment before unconsciousness, the thought flickered and fled that there was something terribly familiar about his face.

It rained the next day. East 52nd Street was slick and shining with the oil rainbows. The rain washed the dog turds into the gutters and nudged them down and down to the catch-basin openings. People bent against the slanting rain, hidden beneath umbrellas, looking like enormous, scurrying black mushrooms. Beth went out to get the newspapers after the police had come and gone.

The news reports dwelled with loving emphasis on the twenty-six tenants of the building who had watched in cold interest as Leona Ciarelli, 37 of 455 Fort Washington Avenue, Manhattan, had been systematically stabbed to death by Burton H. Wells, 41, an unemployed electrician, who had been subsequently shot to death by two off-duty police officers when he burst into Michael's Pub on 55th Street, covered with blood and brandishing a knife that authorities later identified as the murder weapon.

Your own self is your own Cain that murders your own Abel. For every action and motion of self has the spirit of Anti-Christ and murders the divine life within you.

William Law

She had thrown up twice that day. Her stomach seemed incapable of retaining anything solid, and the taste of bile lay along the back of her tongue. She could not blot the scenes of the night before from her mind; she re-ran them again and again, every movement of that reaper arm playing over and over as though on a short loop of memory. The woman's head thrown back for silent screams. The blood. Those eyes in the fog.

She was drawn again and again to the window, to stare down into the courtyard and the street. She tried to superimpose over the bleak Manhattan concrete the view from her window in Swann House at Bennington: the little yard and another white, frame dormitory; the fantastic apple trees; and from the other window the rolling hills and gorgeous Vermont countryside; her memory skittered through the change of seasons. But there was always concrete and the rain-slick streets; the rain on the pavement was black and shiny as blood.

She tried to work, rolling up the tambour closure of the old rolltop desk she had bought on Lexington Avenue and hunching over the graph sheets of choreographer's charts. But Labanotation was merely a Jackson Pollock jumble of arcane hieroglyphics to her today, instead of the careful representation of eurhythmics she had studied four years to perfect. And before that, Farmington.

The phone rang. It was the secretary from the Taylor Dance Company, asking when she would be free. She had to beg off. She looked at her hand, lying on the graph-sheets of figures Laban had devised, and she saw her fingers trembling. She had to beg off. Then she called Guzman at the Downtown Ballet Company, to tell him she would be late with the charts.

"My God, lady, I have ten dancers sitting around in a rehearsal hall getting their leotards sweaty! What do you expect me to do?"

She explained what had happened the night before. And as she told him, she realized the newspapers had been justified in holding that tone against the twenty-six witnesses to the death of Leona Ciarelli. Paschal Guzman listened, and when he spoke again, his voice was several octaves lower, and he spoke more slowly. He said he understood and she could take a little longer to prepare the charts. But there was a distance in his voice, and he hung up while she was thanking him.

She dressed in an argyle sweater vest in shades of dark purple, and a pair of fitted khaki gabardine trousers. She had to go out, to walk around. To do what? To think about other things. As she pulled on the Fred Braun chunky heels, she idly wondered if that heavy silver bracelet was still in the window of Georg Jensen's. In the elevator, the young man from the window across the courtyard stared at her. Beth felt her body begin to tremble again. She went deep into the corner of the box when he entered behind her.

Between the fifth and fourth floors, he hit the *off* switch and the elevator jerked to a halt.

Beth stared at him and he smiled innocently.

"Hi. My name's Gleeson, Ray Gleeson, I'm in 714."

She wanted to demand he turn the elevator back on, by what right did he pre*sume* to do such a thing, what did he mean by this, turn it on at once or suffer the consequences. That was what she *wanted* to do. Instead, from the same place she had heard the gibbering laughter the night before, she heard her voice, much smaller and much less possessed than she had trained it to be, saying, "Beth

O'Neill, I live in 701."

The thing about it, was that *the elevator was stopped.* And she was frightened. But he leaned against the paneled wall, very well-dressed, shoes polished, hair combed and probably blown dry with a hand drier, and he *talked* to her as if they were across a table at L'Argenteuil. "You just moved in, huh?"

"About two months ago."

"Where did you go to school? Bennington or Sarah Lawrence?"

"Bennington. How did you know?"

He laughed, and it was a nice laugh. "I'm an editor at a religious book publisher; every year we get half a dozen Bennington, Sarah Lawrence, Smith girls. They come hopping in like grasshoppers, ready to revolutionize the publishing industry."

"What's wrong with that? You sound like you don't care for them."

"Oh, I *love* them, they're marvelous. They think they know how to write better than the authors we publish. Had one darlin' little item who was given galleys of three books to proof, and she rewrote all three. I think she's working as a table-swabber in a Horn & Hardart's now."

She didn't reply to that. She would have pegged him as an anti-feminist, ordinarily; if it had been anyone else speaking. But the eyes. There was something terribly

familiar about his face. She was enjoying the conversation;
she rather liked him.

"What's the nearest big city to Bennington?"

"Albany, New York. About sixty miles."

"How long does it take to drive there?"

"From Bennington? About an hour and a half."

"Must be a nice drive, that Vermont country, really
pretty. It's an all-girls' school, they haven't thought of
making it co-ed? How many girls enrolled there?"

"Approximately."

"Yes, approximately."

"About four hundred."

"What did you major in?"

"I was a dance major, specializing in Labanotation.
That's the way you write choreography."

"It's all electives, I gather. You don't have to take
anything required, like sciences, for example." He didn't
change tone as he said, "That was a terrible thing last
night. I saw you watching. I guess a lot of us were watching. It was really a terrible thing."

She nodded dumbly. Fear came back.

"I understand the cops got him. Some nut, they don't
even know why he killed her, or why he went charging into
that bar. It was really an awful thing. I'd very much like to

have dinner with you one night soon, if you're not attached."

"That would be all right."

"Maybe Wednesday. There's an Argentinian place I
know. You might like it."

"That would be all right."

"Why don't you turn on the elevator, and we can go,"
he said, and smiled again. She did it, wondering why it
was he had stopped the elevator in the first place.

On her third date with him, they had their first fight. It
was at a party thrown by a director of television commercials. He lived on the ninth floor of their building. He
had just done a series of spots for *Sesame Street* (the letters
"U" for Underpass, "T" for Tunnel, lower-case "b" for
boats, "C" for cars; the numbers 1 to 6 and the numbers
1 to 20; the words *light* and *dark*) and was celebrating his
move from the arena of commercial tawdriness and its
attendant $75,000 a year to the sweet fields of educational
programming and its accompanying descent into low-pay
respectability. There was a logic in his joy Beth could not
quite understand, and when she talked with him about it,
in a far corner of the kitchen, his arguments didn't seem to
parse. But he seemed happy, and his girl friend, a long-
legged ex-model from Philadelphia, continued to drift to
him and away from him, like some exquisite undersea
plant, touching his hair and kissing his neck, murmuring
words of pride and barely-submerged sexuality. Beth

found it bewildering, though the celebrants were all bright and lively.

In the living room, Ray was sitting on the arm of the sofa, hustling a stewardess named Luanne. Beth could tell he was hustling: he was trying to look casual. When he *wasn't* hustling, he was always intense, about everything. She decided to ignore it, and wandered around the apartment, sipping at a Tanqueray and tonic.

There were framed prints of abstract shapes clipped from a calendar printed in Germany. They were in metal Crosse frames.

In the dining room a huge door from a demolished building somewhere in the city had been handsomely stripped, teaked and refinished. It was now the dinner table.

A Lightolier fixture attached to the wall over the bed swung out, levered up and down, tipped, and its burnished globe-head revolved a full three hundred and sixty degrees.

She was standing in the bedroom, looking out the window, when she realized this had been one of the rooms in which light had gone on, gone off; one of the rooms that had contained a silent watcher in the death of Leona Ciarelli.

When she returned to the living room, she looked around more carefully. With only three or four exceptions — the stewardess, a young married couple from the second floor, a stockbroker from Hemphill, Noyes — everyone at the party had been a witness to the slaying.

"I'd like to go." she told him.

"Why, aren't you having a good time?" asked the

The Fear

Andrew Young

How often I turn round
To face the beast that bound by bound
Leaps on me from behind,
Only to see a bough that heaves
With sudden gust of wind
Or blackbird raking withered leaves

A dog may find me out
Or badger toss a white-lined snout;
And one day as I softly trod
Looking for nothing stranger than
A fox or stoat I met a man
And even that seemed not too odd.

And yet in any place I go
I watch and listen as all creatures do
For what I cannot see or hear,
For something warns me everywhere
That even in my land of birth
I trespass on the earth.

stewardess, a mocking smile crossing her perfect little face.

"Like all Bennington ladies," Ray said, answering for Beth, "she is enjoying herself most by not enjoying herself at all. It's a trait of the anal retentive. Being here in someone else's apartment, she can't empty ashtrays or rewind the toilet paper roll so it doesn't hang a tongue, and being tightassed, her nature demands we go."

"All right, Beth, let's say our goodbyes and take off. The Phantom Rectum strikes again."

She slapped him and the stewardess's eyes widened. But the smile stayed frozen where it had appeared.

He grabbed her wrist before she could do it again. "Garbanzo beans, baby," he said, holding her wrist tighter than necessary.

They went back to her apartment, and after sparring silently with kitchen cabinet doors slammed and the television being tuned too loud, they got to her bed, and he tried to perpetuate the metaphor by fucking her in the ass. He had her on elbows and knees before she realized what he was doing; she struggled to turn over and he rode her bucking and tossing without a sound. And when it was clear to him that she would never permit it, he grabbed her breast from underneath and squeezed so hard she howled in pain. He dumped her on her back, rubbed himself between her legs a dozen times, and came on her stomach.

Beth lay with her eyes closed and an arm thrown across her face. She wanted to cry, but found she could not. Ray lay on her and said nothing. She wanted to rush to the bathroom and shower, but he did not move, till long after his semen had dried on their bodies.

"Who did you date at college?" he asked.

"I didn't date anyone very much." Sullen.

"No heavy makeouts with wealthy lads from Williams and Dartmouth ... no Amherst intellectuals begging you to save them from creeping faggotry by permitting them to

stick their carrots in your sticky little slit?''

''Stop it!''

''Come on, baby, it couldn't all have been knee socks and little round circle-pins. You don't expect me to believe you didn't get a little mouthful of cock from time to time. It's only, what? about fifteen miles to Williamstown? I'm sure the Williams werewolves were down burning the highway to your cunt on weekends, you can level with old Uncle Ray....''

''*Why are you like this?!*'' She started to move, to get away from him, and he grabbed her by the shoulder, forced her to lie down again. Then he rose up over her and said, ''I'm like this because I'm a New Yorker, baby. Because I live in this fucking city every day. Because I have to play patty-cake with the ministers and other sanctified holy-joe assholes who want their goodness and lightness tracts published by the Blessed Sacrament Publishing and Storm Window Company of 277 Park Avenue, when what I *really* want to do is toss the stupid psalm-suckers out the thirty-seventh floor window and listen to them quote chapter-and-worse all the way down. Because I've lived in this great big snapping dog of a city all my life and I'm mad as a mudfly, for chrissakes!''

She lay unable to move, breathing shallowly, filled with a sudden pity and affection for him. His face was white and strained, and she knew he was saying things to her that only a bit too much *Almadén* and exact timing would have let him say.

''What do you expect from me,'' he said, his voice softer now, but no less intense, ''do you expect kindness and gentility and understanding and a hand on *your* hand when the smog burns your eyes? I can't do it, I haven't got it. No one has it in this cesspool of a city. Look around you; what do you think is happening here? They take rats and they put them in boxes and when there are too many of them, some of the little fuckers go out of their minds

and start gnawing the rest to death. *It ain't no different here, baby!* It's rat time for everybody in this madhouse. You can't expect to jam as many people into this stone thing as we do, with buses and taxis and dogs shitting themselves scrawny and noise night and day and no money and not enough places to live and no place to go have a decent think...you can't do it without making the time right for some god-forsaken other kind of thing to be born! You can't hate everyone around you, and kick every beggar and nigger and *mestizo* shithead, you can't have cabbies stealing from you and taking tips they don't deserve, and then cursing you, you can't walk in the soot till your collar turns black, and your body stinks with the smell of flaking brick and decaying brains, you can't do it without calling up some kind of awful —''

He stopped.

His face bore the expression of a man who has just received brutal word of the death of a loved one. He suddenly lay down, rolled over, and turned off.

She lay beside him, trembling, trying desperately to remember where she had seen his face before.

He didn't call her again, after the night of the party. And when they met in the hall, he pointedly turned away, as though he had given her some obscure chance and she had refused to take it. Beth thought she understood: though Ray Gleeson had not been her first affair, he had been the first to reject her so completely. The first to put her not only out of his bed and his life, but even out of his world. It was as though she were invisible, not even beneath contempt, simply not there.

If thou has not seen the devil, look at thine own self.

Jalal-uddin Rumi

She busied herself with other things.

She took on three new charting jobs for Guzman and a new group that had formed on Staten Island, of all places. She worked furiously and they gave her new assignments; they even paid her.

She tried to decorate the apartment with a less precise touch. Huge poster blowups of Merce Cunningham and Martha Graham replaced the Brueghel prints that had reminded her of the view looking down the hill toward Williams. The tiny balcony outside her window, the balcony she swept and set about with little flower boxes in night of the slaughter, the night of the fog with eyes, that balcony she swept and set about with flower boxes in which she planted geraniums, petunias, dwarf zinnias and other hardy perennials. Then, closing the window, she went to give herself, to involve herself in this city to which she had brought her ordered life.

And the city responded to her overtures:

Seeing off an old friend from Bennington, at Kennedy International, she stopped at the terminal coffee shop to have a sandwich. The counter circled like a moat a center service island that had huge advertising cubes rising above it on burnished poles. The cubes proclaimed the delights of Fun City. *New York is a Summer Festival,* they said, and *Joseph Papp Presents Shakespeare in Central Park* and *Visit the Bronx Zoo* and *You'll Adore our Contentious but Lovable Cabbies.* The food emerged from a window far down the service area and moved slowly on a conveyor belt through the hordes of screaming waitresses who slathered the counter with redolent washcloths. The lunchroom had all the charm and dignity of a steel rolling mill, and approximately the same noise-level. Beth ordered a cheeseburger that cost a dollar and a quarter, and a glass of milk.

When it came, it was cold, the cheese unmelted, and the patty of meat resembling nothing so much as a dirty scouring pad. The bun was cold and untoasted. There was no lettuce under the patty.

Beth managed to catch the waitress's eye. The girl approached with an annoyed look. "Please toast the bun and may I have a piece of lettuce?" Beth said.

"We dun' do that," the waitress said, turned half away as though she would walk in a moment.

"You don't do what?"

"We dun' toass the bun here."

"Yes, but I *want* the bun toasted," Beth said, firmly.

Man has become alienated from his own basic nature by the artificiality of society.

Rousseau

"An' you got to pay for extra lettuce."

"If I was asking for *extra* lettuce," Beth said, getting annoyed, "I would pay for it, but since there's *no* lettuce here, I don't think I should be charged extra for the first piece."

"We dun' do that."

The waitress started to walk away. "Hold it," Beth said, raising her voice just enough so the assembly-line eaters on either side stared at her. "You mean to tell me I have to pay a dollar and a quarter and I can't get a piece of lettuce or even get the bun toasted?"

"Ef you dun' like it...."

"Take it back."

"You gotta pay for it, you order it."

"I said take it back, I don't want the fucking thing!"

The waitress scratched it off the check. The milk cost 27c and tasted going-sour. It was the first time in her life that Beth had said that word aloud.

At the cashier's stand, Beth said to the sweating man with the felt-tip pens in his shirt pocket, "Just out of curiosity, are you interested in complaints?"

"No!" he said, snarling, quite literally snarling. He did not look up as he punched out 73c and it came rolling down the chute.

The city responded to her overtures:

It was raining again. She was trying to cross Second Avenue, with the light. She stepped off the curb and a car came sliding through the red and splashed her. "Hey!" she yelled.

"Eat shit, sister!" the driver yelled back, turning the corner.

Her boots, her legs and her overcoat were splattered with mud. She stood trembling on the curb.

The city responded to her overtures:

She emerged from the building at One Astor Place with her big briefcase full of Laban charts; she was adjusting her rain scarf about her head. A well-dressed man with an attaché case thrust the handle of his umbrella up between her legs from the rear. She gasped and dropped her case.

The city responded and responded and responded.

Her overtures altered quickly.

The old drunk with the stippled cheeks extended his hand and mumbled words. She cursed him and walked on up Broadway past the beaver film houses.

She crossed against the lights on Park Avenue, making hackies slam their brakes to avoid hitting her; she used that word frequently now.

When she found herself having a drink with a man who had elbowed up beside her in the singles' bar, she felt faint and knew she should go home.

But Vermont was so far away.

Nights later. She had come home from the Lincoln Center ballet, and gone straight to bed. She heard a sound in the bedroom. One room away, in the living room, in the dark, there was a sound. She slipped out of bed and went to the door between the rooms. She fumbled silently for the switch on the lamp just inside the living room, and found it, and clicked it on. A black man in a leather car coat was trying to get *out* of the apartment. In that first flash of light filling the room she noticed the television set beside him on the floor as he struggled with the door, she noticed the police lock and bar had been broken in a new and clever manner *New York Magazine* had not yet reported in a feature article on apartment ripoffs, she noticed that he had gotten his foot tangled in the telephone cord that she had requested be extra-long so she could carry the instrument into the bathroom, I don't want to miss any business calls when the shower is running; she noticed all things in perspective and one thing with sharpest clarity: the expression on the burglar's face.

There was something familiar in that expression.

He almost had the door open, but now he closed it, and slipped the police lock. He took a step toward her.

Beth went back, into the darkened bedroom.

The city responded to her overtures.

She backed against the wall at the head of the bed. Her hand fumbled in the shadows for the telephone. His shape

In silhouette it should not have been possible to tell, but somehow she knew he was wearing gloves and the only marks he would leave would be deep bruises, very blue, almost black, with the tinge under them of blood that had

been stopped in its course.

He came for her, arms hanging casually at his sides. She tried to climb over the bed, and he grabbed her from behind, ripping her nightgown. Then he had a hand around her neck and he pulled her backward. She fell off the bed, landed at his feet and his hold was broken. She scuttled across the floor and for a moment she had the respite to feel terror. She was going to die, and she was frightened.

He trapped her in the corner between the closet and the bureau and kicked her. His foot caught her in the thigh as she folded tighter, smaller, drawing her legs up. She was cold.

Then he reached down with both hands and pulled her erect by her hair. He slammed her head against the wall. Everything slid up in her sight as though running off the edge of the world. He slammed her head against the wall again, and she felt something go soft over her right ear.

When he tried to slam her a third time she reached out blindly for his face and ripped down with her nails. He howled in pain and she hurled herself forward, arms wrapping themselves around his waist. He stumbled backward and in a tangle of thrashing arms and legs they fell out onto the little balcony.

Beth landed on the bottom, feeling the window boxes jammed up against her spine and legs. She fought to get to her feet, and her nails hooked into his shirt under the open jacket, ripping. Then she was on her feet again and they struggled silently.

He whirled her around, bent her backward across the wrought iron railing. Her face was turned outward.

They were standing in their windows, watching.

Through the fog she could see them watching. Through the fog she recognized their expressions. Through the fog she heard them breathing in unison, bellows breathing of expectation and wonder. Through the fog.

And the black man punched her in the throat. She gagged and started to black out and could not draw air into her lungs. Back, back, he bent her further back and she was looking up, straight up, toward the ninth floor and higher …

Up there: eyes.

The words Ray Gleeson had said in a moment filled with what he had become, with the utter hopelessness and finality of the choice the city had forced on him, the words came back. *You can't live in this city and survive unless you have protection…you can't live this way, like rats driven mad, without making the time right for some god-forsaken other kind of thing to be born…you can't do it without calling up some kind of awful….*

God! A new God, an ancient God come again with the eyes and hunger of a child, a deranged blood God of fog and street violence. A God who needed worshippers and offered the choices of death as a victim or life as an eternal witness to the deaths of *other* chosen victims. A God to fit the times, a God of streets and people.

She tried to shriek, to appeal to Ray, to the director in the bedroom window of his ninth-floor apartment with his long-legged Philadelphia model beside him and his fingers inside her as they worshipped in their holiest of ways, to the others who had been at the party that had been Ray's offer of a chance to join their congregation. She wanted to be saved from having to make that choice.

But the black man had punched her in the throat, and now his hands were on her, one on her chest, the other in her face, the smell of leather filling her where the nausea could not. And she understood Ray had *cared,* had wanted her to take the chance offered: but she had come from a world of little white dormitories and Vermont countryside; it was not a real world. *This* was the real world and up there was the God who ruled this world, and she had rejected him, had said no to one of his priests and servitors. *Save me! Don't make me do it!*

She knew she had to call out, to make appeal, to try and win the approbation of that God. *I can't...save me!*

She struggled and made terrible little mewling sounds trying to summon the words to cry out, and suddenly she crossed a line, and screamed up into the echoing courtyard with a voice Leona Ciarelli had never known enough to use.

"Him! Take him! Not me! I'm yours, I love you, I'm yours! Take him, not me, please not me, take him, take him, I'm yours!"

And the black man was suddenly lifted away, wrenched off her, and off the balcony, whirled straight up into the fog-thick air in the courtyard, as Beth sank to her knees on the ruined flower boxes.

She was half-conscious, and could not be sure she saw it just that way, but up he went, end over end, whirling and spinning like a charred leaf.

And the form took firmer shape. Enormous paws with claws and shapes that no animal she had ever seen had ever possessed, and the burglar, black, poor, terrified, whimpering like a whipped dog, was stripped of his flesh. His body was opened with a thin incision, and there was a rush as all the blood poured from him like a sudden cloudburst, and yet he was still alive, twitching with the involuntary horror of a frog's leg shocked with an electric current. Twitched, and twitched again as he was torn piece by piece to shreds. Pieces of flesh and bone and half a face with an eye blinking furiously, cascaded down past Beth, and hit the cement below with sodden thuds. And still he was alive, as his organs were squeezed and musculature and bile and shit and skin were rubbed, sandpapered together and let fall. It went on and on, as the death of Leona Ciarelli had gone on and on, and she understood with the blood-knowledge of survivors *at any cost* that the reason the witnesses to the death of Leona Ciarelli had done nothing was not that they had been frozen with

horror, that they didn't want to get involved, or that they were inured to death by years of television slaughter.

They were worshippers at a black mass the city had demanded be staged, not once, but a thousand times a day in this insane asylum of steel and stone.

Now she was on her feet, standing half-naked in her ripped nightgown, her hands tightening on the wrought iron railing, begging to see more, to drink deeper.

Now she was one of them, as the pieces of the night's sacrifice fell past her, bleeding and screaming.

Tomorrow the police would come again, and they would question her, and she would say how terrible it had been, that burglar, and how she had fought, afraid he would rape her and kill her, and how he had fallen, and she had no idea how he had been so hideously mangled and ripped apart, but a seven-storey fall, after all....

Tomorrow she would not have to worry about walking in the streets, because no harm could come to her. Tomorrow she could even remove the police lock. Nothing in the city could do her any further evil, because she had made the only choice. She was now a dweller in the city, now wholly and richly a part of it. Now she was taken to the bosom of her God.

She felt Ray beside her, standing beside her, holding her, protecting her, his hand on her naked backside, and she watched the fog swirl up and fill the courtyard, fill the city, fill her eyes and her soul and her heart with its power. As Ray's naked body pressed tightly in to her, she drank deeply of the night, knowing whatever voices she heard from this moment forward, they would be the voices not of whipped dogs, but those of strong, meat-eating beasts.

At last she was unafraid, and it was so good, so very good not to be afraid.

"When inward life dries up, when feeling decreases and apathy increases, when one cannot affect or even genuinely *touch* another person, violence flares up as a daimonic necessity for contact, a mad drive forcing touch in the most direct way possible."
— Rollo May, *Love and Will*

The mind is on fire, thoughts are on fire. Mind-consciousness and the impressions received by the mind, and the sensations that arise from the impressions that the mind receives — these too are on fire.

And with what are they on fire? With the fire of greed, with the fire of resentment, with the fire of infatuation; with birth, old age and death, with sorrow and lamentation, with misery and grief and despair they are on fire.

From the Buddha's Fire Sermon

all the trees coloured were
Joy Kogawa

all the trees coloured were
bird full and song ready to move
the forests alive with leaf swish and
ballet shoes on when suddenly
the "no" storm fell cloud down
and curtain heavy i
cocoon the dark grope
my fingernails black
the strange—
everywhere the strange
no colours left—

We need not be unaware of the "inner" world. We do
not realize its existence most of the time. But many
people enter it — unfortunately without guides, con-
fusing outer with inner realities, and inner with outer...

R.D. Laing, *The Politics of Experience* (1967)

Man knows of chaos and creation in the cosmogonic
myth and he learns that chaos and creation take place
in himself, but he does not see the former and the latter
together; he listens to the myth of Lucifer and hushes
it up in his own life.

Martin Buber

The Door
E.B. White

Everything (he kept saying) is something it isn't. And everybody is always somewhere else. Maybe it was the city, being in the city, that made him feel how queer everything was and that it was something else. Maybe (he kept thinking) it was the names of the things. The names were tex and frequently koid. Or they were flex and oid or they were duroid (sani) or flexsan (duro), but everything was glass (but not quite glass) and the thing that you touched (the surface, washable, crease-resistant) was rubber, only it wasn't quite rubber and you didn't quite touch it but almost. The wall, which was glass but thrutex, turned out on being approached not to be a wall, it was something else, it was an opening or doorway — and the doorway (through which he saw himself approaching) turned out to be something else, it was a wall. And what he had eaten not having agreed with him.

He was in a washable house, but he wasn't sure. Now about those rats, he kept saying to himself. He meant the rats that the Professor had driven crazy by forcing them to deal with problems which were beyond the scope of rats, the insoluble problems. He meant the rats that had been trained to jump at the square card with the circle in the middle, and the card (because it was something it wasn't) would give way and let the rat into a place where the food was, but then one day it would be a trick played on the rat, and the card would be changed, and the rat would jump but the card wouldn't give way, and it was an impossible situation (for a rat) and the rat would go insane and into its eyes would come the unspeakable bright imploring look of the frustrated, and after the convulsions were over and the frantic racing around, then the passive stage would set in and the willingness to let anything be done to it, even if it was something else.

He didn't know which door (or wall) or opening in the house to jump at, to get through, because one was an opening that wasn't an opening, it was a sanitary cupboard of the same color. He caught a glimpse of his eyes staring into his eyes, in the thrutex, and in them was the expression he had seen in the picture of the rats — weary after convulsions and the frantic racing around, when they were willing and did not mind having anything done to them. More and more (he kept saying) I am confronted by a problem which is incapable of solution (for this time even if he chose the right door, there would be no food behind it) and that is what madness is, and things seeming different from what they are. He heard, in the house where he was, in the city to which he had gone (as toward a door which might, or might not, give way), a noise — not a loud noise but more of a low prefabricated humming. It came from a place in the base of the wall (or stat) where the flue carrying the filterable air was, and not far from the Minipiano, which was made of the same material nailbrushes are made of, and which was under the stairs. "This, too, has been tested," she said, pointing, but not

When we meet impass and failure in the pursuit of our projects, then our habits and concepts...are challenged. Failure of our projects give us a whiff of the stink of chaos, and this can be terrifying.
...If we experience the pure nothingness, we panic, and seek quickly to shore up the collapsing world, to daub clay into the cracks of our concepts.

Sidney M. Jourard, *"Growing Awareness and the Awareness of Growth"* in *Ways of Growth* (1963)

If the only tool you have is a hammer, you tend to treat everything as if it were a nail.

Abraham Maslow, *The Psychology of Science: a Reconnaissance* (1966)

at it, "and found viable." It wasn't a loud noise, he kept thinking, sorry that he had seen his eyes, even though it was through his own eyes that he had seen them.

First will come the convulsions (he said), then the exhaustion, then the willingness to let anything be done. "And you better believe it *will* be."

All his life he had been confronted by situations which were incapable of being solved, and there was a deliberateness behind all this, behind this changing of the card (or door), because they would always wait till you had learned to jump at the certain card (or door) — the one with the circle — and then they would change it on you. There have been so many doors changed on me, he said, in the last twenty years, but it is now becoming clear that it is an impossible situation, and the question is whether to jump again, even though they ruffle you in the rump with a blast of air — to make you jump. He wished he wasn't standing by the Minipiano. First they would teach you the prayers and the Psalms, and that would be the right door (the one with the circle), and the long sweet words with the holy sound, and that would be the one to jump at to get where the food was. Then one day you jumped and it didn't give way, so that all you got was the bump on the nose, and the first bewilderment, the first young bewilderment.

I don't know whether to tell her about the door they substituted or not, he said, the one with the equation on it and the picture of the amoeba reproducing itself by division. Or the one with the photostatic copy of the check for thirty-two dollars and fifty cents. But the jumping was so long ago, although the bump is...how those old wounds hurt! Being crazy this way wouldn't be so bad if only, if only. If only when you put your foot forward to take a step, the ground wouldn't come up to meet your foot the way it does. And the same way in the street (only I may never get back to the street unless I jump at the right door), the curb coming up to meet your foot, anticipating ever so delicately the weight of the body, which is somewhere else. "We could take your name," she said, "and send it to you." And it wouldn't be so bad if only you could read a sentence all the way through without jumping (your eye) to something else on the same page; and then (he kept thinking) there was that man out in Jersey, the one who started to chop his trees down, one by one, the man who began talking about how he would take his house to pieces, brick by brick, because he faced a problem incapable of solution, probably, so he began to hack at the trees in the yard, began to pluck with trembling fingers at the bricks in the house. Even if a house is not washable, it is worth taking down. It is not till later that the exhaustion sets in.

But it is inevitable that they will keep changing the doors on you, he said, because that is what they are for; and the thing is to get used to it and not let it unsettle the mind. But that would mean not jumping, and you can't. Nobody can not jump. There will be no not-jumping. Among rats, perhaps, but among people never. Everybody

has to keep jumping at a door (the one with the circle on it) because that is the way everybody is, specially some people. You wouldn't want me, standing here, to tell you, would you, about my friend the poet (deceased) who said, "My heart has followed all my days something I cannot name"? (It had the circle on it.) And like many poets, although few so beloved, he is gone. It killed him, the jumping. First, of course, there were the preliminary bouts, the convulsions, and the calm and the willingness.

I remember the door with the picture of the girl on it (only it was spring), her arms outstretched in loveliness, her dress (it was the one with the circle on it) uncaught, beginning the slow, clear, blinding cascade — and I guess we would all like to try that door again, for it seemed like the way and for a while it was the way, the door would open and you would go through winged and exalted (like any rat) and the food would be there, the way the Professor had it arranged, everything O.K., and you had chosen the right door for the world was young. The time they changed that door on me, my nose bled for a hundred hours — how do you like that, Madam? Or would you prefer to show me further through this so strange house, or you could take my name and send it to me, for although my heart has followed all my days something I cannot name, I am tired of the jumping and i do not know which way to go, Madam, and I am not even sure that I am not tried beyond the endurance of man (rat, if you will) and have taken leave of sanity. What are you following these days, old friend, after your recovery from the last bump? What is the name, or is it something you cannot name? The rats have a name for it by this time, perhaps, but I don't know what they call it. I call it plexikoid and it comes in sheets, something like insulating board, unattainable and ugli-proof.

And there was the man out in Jersey, because I keep thinking about his terrible necessity and the passion and trouble he had gone to all those years in the indescribable abundance of a householder's detail, building the estate and the planting of the trees and in spring the lawn-dressing and in fall the bulbs for the spring burgeoning, and the watering of the grass on the long light evenings in summer and the gravel for the driveway (all had to be thought out, planned) and the decorative borders, probably, the perennials and the bug spray, and the building of the house from plans of the architect, first the sills, then the studs, then the full corn in the ear, the floors laid on the floor timbers, smoothed, and then the carpets upon the smooth floors and the curtains and the rods therefor. And then, almost without warning, he would be jumping at the same old door and it wouldn't give: they had changed it on him, making life no longer supportable under the elms in the elm shade, under the maples in the maple shade.

"Here you have the maximum of openness in a small room."

It was impossible to say (maybe it was the city) what made him feel the way he did, and I am not the only one either, he kept thinking — ask any doctor if I am. The doctors, they know how many there are, they even know where the trouble is only they don't like to tell you about the prefrontal lobe because that means making a hole in your skull and removing the work of centuries. It took so long coming, this lobe, so many, many years. (Is it something you read in the paper, perhaps?) And now, the strain being so great, the door having been changed by the Professor once too often...but it only means a whiff of ether, a few deft strokes, and the higher animal becomes a little easier in his mind and more like the lower one. From now on, you see, that's the way it will be, the ones with the small prefrontal lobes will win because the other ones are hurt too much by this incessant bumping. They can stand just so much, eh, Doctor? (And what is that, pray, that you have in your hand?) Still, you never can tell, eh, Madam?

He crossed (carefully) the room, the thick carpet under him softly, and went toward the door carefully, which was glass and he could see himself in it, and which, at his approach, opened to allow him to pass through; and beyond he half expected to find one of the old doors that he had known, perhaps the one with the circle, the one with the girl her arms outstretched in loveliness and beauty before him. But he saw instead a moving stairway, and descended in light (he kept thinking) to the street below and to the other people. As he stepped off, the ground came up slightly, to meet his foot.

Imaginary experience is constitutive of man, no less certainly than everyday experience and practical activities. Although its structure is not homologous with the structures of "objective" realities, the world of the imaginary is not "unreal".

Mircea Eliade, *Myths, Dreams, and Mysteries* (1957)

Minotaur

Michael Ayrton

What is a man that I am not a man
Sitting cramped pupate in this chrysalis?
My tongue is gagged with cud and lolls round words
To speak impeded of my legend death.
My horns lack weapon purpose, cannot kill
And cannot stab the curtain of the dark.

**In the depths of the human personality, the un-
conscious and the supernatural are united in the form
of dynamic images transcending any actual human
experience: demons, monsters, dragons, angels, gods
take possession of the dreamer and become more
obsessively real than the actual world of here and
now....With these overpowering images, independent
and autonomous, sometimes as vivid in daylight as in
sleep, man went farther in the direction of detachment
and projection: detachment from the animal,
projection of the superhuman and the divine.**

Lewis Mumford, *The Transformations of Man* (1962)

The Trap

Jon Stallworthy

The first night that the monster lurched
Out of the forest on all fours,
He saw its shadow in his dream
Circle the house, as though it searched
For one it loved or hated. Claws
On gravel and a rabbit's scream
Ripped the fabric of his dream.

Waking between dark and dawn
And sodden sheets, his reason quelled
The shadow and the nightmare sound.
The second night it crossed the lawn
A brute voice in the darkness yelled.
He struggled up, woke raving, found
His wall-flowers trampled to the ground.

When rook wings beckoned the shadows back
He took his rifle down, and stood
All night against the leaded glass.
The moon ticked round. He saw the black
Elm-skeletons in the doomsday wood,
The sailing and the failing stars
And red coals dropping between bars.

The third night such a putrid breath
Fouled, flared his nostrils, that he turned,
Turned, but could not lift, his head.
A coverlet as thick as death
Oppressed him: he crawled out: discerned
Across the door his watchdog, dead.
"Build a trap," the neighbours said.

All that day he built his trap
With metal jaws and a spring as thick
As the neck of a man. One touch
Triggered the hanging teeth: jump, snap,
And lightning guillotined the stick
Thrust in its throat. With gun and torch
He set his engine in the porch.

The forth night in their beds appalled
His neighbours heard the hunting roar
Mount, mount to an exultant shriek.
At daybreak timidly they called
His name, climbed through the splintered door
And found him sprawling in the wreck,
Naked, with a severed neck.

Antichrist as a Child
James Reaney

When Antichrist was a child
He caught himself tracing
The capital letter A
On a window sill
And wondered why
Because his name contained no A.
And as he crookedly stood
In his mother's flower-garden
He wondered why she looked so sadly
Out of an upstairs window at him.
He wondered why his father stared so
Whenever he saw his little son
Walking in his soot-colored suit.
He wondered why the flowers
And even the ugliest weeds
Avoided his fingers and his touch.
And when his shoes began to hurt
Because his feet were becoming hooves
He did not let on to anyone
For fear they would shoot him for a monster.
He wondered why he more and more
Dreamed of eclipses of the sun,
Of sunsets, ruined towns and zeppelins,
And especially inverted, upside down churches.

The "sanity" of modern man is about as useful to him as the huge bulk and muscles of the dinosaur. If he were a little less sane, a little more doubtful, a little more aware of his absurdities and contradictions, perhaps there might be a possibility of his survival. But if he is sane, too sane...

Thomas Merton, *Raids on the Unspeakable* (1970)

Paranoid
P.K. Page

He loved himself too much. As a child was god.
Thunder stemmed from his whims,
flowers were his path.
Throughout those early days his mother was all love,
a warm projection of him
like a second heart.

In adolescence, dark and silent, he was perfect;
still godlike and like a god
cast the world out.
Crouching in his own torso as in a chapel
the stained glass of his blood
glowed in the light.

Remained a god. Each year he grew more holy
and more wholly himself.
The self spun
thinner and thinner like a moon forming
slowly from that other self
the dead sun.

Until he was alone, revolved in ether
light years from the world,
cold and remote.
Thinking he owned the heavens too, he circled,
wanly he turned and whirled
reflecting light.

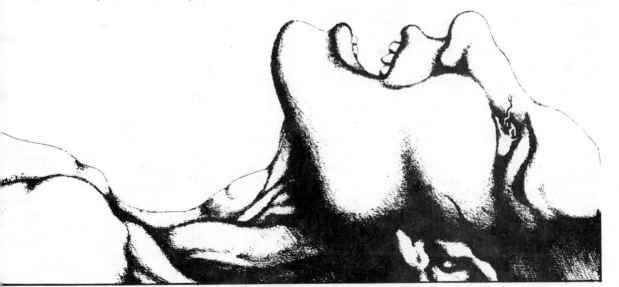

The Outsider

H.P. Lovecraft

That night the Baron dreamt of many a wo;
And all his warrior-guests, with shade and form
Of witch, and demon, and large coffin-worm,
Were long be-nightmared-Keats.

Unhappy is he to whom the memories of childhood bring only fear and sadness. Wretched is he who looks back upon lone hours in vast and dismal chambers with brown hangings and maddening rows of antique books, or upon awed watches in twilight groves of grotesque, gigantic, and vine-encumbered trees that silently wave twisted branches far aloft. Such a lot the gods gave to me — to me, the dazed, the disappointed; the barren, the broken. And yet I am strangely content and cling desperately to those sere memories, when my mind momentarily threatens to reach beyond to *the other*.

I know not where I was born, save that the castle was infinitely old and infinitely horrible, full of dark passages and having high ceilings where the eye could find only cobwebs and shadows. The stones in the crumbling corridors seemed always hideously damp, and there was an accursed smell everywhere, as of the piled-up corpses of dead generations. It was never light, so that I used sometimes to light candles and gaze steadily at them for relief, nor was there any sun outdoors, since the terrible trees grew high above the topmost accessible tower. There was one black tower which reached above the trees into the unknown outer sky, but that was partly ruined and could not be ascended save by a well-nigh impossible climb up the sheer wall, stone by stone.

I must have lived years in this place, but I cannot measure the time. Beings must have cared for my needs, yet I cannot recall any person except myself, or anything alive but the noiseless rats and bats and spiders. I think that whoever nursed me must have been shockingly aged, since my first conception of a living person was that of somebody mockingly like myself, yet distorted, shrivelled, and decaying like the castle. To me there was nothing grotesque in the bones and skeletons that strewed some of the stone crypts deep down among the foundations. I fantastically associated these things with everyday events, and thought them more natural than the colored pictures of living beings which I found in many of the mouldy books. From such books I learned all that I know. No teacher urged or guided me, and I do not recall hearing any human voice in all those years — not even my own; for although I had read of speech, I had never thought to try to speak aloud. My aspect was a matter equally unthought of, for there were no mirrors in the castle, and I merely regarded myself by instinct as akin to the youthful figures I saw drawn and painted in the books. I felt conscious of youth because I remembered so little.

Outside, across the putrid moat and under the dark mute trees, I would often lie and dream for hours about what I read in the books; and would longingly picture myself amidst gay crowds in the sunny world beyond the endless forests. Once I tried to escape from the forest, but as I went farther from the castle the shade grew denser and the air more filled with brooding fear; so that I ran frantically back lest I lose my way in a labyrinth of nighted silence.

So through endless twilights I dreamed and waited, though I knew not what I waited for. Then in the shadowy solitude my longing for light grew so frantic that I could rest no more, and I lifted entreating hands to the single black ruined tower that reached above the forest into the unknown outer sky. And at last I resolved to scale that tower, fall though I might; since it were better to glimpse the sky and perish, than to live without ever beholding day.

In dealing with symbols and myths...we are really conversing...with a part of ourselves...as unfamiliar to our conscious being as the interior of the earth to the student of geology.

Heinrich Zimmer

In the dank twilight I climbed the worn and aged stone stairs till I reached the level where they ceased, and thereafter clung perilously to small footholds leading upward. Ghastly and terrible was that dead, stairless cylinder of rock; black, ruined, and deserted, and sinister with startled bats whose wings made no noise. But more ghastly and terrible still was the slowness of my progress; for climb as I might, the darkness overhead grew no thinner, and a new chill as of haunted and venerable mould assailed me. I shivered as I wondered why I did not reach the light, and would have looked down had I dared. I fancied that night had come suddenly upon me, and vainly groped with one free hand for a window embrasure, that I might peer out and above, and try to judge the height I had attained.

All at once, after an infinity of awesome, sightless, crawling up that concave and desperate precipice, I felt my head touch a solid thing, and knew I must have gained the roof, or at least some kind of floor. In the darkness I raised my free hand and tested the barrier, finding it stone and immovable. Then came a deadly circuit of the tower, clinging to whatever holds the slimy wall could give; till finally my testing hand found the barrier yielding, and I turned upward again, pushing the slab or door with my head as I used both hands in my fearful ascent. There was no light revealed above, and as my hands went higher I knew that my climb was for the nonce ended; since the slab was the trap-door of an aperture leading to a level stone surface of greater circumference than the lower tower, no doubt the floor of some lofty and capacious observation chamber. I crawled through carefully, and tried to prevent the heavy slab from falling back into place, but failed in the latter attempt. As I lay exhausted on the stone floor I heard the eerie echoes of its fall, but hoped when necessary to pry it up again.

Believing I was now at prodigious height, far above the accursed branches of the wood, I dragged myself up from the floor and fumbled about for windows, that I might look for the first time upon the sky, and the moon and stars of which I had read. But on every hand I was disappointed; since all that I found were vast shelves of marble, bearing odious oblong boxes of disturbing size. More and more I reflected, and wondered what hoary secrets might abide in this high apartment so many aeons cut off from the castle below. Then unexpectedly my hands came upon a doorway, where hung a portal of stone, rough with strange chiselling. Trying it, I found it locked; but with a supreme burst of strength I overcame all obstacles and dragged it open inward. As I did so there came to me the purest ecstasy I have ever known; for shining tranquilly through an ornate grating of iron, and down a short stone passageway of steps that ascended from the newly found doorway, was the radiant full moon, which I had never before seen save in dreams and in vague visions I dared not call memories.

Fancying now that I had attained the very pinnacle of the castle, I commenced to rush up the few steps beyond the door; but the sudden veiling of the moon by a cloud caused me to stumble, and I felt my way more slowly in the dark. It was still very dark when I reached the grating — which I tried carefully and found unlocked, but which I did not open for fear of falling from the amazing height to which I had climbed. Then the moon came out.

Most demoniacal of all shocks is that of the abysmally unexpected and grotesquely unbelievable. Nothing I had before undergone could compare in terror with what I now saw; with the bizarre marvels that sight implied. The sight itself was as simple as it was stupefying, for it was merely this: instead of a dizzying prospect of treetops seen from a lofty eminence, there stretched around me on the level through the grating nothing less than *the solid ground*, decked and diversified by marble slabs and columns, and overshadowed by an ancient stone church, whose ruined spire gleamed spectrally in the moonlight.

Half unconscious, I opened the grating and staggered out upon the white gravel path that stretched away in two directions. My mind, stunned and chaotic as it was, still held the frantic craving for light; and not even the fantastic wonder which had happened could stay my course. I neither knew nor cared whether my experience was insanity, dreaming, or magic; but was determined to gaze on brilliance and gaiety at any cost. I knew not who I was or what I was, or what my surroundings might be; though as I continued to stumble alone I became conscious of a kind of fearsome latent memory that made my progress not wholly fortuitous. I passed under an arch out of that region of slabs and columns, and wandered through the open country; sometimes following the visible road, but

sometimes leaving it curiously to tread across meadows where only occasional ruins bespoke the ancient presence of a forgotten road. Once I swam across a swift river where crumbling, mossy masonry told of a bridge long vanished.

Over two hours must have passed before I reached what seemed to be my goal, a venerable ivied castle in a thickly wooded park, maddeningly familiar, yet full of perplexing strangeness to me. I saw that the moat was filled in, and that some of the well-known towers were demolished; whilst new wings existed to confuse the beholder. But what I observed with chief interest and delight were the open windows — gorgeously ablaze with light and sending forth sound of the gayest revelry. Advancing to one of these I looked in and saw an oddly dressed company, indeed; making merry, and speaking brightly to one another. I had never, seemingly, heard human speech before and could guess only vaguely what was said. Some of the faces seemed to hold expressions that brought up incredibly remote recollections, others were utterly alien.

I now stepped through the low window into the brilliantly lighted room, stepping as I did so from my single bright moment of hope to my blackest convulsion of despair and realization. The nightmare was quick to come, for as I entered, there occurred immediately one of the most terrifying demonstrations I had ever conceived. Scarcely had I crossed the sill when there descended upon the whole company a sudden and unheralded fear of hideous intensity, distorting every face and evoking the most horrible screams from nearly every throat. Flight was universal, and in the clamour and panic several fell in a swoon and were dragged away by their madly fleeing companions. Many covered their eyes with their hands, and plunged blindly and awkwardly in their race to escape, overturning furniture and stumbling against the walls before they managed to reach one of the many doors.

The possibility of a relapse into the old superstitions has to be rejected...so that another group of outlets has to be found. There is...reason to think that the chief one of these has been the increase in individual psychoneuroses.

Ernest Jones, *On the Nightmare* (1951)

The cries were shocking; and as I stood in the brilliant apartment alone and dazed, listening to their vanishing echoes, I trembled at the thought of what might be lurking near me unseen. At a casual inspection the room seemed deserted, but when I moved towards one of the alcoves I thought I detected a presence there — a hint of motion beyond the golden-arched doorway leading to another and somewhat similar room. As I approached the arch I began to perceive the presence more clearly; and then, with the first and last sound I ever uttered — a ghastly ululation that revolted me almost as poignantly as its noxious cause — I beheld in full, frightful vividness the inconceivable, indescribable, and unmentionable monstrosity which had by its simple appearance changed a merry company to a herd of delirious fugitives.

I cannot even hint what it was like, for it was a compound of all that is unclean, uncanny, unwelcome, abnormal, and detestable. It was the ghoulish shade of decay, antiquity, and dissolution; the putrid, dripping eidolon of unwholesome revelation, the awful baring of that which the merciful earth should always hide. God knows it was not of this world — or no longer of this world — yet to my horror I saw in its eaten-away and bone-revealing outlines a leering, abhorrent travesty on the human shape; and in its mouldy, disintegrating apparel an unspeakable quality that chilled me even more.

I was almost paralysed, but not too much so to make a feeble effort towards flight; a backward stumble which failed to break the spell in which the nameless, voiceless monster held me. My eyes bewitched by the glassy orbs which stared loathsomely into them, refused to close; though they were mercifully blurred, and showed the terrible object but indistinctly after the first shock. I tried to raise my hand to shut out the sight, yet so stunned were my nerves that my arm could not fully obey my will. The attempt, however, was enough to disturb my balance; so that I had to stagger forward several steps to avoid falling. As I did so I became suddenly and agonizingly aware of the *nearness* of the carrion thing, whose hideous hollow breathing I half fancied I could hear. Nearly mad, I found myself yet able to throw out a hand to ward off the foetid apparition which pressed so close; when in one cataclysmic second of cosmic nightmarishness and hellish accident *my fingers touched the rotting outstretched paw of the monster beneath the golden arch.*

I did not shriek, but all the fiendish ghouls that ride the night-wind shrieked for me as in that same second there crashed down upon my mind a single and fleeting avalanche of soul-annihilating memory. I knew in that second all that had been; I remembered beyond the frightful castle and the trees, and recognized the altered edifice in which I now stood; I recognized, most terrible of all, the unholy abomination that stood leering before me as I withdrew my sullied fingers from its own.

But in the cosmos there is balm as well as bitterness, and that balm is nepenthe. In the supreme horror of that second I forgot what had horrified me, and the burst of black memory vanished in a chaos of echoing images. In a dream I fled from that haunted and accursed pile, and ran swiftly and silently in the moonlight. When I returned to the churchyard place of marble and went down the steps I found the stone trap-door immovable; but I was not sorry, for I had hated the antique castle and the trees. Now I ride with the mocking and friendly ghouls on the night-wind, and play by day amongst the catacombs of Nephren Ka in the sealed and unknown valley of Hadoth by the Nile. I know that light is not for me, save that of the moon over the rock tombs of Neb, nor any gaiety save the unnamed feasts of Nitokris beneath the Great Pyramid; yet in my new wildness and freedom I almost welcome the bitterness of alienage.

For although nepenthe has calmed me, I know always that I am an outsider; a stranger in this century and among those who are still men. This I have known ever since I stretched out my fingers to the abomination within that great gilded frame; stretched out my fingers and touched *a cold and unyielding surface of polished glass.*

I'm just a collection of mirrors, reflecting what everyone else expects of me.

Rollo May, *Man's Search for Himself* (1953)

The Kraken

Alfred, Lord Tennyson

Below the thunders of the upper deep,
Far, far beneath in the abysmal sea,
His ancient, dreamless, uninvaded sleep
The Kraken sleepeth: faintest sunlights flee
About his shadowy sides; above him swell
Huge sponges of milennial growth and height;
And far away into the sickly light,
From many a wondrous grot and secret cell
Unnumber'd and enormous polypi
Winnow with giant arms the slumbering green.
There hath he lain for ages, and will lie
Battening upon huge sea-worms in his sleep,
Until the lattèr fire shall heat the deep;
Then once by man and angels to be seen,
In roaring he shall rise and on the surface die.

The brain is an obstacle in the sense that it is the co-ordinating centre for human movements and appetites. It is necessary to think *in opposition* to the brain.

Gaston Bachelard

The dragon is the great mystery itself. Hidden in the caverns of inaccessible mountains, or coiled in the unfathomed depths of the sea, he awaits the time when he slowly rouses himself to activity. He unfolds himself in the storm clouds; he washes his mane in the blackness of the seething whirlpools. His claws are in the forks of the lightning, his scales begin to glisten in the bark of rainswept pine trees. His voice is heard in the hurricane which, scattering the withered leaves of the forest, quickens the new spring. The dragon reveals himself only to vanish.

Okakura Kakuzo

People who have lost the sense of their identity as selves also tend to lose their sense of relatedness to nature.

Rollo May, *Man's Search for Himself* (1953)

City lights at night, from the air, receding, like these words, atoms each containing its own world and every other world. Each a fuse to set you off...
If I could turn you on, if I could drive you out of your wretched mind, if I could tell you I would let you know.

R.D. Laing, *The Bird of Paradise* (1967)

In a Dark Time

Theodore Roethke

In a dark time, the eye begins to see,
I meet my shadow in the deepening shade;
I hear my echo in the echoing wood—
A lord of nature weeping to a tree.
I live between the heron and the wren,
Beasts of the hill and serpents of the den.

What's madness but nobility of soul
At odds with circumstance? The day's on fire!
I know the purity of pure despair,
My shadow pinned against a sweating wall.
That place among the rocks—is it a cave,
Or winding path? The edge is what I have.

A steady storm of correspondences!
A night flowing with birds, a ragged moon,
And in broad day the midnight come again!
A man goes far to find out what he is—
Death of the self in a long, tearless night,
All natural shapes blazing unnatural light.

Dark, dark my light, and darker my desire.
My soul, like some heat-maddened summer fly,
Keeps buzzing at the sill. Which I is *I*?
A fallen man, I climb out of my fear.
The mind enters itself, and God the mind,
And one is One, free in the tearing wind.

When God is about to justify a man, he damns him. Whom he would make alive he must first kill. God's favour is so communicated in the form of wrath that it seems furthest when it is at hand. Man must first cry out that there is no health in him. He must be consumed with horror. This is the pain of purgatory...In this disturbance salvation begins. When a man believes himself to be utterly lost, light breaks.

Martin Luther

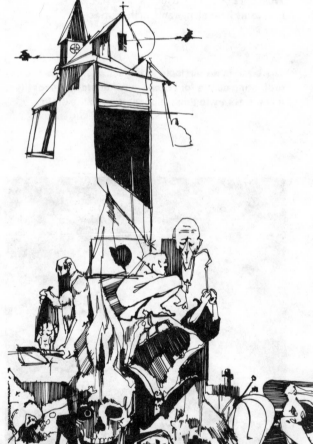

"By inquiring into the doctrines, he has come to understand something, he has found the traces. He now knows that the objective world is a reflection of the Self. Yet, he is unable to distinguish what is good from what is not, his mind is still confused as to truth and falsehood. As he has not yet entered the gate, he is provisionally said to have noticed the traces."

SEEING THE TRACES

CIBERATION

"The boy finds the way by the sound he hears; he sees thereby into the origin of things, and all his senses are in harmonious order. In all his activities, it is manifestly present. [It is there though not distinguishable as an individual entity.] When the eye is properly directed, he will find that it is no other than himself."

SEEING THE OX

Waiting
Joy Kogawa

A very quiet
        very quiet ticking
In the room where the child
Stays by the window
Watching
While outside innumerable snow feathers
Touch melt
        touch melt
                touch melt

Time is what keeps the light from reaching us. There is no greater obstacle to God than time. And not only time but temporalities, not only temporal things but temporal affections; not only temporal affections but the very taint and smell of time.

Meister Eckhart

The Weed of Time
Norman Spinrad

I, me, the spark of mind that is my consciousness, dwells in a locus that is neither place nor time. The objective duration of my lifespan is one hundred ten years, but from my own locus of consciousness, I am immortal — my awareness of my own awareness can never cease to be. I am an infant am a child am a youth am an old, old man dying on clean white sheets. I am all these mes, have always been all these mes, will always be all these mes in the place where my mind dwells in an eternal moment divorced from time....

A century and a tenth is my eternity. My life is like a biography in a book: immutable, invariant, fixed in length, limitless in duration. On April 3, 2040, I am born. On December 2, 2150, I die. The events in between take place in a single instant. Say that I range up and down them at will, experiencing each of them again and again eternally. Even this is not really true; I experience all moments in my century and a tenth simultaneously, once and forever....How can I tell my story? How can I make you understand? The language we have in common is based on concepts of time which we do not share.

For me, time as you think of it does not exist. I do not move from moment to moment sequentially like a blind man groping his way through a tunnel. I am at all points in the tunnel simultaneously, and my eyes are open wide. Time is to me, in a sense, what space is to you, a field over which I move in more directions than one.

How can I tell you? How can I make you understand? We are all of us men born of women, but in a way you have less in common with me than you do with an ape or

On Seeing
Dorothy Livesay

Far-fetched the eye of childhood sees the whole,
Essentializes figures to the brief
Recording of a rounded head
And outlets for the senses—
Eyes, ears, astonished hands;
And then takes on at puberty
A pained perception of the detailed self:
An agonizing analyst with eyes
Shaped to the comic strips
And women puffed like robins for a worm.

The inward eye begins as infantile,
Sees only the broad outline of the self;
Until some blinding day
Stricken on Damascus way
The details are revealed:
Gnarled hands of age, distorted love,
The skin of sickness stretched upon a soul;
The look "I hate," the voice "I scorn,"
The cry upon the deadly thorn.

This clarity is mercy for our sight:
Deformed, we seek the therapy of light.

an amoeba. Yet I *must* tell you, somehow. It is too late for me, will be too late, has been too late. I am trapped in this eternal hell and I can never escape, not even into death. My life is immutable, invariant, for I have eaten of Temp, the Weed of Time. But you must not! You must listen! You must understand! Shun the Weed of Time! I must try to tell you in my own way. It is pointless to try to start at the beginning. There is no beginning. There is no end. Only significant time-loci. Let me describe these loci. Perhaps I can make you understand....

In other living creatures ignorance of self is nature; in man it is vice.

Boethius

September 8, 2050. I am ten years old. I am in the office of Dr. Phipps, who is the director of the mental hospital in which I have been for the past eight years. On June 12, 2053, they will finally understand that I am not insane. It is all they will understand, but it will be enough for them to release me. But on September 8, 2050, I am in a mental hospital.

September 8, 2050, is the day the first expedition returns from Tau Ceti. The arrival is to be televised, and that is why I am in Dr. Phipps' office watching television

with the director. The Tau Ceti expedition is the reason I am in the hospital. I have been babbling about it for the previous ten years. I have been demanding that the ship be quarantined, that the plant samples it will bring back be destroyed, not allowed to grow in the soil of Earth. For most of my life this has been regarded as an obvious symptom of schizophrenia — after all, before July 12, 2048, the ship has not left for Tau Ceti, and until today it has not returned.

But on September 8, 2050, they wonder. This is the day I have been babbling about since I emerged from my mother's womb, and now it is happening. So now I am alone with Dr. Phipps as the image of the ship on the TV set lands on the image of a wide concrete apron....

"Make them understand!" I shout, knowing that it is futile. "Stop them, Dr. Phipps, stop them!"

Dr. Phipps stares at me uneasily. His small blue eyes show a mixture of pity, confusion, and fright. He is all too familiar with my case. Sharing his desktop with the portable television set is a heavy oaktag folder filled with my case history, filled with hundreds of therapy session records. In each of these records, this day is mentioned: September 8, 2050. I have repeated the same story over and over and over again. The ship will leave for Tau Ceti on July 12, 2048. It will return on September 8, 2050. The expedition will report that Tau Ceti has twelve planets ... The fifth alone is Earthlike and bears plant and animal life. ...The expedition will bring back samples and seeds of a

Supposing that suddenly ... the law of mind should change, and, a great average being struck, we should all ... henceforward see every thing precisely alike, and precisely alike be affected by every thing which we saw — it seems to me that a worse calamity could not happen to mankind. The wheels of our spiritual progress now roll somewhat erratically, it is true, as the impulse of the hosts who urge on the chariot is stronger now on this side, now on that, but the resultant of all the forces is a rapid and a forward motion. The check which would ensue to that progress from the coming in of an entire uniformity would be sufficient to retard for centuries the millennium of mind.

Fitz Hugh Ludlow, *The Hashish Eater* (1857)

small Cetan plant with broad green leaves and small purple flowers....The plant will be named *tempis ceti*.... It will become known as Temp....Before the properties of the plant are fully understood, seeds will somehow become scattered and Temp will flourish in the soil of Earth.... Somewhere, somehow, people will begin to eat the leaves of the Temp plant. They will become changed. They will babble of the future, and they will be considered mad — until the future events of which they speak begin to come to pass....

Then the plant will be outlawed as a dangerous narcotic. Eating Temp will become a crime....But as with all forbidden fruit, Temp will continue to be eaten....And, finally, Temp addicts will become the most sought-after criminals in the world. The governments of the Earth will attempt to milk the secrets of the future from their tortured minds....

All this is in my case history, with which Dr. Phipps is familiar. For eight years, this has been considered only a remarkably consistent psychotic delusion.
tent psychotic delusion.

But now it is September 8, 2050. As I have predicted, the ship has returned from Tau Ceti. Dr. Phipps stares at me woodenly as the gangplank is erected and the crew begins to debark. I can see his jaw tense as the reporters gather around the captain, a tall, lean man carrying a small sack.

The captain shakes his head in confusion as the reporters besiege him. "Let me make a short statement first," he says crisply. "Save wear and tear on all of us."

The captain's thin, hard, pale face fills the television screen. "The expedition is a success," he says. "The Tau Ceti system was found to have twelve planets, and the fifth is Earthlike and bears plant and simple animal life — very peculiar animal life...."

"What do you mean, 'peculiar'?" a reporter shouts.

The captain frowns and shrugs his wide shoulders. "Well, for one thing, they all seem to be herbivores and they seem to live off one species of plant which dominates the planetary flora. No predators. And it's not hard to see why. I don't quite know how to explain this, but all the critters seem to know what the other animals will do before they do it. And what we were going to do, too. We had one hell of a time taking specimens. We think it has something to do with the plant. Does something strange to their time sense."

"What makes you say that?" a reporter asks.

"Well, we fed some of the stuff to our lab animals. Same thing seemed to happen. It became virtually impossible to lay a hand on 'em. They seemed to be living a moment in the future, or something. That's why Dr. Lominov has called the plant *tempis ceti*."

"What's this *tempis* look like?" a reporter says.

"Well, it's sort of..." the captain begins. "Wait a minute," he says, "I've got a sample right here."

He reaches into the small sack and pulls something out. The camera zooms in on the captain's hand.

He is holding a small plant. The plant has broad green leaves and small purple blossoms.

Dr. Phipps' hands begin to tremble uncontrollably. He stares at me. He stares and stares and stares....

May 12, 2062. I am in a small room. Think of it as a hospital room, think of it as a laboratory, think of it as a cell; it is all three. I have been here for three months.

I am seated on a comfortable lounge chair. Across a table from me sits a man from an unnamed government intelligence bureau. On the table is a tape recorder. It is running. The man seated opposite is frowning in exasperation.

...It is this. That the soul in itself is capable of receiving all the impressions of all the senses from the action of the object which produces an impression upon a single sense; that in the bodily organs only and the media of transmission, which are relevant to the organs alone, lies the necessity for a divisory action; and, finally, as a consequence of these propositions, that the soul, either wholly freed from its present gross body, or so awakened, by any cause, as to be partially independent of the intervention of the corporeal organs, may behold the manifold impression from an object which now gives it only the fractional, thus seeing, hearing, smelling, tasting, and feeling in the most exquisite degree the thing which, in the state of bodily dominance, was the source of but one of these.

Fitz Hugh Ludlow *The Hashish Eater* (1857)

Luckily for...[mankind] there are always enough adults who retain their juvenile inventiveness and curiosity and who enable populations to progress and expand.

Desmond Morris, *The Naked Ape* (1967)

"The subject is December, 2081," he says. "You will tell me all you know of the events of December, 2081."

I stare at him silently, sullenly. I am tired of all the men from intelligence sections, economic councils, and scientific bureaus, with their endless, futile demands.

"Look," the man snaps, "we know better than to appeal to your nonexistent sense of patriotism. We are all too well aware that you don't give a damn about what the knowledge you have can mean to your country. But just remember this: you're a convicted criminal. Your sentence is indeterminate. Cooperate, and you'll be released in two years. Clam up, and we'll hold you here till you rot or until you get it through your head that the only way for you to get out is to talk. The subject is the month of December in the year 2081. Now, *give!*"

I sigh, I know that it is no use trying to tell any of them that knowledge of the future is useless, that the future cannot be changed because it was not changed because it will not be changed. They will not accept the fact that choice is an illusion caused by the fact that future time-loci are hidden from those who advance sequentially along the timestream one moment after the other in blissful ignorance. They refuse to understand that moments of future time are no different from moments of past or present time: fixed, immutable, invariant. They live in the illusion of sequential time.

So I begin to speak of the month of December in the year 2081. I know they will not be satisfied until I have told them all I know of the years between this time-locus and December 2, 2150. I know they will not be satisfied because they are not satisfied, have not been satisfied, will not be satisfied....

So I tell them of that terrible December nine years in their future....

December 2, 2150. I am old, old, a hundred ten years old. My age-ruined body lies on the clean white sheets of a hospital bed, lungs, heart, blood vessels, and organs all failing. Only my mind is forever untouched, the mind of an infant-child-youth-man-ancient. I am, in a sense, dying. Beyond this day, December 2, 2150, my body no longer exists as a living organism. Time to me forward of this date is as blank to me as time beyond April 3, 2040, is in the other temporal direction.

In a sense, I am dying. But in another sense, I am immortal. The spark of my consciousness will not go out. My mind will not come to an end, for it has neither end nor beginning. I exist in one moment that lasts forever and spans one hundred ten years.

Think of my life as a chapter in a book, the book of eternity, a book with no first page and no last. The chapter that is my lifespan is one hundred ten pages long. It has a starting point and an ending point, but the chapter exists as long as the book exists, the infinite book of eternity....

Or, think of my life as a ruler one hundred ten inches long. The ruler "begins" at one and "ends" at one hundred ten, but "begins" and "ends" refer to length, not duration.

I am dying. I experience dying always, but I never experience death. Death is the absence of experience. It can never come for me.

December 2, 2150, is but a significant time-locus for me, a dark wall, an endpoint beyond which I cannot see. The other wall has the time-locus April 3, 2040....

April 3, 2040. Nothingness abruptly ends, non-nothingness abruptly begins. I am born.

What is it like for me to be born? How can I tell you? How can I make you understand? My life, my whole lifespan of one hundred ten years, comes into being at once, in an instant. At the "moment" of my birth I am at the moment of my death and all moments in between. I emerge from my mother's womb and I see my life as one sees a painting, a painting of some complicated landscape: all at once, whole, a complete gestalt. I see my strange, strange infancy, the incomprehension as I emerge from the womb speaking perfect English, marred only by my undeveloped vocal apparatus, as I emerge from my mother's womb demanding that the ship from Tau Ceti in the time-locus of September 8, 2050, be quarantined, knowing that my demand will be futile because it was futile, will be futile, is futile, knowing that at the moment of my birth I am have been will be all that I ever was-am-will be and that I cannot change a moment of it.

I emerge from my mother's womb and I am dying in clean white sheets and I am in the office of Dr. Phipps watching the ship land and I am in the government cell for two years babbling of the future and I am in a clearing in some woods where a plant with broad green leaves and small purple flowers grows and I am picking the plant and

I was told, "Thou hast lifted thyself above humanity to peer into the speechless secrets before thy time; and thou shalt be smitten — smitten — smitten." As the last echo of the sentence died away, it always began its execution in Promethean pangs. At last even the faintest suggestion of the presence of Deity possessed a power to work me ill which hardly the haunting of demons had been able to produce before. At one time I well remember beholding a colossal veiled figure part the drapery of sombre clouds which hung over the horizon, and appear upon a platform which I supposed to be the stage of the universe. No sound, no radiance issued from behind the veil, yet when the mysterious figure lifted his hands, I cried, "It is the Day of Judgment, and my doom is being pronounced!" Then I fled for my soul, and cowered in the darkest spot that I could find.

Fitz Hugh Ludlow, *The Hashish Eater* (1857)

eating it as I know I will do have done am doing....

I emerge from my mother's womb and I see the gestalt painting of my lifespan, a pattern of immutable events painted on the stationary and eternal canvas of time....

But I do not merely *see* the "painting," I *am* the "painting" and I am the painter and I am also outside the painting viewing the whole and I am none of these.

And I see the immutable time-locus that determines all the rest — March 4, 2060. Change that and the painting dissolves and I live in time like any other man, moment after blessed moment, freed from this all-knowing hell. But change itself is illusion.

March 4, 2060 in a wood not too far from where I was born. But knowledge of the horror that day brings, has brought, will bring, can change nothing. I will do as I am doing will do did because I did it will do it am doing it..... .

April 3, 2040, and I emerge from my mother's womb, an infant-child-youth-man-ancient, in a government cell in a mental hospital dying in clean white sheets....

March 4, 2060. I am twenty. I am in a clearing in the woods. Before me grows a small plant with broad green leaves and purple blossoms — Temp, the Weed of Time, which has haunted, haunts, will haunt my never-ending life. I know what I am doing will do have done because I will do have done am doing it.

How can I explain? How can I make you understand that this moment is unavoidable, invariant, that though I have known, do know, will know its dreadful consequences, I can do nothing to alter it?

The language is inadequate. What I have told you is an unavoidable half-truth. All actions I perform in my one-hundred-ten-year lifespan occur simultaneously. But even that statement only hints around the truth, for "simultaneously" means "at the same time," and "time" as you understand the word has no relevance to my life. But let me approximate: let me say that all actions I have ever performed, will perform, do perform, occur simultaneously. Thus no knowledge inherent in any particular time-locus can effect any action performed at any other locus in time. Let me construct another useful lie. Let me say that, for me, action and perception are totally independent of each other. At the moment of my birth, I did everything I ever would do in my life, instantly, blindly, in one total gestalt. Only in the next "moment" do I perceive the results of all those myriad actions, the horror that March 4, 2060, will make has made is making of my life.

Or ... they say that at the moment of death, one's entire life flashes instantaneously before one's eyes. At the moment of my birth, my whole life flashed before me, not merely before my eyes, but in reality. I cannot change any of it because change is something that exists only as a function of the relationship between different moments in time, and for me life is one eternal moment that is one hundred ten years long....

So this awful moment is invariant, inescapable.

March 4, 2060. I reach down, pluck the Temp plant. I pull off a broad green leaf, put it in my mouth. It tastes

44

bitter-sweet, woody, unpleasant. I chew it, bolt it down.

The Temp travels to my stomach, is digested, passes into my bloodstream, reaches my brain. There changes occur which better men than I are powerless, will be powerless, to understand, at least up till December 2, 2150, beyond which is blankness. My body remains in the objective timestream, to age, grow old, decay, die. But my mind is abstracted out of time to experience all moments as one.

It is like a déjà vu. Because this happened on March 4, 2060, I have already experienced it in the twenty years since my birth. Yet this is the beginning point for my Temp-consciousness in the objective timestream. But the objective timestream has no relevance to what happens...

The language, the very thought patterns, are inadequate. Another useful lie: in the objective timestream I was a normal human being until this dire March 4, experiencing each moment of the previous twenty years sequentially, in order, moment after moment after moment....

Now on March 4, 2060, my consciousness expands in two directions in the timestream to fill my entire lifespan: forward to December 2, 2150, and my death, backward to April 3, 2040, and my birth. As this time-locus of March 4 "changes" my future, so, too, it "changes" my past, expanding my Temp-consciousness to both extremes of my lifespan.

But once the past is changed, the previous past has never existed and I emerge from my mother's womb an infant-child-youth-man-ancient in a government cell a mental hospital dying in clean white sheets....And —

I, me, the spark of mind that is my consciousness, dwells in a locus that is neither place nor time. The objective duration of my lifespan is one hundred ten years, but from my own locus of consciousness, I am immortal — my awareness of my own awareness can never cease to be. I am an infant am a child am a youth am an old, old man dying on clean white sheets. I am all these mes, have always been all these mes will always be all these mes in the place where my mind dwells in an eternal moment divorced from time.

The primal powers never come to a standstill; the cycle of becoming continues uninterruptedly....Between the two primal powers there arises again and again a state of tension, a potential that keeps the powers in motion and causes them to unite, whereby they are constantly regenerated.

I Ching

from **Strange World**

Frank Edwards

[The] young woman could apparently see through her finger tips....the Institute of Biophysics of the Soviet Academy of Science invited her to the Institute for tests....she had discovered the strange talent by accident when she was sixteen years old, when both her eyes were heavily bandaged following an accident. The skeptical scientists bandaged her eyes with adhesive tape and metal foil...and even had her put a metal diving helmet over her head in some of the tests to preclude any possibility of fraud. Without hesitation the young woman read page after page of books and magazines they put before her. Without error she described the photographs in the publications and could even correctly name the colors in the various pictures.

...The Soviet Academy of Science agrees that she does indeed ''see'' with her finger tips...but how she does it they have no idea.

This talent is rare...but by no means unprecedented. In 1898, Doctor Khovrin of the Neuro-Psychiatric Hospital in Tambov tested such a case at great length and published his findings. During the 1920's Dr. Jules Romain of Paris tested more than a score of blind persons who demonstrated the ability to see with their skin. And in our own country, teenager Margaret Foos, daughter of an Elkton, Virginia, railroad worker, baffled the scientists in 1961, with her ability to see without use of her eyes.

Man is thrown into this world without his knowledge, consent or will, and he is removed from it again without his consent or will. In this respect he is not different from the animal, from the plants, or from inorganic matter. But being endowed with reason and imagination, he cannot be content with the passive role. ...He is driven by the urge to transcend...by becoming a"creator".

Erich Fromm, *The Sane Society* (1955)

The thing Seth has said that really excites me is that we make our own reality. I think the greatest thing one can do is to help show other people how their feelings and thoughts *do* form their world — from their daily family life, to their nation, to their world. This is the most liberating knowledge that anyone can possess. It frees people in all other areas of life. Whatever one does on the *outside* is not going to make a damn bit of difference unless he has changed his *thought pattern*.

Jane Roberts, *The Seth Material* (1972)

The Shell
James Stephens

I

And then I pressed the shell
Close to my ear,
And listened well.

And straightway, like a bell,
Came low and clear
The slow, sad, murmur of far distant seas

Whipped by an icy breeze
Upon a shore
Wind-swept and desolate.

It was a sunless strand that never bore
The footprint of a man,
Nor felt the weight

Since time began
Of any human quality or stir,
Save what the dreary winds and wave incur.

II

And in the hush of waters was the sound
Of pebbles, rolling round;
For ever rolling, with a hollow sound:

And bubbling sea-weeds, as the waters go
Swish to and fro
Their long cold tentacles of slimy grey:

There was no day;
Nor ever came a night
Setting the stars alight

To wonder at the moon:
Was twilight only, and the frightened croon,
Smitten to whimpers, of the dreary wind

And waves that journeyed blind ...
And then I loosed an ear—Oh, it was sweet
To hear a cart go jolting down the street.

Noise
Jack Vance

I

Captain Hess placed a notebook on the desk and hauled a chair up under his sturdy buttocks. Pointing to the notebook, he said, ''That's the property of your man Evans. He left it aboard the ship.''

Galispell asked in faint surprise, ''There was nothing else? No letter?''

''No, sir, not a thing. That notebook was all he had when we picked him up.''

Galispell rubbed his fingers along the scarred fibers of the cover. ''Understandable, I suppose.'' He flipped back the cover. ''Hmmmm.''

Hess asked tentatively, ''What's been your opinion of Evans? Rather a strange chap?''

''Howard Evans? No, not at all. He's been a very valuable man to us. Why do you ask?''

Hess frowned, searching for the precise picture of Evans' behavior. ''I considered him erratic, or maybe emotional.''

Galispell was genuinely startled. ''Howard Evans?''

Hess's eyes went to the notebook. ''I took the liberty of looking through his log, and...well —''

''And you took the impression he was...strange.''

''Maybe everything he writes is true,'' said Hess stubbornly. ''But I've been poking into odd corners of space all my life and I've never seen anything like it.''

''Peculiar situation,'' said Galispell in a neutral voice. He looked into the notebook.

II

Journal of Howard Charles Evans

I commence this journal without pessimism but certainly without optimism. I feel as if I have already died once. My time in the lifeboat was at least a foretaste of death. I flew on and on through the dark, and a coffin could be only slightly more cramped. The stars were above, below, ahead, astern. I have no clock, and I can put no duration to my drifting. It was more than a week, it was less than a year.

So much for space, the lifeboat, the stars. There are not too many pages in this journal. I will need them all to chronicle my life on this world which, rising up under me, gave me life.

There is much to tell and many ways in the telling. There is myself, my own response to this rather dramatic situation. But lacking the knack for tracing the contortions of my psyche, I will try to detail events as objectively as possible.

I landed the lifeboat on as favorable a spot as I had opportunity to select. I tested the atmosphere, temperature, pressure, and biology; then I ventured outside. I rigged an antenna and dispatched my first SOS.

Shelter is no problem; the lifeboat serves me as a bed, and, if necessary, a refuge. From sheer boredom later on I may fell a few of these trees and build a house. But I will wait; there is no urgency.

A stream of pure water trickles past the lifeboat; I have abundant concentrated food. As soon as the hydroponic tanks begin to produce, there will be fresh fruits and vegetables and yeast proteins.

Survival seems no particular problem.

The sun is a ball of dark crimson, and casts hardly more light than the full moon of Earth. The lifeboat rests on a meadow of thick black-green creeper, very pleasant underfoot. A hundred yards distant in the direction I shall call south lies a lake of inky water, and the meadow slopes smoothly down to the water's edge. Tall sprays of rather pallid vegetation — I had best use the word "trees" — bound the meadow on either side.

Behind is a hillside, which possibly continues into a range of mountains; I can't be sure. This dim red light makes vision uncertain after the first few hundred feet.

The total effect is one of haunted desolation and peace. I would enjoy the beauty of the situation if it were not for the uncertainties of the future.

The breeze drifts across the lake, smelling pleasantly fragrant, and it carries a whisper of sound from off the waves. I have assembled the hydroponic tanks and set out cultures of yeast. I shall never starve or die of thirst. The lake is smooth and inviting; perhaps in time I will build a little boat. The water is warm, but I dare not swim. What could be more terrible than to be seized from below and dragged under?

There is probably no basis for my misgivings. I have seen no animal life of any kind: no birds, fish, insects, crustacea. The world is one of absolute quiet, except for the whispering breeze.

The scarlet sun hangs in the sky, remaining in place during many of my sleeps. I see it is slowly westering; after this long day how long and how monotonous will be the night!

I have sent off four SOS sequences; somewhere a monitor station must catch them.

A machete is my only weapon, and I have been reluctant to venture far from the lifeboat. Today (if I may use the word) I took my courage in my hands and started around the lake. The trees are rather like birches, tall and supple. I think the bark and leaves would shine a clear silver in light other than this wine-coloured gloom. Along the lakeshore they stand in a line, almost as if long ago they had been planted by a wandering gardener. The tall branches sway in the breeze, glinting scarlet with purple overtones, a strange and wonderful picture which I am alone to see.

I have heard it said that enjoyment of beauty is magnified in the presence of others: that a mysterious rapport comes into play to reveal subtleties which a single mind is unable to grasp. Certainly as I walked along the avenue of trees with the lake and the scarlet sun behind, I would have been grateful for companionship — but I believe that something of peace, the sense of walking in an ancient, abandoned garden, would be lost.

The lake is shaped like an hourglass; at the narrow waist I could look across and see the squat shape of the lifeboat. I sat down under a bush, which continually nodded red and black flowers in front of me.

Mist fibrils drifted across the lake and the wind made low musical sounds.

I rose to my feet, continued around the lake.

I passed through forests and glades and came once more to my lifeboat.

I went to tend my hydroponic tanks, and I think the yeast had been disturbed, prodded at curiously.

The dark red sun is sinking. Every day — it must be clear that I use "day" as the interval between my sleeps — finds it lower in the sky. Night is almost upon me, long night. How shall I spend my time in the dark?

I have no gauge other than my mind, but the breeze seems colder. It brings long, mournful chords to my ears, very sad, very sweet. Mist-wraiths go fleeting across the meadow.

Wan stars already show themselves, ghost-lamps without significance.

I have been considering the slope behind my meadow; tomorrow I think I will make the ascent. I have plotted the position of every article I possess. I will be gone some hours; if a visitor meddles with my goods — I will know his presence for certain.

The sun is low, the air pinches at my cheeks. I must hurry if I wish to return while light still shows me the landscape. I picture myself lost; I see myself wandering the face of this world, groping for my precious lifeboat, my tanks, my meadow.

Anxiety, curiosity, obstinacy all spurring me, I set off up the slope at a half-trot.

Becoming winded almost at once, I slowed my pace. The turf of the lakeshore had disappeared; I was walking on bare rock and lichen. Below me the meadow became a patch, my lifeboat a gleaming spindle. I watched for a moment. Nothing stirred anywhere in my range of vision.

I continued up the slope and finally breasted the ridge. A vast valley fell off below me. Far away a range of great mountains stood into the dark sky. The wine-colored light slanting in from the west lit the prominences, the frontal bluffs, left the valleys in gloom: an alternate sequence of red and black beginning far in the west, continuing past, far to the east.

I looked down behind me, down to my own meadow, and was hard put to find it in the fading light. There it was, and there the lake, a sprawling hourglass. Beyond was dark forest, then a strip of old rose savanna, then a dark strip of woodland, then laminae of colorings to the horizon.

The sun touched the edge of the mountains, and with what seemed almost a sudden lurch, fell half below the horizon. I turned downslope; a terrible thing to be lost in the dark. My eye fell upon a white object, a hundred yards along the ridge. I walked nearer. Gradually it assumed form: a thimble, a cone, a pyramid — a cairn of white rocks.

A cairn, certainly. I stood looking down on it.

I turned, looked over my shoulder. Nothing in view. I looked down to the meadow. Swift shapes? I strained through the gathering murk. Nothing.

I tore at the cairn, threw rocks aside. What was below? Nothing.

In the ground a faintly marked rectangle three feet long was perceptible. I stood back. No power I knew of could induce me to dig into that soil.

The sun was disappearing. Already at the south and north the afterglow began, lees of wine: the sun moved with astounding rapidity; what manner of sun was this, dawdling at the meridian, plunging below the horizon?

I turned downslope, but darkness came faster. The scarlet sun was gone; in the west was the sad sketch of departed flame. I stumbled, I fell. I looked into the east. A marvelous zodiacal light was forming, a strengthening blue triangle.

I watched, from my hands and knees. A cusp of bright blue lifted into the sky. A moment later a flood of sapphire washed the landscape. A new sun of intense indigo rose into the sky.

The world was the same and yet different; where my eyes had been accustomed to red and the red subcolors, now I saw the intricate cycle of blue.

When I returned to my meadow the breeze carried a new sound: bright chords that my mind could almost form into melody. For a moment I so amused myself, and thought to see dance-motion in the wisps of vapor which for the last few days had been noticeable over my meadow.

In what I will call a peculiar frame of mind I crawled into the lifeboat and went to sleep.

I crawled out of the lifeboat into an electric world. I listened. Surely that was music — faint whispers drifting in on the wind like a fragrance.

I went down to the lake, as blue as a ball of that cobalt dye so aptly known as bluing.

The music came louder; I could catch snatches of melody — sprightly, quick-step phrases. I put my hands to my ears; if I were experiencing hallucinations, the music would continue. The sound diminished, but did not fade entirely; my test was not definitive. But I felt sure it was real. And where music was there must be musicians....I ran forward, shouted, "Hello!"

"Hello!" came the echo from across the lake.

The music faded a moment, as a cricket chorus quiets when disturbed, then gradually I could hear it again — distant music, "horns of elf-land faintly blowing."

It went completely out of perception. I was left standing in the blue light, alone on my meadow.

I washed my face, returned to the lifeboat, sent out another set of SOS signals.

...When my concept, of myself, of you, of cars, of cows, trees and refrigerators, are shattered; and when I again face the world with a questioning attitude; when I face the being in question and *let it disclose itself to me* ...I will receive...disclosure and change my concepts, and I will have grown.

John Taylor, *The Shape of Minds To Come* (1971)

Possibly the blue day is shorter than the red day; with no clock I can't be sure. But with my new fascination in the music and its source, the blue day seems to pass swifter.

Never have I caught sight of the musicians. Is the sound generated by the trees, by diaphanous insects crouching out of my vision?

One day I glanced across the lake, and — wonder of wonders! — a gay town spread along the opposite shore. After a first dumbfounded gaze, I ran down to the water's edge, stared as if it were the most precious sight of my life.

Pale silk swayed and rippled: pavilions, tents, fantastic edifices....Who inhabited these places? I waded knee-deep into the lake, and thought to see flitting shapes.

I ran like a madman around the shore. Plants with pale blue blossoms succumbed to my feet; I left the trail of an elephant through a patch of delicate reeds.

And when I came panting to the shore opposite my meadow, what was there? Nothing.

The city had vanished like a dream. I sat down on a rock. Music came clear for an instant, as if a door had momentarily opened.

I jumped to my feet. Nothing to be seen. I looked back across the lake. There — on my meadow — a host of gauzy shapes moved like May flies over a still pond.

When I returned, my meadow was vacant. The shore across the lake was bare.

So goes the blue day; and now there is amazement to my life. Whence comes the music? Who and what are these flitting shapes, never quite real but never entirely out of mind? Four times an hour I press a hand to my forehead, fearing the symptoms of a mind turning in on itself....If music actually exists on this world, actually vibrates the air, why should it come to my ears as Earth music? These chords I hear might be struck on familiar instruments; the harmonies are not all alien....And these pale plasmic wisps that I forever seem to catch from the corner of my eye: the style is that of gay and playful humanity. The tempo of their movement is the tempo of the music.

So goes the blue day. Blue air, blue-black turf, ultramarine water, and the bright blue star bent to the west.... How long have I lived on this planet? I have broadcast the SOS sequence until now the batteries hiss with exhaustion; soon there will be an end to power. Food, water are no problem to me, but what use is a lifetime of exile on a world of blue and red?

The blue day is at its close. I would like to mount the slope and watch the blue sun's passing — but the remembrance of the red sunset still provokes a queasiness in my stomach. So I will watch from my meadow, and then, if there is darkness, I will crawl into the lifeboat like a bear into a cave, and wait the coming of light.

The blue day goes. The sapphire sun wanders into the western forest, the sky glooms to blue-black, the stars show like unfamiliar home-places.

The significance of Brahman is expressed by *neti neti* (not so, not so); for beyond this, that you say it is not so, there is nothing further. Its name, however, is "the Reality of reality." That is to say, the senses are real, and the Brahman is their Reality.

Brhadaranyaka Upanishad

For some time now I have heard no music; perhaps it has been so all-present that I neglect it.

The blue star is gone, the air chills. I think that deep night is on me indeed....I hear a throb of sound, I turn my head. The east glows pale pearl. A silver globe floats up into the night: a great ball six times the diameter of Earth's full moon. Is this a sun, a satellite, a burnt-out star? What a freak of cosmology I have chanced upon!

The silver sun — I must call it a sun, although it casts a cool satin light — moves in an aureole like an oyster shell. Once again the color of the planet changes. The lake glistens like quicksilver, the trees are hammered metal.... The silver star passes over a high wrack of clouds, and the music seems to burst forth as if somewhere someone flung wide curtains.

I wander down to the lake. Across on the opposite shore once more I see the town. It seems clearer, more substantial; I note details that shimmered away to vagueness before — a wide terrace beside the lake, spiral columns, a row of urns. The silhouette is, I think, the same as when I saw it under the blue sun: silken tents; shimmering, reflecting cusps of light; pillars of carved stone, lucent as milk-glass; fantastic fixtures of no obvious purpose.... Barges drift along the quicksilver lake like moths, great sails bellying, the rigging a mesh of cobweb. Nodules of light hang on the stays, along the masts....On sudden thought, I turn, look up to my own meadow. I see a row of booths as at an oldtime fair, a circle of pale stone set in the turf, a host of filmy shapes.

Step by step I edge toward my lifeboat. The music waxes. I peer at one of the shapes, but the outlines waver. It moves to the emotion of the music — or does the motion of the shape generate the music?

I run forward, shouting. One of the shapes slips past me, and I look into a blur where a face might be. I come to a halt, panting hard; I stand on the marble circle. I stamp; it rings solid. I walk toward the booths, they seem to display complex things of pale cloth and dim metal — but as I look my eyes mist over as with tears. The music goes far, far away, my meadow lies bare and quiet. My feet press into silver-black turf; in the sky hangs the silver-black star.

I am sitting with my back to the lifeboat, staring across the lake, which is still as a mirror. I have arrived at a set of theories.

My primary proposition is that I am sane — a necessary article of faith; why bother even to speculate otherwise? So — events occurring outside my own mind cause everything I have seen and heard. But — note this! — these sights and sounds do not obey the laws of science; in many respects they seem particularly subjective.

It must be, I tell myself, that both objectivity and subjectivity enter into the situation. I receive impressions which my brain finds unfamiliar, and so translates to the concept most closely related. By this theory the inhabitants of this world are constantly close; I move unknowingly through their palaces and arcades; they dance incessantly around me. As my mind gains sensitivity, I verge upon rapport with their way of life and I see them. More exactly, I sense something which creates an image in the visual region of my brain. Their emotions, the pattern of their life sets up a kind of vibration which sounds in my brain as music....The reality of these creatures I am sure I will never know. They are diaphane, I am flesh; they live in a world of spirit, I plod the turf with my heavy feet.

These last days I have neglected to broadcast the SOS. Small lack; the batteries are about done.

The silver sun is at the zenith, and leans westward. What comes next? Back to the red sun? Or darkness? Certainly this is no ordinary planetary system; the course of this world along its orbit must resemble one of the pre-Copernican epicycles.

I belive that my brain is gradually tuning into phase with this world, reaching a new high level of sensitivity. If my theory is correct, the *elän-vital* of the native beings expresses itself in my brain as music. On Earth we would perhaps use the word "telepathy." So I am practicing, concentrating, opening my consciousness wide to these new perceptions. Ocean mariners know a trick of never looking directly at a far light lest it strike the eyes' blind spot. I am using a similar device of never staring directly at one of the gauzy beings. I allow the image to establish itself, build itself up, and by this technique they appear quite definitely human. I sometimes think I can glimpse the features. The women are like sylphs, achingly beautiful; the men — I have not seen one in detail, but their carriage, their form is familiar.

The music is always part of the background, just as rustling of leaves is part of a forest. The mood of these creatures seems to change with their sun, so I hear music to suit. The red sun gave them passionate melancholy, the blue sun merriment. Under the silver star they are delicate, imaginative, wistful.

The silver day is on the wane. Today I sat beside the lake with the trees a screen of filigree, watching the moth-barges drift back and forth. What is their function? Can life such as this be translated in terms of economics, ecology, sociology? I doubt it. The word intelligence may not even enter the picture; is not our brain a peculiarly anthropoid characteristic, and is not intelligence a function of our peculiarly anthropoid brain?...A portly barge sways near, with swamp-globes in the rigging, and I forget my hypotheses. I can never know the truth, and it is perfectly possible that these creatures are no more aware of me that I originally was aware of them.

Time goes by; I return to the lifeboat. A young womanshape whirls past. I pause, peer into her face; she tilts her head, her eyes burn into mine as she passes....I try an SOS — listlessly, because I suspect the batteries to be dank and dead.

And indeed they are.

The silver star is like an enormous Christmas tree bauble, round and glistening. It floats low, and once more I stand irresolute, half expecting night.

The star falls; the forest receives it. The sky dulls, and night has come.

I face the east, my back pressed to the hull of my lifeboat. Nothing.

I have no conception of the passage of time. Darkness, timelessness. Somewhere clocks turn minute hands, second hands, hour hands — I stand staring into the night, perhaps as slow as a sandstone statue, perhaps as feverish as a salamander.

In the darkness there is a peculiar cessation of sound. The music has dwindled; down through a series of wistful chords, a forlorn last cry....

A glow in the east, a green glow, spreading. Up rises a magnificent green sphere, the essence of all green, the tincture of emeralds, deep as the sea.

A throb of sound; rhythmical, strong music, swinging and veering.

The green light floods the planet, and I prepare for the green day.

I am almost one with the natives. I wander among their pavilions, I pause by their booths to ponder their stuffs and wares: silken medallions, spangles and circlets of woven metal, cups of fluff and iridescent puff, puddles of color and wafts of light-shot gauze. There are chains of green glass; captive butterflies; spheres which seem to hold all the heavens, all the clouds, all the stars.

And to all sides of me go the flicker and flit of the dreampeople. The men are all vague, but familiar; the women turn me smiles of ineffable provocation. But I will drive myself mad with temptations; what I see is no more than the formulation of my own brain, an interpretation. ... And this is tragedy, for there is one creature so unutterably lovely that whenever I see the shape that is she my throat aches and I run forward, to peer into her eyes that are not eyes....

Today I clasped my arms around her, expecting yielding wisp. Surprisingly, there was the feel of supple flesh. I kissed her, cheek, chin, mouth. Such a look of perplexity on the face as I have never seen; heaven knows what strange act the creature thought me to be performing.

She went her way, but the music is strong and triumphant: the voice of cornets, the resonant bass below.

A man comes past; something in his stride, his posture, plucks at my memory. I step forward; I will gaze into his face, I will plumb the vagueness.

He whirls past like a figure on a carousel; he wears flapping ribbons of silk and pompoms of spangled satin. I pound after him, I plant myself in his path. He strides past with a side-glance, and I stare into the rigid face.

It is my own face.

He wears my face, he walks with my stride. He is I.

Already is the green day gone?

The green sun goes, and the music takes on depth. No cessation now; there is preparation, imminence....What is that other sound? A far spasm of something growling and clashing like a broken gear box.

It fades out.

The green sun goes down in a sky like a peacock's tail. The music is slow, exalted.

The west fades, the east glows. The music goes toward the east, to the great bands of rose, yellow, orange,

52

lavender. Cloud-flecks burst into flame. A golden glow consumes the sky.

The music takes on volume. Up rises the new sun — a gorgeous golden ball. The music swells into a paean of light, fulfillment, regeneration....Hark! A second time the harsh sound grates across the music.

Into the sky, across the sun, drifts the shape of a spaceship. It hovers over my meadow, the landing jets come down like plumes.

The ship lands.

I hear the mutter of voices — men's voices.

The music is vanished; the marble carvings, the tinsel booths, the wonderful silken cities are gone.

III

Galispell rubbed his chin.

Captain Hess asked anxiously, "What do you think of it?"

Galispell looked for a long moment out the window. "What happened after you picked him up? Did you see any of these phenomena he talks about?"

"Not a thing." Captain Hess shook his big round head. "Sure, the system was a fantastic gaggle of dark stars and fluorescent planets and burnt-out old suns; maybe all these things played hob with his mind. He didn't seem too overjoyed to see us, that's a fact — just stood there, staring at us as if we were trespassers. 'We got your SOS,' I told him. 'Jump aboard, wrap yourself around a good meal!' He came walking forward as if his feet were dead.

"Well, to make a long story short, he finally came aboard. We loaded on his lifeboat and took off."

"During the voyage back he had nothing to do with anybody — just kept to himself, walking up and down the promenade."

"He had a habit of putting his hands to his head; one time I asked him if he was sick, if he wanted the medic to look him over. He said no, there was nothing wrong with him. That's about all I know of the man."

"We made Sun, and came down toward Earth. Personally, I didn't see what happened because I was on the bridge, but this is what they tell me:

"As Earth got bigger and bigger Evans began to act more restless than usual, wincing and turning his head back and forth. When we were about a thousand miles out, he gave a kind of furious jump.

" 'The noise!' he yelled. 'The horrible *noise!*' And with that he ran astern, jumped into his lifeboat, cast off, and they tell me disappeared back the way we came."

"And that's all I got to tell you, Mr. Galispell. It's too bad, after our taking all that trouble to get him, Evans decided to pull up stakes — but that's the way it goes."

"He took off back along your course?"

"That's right. If you're wanting to ask, could he have made the planet where we found him, the answer is, not likely."

"But there's a chance?"

"Oh, sure," said Captain Hess. "There's a chance."

The further one travels, the less one knows.

Lao Tzu

If thou shouldst say, "It is enough, I have reached perfection," all is lost. For it is the function of perfection to make one know one's imperfection.

St. Augustine

The Tale of the Sands

Idries Shah

A stream, from its source in far-off mountains, passing through every kind and description of countryside, at last reached the sands of the desert. Just as it had crossed every other barrier, the stream tried to cross this one, but it found that as fast as it ran into the sand, its waters disappeared.

It was convinced, however, that its destiny was to cross this desert, and yet there was no way. Now a hidden voice, coming from the desert itself, whispered: 'The Wind crosses the desert, and so can the stream.'

The stream objected that it was dashing itself against the sand, and only getting absorbed: that the wind could fly, and this was why it could cross a desert.

'By hurtling in your own accustomed way you cannot get across. You will either disappear or become a marsh. You must allow the wind to carry you over, to your destination.'

But how could this happen? 'By allowing yourself to be absorbed in the wind.'

This idea was not acceptable to the stream. After all, it had never been absorbed before. It did not want to lose its individuality. And, once having lost it, how was one to know that it could ever be regained?

'The wind', said the sand, 'performs this function. It takes up water, carries it over the desert, and then lets it fall again. Falling as rain, the water again becomes a river.'

'How can I know that this is true?'

'It is so, and if you do not believe it, you cannot become more than a quagmire, and even that could take many, many years; and it certainly is not the same as a stream.'

'But can I not remain the same stream that I am today?'

'You cannot in either case remain so,' the whisper said. 'Your essential part is carried away and forms a stream again. You are called what you are even today because you do not know which part of you is the essential one.'

When he heard this, certain echoes began to arise in the thoughts of the stream. Dimly, he remembered a state in which he — or some part of him, was it? — had been held in the arms of a wind. He also remembered — or did he? — that this was the real thing, not necessarily the obvious thing, to do.

And the stream raised his vapour into the welcoming arms of the wind, which gently and easily bore it upwards and along, letting it fall softly as soon as they reached the roof of a mountain, many, many miles away. And because he had had his doubts, the stream was able to remember and record more strongly in his mind the details of the experience. He reflected, 'Yes, now I have learned my true identity.'

The stream was learning. But the sands whispered: 'We know, because we see it happen day after day: and because we, the sands, extend from the riverside all the way to the mountain.'

And that is why it is said that the way in which the Stream of Life is to continue on its journey is written in the Sands.

O nobly born, the time has now come for thee to seek the Path. Thy breathing is about to cease. In the past thy teacher hath set thee face to face with the Clear Light; and now thou art about to experience it in its Reality in the *Bardo* state (the "intermediate state" immediately following death, in which the soul is judged — or rather judges itself by choosing, in accord with the character formed during its life on earth, what sort of an after-life it shall have). In this *Bardo* state all things are like the cloudless sky, and the naked, immaculate Intellect is like unto a translucent void without circumference or centre. At this moment know thou thyself and abide in that state. I too, at this time, am setting thee face to face.

The Tibetan Book of the Dead

When the walls come tumbling down, you are left without supports, but you can also see a lot further.

R.E. Masters and J. Houston, *The Varieties of Post-psychedelic Experience* (1966)

Vision is the perception of the human in all things. All nature is a projection of ourselves. As a man is, so he sees. Each person sees the universe in his own way.

William Blake

The poet is a seer, gifted with a peculiar insight into the nature of reality. And this reality is a timeless, unchanging, complete order, of which the familiar world is but a broken reflection.

Northrop Frye, *Fearful Symmetry* (1947)

The Awakening

Arthur C. Clarke

Marlan was bored, with the ultimate boredom that only Utopia can supply. He stood before the great window and stared down at the scudding clouds, driven by the gale that was racing past the foothills of the city. Sometimes, through a rent in the billowing white blanket, he could catch a glimpse of lakes and forests and the winding ribbon of the river that flowed through the empty land he now so seldom troubled to visit. Twenty miles away to the west, rainbow-hued in the sunlight, the upper peaks of the artificial mountain that was City Nine floated above the clouds, a dream island adrift in the cold wastes of the stratosphere. Marlan wondered how many of its inhabitants were staring listlessly across at him, equally dissatisfied with life.

There was, of course, one way of escape, and many had chosen it. But that was so obvious, and Marlan avoided the obvious above all things. Besides, while there was still a chance that life might yet hold some new experience, he would not pass through the door that led to oblivion.

Out of the mist that lay beneath him, something bright and flaming burst through the clouds and dwindled swiftly toward the deep blue of the zenith. With lack-lustre eyes, Marlan watched the ascending ship: once — how long ago! — the sight would have lifted his heart. Once he too had gone on such journeys, following the road along which Man had found his greatest adventures. But now on the twelve planets and the fifty moons there was nothing one could not find on Earth. Perhaps, if only the stars could have been reached, humanity might have avoided the cul-de-sac in which it was now trapped; there would still have remained endless vistas of exploration and discovery. But the spirit of mankind had quailed before the awful immensities of interstellar space. Man had reached the planets while he was still young, but the stars had remained forever beyond his grasp.

And yet — Marlan stiffened at the thought and stared along the twisting vapor-trail that marked the path of the departed ship — if Space had defeated him, there was still another conquest to be attempted. For a long time he stood in silent thought, while, far beneath, the storm's ragged hem slowly unveiled the buttresses and ramparts of the city, and below those, the forgotten fields and forests which had once been Man's only home.

The idea appealed to Sandrak's scientific ingenuity; it presented him with interesting technical problems which would keep him occupied for a year or two. That would give Marlan ample time to wind up his affairs, or, if necessary, to change his mind.

If Marlan felt any last-minute hesitations, he was too proud to show it as he said good-bye to his friends. They had watched his plans with morbid curiosity, convinced that he was indulging in some unusually elaborate form of

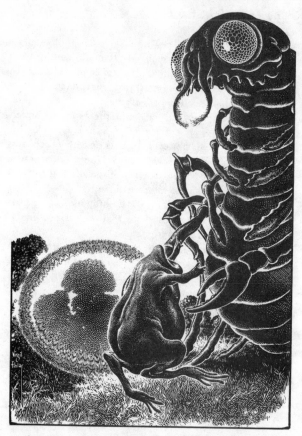

euthanasia. As the door of the little spaceship closed behind Marlan, they walked slowly away to resume the pattern of their aimless lives; and Roweena wept, but not for long.

While Marlan made his final preparations, the ship climbed on its automatic course, gaining speed until the Earth was a silver crescent, then a fading star lost against the greater glory of the sun. Rising upward from the plane in which the planets move, the ship drove steadily toward the stars until the sun itself had become no more than a blazing point of light. Then Marlan checked his outward speed, swinging the ship round into an orbit that made it the outermost of all the sun's children. Nothing would ever disturb it here; it would circle the sun for eternity, unless by some inconceivable chance it was captured by a wandering comet.

For the last time Marlan checked the instruments that Sandrak had built. Then he went to the innermost chamber and sealed the heavy metal door. When he opened it again, it would be to learn the secret of human destiny.

His mind was empty of all emotion as he lay on the thickly padded couch and waited for the machines to do their duty. He never heard the first whisper of gas through the vents; but consciousness went out like an ebbing tide.

Presently the air crept hissing from the little chamber, and its store of heat drained outward into the ultimate cold of space. Change and decay could never enter here; Marlan lay in a tomb that would outlast any that man had ever built on Earth, and might indeed outlast the Earth itself. Yet it was more than a tomb, for the machines it carried were biding their time, and every hundred years a circuit opened and closed, counting the centuries.

So Marlan slept, in the cold twilight beyond Pluto. He knew nothing of the life that ebbed and flowed upon Earth and its sister planets while the centuries lengthened into millennia, the millennia into eons. On the world that had once been Marlan's home, the mountains crumbled and were swept into the sea; the ice crawled down from the Poles as it had done so many times before and would do many times again. On the ocean beds the mountains of the future were built layer by layer from the falling silt, and presently rose into the light of day, and in a little while followed the forgotten Alps and Himalayas to their graves.

The sun had changed very little, all things considered, when the patient mechanism of Marlan's ship reawakened from their long sleep. The air hissed back into the chamber, the temperature slowly climbed from the verge of absolute zero to a level at which life might start again. Gently, the handling machines began the delicate series of tasks which should revitalize their master.

Yet he did not stir. During the long ages that had passed since Marlan began his sleep, something had failed among the circuits that should have awakened him. Indeed, the marvel was that so much had functioned correctly; for Marlan still eluded Death, though his servants would never recall him from his slumbers.

And now the wonderful ship remembered the commands it had been given so long ago. For a little while, as its multitudinous mechanisms slowly warmed to life, it floated inert with the feeble sunlight glinting on its walls. Then, ever more swiftly, it began to retrace the path along

We commonly think of ourselves as the lords and conquerors of nature. But insects had thoroughly mastered the world and taken full possession of it before man began the attempt....If they want our crops, they still help themselves to them. If they wish the blood of our domestic animals, they pump it out of the veins of our cattle and our horses....We cannot even protect our very persons from their annoying and pestiferous attacks....

An insect has a strong exterior skeleton and seems disproportionately powerful in relation to its size (an ant can lift 50 times its own weight). Its capacity for flight...attained about 100 million years before the first flying reptiles or birds, enables it to escape its enemies and range far and wide in search of food. The insect's small size frees it from the need to compete with many larger animals for a place in the en-vironment; its simple physiology enables it to endure conditions that kill other animals. Some insects can survive temperatures as low as -30 degrees F. or as high as 120 degrees F.

Time, July 12, 1976.

To those who think that the law of gravity interferes with their freedom, there is nothing to say. To most sensible people, this law is simply something that has to be taken into account in dealing with the world....In the behavioral sphere, we may be ingoring laws just as fundamental.

Tiger and Fox, *Time,* April 2, 1973

which it had traveled when the world was young. It did not check its speed until it was once more among the inner planets, its metal hull warming beneath the rays of the ancient unwearying sun. Here it began its search, in the temperate zone where the Earth had once circled; and here it presently found a planet it did not recognize.

The size was correct, but all else was wrong. Where were the seas that once had been Earth's greatest glory? Not even their empty beds were left: the dust of vanished continents had clogged them long ago. And where, above all, was the Moon? Somewhere in the forgotten past it had crept earthward and met its doom, for the planet was now girdled, as once only Saturn had been, by a vast, thin halo of circling dust.

For a while the robot controls searched through their electronic memories as the ship considered the situation. Then it made its decision, if a machine could have shrugged its shoulders, it would have done so. Choosing a landing place at random, it fell gently down through the thin air and came to rest on a flat plain of eroded sandstone. It had brought Marlan home; there was nothing more that it could do. If there was still life on the Earth, sooner or later it would find him.

And here, indeed, those who were now masters of Earth presently came upon Marlan's ship. Their memories were long, and the tarnished metal ovoid lying upon the sandstone was not wholly strange to them. They conferred among each other with as much excitement as their natures allowed and, using their own strange tools, began to break through the stubborn walls until they reached the chamber where Marlan slept.

In their way, they were very wise, for they could understand the purpose of Marlan's machines and could tell where they had failed in their duty. In a little while the scientists had made what repairs were necessary, though they were none too hopeful of success. The best that they could expect was that Marlan's mind might be brought, if only for a little while, back to the borders of consciousness before Time exacted its long-deferred revenge.

The light came creeping back into Marlan's brain with the slowness of a winter dawn. For ages he lay on the frontiers of self-awareness, knowing that he existed but not knowing who he was or whence he had come. Then fragments of memory returned, and fitted one by one into the intricate jigsaw of personality, until at last Marlan knew that he was — Marlan. Despite his weakness, the knowledge of success brought him a deep and burning sense of satisfaction. The curiosity that had driven him down the ages when his fellows had chosen the blissful sleep of euthanasia would soon be rewarded: he would know what manner of men had inherited the earth.

Strength returned. He opened his eyes. The light was gentle, and did not dazzle him, but for a moment all was blurred and misty. Then he saw figures looming dimly above him, and was filled with a sense of dreamlike wonder, for he remembered that he should have been alone on his return to life, with only his machines to tend him.

And now the scene came swiftly into focus, and staring back at him, showing neither enmity nor friendship, neither excitement nor indifference, were the fathomless eyes of the Watchers. The thin, grotesquely articulated figures stood around him in a close-packed circle, looking down at him across a gulf which neither his mind nor theirs could ever span.

Other men would have felt terror, but Marlan only smiled, a little sadly, as he closed his eyes forever. His questing spirit had reached its goal; he had no more riddles to ask of Time. For in the last moment of his life, as he saw those waiting round him, he knew that the ancient war between Man and insect had long ago been ended, and that Man was not the victor.

If any living species is to inherit the earth, it will not be man.

David Seltzer, *The Hellstrom Chronicle* (1971)

When...all life shall be on the very last verge of extinction on this globe; then, on a bit of lichen...shall be seated a tiny insect, preening its antennae in the glow of the worn-out sun, representing the sole survival of animal life on this earth — a melancholy BUG.

W.J. Holland, *The Moth Book* (1904)

Winter Evening
Archibald Lampman

Tonight the very horses springing by
Toss gold from whitened nostrils. In a dream
The streets that narrow to the westward gleam
Like rows of golden palaces; and high
From all the crowded chimneys tower and die
A thousand aureoles. Down in the west
The brimming plains beneath the sunset rest,
One burning sea of gold. Soon, soon shall fly
The glorious vision, and the hours shall feel
A mightier master; soon from height to height,
With silence and the sharp unpitying stars,
Stern creeping frosts, and winds that touch like steel,
Out of the depth beyond the eastern bars,
Glittering and still shall come the awful night.

The Man Who Was Put in a Cage

Rollo May

One evening a king of a far land was standing at his window, vaguely listening to some music drifting down the corridor from the reception room in the other wing of the palace. The king was wearied from the diplomatic reception he had just attended, and he looked out of the window pondering about the ways of the world in general and nothing in particular. His eye fell upon a man in the square below — apparently an average man, walking to the corner to take the tram home, who had taken that same route five nights a week for many years. The king followed this man in his imagination — pictured him arriving home, perfunctorily kissing his wife, eating his late meal, inquiring whether everything was right with the children, reading the paper, going to bed, perhaps engaging in the love act with his wife or perhaps not, sleeping, and getting up and going off to work again the next day.

And a sudden curiosity seized the king which for a moment banished his fatigue, "I wonder what would happen if a man were kept in a cage, like the animals at the zoo?"

So the next day the king called in a psychologist, told him of his idea, and invited him to observe the experiment. Then the king caused a cage to be brought from the zoo, and the average man was brought and placed therein.

At first the man was simply bewildered, and he kept saying to the psychologist who stood outside the cage, "I have to catch the tram, I have to get to work, look what time it is, I'll be late for work!" But later on in the afternoon the man began soberly to realize what was up, and then he protested vehemently, "The king can't do this to me! It is unjust, and against the laws." His voice was strong, and his eyes full of anger.

During the rest of the week the man continued his vehement protests. When the king would walk by the cage, as he did every day, the man made his protests directly to the monarch. But the king would answer, "Look here, you get plenty of food, you have a good bed, and you don't have to work. We take good care of you — so why are you objecting?" Then after some days the man's protests lessened and then ceased. He was silent in his cage, refusing generally to talk, but the psychologist could see hatred glowing like a deep fire in his eyes.

But after several weeks the psychologist noticed that more and more it now seemed as if the man were pausing a moment after the king's daily reminder to him that he was being taken good care of — for a second the hatred was postponed from returning to his eyes — as though he were asking himself if what the king said were possibly true.

And after a few weeks more, the man began to discuss with the psychologist how it was a useful thing if a man were given food and shelter, and that man had to live by his fate in any case and the part of wisdom was to accept his fate. So when a group of professors and graduate students came in one day to observe the man in the cage, he was friendly toward them and explained to them that he had chosen this way of life, that there are great values in security and being taken care of, that they would of course see how sensible his course was, and so on. How strange! thought the psychologist, and how pathetic — why is it he struggles so hard to get them to approve of his way of life?

In the succeeding days when the king would walk through the courtyard, the man would fawn upon him from behind the bars in his cage and thank him for the food and shelter. But when the king was not in the yard and the man was not aware that the psychologist was present, his expression was quite different — sullen and morose. When his food was handed to him through the bars by the keeper, the man would often drop the dishes or dump over the water and then be embarrassed because of his stupidity and clumsiness. His conversation became increasingly one-tracked: and instead of the involved philosophical theories about the value of being taken care of, he had gotten down to simple sentences like "It is fate," which he would say over and over again, or just mumble to himself, "It is."

It was hard to say just when the last phase set in. But the psychologist became aware that the man's face seemed to have no particular expression: his smile was no longer fawning, but simply empty and meaningless, like the

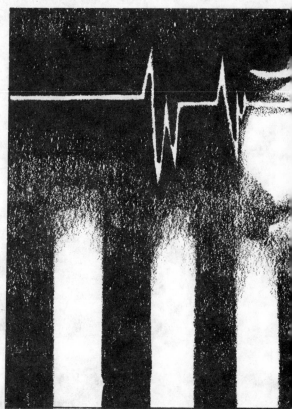

grimace a baby makes when there is gas on its stomach. The man ate his food, and exchanged a few sentences with the psychologist from time to time; his eyes were distant and vague, and though he looked at the psychologist, it seemed that he never really *saw* him.

And now the man, in his desultory conversations, never used the word "I" any more. He had accepted the cage. He had no anger, no hate, no rationalizations. But he was now insane.

That night the psychologist sat in his parlor trying to write a concluding report. But it was very difficult for him to summon up words, for he felt within himself a great emptiness. He kept trying to reassure himself with the words, "They say that nothing is ever lost, that matter is merely changed to energy and back again." But he couldn't help feeling something *had* been lost, something had been taken out of the universe in this experiment, and there was left only a void.

For too many maturity means a narrowing into a dull or resigned acceptance of a limited representative self and a disavowal or oblivion of the real self.

William Walsh, *The Use of Imagination* (1959)

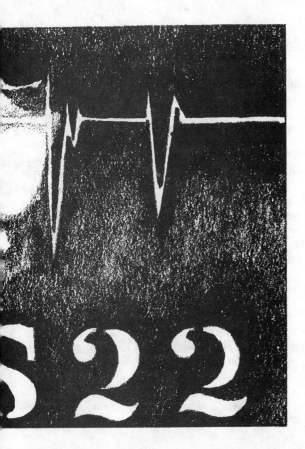

Hughes led a 'half-lunatic life'

New York (AP-Reuter) — For the last 15 years of his life billionaire Howard Hughes "lived a sunless, joyless, half-lunatic life" in tightly-curtained hotel rooms — often lying naked in bed watching movies over and over again....

The mysterious industrialist, pilot and film promoter is depicted as being in appalling physical condition and dependent on drugs. He had shrunk three inches from his former six-foot, four-inch frame and his weight fluctuated between 90 to 130 pounds.

He suffered from anemia, arthritis and other ills before he died at the age of 70.

Because Hughes could not walk during his last three years Margulis...carried him whenever he had to be moved.

In 1972, Hughes moved from Nicaragua to Vancouver Margulis recalls...that after entering his suite, the billionaire lingered by the window of the sitting room admiring the view.

"The aides didn't like that one bit," Margulis recalls. "They told me to get him away from the window and into his bedroom.

"Then something happened that really frosted me" he continues. "The boss said he liked the big room and the view and said it would make a nice sitting room for him.

"He hadn't had a sitting room for years, and he'd always had the windows taped and never looked out. They warned him that somebody could fly past the sitting room in a helicopter and shoot his picture with a telephoto lens.

"They told him 'here's your room' — and took him into another little blacked-out bedroom, with the draperies all taped down tight.

"He just went along with them and they had him back in his cage again," Margulis says.

Animals do not devise the concentration camps....But neither do they staff them; it is not true that the camps were run by beasts — they were run by men; the pleasure is as peculiar to man as the invention.

J. Bronowski, *The Identity of Man* (1965)

A man has many skins in himself, covering the depths of his heart. Man knows so many things; he does not know himself. Why, thirty or forty skins or hides, just like an ox's or a bear's, so thick and hard, cover the soul. Go into your own ground and learn to know yourself there.

Meister Eckhart

Lines Composed a Few Miles
above Tintern Abbey

Willian Wordsworth

Five years have passed; five summers, with the length
Of five long winters! and again I hear
These waters, rolling from their mountain-springs
With a soft inland murmur. Once again
Do I behold these steep and lofty cliffs,
That on a wild secluded scene impress
Thoughts of more deep seclusion; and connect
The landscape with the quiet of the sky.
The day is come when I again repose
Here, under this dark sycamore, and view
These plots of cottage-ground, these orchard tufts,
Which at this season, with their unripe fruits,
Are clad in one green hue, and lose themselves
 Mid groves and copses. Once again I see
These hedge-rows, hardly hedge-rows, little lines
Of sportive wood run wild: these pastoral farms,
Green to the very door; and wreaths o. smoke
Sent up, in silence, from among the trees!
With some uncertain notice, as might seem
Of vagrant dwellers in the houseless woods,
Or of some hermit's cave, where by his fire
The hermit sits alone.
                          These beauteous forms,
Through a long absence, have not been to me
As is a landscape to a blind man's eye;
But oft, in lonely rooms, and 'mid the din
Of towns and cities, I have owed to them,
In hours of weariness, sensations sweet,
Felt in the blood, and felt along the heart;
And passing even into my purer mind,
With tranquil restoration—feelings too
Of unremembered pleasure: such, perhaps,
As have no slight or trivial influence
On that best portion of a good man's life,
His little, nameless, unremembered acts
Of kindness and of love. Nor less, I trust,
To them I may have owed another gift,
Of aspect more sublime; that bless'ed mood,
In which the burthen of the mystery,
In which the heavy and the weary weight
Of all this unintelligible world,
Is lightened—that serene and bless'ed mood,
In which the affections gently lead us on—
Until, the breath of this corporeal frame
And even the motion of our human blood
Almost suspended, we are laid asleep
In body, and become a living soul;
While with an eye made quiet by the power
Of harmony, and the deep power of joy,
We see into the life of things.
                          If this
Be but a vain belief, yet, oh! how oft—

In darkness and amid the many shapes
Of joyless daylight; when the fretful stir
Unprofitable, and the fever of the world,
Have hung upon the beatings of my heart—
How oft, in spirit, have I turned to thee,
O sylvan Wye! thou wanderer through the woods,
How often has my spirit turned to thee!

  And now, with gleams of half-extinguished thought,
With many recognitions dim and faint,
And somewhat of a sad perplexity,
The picture of the mind revives again;
While here I stand, not only with the sense
Of present pleasure, but with pleasing thoughts
That in this moment there is life and food
For future years. And so I dare to hope,
Though changed, no doubt, from what I was when first
I came among these hills; when like a roe
I bounded o'er the mountains, by the sides
Of the deep rivers, and the lonely streams,
Wherever nature led: more like a man
Flying from something that he dreads than one
Who sought the thing he loved. For nature then
(The coarser pleasures of my boyish days,
And their glad animal movements all gone by)
To me was all in all—I cannot paint

When followers of Zen fail to go beyond the world of their senses and thoughts, all their doings and movements are of no significance. But when the senses and thoughts are annihilated, all the passages to Universal Mind are blocked, and no entrance then becomes possible. The original Mind is to be recognized along with the working of the senses and thoughts — only it does not belong to them, nor yet is it independent of them. Do not build up your views upon your senses and thoughts, do not base your understanding upon your senses and thoughts; but at the same time do not seek the Mind away from your senses and thoughts, do not try to grasp Reality by rejecting your senses and thoughts. When you are neither attached to, nor detached from, them, then you enjoy your perfect unobstructed freedom, then you have your seat of enlightenment.

Huang-Po

Mysticism strives...to bring back the old unity which religion has destroyed, but on a new plane, where the world of mythology and that of revelation meet in the soul of man.

Gershom G. Scholem, *Major Trends in Jewish Mysticism* (1955)

What then I was. The sounding cataract
Haunted me like a passion; the tall rock,
The mountain, and the deep and gloomy wood,
Their colors and their forms, were then to me
An appetite; a feeling and a love,
That had no need of a remoter charm,
By thought supplied, nor any intrest
Unborrowed from the eye. That time is past,
And all its aching joys are now no more,
And all its dizzy raptures. Not for this
Faint I, nor mourn nor murmur; other gifts
Have followed; for such loss, I would believe,
Abundant recompense. For I have learned
To look on nature, not as in the hour
Of thoughtless youth; but hearing oftentimes
The still, sad music of humanity,
Nor harsh nor grating, though of ample power
To chasten and subdue. And I have felt
A presence that disturbs me with the joy
Of elevated thoughts; a sense sublime
Of something far more deeply interfused,
Whose dwelling is the light of setting suns,
And the round ocean and the living air,
And the blue sky, and in the mind of man:
A motion and a spirit, that impels
All thinking things, all objects of all thought,
And rolls through all things. Therefore am I still
A lover of the meadows and the woods
And mountains; and of all that we behold
From this green earth; of all the mighty world
Of eye, and ear—both what they half create,
And what perceive; well pleased to recognize
In nature and the language of the sense

In archery a man must die to his purer nature, the one
which is free from all artificiality and deliberation, if he
is to reach perfect enjoyment of Tao. He must learn
how to control the emittance of truth, flowing like an
eternal spring. Finally, he must be able to reveal Tao in
his own attitude on the basis of true "insight." This
way is a very easy and direct one. The most difficult
thing is to let oneself die completely in the very act of
shooting.

Karlfried von Durkheim, *The Japanese Cult of
Tranquility* (1972)

Every living thing is a symbol of everlasting powers,
and it is these which one wishes to grasp and to understand.

C.M. Bowra, *The Romantic Imagination* (1961)

The anchor of my purest thoughts, the nurse,
The guide, the guardian of my heart, and soul
Of all my moral being.
                              Nor perchance,
If I were not thus taught, should I the more
Suffer my genial spirits to decay:
For thou art with me here upon the banks
Of this fair river; though my dearest Friend,
My dear, dear Friend; and in thy voice I catch
The language of my former heart, and read
My former pleasures in the shooting lights
Of thy wild eyes. Oh! yet a little while
May I behold in thee what I was once,
My dear, dear Sister! and this prayer I make,
Knowing that Nature never did betray
The heart that loved her; 'tis her privilege,
Through all the years of this our life, to lead
From joy to joy: for she can so inform
The mind that is within us, so impress
With quietness and beauty, and so feed
With lofty thoughts, that neither evil tongues,
Rash judgments, nor the sneers of selfish men,
Nor greetings where no kindness is, nor all
The dreary intercourse of daily life,
Shall e'er prevail against us, or disturb
Our cheerful faith that all which we behold
Is full of blessings. Therefore let the moon
Shine on thee in thy solitary walk;
And let the misty mountain-winds be free
To blow against thee: and, in after years,
When these wild ecstasies shall be matured
Into a sober pleasure; when thy mind
Shall be a mansion for all lovely forms,
Thy memory be as a dwelling-place
For all sweet sounds and harmonies; oh! then,
If solitude, or fear, or pain, or grief,
Should be thy portion, with what healing thoughts
Of tender joy wilt thou remember me,
And these my exhortations! Nor, perchance—
If I should be where I no more can hear
Thy voice, nor catch from thy wild eyes these gleams
Of past existence—wilt thou then forget
That on the banks of this delightful stream
We stood together; and that I, so long
A worshiper of Nature, hither came
Unwearied in that service; rather say
With warmer love—oh! with far deeper zeal
Of holier love. Nor wilt thou then forget,
That after many wanderings, many years
Of absence, these steep woods and lofty cliffs,
And this green pastoral landscape, were to me
More dear, both for themselves and for thy sake!

62

The moon, the snow,
   And now besides—through mist,
     the morning glow!

Michihko

A deer along with it,
   the mountain's shadow at the temple gate—
     the setting sun.

Buson

The moon on the pine:
   I keep hanging it—taking it off—
     and gazing each time.

Hokushi

A lightning gleam:
   into darkness travels
     a night heron's scream.

Basho

...any personal, direct awareness of the inner world has already grave risks.

But since society, without knowing it, is *starving* for the inner, the demands on people to evoke its presence in a "safe" way, in a way that need not be taken seriously, etc., is tremendous.

R.D. Laing, *The Politics of Experience* (1967)

If we insist on deriving the vision from a personal experience, we must treat the former as something secondary — as a mere substitute for reality. The result is that we strip the vision of its primordial quality and take it as nothing but a sympton. The pregnant chaos then shrinks to the proportions of a psychic disturbance....The frightening revelation of abysses that defy the human understanding is dismissed as illusion, and the poet is regarded as a victim and perpetrator of deception.

C.G. Jung, *Modern Man in Search of a Soul* (1933)

Appear, appear, what so thy shape or name,
O Mountain Bull, Snake of the Hundred Heads,
Lion of the Burning Flame!
O God, Beast, Mystery, come!

Euripides

This Whole
Of suns, and worlds, and men, and beasts, and flowers,
With all the silent or tempestuous workings
By which they have been, are, or cease to be,
Is but a vision; — all that it inherits
Are motes of a sick eye, bubbles and dreams;
Thought is its cradle, and its grave, nor less
The future and the past are idle shadows
Of thought's eternal flight — they have no being:
Nought is but that which feels itself to be.

Percy Bysshe Shelley

In a dark tree there hides
A bough, all golden, leaf and pliant stem,
Sacred to Proserpine. This all the grove
Protects, and shadows cover it with darkness.
Until this bough, this bloom of light, is found,
No one receives his passport to the darkness
Whose queen requires this tribute. In succession,
After the bough is plucked, another grows,
Gold-Green with the same metal. Raise the eyes,
Look up, reach up the hand.

Virgil

A man, just one—
    also a fly, just one—
        in the huge drawing room.

Issau

On the temple bell
    has settled, and is fast asleep,
        a butterfly.

Buson

Icy the moonshine:
    shadow of a tombstone,
        shadow of a pine.

Kyoshi

No sky at all;
    no earth at all—and still
        the snowflakes fall....

Hashin

**To be enlightened is to be aware, always, of total
reality in its immanent otherness — to be aware of it and
yet to remain in a condition to survive as an animal....
Our goal is to discover that we have always been where
we ought to be.**

Aldous Huxley, *The Doors of Perception* (1954)

Not Ideas About The Thing
But The Thing Itself
Wallace Stevens

At the earliest ending of winter,
In March, a scrawny cry from outside
Seemed like a sound in his mind.

He knew that he heard it,
A bird's cry, at daylight or before,
In the early March wind.

The sun was rising at six,
No longer a battered panache above snow...
It would have been outside.

It was not from the vast ventriloquism
Of sleep's faded papier-mâché...
The sun was coming from outside.

That scrawny cry—it was
A chorister whose c preceded the choir.
It was part of the colossal sun,

Surrounded by its choral rings,
Still far away. It was like
A new knowledge of reality.

The Player can't be worrying about the past or the future or the crowd or some other extraneous event. He must be able to respond in the here and now.... Sometimes in the heat of the game a player's perception and coordination improve dramatically. At times, I experience a kind of clarity that I've never seen described in any football story, sometimes time seems to slow way down, as if everyone were moving in slow motion. It seems as if I have all the time in the world to watch the receivers run their patterns, and yet I know the defensive line is coming at me just as fast as ever...the whole thing seems like a movie or a dance in slow motion. It's beautiful.

John Brodie, *San Francisco 49ers*

Sport anticipates what the Divine Essence is. Sport is a Western yoga. The Dance of Shiva. Pure play, the delight in the moment, the Now. We need a more balanced and evolutionary culture. We already have physical mobility, why shouldn't we have psychic mobility, the ability to move physically into different states.

Michael Murphy, *Esalen Institute*

from **The One Quest**
Claudio Naranjo

But in the midst of this deadness we can see the emergence of new life. The time will probably come when a completely new foliage of social forms will evolve. Man, in an unacknowledged thirst for selfknowledge, once set out to explore the whole universe. Disappointed but hopeful he now turns with his amassed knowledge toward himself. Today the value is in the search, in the exploration of chaos and of identities, in the renewal of meanings. This expression of yearning in the midst of a dying speculative philosophy is a return to the Problem of Man and a bowing of reason to experience, both dominant traits of existentialism which, among present philosophies, seems to monopolize all vitality. But just as philosophy in turning to Man generated existentialism, science, in turning to Man, generated today's psychology and sociology. Yet, even within the dawn of psychology there has been a conceptual transition from the mechanics of behaviour — man the robot — to the properly human aspects of man the pilot. For the first time, physiologists and psychologists have begun to speak of a ''science of consciousness.''

Nature gives me my model, life and thought; the nostrils breathe, the heart beats, the lungs inhale, the being thinks, and feels, has pains and joys, ambitions, passions and emotions. These I must express. What makes my Thinker think is that he thinks not only with his brain, with his knitted brow, his distended nostrils and compressed lips, but with every muscle of his arms, back and legs, with his clenched fist and gripping toes.

The main thing is to feel emotion, to love, to hope, to quiver, to live.

Auguste Rodin

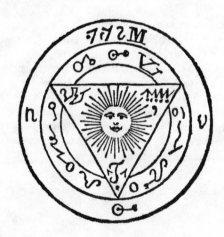

"Long lost in the wilderness, the boy has at last found the ox and his hands are on him. But, owing to the overwhelming pressure of the outside world, the ox is hard to keep under control. The wild nature is still unruly, and altogether refuses to be broken. If the oxherd wishes to see the ox completely in harmony with himself, he has surely to use the whip freely. With the energy of his whole being, the boy has at last taken hold of the ox: But how wild his will, how ungovernable his power!"

CATCHING THE OX

CREATIVITY

"When a thought moves, another follows, and then another — an endless train of thoughts is thus awakened. Through enlightenment all this turns into truth; but falsehood asserts itself when confusion prevails. Things oppress us not because of an objective world, but because of a self-deceiving mind. The boy is not to separate himself with his whip and tether, lest the animal should wander away into a world of defilements; when the ox is properly tended to, he will grow pure and docile; without a chain, nothing binding, he will by himself follow the oxherd."

HERDING THE OX

Time One is the way I experience time when I am passive and unfocussed.

Time Two is the way I experience time when my mind becomes self-governing, which is what happens when it focusses on *meaning*.

Time Three is the way I experience time when the creative chain reaction begins, when I experience a sense of total control of my mental processes and unwavering perception of meaning.

J.B. Priestly, *History and Present State of Discoveries Relating to Vision, Light and Color* (1772)

Dwarf Trees
Joy Kogawa

Out of the many small embarrassments of the day
Grew a miniature personality
Leafing itself gingerly in whatever genuine smile
It recognized in the thick undergrowth.
Dwarf trees planted in a fertile gentleness
Beside lush vegetation and sheltering green fans
Grew angular and stunted in a constant adjustment to cutting.
Horns of new growths sprouted
To bleed into warts and tiny anxieties.
Glances of disapproval felt as sharply
As salivating fangs tore at limbs.
Men developed into twisted sculptures of endurance
Bowing and smiling in civilized anger
And old women pruned daily into careful beauty
Glanced away in a cultivated shyness
Hiding smiles with humpbacked hands
Symbolizing by small gestures
Tiny treasures from a hidden childhood.

Reality Is an Activity of the Most August Imagination
Wallace Stevens

Last Friday, in the big light of last Friday night,
We drove home from Cornwall to Hartford, late.

It was not a night blown at a glassworks in Vienna
Or Venice, motionless, gathering time and dust.

There was a crush of strength in a grinding going round,
Under the front of the westward evening star,

The vigor of glory, a glittering in the veins,
As things emerged and moved and were dissolved,

Either in distance, change or nothingness,
The visible transformations of summer night,

An argentine abstraction approaching form
And suddenly denying itself away.

There was an insolid billowing of the solid.
Night's moonlight lake was neither water nor air.

Hush!

Zenna Henderson

June sighed and brushed her hair back from her eyes automatically as she marked her place in her geometry book with one finger and looked through the dining-room door at Dubby lying on the front-room couch.

"Dubby, *please,*" she pleaded. "You promised your mother that you'd be quiet tonight. How can you get over your cold if you bounce around making so much noise?"

Dubby's fever-bright eyes peered from behind his tented knees where he was holding a tin truck which he hammered with a toy guitar.

"I am quiet, June. It's the truck that made the noise. See?" And he banged on it again. The guitar splintered explosively and Dubby blinked in surprise. He was wavering between tears at the destruction and pleased laughter for the awful noise it made. Before he could decide, he began to cough, a deep-chested pounding cough that shook his small body unmercifully.

"That's just about enough out of you, Dubby," said June firmly, clearing the couch of toys and twitching the covers straight with a practiced hand. "You have to go to your room in just fifteen minutes anyway — or right now if you don't settle down. Your mother will be calling at seven to see if you're okay. I don't want to have to tell her you're worse because you wouldn't be good. Now read your book and keep quiet. I've got work to do."

There was a brief silence broken by Dubby's sniffling and June's scurrying pencil. Then Dubby began to chant:

"Shrimp boatses running a dancer tonight
 Shrimp boatses *run*ning a *dan*cer *tonight*
 SHRIMP BOATses RUNning a DANcer to-NIGHT —"

"Dub-by!" called June, frowning over her paper at him.

"That's not noise," protested Dubby. "It's singing. *Shrimp boatses —*" The cough caught him in mid-phrase and June busied herself providing Kleenexes and comfort until the spasm spent itself.

"See?" she said. "Your cough thinks it's noise."

"Well, what can I do then?" fretted Dubby, bored by four days in bed and worn out by the racking cough that still shook him. "I can't sing and I can't play. I want something to do."

"Well," June searched the fertile pigeonholes of her baby sitter's repertoire and came up with an idea that Dubby had once originated himself and dearly loved.

"Why not play-like? Play-like a zoo. I think a green giraffe with a mop for a tail and roller skates for feet would be nice, don't you?"

Dubby considered the suggestion solemnly. "If he had egg beaters for ears," he said, overly conscious as always of ears, because of the trouble he so often had with his own.

"Of course he does," said June. "Now you play-like one."

"Mine's a lion," said Dubby, after mock consideration. "Only he has a flag for a tail — a pirate flag — and he wears yellow pajamas and airplane wings sticking out of his back and his ears turn like propellers."

"That's a good one," applauded June. "Now mine is an eagle with rainbow wings and roses growing around his neck. And the only thing he ever eats is the song of birds, but the birds are scared of him and so he's hungry nearly all the time — pore ol' iggle!"

Dubby giggled. "Play-like some more," he said, settling back against the pillows.

"No, it's your turn. Why don't you play-like by yourself now? I've just got to get my geometry done."

Dubby's face shadowed and then he grinned. "Okay."

June went back to the table, thankful that Dubby was a nice kid and not like some of the brats she had met in her time. She twined both legs around the legs of her chair, running both hands up through her hair. She paused before tackling the next problem to glance in at Dubby. A worry nudged at her heart as she saw how pale and fine-drawn his features were. It seemed, everytime she came over, he was more nearly transparent.

She shivered a little as she remembered her mother saying, "Poor child. He'll never have to worry about old age. Have you noticed his eyes, June? He has wisdom in them now that no child should have. He has looked too often into the Valley."

June sighed and turned to her work.

The heating system hummed softly and the out-of-joint day settled into a comfortable accustomed evening. Mrs. Warren rarely ever left Dubby because he was ill so much of the time, and she practically never left him until he was settled for the night. But today when June got home from school, her mother had told her to call Mrs. Warren.

"Oh June," Mrs. Warren had appealed over the phone, "could you possibly come over right now?"

"Now?" asked June, dismayed, thinking of her hair and nails she'd planned to do, and the tentative date with Larryanne to hear her new album.

"I hate to ask it," said Mrs. Warren. "I have no patience with people who make last minute arrangements, but Mr. Warren's mother is very ill again and we just have to go over to her house. We wouldn't trust Dubby with anyone but you. He's got that nasty bronchitis again, so we can't take him with us. I'll get home as soon as I can, even if Orin has to stay. He's home from work right now, waiting for me. So please come, June!"

"Well," June melted to the tears in Mrs. Warren's voice. She could let her hair and nails and album go and she could get her geometry done at the Warrens' place. "Well, okay. I'll be right over."

"Oh, bless you, child," cried Mrs. Warren. Her voice faded away from the phone. "Orin, she's coming —" and the receiver clicked.

"June!" He must have called several times before June

Virgil Finlay

began to swim back up through the gloomy haze of the new theorem.

"Joo-un!" Dubby's plaintive voice reached down to her and she sighed in exasperation. She had nearly figured out how to work the problem.

"Yes, Dubby." The exaggerated patience in her voice signaled her displeasure to him.

"Well," he faltered, "I don't want to play-like anymore. I've used up all my thinkings. Can I make something now? Something for true?"

"Without getting off the couch?" asked June cautiously, wise from past experience.

"Yes," grinned Dubby.

"Without my to-ing and fro-ing to bring you stuff?" she questioned, still wary.

"Uh-huh," giggled Dubby.

...according to the *Courrier de l'Isere,* two little girls, last of December, 1842, were picking leaves from the ground, near Clavaux (Livet), France, when they saw stones falling around them. The stones fell with uncanny slowness. The children ran to their homes, and told of the phenomenon, and returned with their parents. Again stones fell, and with the same uncanny slowness....There was another phenomenon, an upward current, into which the children were dragged, as if into a vortex. We might have had data of mysterious disappearances of children, but the parents, who were unaffected by the current, pulled them back.

Charles Fort, *The Book of the Damned* (1919)

"What can you make for true without anything to make it with?" June asked skeptically.

Dubby laughed. "I just thought it up." Then all in one breath, unable to restrain his delight: "It's-really-kinda-like-play-like, but-I'm going-to-make-something-that-isn't-like-anything-real-so it'll-be-for-true, cause-it-won't-be-play-like-anything-that's-real!"

"Huh? Say that again," June challenged. "I bet you can't do it."

Dubby was squirming with excitement. He coughed tentatively, found it wasn't a prelude to a full production and said: "I can't say it again, but I can do it, I betcha. Last time I was sick, I made up some new magic words. They're real good. I betcha they'll work real good like anything."

"Okay, go ahead and make something," said June. "Just so it's quiet."

"Oh, it's *real* quiet," said Dubby in a hushed voice. "Exter quiet. I'm going to make a Noise-eater."

"A Noise-eater?"

"Uh-huh!" Dubby's eyes were shining. "It'll eat up all the noises. I can make lotsa racket then, 'cause it'll eat it all up and make it real quiet for you so's you can do your jommety."

"Now that's right thunkful of you, podner," drawled June. "Make it a good one, because little boys make a lot of noise."

"Okay." And Dubby finally calmed down and settled back against his pillows.

The heating system hummed. The old refrigerator in the kitchen cleared its throat and added its chirking throb to the voice of the house. The mantel clock tocked firmly to itself in the front room. June was absorbed in her homework when a flutter of movement at her elbow jerked her head up.

"Dubby!" she began indignantly.

"Shh!" Dubby pantomimed, finger to lips, his eyes wide with excitement. He leaned against June, his fever radiating like a small stove through his pajamas and robe. His breath was heavy with the odor of illness as he put his mouth close to her ear and barely whispered.

"I made it. The Noise-eater. He's asleep now. Don't make a noise or he'll get you."

"I'll get you, too," said June. "Play-like is play-like, but you get right back on that couch!"

"I'm too scared," breathed Dubby. "What if I cough?"

"You will cough if you —" June started in a normal tone, but Dubby threw himself into her lap and muffled her mouth with his small hot hand. He was trembling.

"Don't! Don't!" he begged frantically. "I'm scared. How do you un-play-like? I didn't know it'd work so good!"

There was a *choonk* and a slither in the front room. June strained her ears, alarm stirring in her chest.

"Don't be silly," she whispered. "Play-like isn't for true. There's nothing in there to hurt you."

A sudden succession of musical pings startled June and threw Dubby back into her arms until she recognized Mrs. Warren's bedroom clock striking seven o'clock — early as usual. There was a soft, drawn-out slither in the front room and then silence.

"Go on, Dubby. Get back on the couch like a nice child. We've played long enough."

"You take me."

June herded him ahead of her, her knees bumping his reluctant back at every step until he got a good look at the whole front room. Then he sighed and relaxed.

"He's gone." he said normally.

"Sure he is," replied June. "Play-like stuff always goes away." She tucked him under his covers. Then, as if hoping to brush his fears — and hers — away, by calmly discussing it, "What did he look like?"

"Well, he had a body like Mother's vacuum cleaner — the one that lies down on the floor — and his legs were like my sled, so he could slide on the floor, and had a nose like the hose on the cleaner only he was able to make it long or short when he wanted to."

Dubby, overstrained, leaned back against his pillows.

The mantel clock began to boom the hour deliberately.

"And he had little eyes like the light inside the refrigerator —"

The symbolic, imaginative view of the world is just as organic a part of the child's life as the view transmitted by the sense organs. It represents a natural and spontaneous striving which adds to man's biological bond a parallel and equivalent psychic bond, thus enriching life by another dimension — and it is eminently this dimension that makes man what he is.

J. Jacobi, *Complex/Archetype/Symbol* (1942)

June heard a *choonk* at the hall door and glanced up. Then with fear-stiffened lips, she continued for him, "And ears like TV antennae because he needs good ears to find the noises." And watched, stunned, as the round metallic body glided across the floor on shiny runners and paused in front of the clock that was deliberating on the sixth stroke.

The long, wrinkly trunk-like nose on the front of the thing flashed upward. The end of it shimmered, then melted into the case of the clock. And the seventh stroke never began. There was a soft sucking sound and the nose dropped free. On the mantel, the hands of the clock dropped soundlessly to the bottom of the dial. In the tight circle of June's arms, Dubby whimpered. June clapped her hand over his mouth. But his shoulders began to shake and he rolled frantic imploring eyes at her as another coughing spell began. He couldn't control it.

June tried to muffle the sound with her shoulder, but over the deep, hawking convulsions, she heard the *choonk* and slither of the creature and screamed as she felt it nudge her knee. Then the long snout nuzzled against her shoulder and she heard a soft hiss as it touched the straining throat of the coughing child. She grabbed the horribly vibrating thing and tried to pull it away, but Dubby's cough cut off in mid-spasm.

In the sudden quiet that followed she heard a gurgle like a straw in the bottom of a soda glass and Dubby folded into himself like an empty laundry bag. June tried to straighten him against the pillows, but he slid laxly down.

June stood up slowly. Her dazed eyes wandered trance-like to the clock, then to the couch, then to the horrible thing that lay beside it. Its glowing eyes were blinking and its ears shifting planes — probably to locate sound.

Her mouth opened to let out the terror that was constricting her lungs, and her frantic scream coincided with the shrill clamor of the telephone. The Eater hesitated, then slid swiftly toward the repeated ring. In the pause after the party line's four identifying rings, it stopped and June clapped both hands over her mouth, her eyes dilated with paralyzed terror.

The primary *imagination* I hold to be the living Power and prime Agent of all human Perception, and as a repetition in the finite mind of the eternal act of creation in the infinite I *am*.

Samuel Taylor Coleridge

The ring began again. June caught Dubby up into her arms and backed slowly toward the front door. The Eater's snout darted out to the telephone and the ring stilled without even an after-resonance.

The latch of the front door gave a rasping click under June's trembling hand. Behind her, she heard the *choonk* and horrible slither as the Eater lost interest in the silenced telephone. She whirled away from the door, staggering off balance under the limp load of Dubby's body. She slipped to one knee, spilling the child to the floor with a thump. The Eater slid toward her, pausing at the hall door, its ears tilting and moving.

June crouched on her knees, staring, one hand caught under Dubby. She swallowed convulsively, then cautiously withdrew her hand. She touched Dubby's bony little chest. There was no movement. She hesitated indecisively, then backed away, eyes intent on the Eater.

Her heart drummed in her burning throat. Her blood roared in her ears. The starchy *krunkle* of her wide skirt rattled in the stillness. The fibers of the rug murmured under her knees and toes. She circled wider, wider, the noise only loud enough to hold the Eater's attention — not to attract him to her. She backed guardedly into the corner by the radio. Calculatingly, she reached over and clicked it on, turning the volume dial as far as it would go.

The Eater slid tentatively toward her at the click of the switch. June backed slowly away, eyes intent on the creature. The sudden insane blare of the radio hit her an almost physical blow. The Eater glided up close against the vibrating cabinet, its snout lifting and drinking in the horrible cacophony of sound.

June lurched for the front door, wrenching frantically at the door knob. She stumbled outside, slamming the door behind her. Trembling, she sank to the top step, wiping the cold sweat from her face with the under side of her skirt. She shivered in the sharp cold, listening to the raucous outpouring from the radio that boomed so loud it was no longer intelligible.

She dragged herself to her feet, pausing irresolutely, looking around at the huddled houses, each set on its own acre of weeds and lawn. They were all dark in the early winter evening.

June gave a little moan and sank on the step again, hugging herself desperately against the penetrating chill. It seemed an eternity that she crouched there before the radio cut off in mid-note.

Fearfully, she roused and pressed her face to one of the door panes. Dimly through the glass curtains she could see the Eater, sluggish and swollen, lying quietly by the radio. Hysteria was rising for a moment, but she resolutely knuckled the tears from her eyes.

The headlights scythed around the corner, glittering swiftly across the blank windows next door as the car crunched into the Warren's driveway and came to a gravel-skittering stop.

June pressed her hands to her mouth, sure that even through the closed door she could hear the *choonk* and slither of the thing inside as it slid to and fro, seeking sound.

The car door slammed and hurried footsteps echoed along the path. June made wild shushing motions with her hands as Mrs. Warren scurried around the corner of the house.

"June!" Mrs. Warren's voice was ragged with worry. "Is Dubby all right? What are you doing out here? What's wrong with the phone?" She fumbled for the door knob.

"No, no!" June shouldered her roughly aside. "Don't go in! It'll get you, too!"

She heard a thud just inside the door. Dimly through the glass she saw the flicker of movement as the snout of the Eater raised and wavered toward them.

"June!" Mrs. Warren jerked her away from the door. "Let me in! What's the matter? Have you gone crazy?"

Mrs. Warren stopped suddenly, her face whitening. *"What have you done to Dubby, June?"*

The girl gulped with the shock of the accusation. "I haven't done anything, Mrs. Warren. He made a Noise-eater and it — it —" June winced away from the sudden blaze of Mrs. Warren's eyes.

"Get away from that door!" Mrs. Warren's face was that of a stranger, her words icy and clipped. "I trusted you with my child. If anything has happened to him —"

"Don't go in — oh, don't go in!" June grabbed at her coat hysterically. "Please, please wait! Let's get —"

"Let go!" Mrs. Warren's voice grated between her tightly clenched teeth. "Let me go, you — you —" Her hand flashed out and the crack of her palm against June's cheek was echoed by a *choonk* inside the house. June was staggered by the blow, but she clung to the coat until Mrs. Warren pushed her sprawling down the front steps and fumbled at the knob, crying, "Dubby! Dubby!"

June, scrambling up the steps on hands and knees, caught a glimpse of a hovering something that lifted and swayed like a waiting cobra. It was slapped aside by the violent opening of the door as Mrs. Warren stumbled into the house, her cries suddenly stilling on her slack lips as she saw her crumpled son by the couch.

She gasped and whispered, "Dubby!" She lifted him into her arms. His head rolled loosely against her shoulder. Her protesting, "No, no, no!" merged into half-articulate screams as she hugged him to her.

And from behind the front door there was a *choonk* and a slither.

June lunged forward and grabbed the reaching thing that was homing in on Mrs. Warren's hysterical grief. Her hands closed around it convulsively, her whole weight dragging backward, but it had a strength she couldn't match. Desperately then, her fists clenched, her eyes tight shut, she screamed and screamed and screamed.

The snout looped almost lazily around her straining throat, but she fought her way almost to the front door before the thing held her, feet on the floor, body at an impossible angle and stilled her frantic screams, quieted her straining lungs and sipped the last of her heartbeats, and let her drop.

Mrs. Warren stared incredulously at June's crumpled body and the horrible creature that blinked its lights and shifted its antennae questingly. With a muffled gasp, she sagged, knees and waist and neck, and fell soundlessly to the floor.

The refrigerator in the kitchen cleared its throat and the Eater turned from June with a *choonk* and slid away, crossing to the kitchen.

The Eater retracted its snout and slid back from the refrigerator. It lay quietly, its ears shifting from quarter to quarter.

The thermostat in the dining room clicked and the hot air furnace began to hum. The Eater slid to the wall under the register that was set just below the ceilings. Its snout extended and lifted and narrowed until the end of it slipped through one of the register openings. The furnace hum choked off abruptly and the snout end flipped back into sight.

Then there was quiet, deep and unbroken until the Eater tilted its ears and slid up to Mrs. Warren.

In such silence, even a pulse was noise.

There was a sound like a straw in the bottom of a soda glass.

A stillness was broken by the shrilling of a siren on the main highway four blocks away.

A *choonk* and a slither and the metallic bump of runners down the three front steps.

And a quiet, quiet house on a quiet side street.

Hush.

from **Fate** November 1960

Her sixteen-year-old girl got out of the car first and ran up a flight of stairs to the front door of their summer cottage. Mrs. Taggart had just started out of the car with her bags of groceries when she heard her daughter's confused cries.

Mrs. Taggart was startled to see Sonette inside the porch, still bearing a heavy load of books and groceries in her arms. Mrs. Taggart had the house keys in her hand, and the front door was definitely locked. Mrs. Taggart had to use her keys in order to open the door so that she could comfort her daughter.

"I questioned my daughter at great length as to what had happened," Mrs. Taggart wrote, "and she told me that she reached the first landing, then all of a sudden she was inside the house. She says the last thing she remembers about the stairs is getting to the landing. My daughter had no reason to fool me or make a joke of this... Anyway, she had no keys. We were both baffled...she didn't try the door or even set her packages down. She merely found herself inside on the porch."

The dreams of three-and four-year-old children...are so strikingly mythological and so fraught with meaning that one would take them at once for the dreams of grown-ups....They are the last vestiges of a dwindling collective psyche which dreamingly reiterates the perennial contents of the human soul.

C.G. Jung, *The Development of Personality CW Vol 17* (1928)

It did not dawn on man's consciousness until many centuries had passed that while his magic had no actual effect on the order of the external world, it did exert an influence on the...force emanating from the depths of his own psyche.

M.E. Harding, *Psychic Energy, Its Source and Its Transformation* (1963)

Shaw.75

from **The Magic Years**

Selma H. Fraiberg

The magician is seated in his high chair and looks upon the world with favor. He is at the height of his powers. If he closes his eyes, he causes the world to disappear. If he opens his eyes, he causes the world to come back. If there is harmony within him, the world is harmonious. If rage shatters his inner harmony, the unity of the world is shattered. If desire arises within him, he utters the magic syllables that causes the desired object to appear. His wishes, his thoughts, his gestures, his noises command the universe.

The magician stands midway between two worlds, but the world he commands at eighteen months is already waiting to take away his magic, and he himself has begun to make certain observations which cast doubt upon his powers. Somewhere around the end of the first year he began to discover that he was not the initiator of all activity, that causes for certain events existed outside of himself, quite independent of his needs and his wishes, but now, in the middle of the second year, the magician makes a discovery which will slowly lead him to his downfall. The magician will be undone by his own magic. For when he ascends to the heights of word-magic, when he discovers he can command with a word, he will be lured into a new world, he will commit himself unknowingly to new laws of thinking, the principles of this second world which oppose magic by means of the word.

Summer

John Ashbery

There is that sound like the wind
Forgetting in the branches that means something
Nobody can translate. And there is the sobering "later
    on,"
When you consider what a thing meant, and put it
    down.

For the time being the shadow is ample
And hardly seen, divided among the twigs of a tree,
The trees of a forest, just as life is divided up
Between you and me, and among all the others out
    there.

And the thinning-out phase follows
The period of reflection. And suddenly, to be dying
Is not a little or mean or cheap thing,
Only wearying, the heat unbearable,

And also the little mindless constructions put upon
Our fantasies of what we did: summer, the ball of pine
    needles,
The loose fates serving our acts, with token smiles,
Carrying out their instructions too accurately—

Too late to cancel them now—and winter, the twitter
Of cold stars at the pane, that describes with broad
    gestures
This state of being that is not so big after all.
Summer involves going down as a steep flight of steps

To a narrow ledge over the water. Is this it, then,
This iron comfort, these reasonable taboos,
Or did you mean it when you stopped? And the face
Resembles yours, the one reflected in the water.

The Hounds of Tindalos

Frank Belknap Long

"I'm glad you came," said Chalmers. He was sitting by the window and his face was very pale. Two tall candles guttered at his elbow and cast a sickly amber light over his long nose and slightly receding chin. Chalmers would have nothing modern about his apartment. He had the soul of a mediaeval ascetic and he preferred illuminated manuscripts to automobiles, and leering stone gargoyles to radios and adding-machines.

As I crossed the room to the settee he had cleared for me I glanced at his desk and was surprised to discover that he had been studying the mathematical formulae of a celebrated contemporary physicist, and that he had covered many sheets of thin yellow paper with curious geometric designs.

"Einstein and John Dee are strange bedfellows," I said as my gaze wandered from his mathematical charts to the sixty or seventy quaint books that comprised his strange little library. Plotinus and Emanuel Moscopulus, St. Thomas Aquinas and Frenicle de Bessy stood elbow to elbow in the somber ebony bookcase, and chairs, table and desk were littered with pamphlets about mediaeval sorcery and witchcraft and black magic, and all of the valiant glamorous things that the modern world has repudiated.

Chalmers smiled engagingly, and passed me a Russian cigarette on a curiously carved tray. "We are just discovering now," he said, "that the old alchemists and sorcerers were two-thirds *right*, and that your modern biologist and materialist is nine-tenths *wrong.*"

"You have always scoffed at modern science," I said, a little impatiently.

"Only at scientific dogmatism," he replied. "I have always been a rebel, a champion of originality and lost causes; that is why I have chosen to repudiate the conclusions of contemporary biologists."

"And Einstein?" I asked.

"A priest of transcendental mathematics!" he murmured reverently. "A profound mystic and explorer of the great *suspected.*"

"Then you do not entirely despise science."

"Of course not," he affirmed. "I merely distrust the scientific positivism of the past fifty years, the positivism of Haeckel and Darwin and of Mr. Bertrand Russell. I believe that biology has failed pitifully to explain the mystery of man's origin and destiny."

"Give them time," I retorted.

Chalmers' eyes glowed. "My friend," he murmured, "your pun is sublime. Give them *time*. That is precisely what I would do. But your modern biologist scoffs at time. He has the key but he refuses to use it. What do we know of time, really? Einstein believes that it is relative, that it can be interpreted in terms of space, of *curved* space. But must we stop there? When mathematics fails us can we not advance by — insight?"

"You are treading on dangerous ground," I replied. "That is a pitfall that your true investigator avoids. That is why modern science has advanced so slowly. It accepts nothing that it cannot demonstrate. But you —"

"I would take hashish, opium, all manner of drugs. I would emulate the sages of the East. And then perhaps I would apprehend — "

"What?"

"The fourth dimension."

"Theosophical rubbish!"

"Perhaps. But I believe that drugs expand human consciousness. William James agreed with me. And I have discovered a new one."

"A new drug?"

"It was used centuries ago by Chinese alchemists, but it is virtually unknown in the West. Its occult properties are amazing. With its aid and the aid of my mathematical knowledge I believe that I can *go back through time.*"

"I do not understand."

"Time is merely our imperfect perception of a new dimension of space. Time and motion are both illusions. Everything that has existed from the beginning of the world *exists now*. Events that occurred centuries ago on this planet continue to exist in another dimension of space. Events that will occur centuries from now *exist already*. We cannot perceive their existence because we

76

cannot enter the dimension of space that contains them. Human beings as we know them are merely fractions, infinitesimally small fractions of one enormous whole. Every human being is linked with *all* the life that has preceded him on this planet. All of his ancestors are parts of him. Only time separates him from his forebears, and time is an illusion and does not exist.''

''I think I understand,'' I murmured.

''It will be sufficient for my purpose if you can form a vague idea of what I wish to achieve. I wish to strip from my eyes the veils of illusion that time has thrown over them, and see the *beginning and the end.*''

''And you think this new drug will help you?''

''I am sure that it will. And I want you to help me. I intend to take the drug immediately. I cannot wait. I must *see.*'' His eyes glittered strangely. ''I am going back, back through time.''

He rose and strode to the mantel. When he faced me again he was holding a small square box in the palm of his hand. ''I have here five pellets of the drug Liao. It was used by the Chinese philosopher Lao Tze, and while under its influence he visioned Tao. Tao is the most mysterious force in the world; it surrounds and pervades all things; it contains the visible universe and everything that we call reality. He who apprehends the mysteries of Tao sees clearly all that was and will be.''

''Rubbish!'' I retorted.

''Tao resembles a great animal, recumbent, motionless, containing in its enormous body all the worlds of our universe, the past, the present and the future. We see portions of this great monster through a slit, which we call time. With the aid of this drug I shall enlarge the slit. I shall behold the great figure of life, the great recumbent beast in its entirety.''

''And what do you wish me to do?''

''Watch, my friend. Watch and take notes. And if I go back too far you must recall me to reality. You can recall me by shaking me violently. If I appear to be suffering acute physical pain you must recall me at once.''

''Chalmers,'' I said, ''I wish you wouldn't make this experiment. You are taking dreadful risks. I don't believe that there is any fourth dimension and I emphatically do not believe in Tao. And I don't approve of your experimenting with unknown drugs.''

''I know the properties of this drug,'' he replied. ''I know precisely how it affects the human animal and I know its dangers. The risk does not reside in the drug itself. My only fear is that I may become lost in time. You see, I shall assist the drug. Before I swallow this pellet I shall give my undivided attention to the geometric and algebraic symbols that I have traced on this paper.'' He raised the mathematical chart that rested on his knee. ''I shall prepare my mind for an excursion into time. I shall approach the fourth dimension with my conscious mind before I take the drug which will enable me to exercise occult powers of perception. Before I enter the dream world of the Eastern mystic I shall acquire all of the mathematical help that modern science can offer. This mathematical knowledge, this conscious approach to an actual apprehension of the fourth dimension of time will supplement the work of the drug. The drug will open up stupendous new vistas — the mathematical preparation will enable me to grasp them intellectually. I have often grasped the fourth dimension in dreams, emotionally, intuitively, but I have never been able to recall, in waking life, the occult splendors that were momentarily revealed to me.

''But with your aid, I believe that I can recall them. You will take down everything that I say while I am under the influence of the drug. No matter how strange or incoherent my speech may become you will omit nothing. When I awake I may be able to supply the key to whatever is mysterious or incredible. I am not sure that I shall succeed, but if I *do* succeed'' — his eyes were strangely luminious — ''*time will exist for me no longer!*''

Were we to plunge down a black hole, we would re-emerge, it is conjectured, in a different part of the universe and in another epoch in time....

Black holes may be entrances to Wonderlands. But are there Alices or white rabbits?

Carl Sagan, *The Cosmic Connection* (1973)

"What we want is *complete* imaginative experience which goes through the whole soul and body: the whole consciousness of men working together in unison and oneness: instinct, intuition, mind, intellect all fused into one complete consciousness, and grasping what we may call a complete truth, or a complete vision, a complete revelation..."

Phoenix

He sat down abruptly. ''I shall make the experiment at once. Please stand over there by the window and watch. Have you a fountain pen?''

I nodded gloomily and removed a pale green Waterman from my upper vest pocket.

''And a pad, Frank?''

I groaned and produced a memorandum book. ''I emphatically disapprove of this experiment,'' I muttered. ''You're taking a frightful risk.''

''Don't be an asinine old woman!'' he admonished. ''Nothing that you can say will induce me to stop now. I entreat you to remain silent while I study these charts.''

He raised the charts and studied them intently. I

watched the clock on the mantel as it ticked óut the seconds, and a curious dread clutched at my heart so that I choked.

Suddenly the clock stopped ticking, and exactly at that moment Chalmers swallowed the drug.

I rose quickly and moved toward him, but his eyes implored me not to interfere. "The clock has stopped," he murmured. "The forces that control it approve of my experiment. *Time* stopped, and I swallowed the drug. I pray God that I shall not lose my way."

He closed his eyes and leaned back on the sofa. All of the blood had left his face and he was breathing heavily. It was clear that the drug was acting with extraordinary rapidity.

"It is beginning to get dark," he murmured. "Write that. It is beginning to get dark and the familiar objects in the room are fading out. I can discern them vaguely through my eyelids, but they are fading swiftly."

I shook my pen to make the ink come and wrote rapidly in shorthand as he continued to dictate.

"I am leaving the room. The walls are vanishing and I can no longer see any of the familiar objects. Your face, though, is still visible to me. I hope that you are writing. I think that I am about to make a great leap — a leap through space. Or perhaps it is through time that I shall make the leap. I cannot tell. Everything is dark, indistinct."

Imagination creates shapes by which reality can be revealed.

C.M. Bowra, *The Romantic Imagination* (1949)

Imagination is a communion of the soul and the external world....

June K. Singer, *The Unholy Bible* (1970)

He sat for a while silent, with his head sunk upon his breast. Then suddenly he stiffened and his eyelids fluttered open. "God in heaven!" he cried. "*I see!*"

He was straining forward in his chair, staring at the opposite wall. But I knew that he was looking beyond the wall and that the objects in the room no longer existed for him. "Chalmers," I cried, "Chalmers, shall I wake you?"

"Do not!" he shrieked. "*I see everything.* All of the billions of lives that preceded me on this planet are before me at this moment. I see men of all ages, all races, all colors. They are fighting, killing, building, dancing, singing. They are sitting about rude fires on lonely gray deserts, and flying through the air in monoplanes. They are riding the seas in bark canoes and enormous steam-

ships; they are painting bison and mammoths on the walls of dismal caves and covering huge canvases with queer futuristic designs. I watch the migrations from Atlantis. I watch the migrations from Lemuria. I see the elder races — a strange horde of black dwarfs overwhelming Asia, and the Neandertalers with lowered heads and bent knees ranging obscenely across Europe. I watch the Achaeans streaming into the Greek islands, and the crude beginnings of Hellenic culture. I am in Athens and Pericles is young. I am standing on the soil of Italy. I assist in the rape of the Sabines; I march with the Imperial Legions. I tremble with awe and wonder as the enormous standards go by and the ground shakes with the tread of the victorious *hastati*. A thousand naked slaves grovel before me as I pass in a litter of gold and ivory drawn by night-black oxen from Thebes, and the flowergirls scream '*Ave Caesar*' as I nod and smile. I am myself a slave on a Moorish galley. I watch the erection of a great cathedral. Stone by stone it rises, and through months and years I stand and watch each stone as it falls into place. I am burned on a cross head downward in the thyme-scented gardens of Nero, and I watch with amusement and scorn the torturers at work in the chambers of the Inquisition.

"I walk in the holiest sanctuaries; I enter the temples of Venus. I kneel in adoration before the Magna Mater, and I throw coins on the bare knees of the sacred courtezans who sit with veiled faces in the groves of Babylon. I creep into an Elizabethan theater and with the stinking rabble about me I applaud *The Merchant of Venice*. I walk with Dante through the narrow streets of Florence. I meet the young Beatrice, and the hem of her garment brushes my sandals as I stare enraptured. I am a priest of Isis, and my magic astounds the nations. Simon Magus kneels before me, imploring my assistance, and Pharaoh trembles when I approach. In India I talk with the Masters and run screaming from their presence, for their revalations are as salt on wounds that bleed.

"I perceive everything *simultaneously*. I perceive everything from all sides; I am a part of all the teeming billions about me. I exist in all men and all men exist in me. I perceive the whole of human history in a single instant, the past and the present.

"By simply *straining* I can see farther and farther back. Now I am going back through strange curves and angles. Angles and curves multiply about me. I perceive great segments of time through *curves*. There is *curved time*, and *angular time*. The beings that exist in angular time cannot enter curved time. It is very strange.

"I am going back and back. Man has disappeared from the earth. Gigantic reptiles crouch beneath enormous palms and swim through the loathly black waters of dismal lakes. Now the reptiles have disappeared. No animals remain upon the land, but beneath the waters, plainly visible to me, dark forms move slowly over the rotting vegetation.

"The forms are becoming simpler and simpler. Now they are single cells. All about me there are angles — strange angles that have no counterparts on the earth. I am desperately afraid.

"There is an abyss of being which man has never fathomed."

I stared. Chalmers had risen to his feet and he was gesticulating helplessly with his arms. "I am passing through unearthly angles; I am approaching — oh, the burning horror of it."

"Chalmers!" I cried. "Do you wish me to interfere?"

He brought his right hand quickly before his face, as though to shut out a vision unspeakable. "Not yet!" he cried; "I will go on. I will see — what — lies — beyond —"

A cold sweat streamed from his forehead and his shoulders jerked spasmodically. "Beyond life there are" — his face grew ashen with terror — "*things* that I cannot distinguish. They move slowly through angles. They have no bodies, and they move slowly through outrageous angles."

It was then that I became aware of the odor in the room. It was a pungent, indescribable odor, so nauseous that I could scarcely endure it. I stepped quickly to the window and threw it open. When I returned to Chalmers and looked into his eyes I nearly fainted.

"I think they have scented me!" he shrieked. "They are slowly turning toward me."

He was trembling horribly. For a moment he clawed at the air with his hands. Then his legs gave way beneath him and he fell forward on his face, slobbering and moaning.

I watched him in silence as he dragged himself across the floor. He was no longer a man. His teeth were bared and saliva dripped from the corners of his mouth.

"Chalmers," I cried. "Chalmers, stop it! Stop it, do you hear?"

As if in reply to my appeal he commenced to utter hoarse convulsive sounds which resembled nothing so much as the barking of a dog, and began a sort of hideous writhing in a circle about the room. I bent and seized him by the shoulders. Violently, desperately, I shook him. He turned his head and snapped at my wrist. I was sick with horror, but I dared not release him for fear that he would destroy himself in a paroxysm of rage.

"Chalmers," I muttered, "you must stop that. There is nothing in this room that can harm you. Do you understand?"

I continued to shake and admonish him, and gradually the madness died out of his face. Shivering convulsively, he crumpled into a grotesque heap on the Chinese rug.

I carried him to the sofa and deposited him upon it. His features were twisted in pain, and I knew that he was still struggling dumbly to escape from abominable memories.

"Whisky," he muttered. "You'll find a flask in the cabinet by the window — upper left-hand drawer."

When I handed him the flask his fingers tightened about it until the knuckles showed blue. "They nearly got me," he gasped. He drained the stimulant in immoderate gulps, and gradually the color crept back into his face.

"That drug was the very devil!" I murmured.

"It wasn't the drug," he moaned.

His eyes no longer glared insanely, but he still wore the look of a lost soul.

"They scented me in time," he moaned. "I went too far."

"What were *they* like." I said, to humor him.

He leaned forward and gripped my arm. He was shivering horribly. "No words in our language can describe them!" He spoke in a hoarse whisper. "They are symbolized vaguely in the myth of the Fall, and in an obscene form which is occasionally found engraved on ancient tablets. The Greeks had a name for them, which veiled their essential foulness. The tree, the snake, and the apple — these are the vague symbols of a most awful mystery."

His voice had risen to a scream. "Frank, Frank, a terrible and unspeakable *deed* was done in the beginning. Before time, the *deed,* and from the deed —"

He had risen and was hysterically pacing the room. "The deeds of the dead move through angles in dim recesses of time. They are hungry and athirst!"

"Chalmers," I pleaded to quiet him. "We are living in the third decade of the Twentieth Century."

"They are lean and athirst!" he shrieked. "*The Hounds of Tindalos!*"

"Chalmers, shall I phone for a physician?"

"A physician cannot help me now. They are horrors of the soul, and yet" — he hid his face in his hands and groaned — "they are real, Frank. I saw them for a ghastly moment. For a moment I stood on the *other side.* I stood on the pale gray shores beyond time and space. In an awful light that was not light, in a silence that shrieked, I saw *them.*

"All the evil in the universe was concentrated in their lean, hungry bodies. Or had they bodies? I saw them only for a moment; I cannot be certain. *But I heard them breathe.* Indescribable for a moment I felt their breath upon my face. They turned toward me and I fled screaming. In a single moment I fled screaming through time. I fled down quintillions of years.

"But they scented me. Men awake in them cosmic hungers. We have escaped, momentarily, from the foulness that rings them round. They thirst for that in us which is clean, which emerged from the deed without stain. There is a part of us which did not partake in the deed, and that they hate. But do not imagine that they are literally, prosaically evil. They are beyond good and evil as we know it. They are that which in the beginning fell away from cleanliness. Through the deed they became bodies of death, receptacles of all foulness. But they are not evil in *our* sense because in the spheres through which they move there is no thought, no moral, no right or wrong as we understand it. There is merely the pure and the foul. The foul expresses itself through angle; the pure through curves. Man, the pure part of him, is descended from a curve. Do not laugh. I mean that literally.''

I rose and searched for my hat. ''I'm dreadfully sorry for you, Chalmers,'' I said, as I walked toward the door. ''But I don't intend to stay and listen to such gibberish. I'll send my physician to see you. He's an elderly, kindly chap and he won't be offended if you tell him to go to the devil. But I hope you'll respect his advice. A week's rest in a good sanitarium should benefit you immeasurably.''

I heard him laughing as I descended the stairs, but his laughter was so utterly mirthless that it moved me to tears.

When Chalmers phoned the following morning my first impulse was to hang up the receiver immediately. His request was so unusual and his voice was so wildly hysterical that I feared any further association with him would result in the impairment of my own sanity. But I could not doubt the genuineness of his misery, and when he broke down completely and I heard him sobbing over the wire I decided to comply with his request.

''Very well,'' I said. ''I will come over immediately and bring the plaster.''

En route to Chalmers' home I stopped at a hardware store and purchased twenty pounds of plaster of Paris. When I entered my friend's room he was crouching by the window watching the opposite wall out of eyes that were feverish with fright. When he saw me he rose and seized the parcel containing the plaster with an avidity that

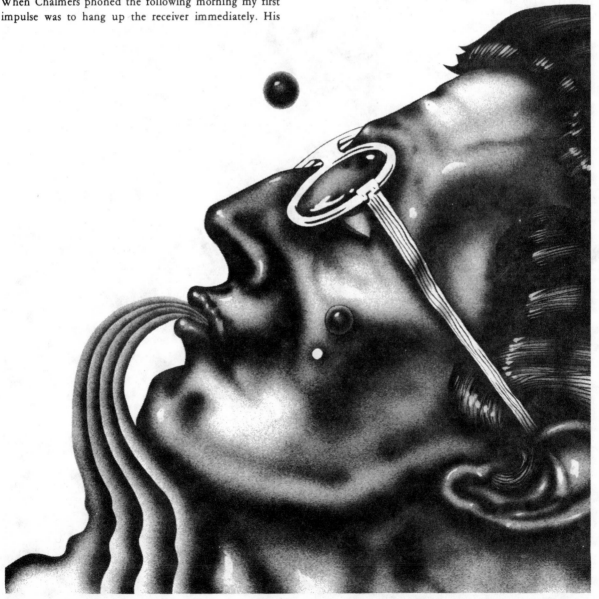

...valued intellectual abilities like learning, insight, curiosity, and imagination can be seen as extensions of juvenile attributes....For most of hominoid evolution adult behaviour has been conservative, acting as a suppressor mechanism preventing change.

David Pilbeam, *The Evolution of Man* (1970)

When one's customary ways of orienting oneself are threatened, and one is without other selves around one, one is thrown back on inner resources and inner strength, and this is what modern people have neglected to develop.

Rollo May, *Man's Search for Himself* (1953)

amazed and horrified me. He had extruded all of the furniture and the room presented a desolate appearance.

"It is just conceivable that we can thwart them!" he exclaimed. "But we must work rapidly. Frank, there is a stepladder in the hall. Bring it here immediately. And then fetch a pail of water."

"What for?" I murmured.

He turned sharply and there was a flush on his face. "To mix the plaster, you fool!" he cried. "To mix the plaster that will save our bodies and souls from a contamination unmentionable. To mix the plaster that will save the world from — Frank, *they must be kept out!*"

"Who?" I murmured.

"The Hounds of Tindalos!" he muttered. "They can only reach us through angles. We must eliminate all angles from this room. I shall plaster up all of the corners, all of

the crevices. We must make this room resemble the interior of a sphere.''

I knew that it would have been useless to argue with him. I fetched the stepladder, Chalmers mixed the plaster, and for three hours we laboured. We filled in four corners of the wall and the intersections of the floor and wall and the wall and ceiling, and we rounded the sharp angles of the window-seat.

"I shall remain in this room until they return in time," he affirmed when our task was completed. "When they discover that the scent leads through curves they will return. They will return ravenous and snarling and unsatisfied to the foulness that was in the beginning, before time, beyond space."

He nodded graciously and lit a cigarette. "It was good of you to help," he said.

"Will you not see a physician, Chalmers?" I pleaded.

"Perhaps — tomorrow," he murmured. "But now I must watch and wait."

"Wait for what?" I urged.

Chalmers smiled wanly. "I know that you think me insane," he said. "You have a shrewd but prosaic mind, and you cannot conceive of an entity that does not depend for its existence on force and matter. But did it ever occur to you, my friend, that force and matter are merely the barriers, to perception imposed by time and space? When one knows, as I do, that time and space are identical and that they are both deceptive because they are merely imperfect manifestations of a higher reality, one no longers seeks in the visible world for an explanation of the mystery and terror of being."

I rose and walked toward the door.

"Forgive me," he cried. "I did not mean to offend you. You have a superlative intellect, but I-I have a *superhuman* one. It is only natural that I should be aware of your limitations."

"Phone if you need me," I said, and descended the stairs two steps at a time. "I'll send my physician over at once," I muttered, to myself. "He's a hopeless maniac, and heaven knows what will happen if someone doesn't take a charge of him immediately."

3

The following is a condensation of two announcements which appeared in the **Partridgeville Gazette** *for July 3, 1928:*

EARTHQUAKE SHAKES FINANCIAL DISTRICT

At 2 o'clock this morning an earth tremor of unusual severity broke several plate-glass windows in Central Square and completely disorganized the electric and street railway systems. The tremor was felt in the outlying districts and the steeple of the First Baptist Church on Angell Hill (designed by Christopher Wren in 1717) was

entirely demolished. Firemen are now attempting to put out a blaze which threatens to destroy the Partridgeville Glue Works. An investigation is promised by the mayor and an immediate attempt will be made to fix responsibility for this disastrous occurrence.

OCCULT WRITER MURDERED BY UNKNOWN GUEST

HORRIBLE CRIME IN CENTRAL SQUARE
Mystery Surrounds Death of Halpin Chalmers

At 9 A.M. today the body of Halpin Chalmers, author and journalist, was found in an empty room above the jewelry store of Smithwich and Isaacs, 24 Central Square. The coroner's investigation revealed that the room had been rented furnished to Mr. Chalmers on May 1, and that he had himself disposed of the furniture a fortnight ago. Chalmers was the author of several recondite books on occult themes, and a member of the Bibliographic Guild. He formerly resided in Brooklyn, New York.

At 7 A.M. Mr. L.E. Hancock, who occupies the apartment opposite Chalmers' room in the Smithwick and Isaacs establishment, smelt a peculiar odor when he opened his door to take in his cat and the morning edition of the *Partridgeville Gazette*. The odor he describes as extremely acrid and nauseous, and he affirms that it was so strong in the vicinity of Chalmer's room that he was obliged to hold his nose when he approached that section of the hall.

He was about to return to his own apartment when it occurred to him that Chalmers might have accidentally forgotten to turn off the gas in his kitchenette. Becoming considerably alarmed at the thought, he decided to investigate, and when repeated tappings on Chalmers' door brought no response he notified the superintendent. The latter opened the door by means of a pass key, and the two men quickly made their way into Chalmers' room. The room was utterly destitute of furniture, and Hancock asserts that when he first glanced at the floor his heart went cold within him, and that the superintendent, without saying a word, walked to the open window and stared at the building opposite for fully five minutes.

Chalmers lay stretched upon his back in the center of the room. He was starkly nude, and his chest and arms were covered with a peculiar bluish pus or ichor. His head lay grotesquely upon his chest. It had been completely severed from his body, and the features were twisted and torn and horribly mangled. Nowhere was there a trace of blood.

The room presented a most astonishing appearance. The intersections of the walls, ceiling and floor had been thickly smeared with plaster of Paris, but at intervals fragments had cracked and fallen off, and someone had grouped these upon the floor about the murdered man so as to form a perfect triangle.

82

Beside the body were several sheets of charred yellow paper. These bore fantastic geometric designs and symbols and several hastily scrawled sentences. The sentences were almost illegible and so absurd in context that they furnished no possible clue to the perpetrator of the crime. "I am waiting and watching," Chalmers wrote. "I sit by the window and watch walls and ceiling. I do not believe they can reach me, but I must beware of the Doels. Perhaps *they* can help them break through. The satyrs will help, and they can advance through the scarlet circles. The Greeks knew a way of preventing that. It is a great pity that we have forgotten so much."

On another sheet of paper, the most badly charred of the seven or eight fragments found by Detective Sergeant Douglas (of the Partridgeville Reserve), was scrawled the following:

"Good God, the plaster is falling! A terrific shock has loosened the plaster and it is falling. An earthquake perhaps! I never could have anticipated this. It is growing dark in the room. I must phone Frank. But can he get here in time? I will try. I will recite the Einstein formula. I will — God, they are breaking through! They are breaking through! Smoke is pouring from the corners of the wall. Their tongues — ahhh —"

In the opinion of Detective Sergeant Douglas, Chalmers was poisoned by some obscure chemical. He has sent specimens of the strange blue slime found on Chalmers' body to the Partridgeville Chemical Laboratories; and he expects the report will shed new light on one of the most mysterious crimes of recent years. That Chalmers entertained a guest on the evening preceeding the earthquake is certain, for his neighbor distinctly heard a low murmur of conversation in the former's room as he passed it on his way to the stairs. Suspicion points strongly to this unknown visitor and the police are diligently endeavoring to discover his identity.

4

Report of James Morton, chemist and bacteriologist:
My dear Mr. Douglas:

The fluid sent to me for analysis is most peculiar that I have ever examined. It resembles living protoplasm, but it lacks the peculiar substances known as enzymes. Enzymes catalyze the chemical reactions occurring in living cells, and when the cell dies they cause it to disintegrate by hydrolyzation. Without enzymes protoplasm should possess enduring vitality, i.e., immortality. Enzymes are the negative components, so to speak, of unicellular organism, which is the basis of all life. That living matter can exist without enzymes biologists emphatically deny. And yet the substance that you have sent me is alive and it lacks these "indispensable" bodies. Good God, sir, do you realize what astounding new vistas this opens up?

5

Excerpt from The Secret Watcher *by the late Halpin Chalmers:*

What if, parallel to the life we know, there is another life that does not die, which lacks the elements that destroy *our* life? Perhaps in another dimension there is a *different* force from that which generates our life. Perhaps this force emits energy, or something similar to energy, which passes from the unknown dimension where *it* is and creates a new form of cell life in our dimension. No one knows that such new cell life does exist in our dimension. Ah, but I have seen *its* manifestations. I have *talked* with them. In my room at night I have talked with the Doels. And in dreams I have seen their maker. I have stood on the dim shore beyond time and matter and seen *it*. It moves through strange curves and outrageous angles. Some day I shall travel in time and meet *it* face to face.

Perhaps there do indeed exist universes interpenetrating with ours; perhaps of a high complexity; perhaps containing their own forms of awareness; constructed out of other particles and other interactions than those we know....

Denys Wilkinson

...a slight tearing of the veil that cuts us off from full awareness of the cosmic truth. And if a tiny hole can be made, perhaps others might rend it even more; make it large enough for all mankind to crawl through.

Zarkon: *The Zarkon Principle* (1975)

The Senoi Dream People

Kilton Stewart

In 1935 a Western scientific expedition first came across this preliterate society of some 12,000 people living in isolated communities in the central mountain range of the Malay Peninsula. The Senoi supported themselves in a mixed hunting-fishing and agricultural economy, lived in peace and harmony, and were very much in touch with their own primordial dream power.

The major authority of the Senoi community, once held by patrilineal elders, had now been passed on to *Halaks,* their primitive psychological healer-educators. But such men only guide and inspire, while the people rule themselves by democratic consensus, unsupported by any coercive structure such as a police force, army, jail or mental hospital. There appears to be no violent crime or seriously destructive conflict within the community. Physical and mental disease is minimal. And there is no war with the surrounding tribes. Extra-communal peace is maintained by encouraging neighbouring groups to believe that the Senoi practice black magic (thus scaring them off without having to fight them).

How is it then that the Senoi are able to maintain this harmony within their own community? Their power rests in their dream psychology which has a twofold emphasis: the interpretation of dreams, and the expression of dreams in voluntary trance states.

Though the Halaks are especially sensitive in such matters, this dream power is common knowledge and everyday practice for all members of the Senoi community. Each small Senoi child learns dream interpretation at family breakfast time when the older family members analyze the dreams the child remembers and reports from the night before. Then the men and the older children gather to describe and explore the dreams which other members of the community share with the group.

Without help, man does himself in, undone by his bewildering dream-beings. But when a Senoi is willing to turn to his brothers for aid, the tortuous dream-beings can be transformed into helpful allies. So it is that when a Senoi child has a nightmare of falling through space, his report is met with delight. He is told that this wonderful dream may lead to many good things if only he will explore the trip of where he would fall to, and what wonders he might discover there. All dream images have purpose and promise for the Senoi adult, so supported has he been as a child in learning to let his dream-creatures befriend him. A dream of falling is transfigured into one of being drawn to the land of falling powers because they love the dreamer and would instruct him in pleasure and spiritual power. Eventually the very dream experience becomes joyful.

The young dreamer learns to thrust himself further and further into each dream. In dreams of danger, he gains the courage to fight on by learning that he can call on the potential ally of any other dream-image to come to his aid. Any foe subdued in the process will return as an ally or servant. Pleasurable dreams are always to be pursued to a point of resolution, which then gives something useful to bring to the other members of his community, while of course adding to his own pleasure as well. So it is that sexual dreams should always continue to orgasm. And from the dream-lover, it is possible to demand a poem, a song or a dance which can later be offered to the group.

There are no taboo images or actions in dreams. Not only is everything permitted, but each aspect can be a source of personal pleasure and communal usefulness. The Senoi know that we need everything we've got. Every aspect of an individual's unconscious is of value to him, if he can learn to enjoy it. Revealing himself to himself and to his brothers is supported in every Senoi from the time he is a small child. Those experiences which first make him anxious, are eventually understood to be sources of pleasure and of power. Social transparency minimizes distrust, and social conflicts revealed in dreams are resolved in the next day's communal exchanges. Nothing human is considered to be alien, and so all men are more aware of the brotherhood of every other man.

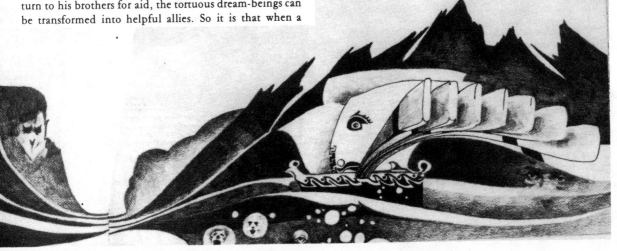

from **The Intellectual Culture of the Iglulik Eskimos**
K. Rasmussen

"In the wilderness I soon became melancholy. I would sometimes fall to weeping and feel unhappy without knowing why. Then for no reason all would suddenly be changed, and I felt great, inexplicable joy, a joy so powerful that I could not restrain it, but had to break into song, a mighty song, with room for only one word: joy, joy! And I had to use the full strength of my voice. And then in the midst of such a fit of mysterious and overwhelming delight I became a shaman, not knowing myself how it came about. But I was a shaman. I could see and hear in a totally different way. I had gained my enlightenment, the shaman's light of brain and body, and this in such a manner that it was not only I who could see through the darkness of life, but the same bright light also shone out from me, imperceptible to human beings but visible to all spirits of earth and sky and sea, and these now came to me to become my helping spirit." *an Eskimo shaman*

Flower Arranger
Joy Kogawa

Among the weedy steel structures
And frenetic flowering of factories
I found a blind flower arranger
In a sketch of a room
Dipping a drop of water
Onto an opening petal
Of a tiny not quite flowering bud.
With his fingertips
He placed gentleness in the air
And everywhere among the blowing weeds
He moved with his outstretched hands
Touching the air
With his transient dew.

I have seen the Bird of Paradise, she has spread herself before me, and I shall never be the same again.
There is nothing to be afraid of. Nothing.
Exactly.
The Life I am trying to grasp is the me that is trying to grasp it.

R.D. Laing, *The Bird of Paradise* (1967)

from **On the Taboo Against Knowing Who You Are**
Alan Watts

Most of us have the sensation that "I myself" is a separate center of feeling and action, living inside and bounded by the physical body — a center which "confronts" an "external" world of people and things, making contact through the senses with a universe both alien and strange. Everyday figures of speech reflect this illusion. "I came into this world." "You must face reality." "The conquest of nature."

This feeling of being lonely and very temporary visitors in the universe is in flat contradiction to everything known about man (and all other living organisms) in the sciences. We do not "come into" this world; we come out of it, as leaves from a tree. As the ocean "waves," the universe "peoples." Every individual is an expression of the whole realm of nature, a unique action of the total universe. This fact is rarely, if ever, experienced by most individuals. Even those who know it to be true in theory do not sense or feel it, but continue to be aware of themselves as isolated "egos" inside bags of skin.

The first result of this illusion is that our attitude to the world "outside" us is largely hostile. We are forever "conquering" nature, space, mountains, deserts, bacteria, and insects instead of learning to co-operate with them in a harmonious order.

Within each of us there is another whom we do not know.

St. John Perse

"The struggle is over; the man is no more concerned with gain and loss. Saddling himself on the ox's back, his eyes are fixed on things not of the earth, earthy. Even if he is called, he will not turn his head; however enticed he will no more be kept back."

COMING HOME ON THE OX'S BACK

NEW JERUSALEM

"When you know that what you need is not the snare or set-net but the hare or fish, it is like gold separated from the dross. The one ray of light serene and penetrating shines even before days of creation. Riding on the animal, he is at last back in his home, where lo! the ox is no more; the man alone sits serenely. Though the red sun is high up he is still quietly dreaming, his whip and rope idly lying."

THE OX FORGOTTEN, LEAVING THE MAN ALONE

Connoisseur of Chaos
Wallace Stevens

I
A.   A violent order is disorder; and
B.   A great disorder is an order. These
Two things are one. (Pages of illustrations.)

II
If all the green of spring was blue, and it is;
If the flowers of South Africa were bright
On the tables of Connecticut, and they are;
If Englishmen lived without tea in Ceylon, and they do;
And if it all went on in an orderly way,
And it does; a law of inherent opposites,
Of essential unity, is as pleasant as port,
As pleasant as the brush-strokes of a bough,
An upper, particular bough in, say, Marchand.

III
After all the pretty contrast of life and death
Proves that these opposite things partake of one,
At least that was the theory, when bishops' books
Resolve the world. We cannot go back to that.
The squirming facts exceed the squamous mind,
If one may say so. And yet relation appears,
A small relation expanding like the shade
Of a cloud on sand, a shape on the side of a hill.

IV
A.   Well, an old order is a violent one.
This proves nothing. Just one more truth, one more
Element in the immense disorder of truths.
B.   It is April as I write. The wind
Is blowing after days of constant rain.
All this, of course, will come to summer soon.
But suppose the disorder of truths should ever come
To an order, most Plantagenet, most fixed...
A great disorder as an order. Now, A
And B are not like statuary, posed
For a vista in the Louvre. They are things chalked
On the sidewalk so that the pensive man may see.

V
The pensive man....He sees that eagle float
For which the intricate Alps are a single nest.

**No man shall ever know
    what is true blessedness**

**Till oneness overwhelm
    and swallow separateness.**

Angelus Silesius

Applelore
Judy Stonehill

Once upon an apple cart
a strange girl threw her lonely limbs.
She swam among the apples there
while singing holy apple hymns.

The maker of the cart turned green
seeing a maiden swimming there.
He leapt into the crimson sea
and tightly pulled her virgin hair.

"Fair Eve, you must climb down at once,
or pay the price of apples sore."
And she replied with tender voice,
"I'm only looking for the core."

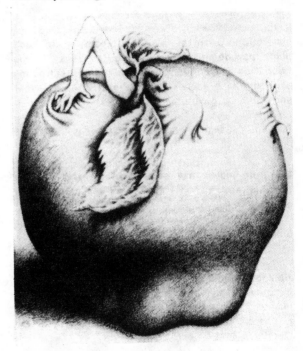

Once upon a time, I, Chuang Tzu, dreamt I was a butterfly, fluttering hither and thither, to all intents and purposes a butterfly. I was conscious only of following my fancies as a butterfly, and was unconscious of my individuality as a man. Suddenly, I awoke, and there I lay, myself again. Now I do not know whether I was then a man dreaming I was a butterfly, or whether I am now a butterfly dreaming I am a man.

Chuang Tzu

The Street
Octavio Paz

The street is very long and filled with silence.
I walk in shadow and I trip and fall,
And then get up and walk with unseeing feet
Over the silent stones and the dry leaves,
And someone close behind, tramples them, too.
If I slow down and stop, he also stops.
If I run, so does he. I look. No one!
The whole street seems so dark, with no way out,
And though I turn and turn, I can't escape.
I always find myself on the same street
Where no one waits for me and none pursues.
Where I pursue, a man who trips and falls
Gets up and seeing me, keeps saying: "No one!"

Imagination makes man's world. This is not to say that his world is a fantasy, his life a dream, or any such poetic pseudo-philosophical thing. It means that his "world" is bigger than the stimuli which surrounds him, and the measure of it is the reach of his coherent and steady imagination.

Susanne K. Langer, *Philosophical Sketches* (1962)

The truth indeed has never been preached by the Buddha, seeing that one has to realize it within oneself.

Sutralamkara

He knoweth nothing as he ought to know, who thinks he knoweth anything without seeing its place and the manner how it relateth to God, angels and men, and to all the creatures in earth, heaven and hell, time and eternity.

Thomas Traherne

The Circular Ruins
Jorge Luis Borges
Translated by James E. Irby

And if he left off dreaming about you....
— *Through the Looking Glass*, VI

No one saw him disembark in the unanimous night, no one saw the bamboo canoe sinking into the sacred mud, but within a few days no one was unaware that the silent man came from the South and that his home was one of the infinite villages upstream, on the violent mountainside, where the Zend tongue is not contaminated with Greek and where leprosy is infrequent. The truth is that the obscure man kissed the mud, came up the bank without pushing aside (probably without feeling) the brambles which dilacerated his flesh, and dragged himself, nauseous and bloodstained, to the circular enclosure crowned by a stone tiger or horse, which once was the color of fire and now was that of ashes. This circle was a temple, long ago devoured by fire, which the malarial jungle had profaned and whose god no longer received the homage of men. The stranger stretched out beneath the pedestal. He was awakened by the sun high above. He evidenced without astonishment that his wounds had closed; he shut his pale eyes and slept, not out of bodily weakness but out of determination of will. He knew that this temple was the place required by his invincible purpose; he knew that, downstream, the incessant trees had not managed to choke the ruins of another propitious temple, whose gods were also burned and dead; he knew that his immediate obligation was to sleep. Towards midnight he was awakened by the disconsolate cry of a bird. Prints of bare feet, some figs and a jug told him that men of the region had respectfully spied upon his sleep and were solicitous of his favor or feared his magic. He felt the chill of fear and sought out a burial niche in the dilapidated wall and covered himself with some unknown leaves.

The purpose which guided him was not impossible, though it was supernatural. He wanted to dream a man: he wanted to dream him with minute integrity and insert him into reality. This magical project had exhausted the entire content of his soul; if someone had asked him his own name or any trait of his previous life, he would not have been able to answer. The uninhabited and broken temple suited him, for it was a minimum of visible world; the nearness of the peasants also suited him, for they would see that his frugal necessities were supplied. The rice and fruit of their tribute were sufficient sustenance for his body, consecrated to the sole task of sleeping and dreaming.

At first, his dreams were chaotic; somewhat later, they were of a dialectical nature. The stranger dreamt that he was in the center of a circular amphitheater which in some way was the burned temple: clouds of silent students filled the gradins; the faces of the last ones hung many centuries away and at a cosmic height, but were entirely clear and precise. The man was lecturing to them on anatomy, cosmography, magic; the countenances listened with eagerness and strove to respond with understanding, as if they divined the importance of the examination which would redeem one of them from his state of vain appearance and interpolate him into the world of reality. The man, both in dreams and awake, considered his phantoms' replies, was not deceived by impostors, divined a growing intelligence in certain perplexities. He sought a soul which would merit participation in the universe.

After nine or ten nights, he comprehended with some bitterness that he could expect nothing of those students who passively accepted his doctrines, but that he could of those who, at times, would venture a reasonable contradiction. The former, though worthy of love and affection, could not rise to the state of individuals; the latter pre-existed somewhat more. One afternoon (now his afternoons too were tributaries of sleep, now he remained awake only for a couple of hours at dawn) he dismissed the vast illusory college forever and kept one single student. He was a silent boy, sallow, sometimes obstinate, with sharp features which reproduced those of the dreamer. He was not long disconcerted by his companions' sudden elimination; his progress, after a few special lessons, astounded his teacher. Nevertheless, catastrophe ensued. The man emerged from sleep one day as if from a viscous desert, looked at the vain light of afternoon, which at first he confused with that of dawn, and understood that he had not really dreamt. All that night and all day, the intolerable lucidity of insomnia weighed upon him. He tried to explore the jungle, to exhaust himself; amidst the hemlocks, he was scarcely able to manage a few snatches of feeble sleep, fleetingly mottled with some rudimentary visions which were useless. He tried to convoke the college and had scarcely uttered a few brief words of exhortation, when it became deformed and was extinguished. In his almost perpetual sleeplessness, his old eyes burned with tears of anger.

He comprehended that the effort to mold the incoherent and vertiginous matter dreams are made of was the most arduous task a man could undertake, though he might penetrate all the enigmas of the upper and lower orders: much more arduous than weaving a rope of sand or coining the faceless wind. He comprehended that an initial failure was inevitable. He swore he would forget the enormous hallucination which had misled him at first, and he sought another method. Before putting it into effect, he dedicated a month to replenishing the powers his delirium had wasted. He abandoned any premeditation of dreaming and, almost at once, was able to sleep for a considerable part of the day. The few times he dreamt during this period, he did not take notice of the dreams. To take up his task again, he waited until the moon's disk was perfect. Then, in the afternoon, he purified himself in the waters of the river, worshipped the planetary gods, uttered the lawful syllables of a powerful name and slept. Almost immediately, he dreamt of a beating heart.

He dreamt it as active, warm, secret, the size of a closed fist, of garnet color in the penumbra of a human body as yet without face or sex; with minute love he dreamt it, for fourteen lucid nights. Each night he perceived it with greater clarity. He did not touch it, but limited himself to witnessing it, observing it, perhaps correcting it with his eyes. He perceived it, lived it, from many distances and many angles. On the fourteenth night he touched the pulmonary artery with his finger, and then the whole heart, inside and out. The examination satisfied him. Deliberately, he did not dream for a night; then he took the heart again, invoked the name of a planet and set about to envision another of the principal organs. Within a year he reached the skelton, the eyelids. The innumerable hair was perhaps the most difficult task. He dreamt a complete man, a youth, but this youth could not rise nor did he speak nor could he open his eyes. Night after night, the man dreamt him as asleep.

In the Gnostic cosmogonies, the demiurgi knead and mold a red Adam who cannot stand alone; as unskillful and crude and elementary as this Adam of dust was the Adam of dreams fabricated by the magician's nights of effort. One afternoon, the man almost destroyed his work but then repented. (It would have been better for him had he destroyed it.) Once he had completed his supplications to the numina of the earth and the river, he threw himself down at the feet of the effigy which was perhaps a tiger and perhaps a horse, and implored its unknown succor. That twilight, he dreamt of the statue. He dreamt of it as a living, tremulous thing: it was not an atrocious mongrel of tiger and horse, but both these vehement creatures at once and also a bull, a rose, a tempest. This multiple god revealed to him that its earthly name was Fire, that in the circular temple (and in others of its kind) people had rendered it sacrifices and cult and that it would magically give life to the sleeping phantom, in such a way that all creatures except Fire itself and the dreamer would believe him to be a man of flesh and blood. The man was ordered by the divinity to instruct his creature in its rites, and send him to the other broken temple whose pyramids survived downstream, so that in this deserted edifice a voice might give glory to the god. In the dreamer's dream, the dreamed one awoke.

The magician carried out these orders. He devoted a period of time (which finally comprised two years) to revealing the arcana of the universe and of the fire cult to his dream child. Inwardly, it pained him to be separated from the boy. Under the pretext of pedagogical necessity, each day he prolonged the hours he dedicated to his dreams. He also redid the right shoulder, which was perhaps deficient. At times, he was troubled by the impression that all this had happened before....In general, his days were happy; when he closed his eyes, he would think: *Now I shall be with my son.* Or, less often: *The child I have engendered awaits me and will not exist if I do not go to him.*

Gradually, he accustomed the boy to reality. Once he ordered him to place a banner on a distant peak. The following day, the banner flickered from the mountain top. He tried other analogous experiments, each more daring than the last. He understood with certain bitterness that his son was ready — and perhaps impatient — to be born. That night he kissed him for the first time and sent him to the other temple whose debris showed white downstream, through many leagues of inextricable jungle and swamp. But first (so that he would never know he was a phantom, so that he would be thought a man like others) he instilled into him a complete oblivion of his years of apprenticeship.

The man's victory and peace were dimmed by weariness. At dawn and at twilight, he would prostrate himself before the stone figure, imagining perhaps that his unreal child was practicing the same rites, in other circular ruins, downstream; at night, he would not dream, or would dream only as all men do. He perceived the sounds and forms of the universe with a certain colorlessness: his absent son was being nurtured with these diminutions of his soul. His life's purpose was complete; the man persisted in a kind of ecstasy. After a time, which some narrators of his story prefer to compute in years and others in lustra, he was awakened one midnight by two boatmen; he could not see their faces, but they told him of a magic man in a temple of the North who could walk upon fire and not be burned. The magician suddenly remembered the words of the god. He recalled that, of all the creatures of the world, fire was the only one that knew his son was a phantom. This recollection, at first soothing, finally tormented him. He feared his son might meditate on his abnormal privilege and discover in some way that his condition was that of a mere image. Not to be a man, to be the projection of another man's dream, what a feeling of humiliation, of vertigo! All fathers are interested in the children they have procreated (they have permitted to exist) in mere confusion or pleasure; it was natural that the magician should fear for the future of that son, created in thought, limb by limb and feature by feature, in a thousand and one secret nights.

The end of his meditations was sudden, though it was foretold in certain signs. First (after a long drought) a faraway cloud on a hill, light and rapid as a bird; then, toward the south, the sky which had the rose color of the leopard's mouth; then the smoke which corroded the metallic nights; finally, the panicky flight of the animals. For what was happening had happened many centuries ago. The ruins of the fire god's sanctuary were destroyed by fire. In a birdless dawn the magician saw the concentric blaze close round the walls. For a moment, he thought of taking refuge in the river, but then he knew that death was coming to crown his old age and absolve him of his labors. He walked into the shreds of flame. But they did not bite into his flesh, they caressed him and engulfed him without heat or combustion. With relief, with humiliation, with terror, he understood that he too was a mere appearance, dreamt by another.

'To the small child his mother and father are as gods... yet when he grows older in experience he sees they are not gods but people like himself save wiser in their years. And so the child becomes a man and takes his place amongst men....So it will be with you, Boaz. Because you are as a child you think us to be gods. Learn from us and you will take your place amongst us. You too will become a god amongst gods. And so may all men if they but watch and listen to our words and keep their hearts and minds pure and open.' *Teramos*

Michel Parry, *Chariots of Fire* (1974)

The Valley Spirit never dies.
It is called the Mysterious Female.
And the doorway of the Mysterious Female
Is the base from which Heaven and Earth spring.
It is there within us all the time.
Draw upon it as you will, it never runs dry.

Lao Tzu

Eros, the god of love, emerged to create the earth.
Before, all was silent, bare, and motionless. Now all
was life, joy, and motion.

Greek Myth

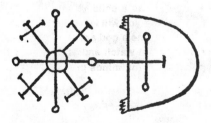

The Man Who Loved the Faioli

Roger Zelazny

It is the story of John Auden and the Faioli, and no one knows it better than I. Listen —

It happened on that evening, as he strolled (for there was no reason not to stroll) in his favorite places in the whole world, that he saw the Faioli near the Canyon of the Dead, seated on a rock, her wings of light flickering, flickering, flickering and then gone, until it appeared that a human girl was sitting there, dressed all in white and weeping, with long black tresses coiled about her waist.

He approached her through the terrible light from the dying, half-dead sun, in which human eyes could not distinguish distances nor grasp perspectives properly (though his could), and he lay his right hand upon her shoulder and spoke a word of greeting and of comfort.

It was as if he did not exist, however. She continued to weep, streaking with silver her cheeks the color of snow or a bone. Her almond eyes looked forward as though they saw through him, and her long fingernails dug into the flesh of her palms, though no blood was drawn.

Then he knew that it was true, the things that are said of the Faioli — that they see only the living and never the dead, and that they are formed into the loveliest women in the entire universe. Being dead himself, John Auden debated the consequences of becoming a living man once again, for a time.

The Faioli were known to come to a man the month before his death — those rare men who still died — and to live with such a man for that final month of his existence, rendering to him every pleasure that it is possible for a human being to know, so that on the day when the kiss of death is delivered, which sucks the remaining life from his body, that man accepts it — no, seeks it — with desire and with grace, for such is the power of the Faioli among all creatures that there is nothing more to be desired after such knowledge.

John Auden considered his life and his death, the conditions of the world upon which he stood, the nature of his stewardship and his curse and the Faioli — who was the loveliest creature he had seen in all of his four hundred thousand days of existence — and he touched the place beneath his left armpit which activated the necessary mechanism to make him live again.

The creature stiffened beneath his touch, for suddenly it was flesh, his touch, and flesh, warm and woman-filled, that he was touching, now that the sensations of life had returned to him. He knew that his touch had become the touch of a man once more.

"I said 'hello, and don't cry,' " he said, and her voice was like the breezes he had forgotten through all the trees that he had forgotten, with their moisture and their odors and their colors all brought back to him thus, "From where do you come, man? You were not here a moment ago."

"From the Canyon of the Dead," he said.

"Let me touch your face," and he did, and she did.

"It is strange that I did not feel you approach."

"This is a strange world," he replied.

"That is true," she said. "You are the only living thing upon it."

And he said, "What is your name?"

She said, "Call me Sythia," and he did.

"My name is John," he told her, "John Auden."

"I have come to be with you, to give you comfort and pleasure," she said, and he knew that the ritual was beginning.

"Why were you weeping when I found you?" he asked.

"Because I thought there was nothing upon this world, and I was so tired from my travels," she told him. "Do you live near here?"

"Not far away," he answered. "Not far away at all."

"Will you take me there? To the place where you live?"

"Yes."

And she rose and followed him into the Canyon of the Dead, where he made his home.

They descended and they descended, and all about them were the remains of people who once had lived. She did not seem to see these things, however, but kept her eyes fixed upon John's face and her hand upon his arm.

"Why do you call this place the Canyon of the Dead?" she asked him.

"Because they are all about us here, the dead," he replied.

"I feel nothing."

"I know."

They crossed through the Valley of the Bones, where millions of the dead from many races and worlds lay stacked all about them, and she did not see these things. She had come to the graveyard of all the worlds, but she did not realize this thing. She had encountered its tender, its keeper, and she did not know what he was, he who staggered beside her like a man drunken.

John Auden took her to his home — not really the place where he lived, but it would be now — and there he activated ancient circuits within the building within the mountain, and in response light leaped forth from the walls, light he had never needed before but now required.

The door slid shut behind them and the temperature built up to a normal warmth. Fresh air circulated and he took it into his lungs and expelled it, glorying in the forgotten sensation. His heart beat within his breast, a red warm thing that reminded him of the pain and of the pleasure. For the first time in ages, he prepared a meal and fetched a bottle of wine from one of the deep, sealed lockers. How many others could have borne what he had borne?

None, perhaps.

She dined with him, toying with the food, sampling a bit of everything, eating very little. He, on the other hand, glutted himself fantastically, and they drank of the wine and were happy.

"This place is so strange," she said. "Where do you sleep?"

"I used to sleep in there," he told her, indicating a room he had almost forgotten; and they entered and he showed it to her, and she beckoned him toward the bed and the pleasures of her body.

That night he loved her, many times, with a desperation that burnt away the alcohol and pushed all of his life forward with something like a hunger, but more.

The following day, when the dying sun had splashed the Valley of the Bones with its pale, moonlike light, he awakened and she drew his head to her breast, not having slept herself, and she asked him, "What is the thing that moves you, John Auden? You are not like one of the men who live and who die, but you take life almost like one of the Faioli, squeezing from it everything that you can and pacing it at a tempo that bespeaks a sense of time no man should know. What are you?"

"I am one who knows," he said. "I am one who knows that the days of a man are numbered and one who covets their dispositions as he feels them draw to a close."

"You are strange," said Sythia. "Have I pleased you?"

"More than anything else I have ever known," he said.

And she sighed, and he found her lips once again.

They breakfasted, and that day they walked in the Valley of the Bones. He could not distinguish distances nor grasp perspectives properly, and she could not see anything that had been living and now was dead. So, of course, as they sat there on a shelf of stone, his arm about her shoulders, he pointed out to her the rocket which had just come down from out of the sky, and she squinted after his gesture. He indicated the robots, which had begun unloading the remains of the dead of many worlds from the hold of the ship, and she cocked her head to one side and stared ahead, but she did not really see what he was talking about.

Even when one of the robots lumbered up to him and held out the board containing the receipt and the stylus, and as he signed the receipt for the bodies received, she did not see or understand what it was that was occuring.

In the days that followed, his life took upon it a dreamlike quality, filled with the pleasure of Sythia and shot through with certain inevitable streaks of pain. Often, she saw him wince, and she asked him concerning his expressions.

And always he would laugh and say, "Pleasure and pain are near to one another," or some thing such as that.

And as the days wore on, she came to prepare the meals and to rub his shoulders and mix his drinks and to recite to him certain pieces of poetry he had somehow once come to love.

A month. A month, he knew, and it would come to an end. The Faioli, whatever they were, paid for the life that they took with the pleasures of the flesh. They always knew when a man's death was near at hand. And in this sense, they always gave more than they received. The life was fleeing anyway, and they enhanced it before they took it

away with them, to nourish themselves most likely, price of the things that they'd given.

John Auden knew that no Faioli in the entire universe had ever met a man such as himself.

Sythia was mother-of-pearl, and her body was alternately cold and warm to his caresses, and her mouth was a tiny flame, igniting wherever it touched, with its teeth like needles and its tongue like the heart of a flower. And so he came to know the thing called love for the Faioli called Sythia.

Nothing much really happened beyond the loving. He knew that she wanted him, to use him ultimately, and he was perhaps the only man in the universe able to gull one of her kind. His was the perfect defense against life and against death. Now that he was human and alive, he often wept when he considered it.

He had more than a month to live.

He had maybe three or four.

This month, therefore, was a price he'd willingly pay for what it was that the Faioli offered.

Sythia racked his body and drained from it every drop of pleasure contained within his tired nerve cells. She turned him into a flame, an iceberg, a little boy, an old man. When they were together, his feelings were such that he considered the *consolamentum* as a thing he might really accept at the end of the month, which was drawing near. Why not? He knew she had filled his mind with her presence, on purpose. But what more did existence hold for him? This creature from beyond the stars had brought him every single thing a man could desire. She had baptized him with passion and confirmed him with the quietude which follows after. Perhaps the final oblivion of her final kiss was best after all.

He seized her and drew her to him. She did not understand him, but she responded.

He loved her for it, and this was almost his end.

There is a thing called disease that battens upon all living things, and he had known it beyond the scope of all living men. She could not understand, woman-thing who had known only life.

So he never tried to tell her, though with each day the taste of her kisses grew stronger and saltier and each seemed to him a strengthening shadow, darker and darker, stronger and heavier, of that one thing which he now knew he desired most.

And the day would come. And come it did.

He held her and caressed her, and the calendars of all his days fell about them.

He knew, as he abandoned himself to her ploys and the glories of her mouth, her breasts, that he had been ensnared, as had all men who had known them, by the power of the Faioli. Their strength was their weakness. They were the ultimate in Woman. By their frailty they begat the desire to please. He wanted to merge himself with the pale landscape of her body, to pass within the circles of her eyes and never depart.

He had lost, he knew. For as the days had vanished about him, he had weakened. He was barely able to scrawl his name upon the receipt proffered him by the robot who had lumbered toward him, crushing rib cages and cracking skulls with each terrific step. Briefly, he envied the thing. Sexless, passionless, totally devoted to duty. Before he dismissed it, he asked it, "What would you do if you had desire and you met with a thing that gave you all things you wished for in the world?"

"I would — try to — keep it," it said, red lights blinking about its dome, before it turned and lumbered off, across the Great Graveyard.

"Yes," said John Auden aloud, "but this thing cannot be done."

Sythia did not understand him, and on that thirty-first day they returned to that place where he had lived for a month and he felt the fear of death, strong, so strong come upon him.

She was more exquisite than ever before, but he feared this final encounter.

"I love you," he said finally, for it was a thing he had never said before, and she stroked his brow and kissed it.

"I know," she told him, "and your time is almost at hand, to love me completely. Before the final act of love, my John Auden, tell me a thing: What is it that sets you apart? Why is it that you know so much more of things-that-are-not-life than mortal man should know? How was it that you approached me on that first night without my knowing it?"

"It is because I am already dead," he told her. "Can't you see it when you look into my eyes? Do you not feel it, as a certain special chill, whenever I touch you? I came here rather than sleep the cold sleep, which would have me to be in a thing like death anyhow, an oblivion wherein I would not even know I was waiting, waiting for the cure which might never happen, the cure for one of the very last fatal diseases remaining in the universe, the disease which now leaves me only small time of life."

"I do not understand," she said.

"Kiss me and forget it," he told her. "It is better this way. There will doubtless never be a cure, for some things remain always dark, and I have surely been forgotten. You must have sensed the death upon me, when I restored my humanity, for such is the nature of your kind. I did it to enjoy you, knowing you to be of the Faioli. So have your pleasure of me now, and know that I share it. I welcome thee. I have courted thee all the days of my life, unknowing."

But she was curious and asked him (using the familiar for the first time), "How then dost thou achieve this balance between life and that-which-is-not-life, this thing which keeps thee conscious yet unalive?"

"There are controls set within this body I happen, unfortunately, to occupy. To touch this place beneath my armpit will cause my lungs to cease their breathing and my heart to stop its beating. It will set into effect an installed electrochemical system, like those my robots (invisible to you, I know) possess. This is my life within death. I asked for it becasue I feared oblivion. I volunteered to be gravekeeper to the universe, because in this place there are none to look upon me and be repelled by my deathlike appearance. This is why I am what I am. Kiss me and end it."

But having taken the form of woman, or perhaps being woman all along, the Faioli who was called Sythia was curious, and she said, "This place?" and she touched the spot beneath his left armpit.

With this he vanished from her sight, and with this also, he knew once again the icy logic that stood apart from emotion. Because of this, he did not touch upon the critical spot once again.

Instead, he watched her as she sought for him about the place where he once had lived.

She checked into every closet and adytum, and when she could not discover a living man, she sobbed once, horribly, as she had on that night when first he had seen her. Then the wings flickered, flickered, weakly flickered, back into existence upon her back, and her face dissolved and her body slowly melted. The tower of sparks that stood before him then vanished, and later on that crazy night during which he could distinguish distances and grasp perspectives once again he began looking for her.

And that is the story of John Auden, the only man who ever loved a Faioli and lived (if you could call it that) to tell of it. No one knows it better than I.

No cure has ever been found. And I know that he walks the Canyon of the Dead and considers the bones, sometimes stops by the rock where he met her, blinks after the moist things that are not there, wonders at the judgment that he gave.

It is that way, and the moral may be that life (and perhaps love also) is stronger than that which it contains, but never that which contains it. But only a Faioli could tell you for sure, and they never come here any more.

...we have untapped intuitive and psychic forces which we must utilize if we are to be saved from all the insanity on this planet.

Edgar Mitchell, *Astronaut on Apollo 14*

Design

Robert Frost

I found a dimpled spider, fat and white,
On a white heal-all, holding up a moth
Like a white piece of rigid satin cloth—
Assorted characters of death and blight
Mixed ready to begin the morning right,
Like the ingredients of a witches' broth—
A snow-drop spider, a flower like a froth,
And dead wings carried like a paper kite.

What had that flower to do with being white,
The wayside blue and innocent heal-all?
What brought the kindred spider to that height,
Then steered the white moth thither in the night?
What but design of darkness to appall?—
If design govern in a thing so small.

**The image of God is found essentially and personally
in all mankind. Each possesses it whole, entire and
undivided, and all together not more than one alone. In
this way we are all one, intimately united in our eternal
image, which is the image of God and the source in us
of all our life. Our created essence and our life are
attached to it without mediation as to their eternal
cause.**

Ruysbroeck

A Recognition

Mark Rudman

There is no end
to being
delivered

midwife
to the self
we play the other

calmly we watch
the dock
sinking

not noticing
who is sitting
on it

and as our nostrils
fill with water
we think

Damn
I should have
known

who else
could it
have been

The Second Coming

W.B. Yeats

Turning and turning in the widening gyre
The falcon cannot hear the falconer;
Things fall apart; the centre cannot hold;
Mere anarchy is loosed upon the world,
The blood-dimmed tide is loosed, and everywhere
The ceremony of innocence is drowned;
The best lack all conviction, while the worst
Are full of passionate intensity.

Surely some revelation is at hand;
Surely the Second Coming is at hand.
The Second Coming! Hardly are those words out
When a vast image out of *Spiritus Mundi*
Troubles my sight: somewhere in sands of the desert
A shape with lion body and the head of a man,
A gaze blank and pitiless as the sun,
Is moving its slow thighs, while all about it
Reel shadows of the indignant desert birds.
The darkness drops again; but now I know
That twenty centuries of stony sleep
Were vexed to nightmare by a rocking cradle,
And what rough beast, its hour come round at last,
Slouches towards Bethlehem to be born?

Virgil Finlay '35

Nine Lives
Ursula K. Le Guin

She was alive inside, but dead outside, her face a black and dun net of wrinkles, tumors, cracks. She was bald and blind. The tremors that crossed Libra's face were mere quiverings of corruption: underneath, in the black corridors, the halls beneath the skin, there were crepitations in darkness, ferments, chemical nightmares that went on for centuries. "Oh the damned flatulent planet," Pugh murmured as the dome shook and a boil burst a kilometer to the southwest, spraying silver pus across the sunset. The sun had been setting for the last two days. "I'll be glad to see a human face."

"Thanks," said Martin.

"Yours is human to be sure," said Pugh, "but I've seen it so long I can't see it."

Radvid signals cluttered the communicator which Martin was operating, faded, returned as face and voice. The face filled the screen, the nose of an Assyrian king, the eyes of a samurai, skin bronze, eyes the color of iron: young, magnificent. "Is that what human beings look like?" said Pugh with awe. "I'd forgotten."

"Shut up, Owen, we're on."

"Libra Exploratory Mission Base, come in please, this is *Passerine* launch."

"Libra here. Beam fixed. Come on down, launch."

"Expulsion in seven E-seconds. Hold on." The screen blanked and sparkled.

"Do they all look like that? Martin, you and I are uglier men than I thought."

"Shut up, Owen...."

For twenty-two minutes Martin followed the landing-craft down by signal and then through the cleared dome they saw it, small star in the blood-colored east, sinking. It came down neat and quiet, Libra's thin atmosphere carrying little sound. Pugh and Martin closed the head-pieces of their imsuits, zipped out of the dome airlocks, and ran with soaring strides, Nijinsky and Nureyev, toward the boat. Three equipment modules came floating down at four-minute intervals from each other and hundred-meter intervals east of the boat. "Come on out," Martin said on his suit radio, "we're waiting at the door."

"Come on in, the methane's fine," said Pugh.

The hatch opened. The young man they had seen on the

screen came out with one athletic twist and leaped down onto the shaky dust and clinkers of Libra. Martin shook his hand, but Pugh was staring at the hatch, from which another young man emerged with the same neat twist and jump, followed by a young woman who emerged with the same neat twist, ornamented by a wriggle, and the jump. They were all tall, with bronze skin, black hair, high-bridged noses, epicanthic fold, the same face. They all had the same face. The fourth was emerging from the hatch with a neat twist and jump. "Martin bach," said Pugh, "we've got a clone."

"Right," said one of them, "we're a tenclone. John Chow's the name. You're Lieutenant Martin?"

"I'm Owen Pugh."

"Alvaro Guillen Martin," said Martin, formal, bowing slightly. Another girl was out, the same beautiful face; Martin stared at her and his eye rolled like a nervous pony's. Evidently he had never given any thought to cloning, and was suffering technological shock. "Steady," Pugh said in the Argentine dialect, "it's only excess twins." He stood close by Martin's elbow. He was glad himself of the contact.

It is hard to meet a stranger. Even the greatest extrovert meeting even the meekest stranger knows a certain dread, though he may not know he knows it. Will he make a fool of me wreck my image of myself invade me destroy me change me? Will he be different from me? Yes, that he will. There's the terrible thing: the strangeness of the stranger.

After two years on a dead planet, and the last half year isolated as a team of two, oneself and one other, after that it's even harder to meet a stranger, however welcome he may be. You're out of the habit of difference, you've lost the touch; and so the fear revives, the primitive anxiety, the old dread.

The clone, five males and five females, had got done in a couple of minutes what a man might have got done in twenty: greeted Pugh and Martin, had a glance at Libra, unloaded the boat, made ready to go. They went, and the dome filled with them, a hive of golden bees. They hummed and buzzed quietly, filled up all silences, all spaces with a honey-brown swarm of human presence. Martin looked bewilderedly at the long-limbed girls, and they smiled at him, three at once. Their smile was gentler than that of the boys, but no less radiantly self-possessed.

"Self-possessed," Owen Pugh murmured to his friend, "that's it. Think of it, to be oneself ten times over. Nine seconds for every motion, nine ayes on every vote. It would be glorious!" But Martin was asleep. And the John Chows had all gone to sleep at once. The dome was filled with their quiet breathing. They were young, they didn't snore. Martin sighed and snored, his hershey-bar colored face relaxed in the dim afterglow of Libra's primary, set at last. Pugh had cleared the dome and stars looked in, Sol among them, a great company of lights, a clone of splendors. Pugh slept and dreamed of a one-eyed giant who chased him through the shaking halls of Hell.

From his sleeping-bag Pugh watched the clone's awakening. They all got up within one minute except for one pair, a boy and a girl, who lay snugly tangled and still sleeping in one bag. As Pugh saw this there was a shock like one of Libra's earthquakes inside him, a very deep tremor. He was not aware of this, and in fact thought he was pleased at the sight; there was no other such comfort on this dead hollow world, more power to them, who made love. One of the others stepped on the pair. They woke and the girl sat up flushed and sleepy, with bare golden breasts. One of her sisters murmured something to her; she shot a glance at Pugh and disappeared in the sleeping-bag, followed by a giant giggle, from another direction a fierce stare, from still another direction a voice: "Christ, we're used to having a room to ourselves. Hope you don't mind, Captain Pugh."

"It's a pleasure," Pugh said half-truthfully. He had to stand up then, wearing only the shorts he slept in, and he felt like a plucked rooster, all white scrawn and pimples. He had seldom envied Martin's compact brownness so much. The United Kingdom had come through the Great Famines well, losing less than half its population: a record achieved by rigorous food-control. Black-marketeers and hoarders had been executed. Crumbs had been shared. Where in richer lands most had died and a few had thriven, in Britain fewer died and none throve. They all got lean. Their sons were lean, their grandsons lean, small, brittle-boned, easily infected. When civilization became a matter of standing in lines, the British had kept queue, and so had replaced the survival of the fittest with the survival of the fair-minded. Owen Pugh was a scrawny little man. All the same, he was there.

At the moment he wished he wasn't.

At breakfast a John said, "Now if you'll brief us, Captain Pugh —"

"Owen, then."

"Owen, we can work out our schedule. Anything new on the mine since your last report to your Mission? We saw your reports when *Passerine* was orbiting Planet V, where they are now."

Martin did not answer, though the mine was his discovery and project, and Pugh had to do his best. It was hard to talk to them. The same faces, each with the same expression of intelligent interest, all leaned toward him across the table at almost the same angle. They all nodded together.

Over the Exploitation Corps insignia on their tunics each had a nameband, first name John and last name Chow of course, but the middle names different. The men were Aleph, Kaph, Yod, Gimel, and Samedh; the women Sadhe, Daleth, Zayin, Beth and Resh. Pugh tried to use the names but gave it up at once; he could not even tell sometimes which one had spoken, for the voices were all alike.

Martin buttered and chewed his toast, and finally interrupted: "You're a team. Is that it?"

"Right," said two Johns.

"God, what a team! I hadn't seen the point. How much do you each know what the others are thinking?"

"Not at all, properly speaking," replied one of the girls, Zayin. The others watched her with the proprietary, approving look they had. "No ESP, nothing fancy. But we think alike. We have exactly the same equipment. Given the same stimulus, the same problem, we're likely to be coming up with the same reactions and solutions at the same time. Explanations are easy — don't even have to make them, usually. We seldom misunderstand each other. It does facilitate our working as a team."

"Christ yes," said Martin. "Pugh and I have spent seven hours out of ten for six months misunderstanding each other. Like most people. What about emergencies, are you as good at meeting the unexpected problem as a nor...an unrelated team?"

"Statistics so far indicate that we are," Zayin answered readily. Clones must be trained, Pugh thought, to meet questions, to reassure and reason. All they said had the slightly bland and stilted quality of answers furnished to the Public. "We can't brainstorm as singletons can, we as a team don't profit from the interplay of varied minds; but we have a compensatory advantage. Clones are drawn from the best human material, individuals of IIQ 99th percentile, Genetic Constitution alpha double A, and so on. We have more to draw on than most individuals do."

"And it's multiplied by a factor of ten. Who is — who was John Chow?"

"A genius surely," Pugh said politely. His interest in cloning was not so new and avid as Martin's.

"Leonardo Complex type," said Yod. "Biomath, also a cellist, and an undersea hunter, and interested in structural engineering problems, and so on. Died before he'd worked out his major theories."

"Then you each represent a different facet of his mind, his talents?"

"No, said Zayin, shaking her head in time with several others. "We share the basic equipment and tendencies, of course, but we're all engineers in Planetary Exploitation. A later clone can be trained to develop other aspects of the basic equipment. It's all training; the genetic substance is identical. We *are* John Chow. But we were differently trained."

Martin looked shell-shocked. "How old are you?"

"Twenty-three."

"You say he died young — Had they taken germ cells from him beforehand or something?"

Gimel took over: "He died at twenty-four in an aircar crash. They couldn't save the brain, so they took some intestinal cells and cultured them for cloning. Reproductive cells aren't used for cloning since they have only half the chromosomes. Intestinal cells happen to be easy to despecialize and reprogram for total growth."

"All chips off the old block," Martin said valiantly. "But how can...some of you be women ...?"

Beth took over: "It's easy to program half the clonal mass back to the female. Just delete the male gene from half the cells and they revert to the basic, that is, the female. It's trickier to go the other way, have to hook in artificial Y chromosomes. So they mostly clone from males, since clones function best bisexually."

Gimel again: "They've worked these matters of technique and function out carefully. The taxpayer wants the best for his money, and of course clones are expensive. With the cell-manipulations, and the incubation in Ngama Placentae, and the maintenance and training of the foster-parent groups, we end up costing about three million apiece."

"For your next generation," Martin said, still struggling, "I suppose you...you breed?"

"We females are sterile," said Beth with perfect equanimity; "you remember that the Y chromosome was deleted from our original cell. The males can interbreed with approved singletons, if they want to. But to get John Chow again as often as they want, they just reclone a cell from this clone."

Martin gave up the struggle. He nodded and chewed cold toast. "Well," said one of the Johns, and all changed mood, like a flock of starlings that change course in one wingflick, following a leader so fast that no eye can see which leads. They were ready to go. "How about a look at the mine? Then we'll unload the equipment. Some nice new models in the roboats; you'll want to see them. Right?" Had Pugh or Martin not agreed they might have

found it hard to say so. The Johns were polite but unanimous; their decisions carried. Pugh, Commander of Libra Base 2, felt a qualm. Could he boss around this superman-woman-entity-of-ten? and a genius at that? He stuck close to Martin as they suited for outside. Neither said anything.

Four apiece in the three large jetsleds, they slipped off north from the dome, over Libra's dun rugose skin, in starlight.

"Desolate," one said.

It was a boy and girl with Pugh and Martin. Pugh wondered if these were the two that had shared a sleeping-bag last night. No doubt they wouldn't mind if he asked them. Sex must be as handy as breathing, to them. Did you two breathe last night?

"Yes," he said, "it is desolate."

"This is our first time Off, except training on Luna." The girl's voice was definitely a bit higher and softer.

"How did you take the big hop?"

"They doped us. I wanted to experience it." That was the boy; he sounded wistful. They seemed to have more personality, only two at a time. Did repetition of the individual negate individuality?

"Don't worry," said Martin, steering the sled, "you can't experience no-time because it isn't there."

"I'd just like to once," one of them said. "So we'd know."

The Mountains of Merioneth showed leprotic in starlight to the east, a plume of freezing gas trailed silvery from a vent-hole to the west, and the sled tilted ground-ward. The twins braced for the stop at one moment, each with a slight protective gesture to the other. Your skin is my skin, Pugh thought, but literally, no metaphor. What would it be like, then, to have someone as close to you as that? Always to be answered when you spoke, never to be in pain alone. Love your neighbor as you love yourself.... That hard old problem was solved. The neighbor was the self: the love was perfect.

And here was Hellmouth, the mine.

Pugh was the Exploratory Mission's ET geologist, and Martin his technician and cartographer; but when in the course of a local survey Martin had discovered the U-mine, Pugh had given him full credit, as well as the onus of prospecting the lode and planning the Exploitation Team's job. These kids had been sent out from Earth years before Martin's report got there, and had not known what their job would be until they got here. The Exploitation Corps simply sent out teams regularly and blindly as a dandelion sends out its seeds, knowing there would be a job for them on Libra or the next planet out or one they hadn't even heard about yet. The Government wanted uranium too urgently to wait while reports drifted home across the light-years. The stuff was like gold, old-fashioned but essential, worth mining extraterrestrially and shipping interstellar. Worth its weight in people, Pugh thought sourly, watching the tall young men and women go one by one, glimmering in starlight, into the black hole Martin had named Hellmouth.

As they went in their homeostatic forehead-lamps brightened. Twelve nodding gleams ran along the moist, wrinkled walls. Pugh heard Martin's radiation counter peeping twenty to the dozen up ahead. "Here's the drop-off," said Martin's voice in the suit intercom, drowning out the peeping and the dead silence that was around them. "We're in a side-fissure; this is the main vertical vent in front of us." The black void gaped, its far side not visible in the headlamp beams. "Last vulcanism seems to have been a couple of thousand years ago. Nearest fault is twenty-eight kilos east, in the Trench. This region seems to be as safe seismically as anything in the area. The big basalt-flow overhead stabilizes all these substructures, so long as it remains stable itself. Your central lode is thirty-six meters down and runs in a series of five bubble-caverns northeast. It is a lode, a pipe of very high-grade ore. You saw the percentage figures, right? Extraction's going to be no problem. All you've got to do is get the bubbles topside."

"Take off the lid and let 'em float up." A chuckle. Voices began to talk, but they were all the same voice and the suit radio gave them no location in space. "Open the thing right up. — Safer that way. — But it's a solid basalt roof, how thick, ten meters here? — Three to twenty, the report said. — Blow good ore all over the lot. — Use this access we're in, straighten it a bit and run slider-rails for the robos. — Import burros. — Have we got enough propping material? — What's your estimate of total payload mass, Martin?"

"Say over five million kilos and under eight."

"Transport will be here in ten E-months. — It'll have to go pure. — No, they'll have the mass problem in NAFAL shipping licked by now; remember it's been sixteen years since we left Earth last Tuesday. — Right, they'll send the whole lot back and purify it in Earth orbit. — Shall we go down, Martin?"

"Go on. I've been down."

The first one — Aleph? (Heb., the ox, the leader) — swung onto the ladder and down; the rest followed. Pugh and Martin stood at the chasm's edge. Pugh set his intercom to exchange only with Martin's suit, and noticed Martin doing the same. It was a bit wearing, this listening to one person think aloud in ten voices, or was it one voice speaking the thoughts of ten minds?

"A great gut," Pugh said, looking down into the black pit, its veined and warted walls catching stray gleams of head-lamps far below. "A cow's bowel. A bloody great constipated intestine."

Martin's counter peeped like a lost chicken. They stood inside the epileptic planet, breathing oxygen from tanks, wearing suits impermeable to corrosives and harmful radiations, resistant to a two-hundred-degree range of temperatures, tear-proof, and as shock-resistant as possible given the soft vulnerable stuff inside.

"Next hop," Martin said, "I'd like to find a planet that has nothing whatever to exploit."

"You found this."

"Keep me home next time."

Pugh was pleased. He had hoped Martin would want to go on working with him, but neither of them was used to talking much about their feelings, and he had hesitated to ask. "I'll try that," he said.

"I hate this place. I like caves, you know. It's why I came in here. Just spelunking. But this one's a bitch. Mean. You can't ever let down in here. I guess this lot can handle it, though. They know their stuff."

"Wave of the future, whatever," said Pugh.

The wave of the future came swarming up the ladder, swept Martin to the entrance, gabbled at and around him: "Have we got enough material for supports? — If we convert one of the extractor-servos to anneal, yes. — Sufficient if we miniblast? — Kaph can calculate stress."

Pugh had switched his intercom back to receive them; he looked at them, so many thoughts jabbering in an eager mind, and at Martin standing silent among them, and at Hellmouth, and the wrinkled plain. "Settled! How does that strike you as a preliminary schedule, Martin?"

"It's your baby," Martin said.

Within five E-days the Johns had all their material and equipment unloaded and operating, and were starting to open up the mine. They worked with total efficiency. Pugh was fascinated and frightened by their effectiveness, their confidence, their independence. He was no use to them at all. A clone, he thought, might indeed be the first truly stable, self-relient human being. Once adult it would need nobody's help. It would be sufficient to itself physically, sexually, emotionally, intellectually. Whatever he did, any member of it would always receive the support and approval of his peers, his other selves. Nobody else was needed.

Two of the clone stayed in the dome doing calculations and paperwork, with frequent sled-trips to the mine for measurements and tests. They were the mathematicians of the clone, Zayin and Kaph. That is, as Zayin explained, all ten had had thorough mathematical training from age three to twenty-one, but from twenty-one to twenty-three she and Kaph had gone on with math while the others intensified other specialties, geology, mining engineering, electronic engineering, equipment robotics, applied atomics, and so on. "Kaph and I feel," she said, "that we're the element of the clone closest to what John Chow was in his singleton lifetime. But of course he was principally in biomath, and they didn't take us far in that."

"They needed us most in this field," Kaph said, with the patriotic priggishness they sometimes evinced.

Pugh and Martin soon could distinguish this pair from the others, Zayin by gestalt, Kaph only by a discolored left fourth fingernail, got from an ill-aimed hammer at the age of six. No doubt there were many such differences, physical and psychological, among them; nature might be identical, nurture could not be. But the differences were hard to find. And part of the difficulty was that they really never talked to Pugh and Martin. They joked with them, were polite, got along fine. They gave nothing. It was nothing one could complain about; they were very pleasant, they had the standardized American friendliness. "Do you come from Ireland, Owen?"

"Nobody comes from Ireland, Zayin."

"There are lots of Irish-Americans."

"To be sure, but no more Irish. A couple of thousand in all the island, the last I knew. They didn't go in for birth-control, you know, so the food ran out. By the Third

Famine there were no Irish left at all but the priesthood, and they were all celibate, or nearly all.''

Zayin and Kaph smiled stiffly. They had no experience of either bigotry or irony. "What are you then, ethnically?" Kaph asked, and Pugh replied, "A Welshman."

"Is it Welsh that you and Martin speak together?"

None of your business, Pugh thought, but said, "No, it's his dialect, not mine: Argentinean. A descendant of Spanish."

"You learned it for private communication?"

"Whom had we here to be private from? It's just that sometimes a man likes to speak his native language."

"Ours is English," Kaph said unsympathetically. Why should they have sympathy? That's one of the things you give because you need it back.

"Is Wells quaint?" asked Zayin.

"Wells? Oh, Wales, it's called. Yes. Wales is quaint." Pugh switched on his rock-cutter, which prevented further conversation by a synapse-destroying whine, and while it whined he turned his back and said a profane word in Welsh.

That night he used the Argentine dialect for private communication. "Do they pair off in the same couples, or change every night?"

Martin looked surprised. A prudish expression, unsuited to his features, appeared for a moment. It faded. He too was curious. "I think it's random."

"Don't whisper, man, it sounds dirty. I think they rotate."

"On a schedule?"

"So nobody gets omitted."

Martin gave a vulgar laugh and smothered it. "What about us? Aren't we omitted."

"That doesn't occur to them."

"What if I proposition one of the girls?"

"She'd tell the others and they'd decide as a group."

"I am not a bull," Martin said, his dark, heavy face heating up. "I will not be judged —"

"Down, down, *machismo*," said Pugh. "Do you mean to proposition one?"

Martin shrugged sullen. "Let 'em have their incest."

"Incest is it, or masturbation?"

"I don't care, if they'd do it out of earshot!"

The clone's early attempts at modesty had soon worn off, unmotivated by any deep defensiveness of self or awareness of others. Pugh and Martin were daily deeper swamped under the intimacies of its constant emotional-sexual-mental interchange: swamped yet excluded.

"Two months to go," Martin said one evening.

"To what?" snapped Pugh. He was edgy lately and Martin's sullenness got on his nerves.

"To relief."

In sixty days the full crew of their Exploratory Mission were due back from their survey of the other planets of the system. Pugh was aware of this.

"Crossing off the days on your calendar?" he jeered.

"Pull yourself together, Owen."

"What do you mean?"

"What I say."

They parted in contempt and resentment.

Pugh came in after a day alone on the Pampas, a vast lava-plain the nearest edge of which was two hours south by jet. He was tired, but refreshed by solitude. They were not supposed to take long trips alone, but lately had often done so. Martin stooped under bright lights, drawing one of his elegant, masterly charts: this one was of the whole face of Libra, the cancerous face. The dome was otherwise empty, seeming dim and large as it had before the clone came. "Where's the golden horde?"

Martin grunted ignorance, crosshatching. He straightened his back to glance around at the sun, which squatted feebly like a great red toad on the eastern plain, and at the clock, which said 18:45. "Some big quakes today," he said, returning to his map. "Feel them down there? Lot of crates were falling around. Take a look at the seismo."

The needle jigged and wavered on the roll. It never stopped dancing here. The roll had recorded five quakes of major intensity back in mid-afternoon; twice the needle had hopped off the roll. The attached computer had been activated to emit a slip reading, "Epicenter 61' N by 4'24'' E."

"Not in the Trench this time."

"I thought it felt a bit different from usual. Sharper."

"In Base One I used to lie awake all night feeling the ground jump. Queer how you get used to things."

"Go spla if you didn't. What's for dinner?"

"I thought you'd have cooked it."

"Waiting for the clone."

Feeling put upon, Pugh got out a dozen dinner-boxes, stuck two in the Instobake, pulled them out. "All right, here's dinner."

"Been thinking," Martin said, coming to the table. "What if some clone cloned itself? Illegally. Made a thousand duplicates — ten thousand. Whole army. They could make a tidy power-grab, couldn't they?"

"But how many millions did this lot cost to rear? Artificial placentae and all that. It would be hard to keep secret, unless they had a planet to themselves....Back before the Famines when Earth had national governments, they talked about that: clone your best soldiers, have whole regiments of them. But the food ran out before they could play that game."

They talked amicably, as they used to do.

"Funny," Martin said, chewing. "They left early this morning, didn't they?"

"All but Kaph and Zayin. They thought they'd get the first payload aboveground today. What's up?"

"They weren't back for lunch."

"They won't starve to be sure."

"They left at seven."

"So they did." Then Pugh saw it. The air-tanks held eight hours supply.

"Kaph and Zayin carried out spare cans when they left. Or they've got a heap out there."

"They did, but they brought the whole lot in to recharge." Martin stood up, pointing to one of the stacks of stuff that cut the dome into rooms and alleys.

"There's an alarm signal on every imsuit."

"It's not automatic."

Pugh was tired and still hungry. "Sit down and eat, man. That lot can look after themselves."

Martin sat down, but did not eat. "There was a big quake, Owen. The first one. Big enough, it scared me."

After a pause Pugh sighed and said, "All right."

Unenthusiastically, they got out the two-man sled that was always left for them, and headed it north. The long sunrise covered everything in poisonous red jello. The horizontal light and shadow made it hard to see, raised walls of fake iron ahead of them through which they slid, turned the convex plain beyond Hellmouth into a great dimple full of bloody water. Around the tunnel entrance a wilderness of machinery stood, cranes and cables and servos and wheels and diggers and robocarts and sliders and controlhuts, all slanting and bulking incoherently in the red light. Martin jumped from the sled, ran into the mine. He came out again, to Pugh. "Oh God, Owen, it's down," he said. Pugh went in and saw, five meters from the entrance, the shiny, moist, black wall that ended the tunnel. Newly exposed to air, it looked organic, like visceral tissue. The tunnel entrance, enlarged by blasting and double-tracked for robocarts, seemed unchanged until he noticed thousands of tiny spiderweb cracks in the walls. The floor was wet with some sluggish fluid.

"They were inside," Martin said.

"They may be still. They surely had extra air-cans —"

"Look, Owen, look at the basalt flow, at the roof; don't you see what the quake did, look at it."

The low hump of land that roofed the caves still had the unreal look of an optical illusion. It had reversed itself, sunk down, leaving a vast dimple or pit. When Pugh walked on it he saw that it too was cracked with many tiny fissures. From some a whitish gas was seeping, so that the sunlight on the surface of the gas-pool was shafted as if by the waters of a dim red lake.

"The mine's not on the fault. There's no fault here!"

Pugh came back to him quickly. "No, there's no fault, Martin. Look, they surely weren't all inside together."

Martin followed him and searched among the wrecked machines dully, then actively. He spotted the airsled. It had come down heading south, and stuck at an angle in a pothole of colloidal dust. It had carried two riders. One was half sunk in the dust, but his suit-meters registered normal functioning; the other hung strapped onto the tilted sled. Her imsuit had burst open on the broken legs, and the body was frozen hard as any rock. That was all they found. As both regulation and custom demanded, they cremated the dead at once with the laser-guns they carried by regulation and had never used before. Pugh, knowing he was going to be sick, wrestled the survivor onto the two-man sled and sent Martin off to the dome with him. Then he vomited, and flushed the waste out of his suit, and finding one four-man sled undamaged followed after Martin, shaking as if the cold of Libra had got through to him.

The survivor was Kaph. He was in deep shock. They found a swelling on the occiput that might mean concussion, but no fracture was visible.

Pugh brought two glasses of food-concentrate and two chasers of aquavit. "Come on," he said. Martin obeyed, drinking off the tonic. They sat down on crates near the cot and sipped the aquavit.

Kaph lay immobile, face like beeswax, hair bright black to the shoulders, lips stiffly parted for faintly gasping breaths.

"It must have been the first shock, the big one," Martin said. "It must have slid the whole structure sideways. Till it fell in on itself. There must be gas layers in the lateral rocks, like those formations in the Thirty-first Quadrant. But there wasn't any sign —" As he spoke the world slid out from under them. Things leaped and clattered, hopped and jigged, shouted Ha! Ha! Ha! "It was like this at fourteen hours," said Reason shakily in Martin's voice; amidst the unfastening and ruin of the world. But Unreason sat up, as the tumult lessened and things ceased dancing, and screamed aloud.

Pugh leaped across his spilled aquavit and held Kaph down. The muscular body flailed him off. Martin pinned the shoulders down. Kaph screamed, struggled, choked; his face blackened. "Oxy," Pugh said, and his hand found the right needle in the medical kit as if by homing instinct; while Martin held the mask he struck the needle home to the vagus nerve, restoring Kaph to life.

"Didn't know you knew that stunt," Martin said, breathing hard.

"The Lazarus Jab; my father was a doctor. It doesn't often work," Pugh said. "I want that drink I spilled. Is the quake over? I can't tell."

"Aftershocks. It's not just you shivering."

"Why did he suffocate?"

"I don't know, Owen. Look in the book."

Kaph was breathing normally and his color was restored, only the lips were still darkened. They poured a new shot of courage and sat down by him again with their medical guide. "Nothing about cyanosis or asphyxiation under 'shock' or 'concussion.' He can't have breathed in anything with his suit on. I don't know. We'd get as much good out of *Mother Mog's Home Herbalist*....'Anal Hemorrhoids,' fy!" Pugh pitched the book to a crate-table. It fell short, because either Pugh or the table was still unsteady.

"Why didn't he signal?"

"Sorry?"

''The eight inside the mine never had time. But he and the girl must have been outside. Maybe she was in the entrance, and got hit by the first slide. He must have been outside, in the control-hut maybe. He ran in, pulled her out, strapped her onto the sled, started for the dome. And all that time never pushed the panic button in his imsuit. Why not?''

''Well, he'd had that whack on his head. I doubt he ever realized the girl was dead. He wasn't in his senses. But if he had been I don't know if he'd have thought to signal us. They looked to one another for help.''

Martin's face was like an Indian mask, grooves at the mouth-corners, eyes of dull coal. ''That's so. What must he have felt, then, when the quake came and he was outside, alone —''

In answer Kaph screamed.

He came up off the cot in the heaving convulsions of one suffocating, knocked Pugh right down with his flailing arm, staggered into a stack of crates and fell to the floor, lips blue, eyes white. Martin dragged him back onto the cot and gave him a whiff of oxygen, then knelt by Pugh, who was just sitting up, and wiped at his cut cheekbone. ''Owen, are you all right, are you going to be all right, Owen?''

''I think I am,'' Pugh said. ''Why are you rubbing that on my face?''

It was a short length of computer-tape, now spotted with Pugh's blood. Martin dropped it. ''Thought it was a towel. You clipped your cheek on that box there.''

''Is he out of it?''

''Seems to be.''

They stared down at Kaph lying stiff, his teeth a white line inside dark parted lips.

''Like epilepsy. Brain damage maybe?''

''What about shooting him full of meprobamate?''

Pugh shook his head. ''I don't know what's in that shot I already gave him for shock. Don't want to overdose him.''

''Maybe he'll sleep it off now.''

''I'd like to myself. Between him and the earthquake I can't seem to keep on my feet.''

''You got a nasty crack there. Go on, I'll sit up a while.''

Pugh cleaned his cut cheek and pulled off his shirt, then paused.

''Is there anything we ought to have done — have tried to do —''

''They're all dead,'' Martin said heavily, gently.

Pugh lay down on top of his sleeping-bag, and one instant later was awakened by a hideous, sucking, struggling noise. He staggered up, found the needle, tried three times to jab it in correctly and failed, began to massage over Kaph's heart. ''Mouth-to-mouth,'' he said, and Martin obeyed. Presently Kaph drew a harsh breath, his heartbeat steadied, his rigid muscles began to relax.

''How long did I sleep?''

''Half an hour.''

They stood up sweating. The ground shuddered, the fabric of the dome sagged and swayed. Libra was dancing her awful polka again, her Totentanz. The sun, though rising, seemed to have grown larger and redder; gas and dust must have been stirred up in the feeble atmosphere.

''What's wrong with him, Owen?''

''I think he's dying with them.''

''Them — But they're dead, I tell you.''

''Nine of them. They're all dead, they were crushed or suffocated. They were all him, he is all of them. They died, and now he's dying their deaths one by one.''

''Oh pity of God,'' said Martin.

The next time was much the same. The fifth time was worse, for Kaph fought and raved, trying to speak but getting no words out, as if his mouth were stopped with rocks or clay. After that the attacks grew weaker, but so did he. The eighth seizure came at about four-thirty; Pugh and Martin worked till five-thirty doing all they could to keep life in the body that slid without protest into death. They kept him, but Martin said, ''The next will finish him.'' And it did; but Pugh breathed his own breath into the inert lungs, until he himself passed out.

He woke. The dome was opaqued and no light on. He listened and heard the breathing of two sleeping men. He slept, and nothing woke him till hunger did.

The sun was well up over the dark plains, and the planet had stopped dancing. Kaph lay asleep. Pugh and Martin drank tea and looked at him with proprietary triumph.

When he woke Martin went to him: ''How do you feel, old man?'' There was no answer. Pugh took Martin's place and looked into the brown, dull eyes that gazed toward but not into his own. Like Martin he quickly turned away. He heated food-concentrate and brought it to Kaph. ''Come on, drink.''

He could see the muscles in Kaph's throat tighten. ''Let me die,'' the young man said.

''You're not dying.''

Kaph spoke with clarity and precision: ''I am nine-tenths dead. There is not enough of me left alive.''

That precision convinced Pugh, and he fought the conviction. ''No,'' he said, peremptory. ''They are dead. The others. Your brothers and sisters. You're not them, you're alive. You are John Chow. Your life is in your own hands.''

The young man lay still, looking into a darkness that was not there.

Martin and Pugh took turns taking the Exploitation hauler and a spare set of robos over to Hellmouth to salvage equipment and protect it from Libra's sinister atmosphere, for the value of the stuff was, literally, astronomical. It was slow work for one man at a time, but they were unwilling to leave Kaph by himself. The one left in the dome did paperwork, while Kaph sat or lay and stared into his darkness, and never spoke. The days went by silent.

The radio spat and spoke: the Mission calling from ship.

"We'll be down on Libra in five weeks, Owen. Thirty-four E-days nine hours I make it as of now. How's tricks in the old dome?"

"Not good, chief. The Exploit team were killed, all but one of them, in the mine. Earthquake. Six days ago."

The radio crackled and sang starsong. Sixteen seconds lag each way; the ship was out around Planet II now. "Killed, all but one? You and Martin were unhurt?"

"We're all right, chief."

thirty-two seconds.

"*Passerine* left an Exploit team out here with us. I may put them on the Hellmouth project then, instead of the Quadrant Seven project. We'll settle that when we come down. In any case you and Martin will be relieved at Dome Two. Hold tight. Anything else?"

"Nothing else."

Thirty-two seconds.

"Right then. So long, Owen."

Kaph had heard all this, and later on Pugh said to him, "The chief may ask you to stay here with the other Exploit team. You know the ropes here." Knowing the exigencies of Far Out Life, he wanted to warn the young man. Kaph made no answer. Since he had said, "There is not enough of me left alive," he had not spoken a word.

"Owen," Martin said on suit intercom, "he's spla. Insane. Psycho."

"He's doing very well for a man who's died nine times."

"Well? Like a turned-off android is well? The only emotion he has left is hate. Look at his eyes."

"That's not hate, Martin. Listen, it's true that he has, in a sense, been dead. I cannot imagine what he feels. But it's not hatred. He can't even see us. It's too dark."

"Throats have been cut in the dark. He hates us because we're not Aleph and Yod and Zayin."

"Maybe. But I think he's alone. He doesn't see us or hear us, that's the truth. He never had to see anyone else before. He never was alone before. He had himself to see, talk with, live with, nine other selves all his life. He doesn't know how you go it alone. He must learn. Give him time."

Martin shook his heavy head. "Spla," he said. "Just remember when you're alone with him that he could break your neck one-handed."

"He could do that," said Pugh, a short, soft-voiced man with a scarred cheekbone; he smiled. They were just outside the dome airlock, programming one of the servos to repair a damaged hauler. They could see Kaph sitting inside the great half-egg of the dome like a fly in amber.

"Hand me the insert pack there. What makes you think he'll get any better?"

"He has a strong personality, to be sure."

"Strong? Crippled. Nine-tenths dead, as he put it."

"But he's not dead. He's a live man: John Kaph Chow. He had a jolly queer upbringing, but after all every boy has got to break free of his family. He will do it."

"I can't see it."

"Think a bit, Martin bach. What's this cloning for? To repair the human race. We're in a bad way. Look at me. My IIQ and GC are half this John Chow's. Yet they wanted me so badly for the Far Out Service that when I volunteered they took me and fitted me out with an artificial lung and corrected my myopia. Now if there were enough good sound lads about would they be taking one-lunged shortsighted Welshmen?"

"Didn't know you had an artifical lung."

"I do then. Not tin, you know. Human, grown in a tank from a bit of somebody; cloned, if you like. That's how they make replacement-organs, the same general idea as cloning, but bits and pieces instead of whole people. It's my own lung now, whatever. But what I am saying is this, there are too many like me these days, and not enough like John Chow. They're trying to raise the level of the human genetic pool, which is a mucky little puddle since the population crash. So then if a man is cloned, he's a strong and clever man. It's only logic, to be sure."

Martin grunted; the servo began to hum.

Kaph had been eating little; he had trouble swallowing his food, choking on it, so that he would give up trying after a few bites. He had lost eight or ten kilos. After three weeks or so, however, his appetite began to pick up, and one day he began to look through the clone's possessions, the sleeping-bags, kits, papers which Pugh had stacked neatly in a far angle of a packing-crate alley. He sorted, destroyed a heap of papers and oddments, made a small packet of what remained, then relapsed into his walking coma.

But now man's confidence in his power to control his world is at a low ebb. Technology is seen as a dangerous ally, and progress is suspect. Even the evolutionists share this unease; their hope lies not in man as he is but in some mutant superman.

Time, April 23, 1973

Two days later he spoke. Pugh was trying to correct a flutter in the tape-player, and failing; Martin had the jet out, checking their maps of the Pampas. "Hell and damnation!" Pugh said, and Kaph said in a toneless voice, "Do you want me to do that?"

Pugh jumped, controlled himself, and gave the machine to Kaph. The young man took it apart, put it back together, and left it on the table.

"Put on a tape," Pugh said with careful casualness, busy at another table.

Kaph put on the topmost tape, a chorale. He lay down on his cot. The sound of a hundred human voices singing together filled the dome. He lay still, his face blank.

In the next days he took over several routine jobs, unasked. He undertook nothing that wanted initiative, and if asked to do anything he made no response at all.

"He's doing well," Pugh said in the dialect of Argentina.

"He's not. He's turning himself into a machine. Does what he's programmed to do, no reaction to anything else. He's worse off than when he didn't function at all. He's not human any more."

Pugh sighed. "Well, good night," he said in English. "Good night, Kaph."

"Good night," Martin said; Kaph did not.

Next morning at breakfast Kaph reached across Martin's plate for the toast. "Why don't you ask for it," Martin said with the geniality of repressed exasperation. "I can pass it."

"I can reach it," Kaph said in his flat voice.

"Yes, but look. Asking to pass things, saying good night or hello, they're not important, but all the same when somebody says something a person ought to answer...."

The young man looked indifferently in Martin's direction; his eyes still did not seem to see clear through to the person he looked toward. "Why should I answer?"

"Because somebody has said something to you."

"Why?"

Martin shrugged and laughed. Pugh jumped up and turned on the rock-cutter.

Later on he said, "Lay off that, please, Martin."

"Manners are essential in small isolated crews, some kind of manners, whatever you work out together. He's been taught that, everybody in Far Out knows it. Why does he deliberately flout it?"

"Do you tell yourself good night?"

"So?"

"Don't you see Kaph's never known anyone but himself?"

Martin brooded and then broke out, "Then by God this cloning business is all wrong. It won't do. What are a lot of duplicate geniuses going to do for us when they don't even know we exist?"

Pugh nodded. "It might be wiser to separate the clones and bring them up with others. But they make such a grand team this way."

"Do they? I don't know. If this lot had been ten average inefficient ET engineers, would they all have been in the same place at the same time? Would they all have got killed? What if, when the quake came and things started caving in, what if all those kids ran the same way, farther into the mine, maybe, to save the one that was farthest in? Even Kaph was outside and went in....It's hypothetical. But I keep thinking, out of ten ordinary confused guys, more might have got out."

"I don't know. It's true that identical twins tend to die at about the same time, even when they have never seen each other. Identity and death, it is very strange...."

The days went on, the red sun crawled across the dark sky, Kaph did not speak when spoken to, Pugh and Martin snapped at each other more frequently each day. Pugh complained of Martin's snoring. Offended, Martin moved his cot clear across the dome and also ceased speaking to Pugh for some while. Pugh whistled Welsh dirges until Martin complained, and then Pugh stopped speaking for a while.

The day before the Mission ship was due, Martin announced he was going over to Merioneth.

"I thought at least you'd be giving me a hand with the computer to finish the rock-analyses," Pugh said, aggrieved.

"Kaph can do that. I want one more look at the Trench. Have fun," Martin added in dialect, and laughed, and left.

"What is that language?"

"Argentinean. I told you that once, didn't I?"

"I don't know." After a while the young man added, "I have forgotten a lot of things, I think."

"It wasn't important, to be sure," Pugh said gently, realizing all at once how important this conversation was. "Will you give me a hand running the computer, Kaph?"

He nodded.

Pugh had left a lot of loose ends, and the job took them all day. Kaph was a good co-worker, quick and systematic, much more so than Pugh himself. His flat voice, now that he was talking again, got on the nerves; but it didn't matter, there was only this one day left to get through and then the ship would come, the old crew, comrades and friends.

During tea-break Kaph said, "What will happen if the Explorer ship crashes?"

"They'd be killed."

"To you, I mean."

"To us? We'd radio SOS all signals, and live on half rations till the rescue cruiser from Area Three Base came. Four and a half E-years away it is. We have life-support here for three men for, let's see, maybe between four and five years. A bit tight, it would be."

"Would they send a cruiser for three men?"

"They would."

Kaph said no more.

"Enough cheerful speculations," Pugh said cheerfully, rising to get back to work. He slipped sideways and the chair avoided his hand; he did a sort of half-pirouette and fetched up hard against the dome-hide. "My goodness," he said, reverting to his native idiom, "what is it?"

"Quake," said Kaph.

The teacups bounced on the table with a plastic cackle, a litter of papers slid off a box, the skin of the dome swelled and sagged. Underfoot there was a huge noise, half sound half shaking, a subsonic boom.

Kaph sat unmoved. An earthquake does not frighten a man who died in an earthquake.

Pugh, white-faced, wiry black hair sticking out, a frightened man, said, "Martin is in the Trench."

"What trench?"

"The big fault line. The epicenter for the local quakes. Look at the seismograph." Pugh struggled with the stuck door of a still-jittering locker.

"Where are you going?"

"After him."

"Martin took the jet. Sleds aren't safe to use during quakes. They go out of control."

"For God's sake, man, shut up."

Kaph stood up, speaking in a flat voice as usual.

"It's unnecessary to go out after him now. It's taking an unnecessary risk."

"If his alarm goes off, radio me," Pugh said, shut the headpiece of his suit, and ran to the lock. As he went out Libra picked up her ragged skirts and danced a belly-dance from under his feet clear to the red horizon.

Inside the dome, Kaph saw the sled go up, tremble like a meteor in the dull red daylight, and vanish to the northeast. The hide of the dome quivered; the earth coughed. A vent south of the dome belched up a slow-flowing bile of black gas.

A bell shrilled and a red light flashed on the central control board. The sign under the light read Suit Two and scribbled under that, A.G.M. Kaph did not turn the signal off. He tried to radio Martin, then Pugh, but got no reply from either.

In the work at the Bioinformation Institute in Moscow a very definite bias in telepathy toward *visual* rather than linguistic transmission has also been noted....A screw driver was received as a "long blackish-handle sort of thing," not as a specific tool. The telepathic sense quite evidently is a survivor of prehistoric eye-mindedness rather than a symbol-sensing development of modern man.

D.E. Carr, *The Forgotten Senses* (1972)

When the aftershocks decreased he went back to work, and finished up Pugh's job. It took him about two hours. Every half hour he tried to contact Suit One, and got no reply, then Suit Two and got no reply. The red light had stopped flashing after an hour.

It was dinnertime. Kaph cooked dinner for one, and ate it. He lay down on his cot.

The aftershocks had ceased except for faint rolling tremors at long intervals. The sun hung in the west, oblate, pale-red, immense. It did not sink visibly. There was no sound at all.

Kaph got up and began to walk about the messy, half-packed-up, overcrowded, empty dome. The silence continued. He went to the player and put on the first tape that came to hand. It was pure music, electronic, without harmonies, without voices. It ended. The silence continued.

Pugh's uniform tunic, one button missing, hung over a stack of rock-samples. Kaph stared at it a while.

The silence continued.

The child's dream: There is no one else alive in the world but me. In all the world.

Low, north of the dome, a meteor flickered.

Kaph's mouth opened as if he were trying to say something, but no sound came. He went hastily to the north wall and peered out into the gelatinous red light.

The little star came in and sank. Two figures blurred the airlock. Kaph stood close beside the lock as they came in. Martin's imsuit was covered with some kind of dust so that he looked raddled and warty like the surface of Libra. Pugh had him by the arm.

"Is he hurt?"

Pugh shucked his suit, helped Martin peel off his. "Shaken up," he said, curt.

"A piece of cliff fell onto the jet," Martin said, sitting down at the table and waving his arms. "Not while I was in it, though. I was parked, see, and poking about that carbon-dust area when I felt things humping. So I went out onto a nice bit of early igneous I'd noticed from above, good footing and out from under the cliffs. Then I saw this bit of the planet fall off onto the flyer, quite a sight it was, and after a while it occurred to me the spare aircans were in the flyer, so I leaned on the panic button. But I didn't get any radio reception, that's always happening here during quakes, so I didn't know if the signal was getting through either. And things went on jumping around and pieces of the cliff coming off. Little rocks flying around, and so dusty you couldn't see a meter ahead. I was really beginning to wonder what I'd do for breathing in the small hours, you know, when I saw old Owen buzzing up the Trench in all that dust and junk like a big ugly bat—"

"Want to eat?" said Pugh.

"Of course I want to eat. How'd you come through the quake here, Kaph? No damage? It wasn't a big one actually, was it, what's the seismo say? My trouble was I was in the middle of it. Old Epicenter Alvaro. Felt like Richter Fifteen there—total destruction of planet—"

"Sit down," Pugh said. "Eat."

After Martin had eaten a little his spate of talk ran dry. He very soon went off to his cot, still in the remote angle where he had removed it when Pugh complained of his snoring. "Good night, you one-lunged Welshman," he said across the dome.

"Good night."

There was no more out of Martin. Pugh opaqued the dome, turned the lamp down to a yellow glow less than a candle's light, and sat doing nothing, saying nothing, withdrawn.

The silence continued.

"I finished the computations."

Pugh nodded thanks.

"The signal from Martin came through, but I couldn't contact you or him."

Pugh said with effort, "I should not have gone. He had two hours of air left even with only one can. He might have been heading home when I left. This way we were all out of touch with one another. I was scared."

The silence came back, punctuated now by Martin's long, soft snores.

"Do you love Martin?"

Pugh looked up with angry eyes: "Martin is my friend. We've worked together, he's a good man." He stopped. After a while he said, "Yes, I love him. Why did you ask that?"

Kaph said nothing, but he looked at the other man. His face was changed, as if he were glimpsing something he had not seen before; his voice too was changed. "How can you...? How do you...?"

But Pugh could not tell him. "I don't know," he said, "it's practice, partly. I don't know. We're each of us alone, to be sure. What can you do but hold your hand out in the dark?"

Kaph's strange gaze dropped, burned out by its own intensity.

"I'm tired," Pugh said. "That was ugly, looking for him in all that black dust and muck, and mouths opening and shutting in the ground....I'm going to bed. The ship will be transmitting to us by six or so." He stood up and stretched.

"It's a clone," Kaph said. "The other Exploit team they're bringing with them."

"Is it, then?"

"A twelveclone. They came out with us on the *Passerine.*"

Kaph sat in the small yellow aura of the lamp seeming to look past it at what he feared: the new clone, the multiple self of which he was not part. A lost piece of a broken set, a fragment, inexpert at solitude, not knowing even how you go about giving love to another individual, now he must face the absolute, closed self-sufficiency of the clone of twelve; that was a lot to ask of the poor fellow, to be sure. Pugh put a hand on his shoulder in passing. "The chief won't ask you to stay here with a clone. You can go home. Or since you're Far Out maybe you'll come on farther out with us. We could use you. No hurry deciding. You'll make out all right."

Pugh's quiet voice trailed off. He stood unbuttoning his coat, stooped a little with fatigue. Kaph looked at him and saw the thing he had never seen before: saw him: Owen Pugh, the other, the stranger who held his hand out in the dark.

"Good night," Pugh mumbled, crawling into his sleeping-bag and half asleep already, so that he did not hear Kaph reply after a pause, repeating, across darkness, benediction.

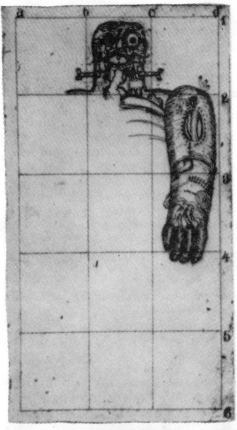

The Bride of Frankenstein
Edward Field

The Baron has decided to mate the monster,
to breed him perhaps,
in the interests of pure science, his only god.

So he goes up into his laboratory
which he has built in the tower of the castle
to be as near the interplanetary forces as possible,
and puts together the prettiest monster-woman you ever
      saw
with a body like a pin-up girl
and hardly any stitching at all
where he sewed on the head of a raped and murdered
      beauty queen.

He sets his liquids burping, and coils blinking and
         buzzing,
and waits for an electric storm to send through the
         equipment
the spark vital for life.
The storm breaks over the castle
and the equipment really goes crazy
like a kitchen full of modern appliances
as the lightning juice starts oozing right into that pretty
      corpse.

He goes to get the monster
so he will be right there when she opens her eyes,
for she might fall in love with the first thing she sees as
      ducklings do.

That monster is already straining at his chains and
         slurping,
ready to go right to it:
He has been well prepared for coupling
by his pinching leering keeper who's been saying for
      weeks,
"Ya gonna get a little nookie, kid,"
or "How do you go for some poontang, baby?"
All the evil in him is focused on this one thing now
as he is led into her very presence.

She awakens slowly,
she bats her eyes,
she gets up out of the equipment,
and finally she stands in all her seamed glory,
a monster princess with a hairdo like a fright wig,
lightning flashing in the background
like a halo and a wedding veil,
like a photographer snapping pictures of great
      moments.

She stands and stares with her electric eyes,
beginning to understand that in this life too
she was just another body to be raped.

The monster is ready to go:
He roars with joy at the sight of her,
so they let him loose and he goes right for those
      knockers.
And she starts screaming to break your heart
and you realize that she was just born:
In spite of her big tits she was just a baby.

But her instincts are right—
rather death than that green slobber:
She jumps off the parapet.
And then the monster's sex drive goes wild.
Thwarted, it turns to violence, demonstrating
      sublimation crudely;
and he wrecks the lab, those burping acids and buzzing
      coils,
overturning the control panel so the equipment goes off
      like a bomb,
and the stone castle crumbles and crashes in the storm
destroying them all...perhaps.

Perhaps somehow the Baron got out of that wreckage of
      his dreams
with his evil intact, if not his good looks,
and more wicked than ever went on with his thrilling
      career.

And perhaps even the monster lived
to roam the earth, his desire still ungratified;
and lovers out walking in shadowy and deserted places
will see his shape loom up over them, their doom—
and children sleeping in their beds
will wake up in the dark night screaming
as his hideous body grabs them.

**"For knowledge is the best gift of God to man, to know
what is the root and principle of all things. The primal
truth is not a body, but it is One, One Truth, One Unity.
All things come from it and through it receive truth and
unity in the perpetual movement of generation and
corruption. There is a hierarchy in things, and lower
things are raised to higher things; and higher things
descend to lower things. Man is a little world reflecting
the great world of the cosmos, but through his intellect
the wise man can raise himself above the seven
heavens."** *Giordano Bruno*

Giordano Bruno
Frances A. Yates, *Giordano Bruno and the Hermetic
Tradition* (1964)

**The radiance of Paradise alternates with deep, dreadful
night.**

Goethe

from The Biological Time Bomb
Gordon Rattray Taylor

Professor S. Zamenhof and his team at the University of
California have tried injecting pregnant mice and rats with
pituitary growth hormone, while the brain of the offspring
was still maturing. They gave injections from the seventh
to the twelfth day of pregnancy. Subsequently they killed
the offspring and examined their brains closely. They
found not only a significant increase in brain weight but
also an increase in the ratio of neurones to the supporting
glial cells. More important still, they discovered that the
density of cells in the cortex, where reasoning is carried
out, was increased and that the number and length of
the dendrites — the branching interconnections — was

At the university of Witwatersrand, the Dean of the
Medical Faculty, Professor O.S. Heyns, developed a
technique of keeping pregnant women with their ab-
domen and pelvis inside a plastic enclosure, the pressure in
which is reduced by a pump to one-fifth atmospheric
pressure, a procedure he calls decompression, or fetal
oxygenation. The treatment is given for half an hour daily,
during the last ten days of pregnancy and during the
beginning of labour. The reduction in pressure on the
uterus was planned to reduce the pains of childbirth, and
it also helps the maternal blood to circulate more freely.

Professor Heyns was surprised when, a year or so after his
first experiments, he began to get reports from their
mothers that the children born in these conditions were
exceptionally intelligent, and certainly forward in their
physical development. At first these reports were ignored
on the grounds that all mothers believe their new baby to
be exceptional. But soon it was found that some of these
super-oxygenated babies really were exceptional — like
Katl Oertel, who was answering the telephone at 13
months, and was speaking in four languages by the age of
three (these babies commonly hear four languages spoken
around them — English, German, Zulu, and Afrikaans —
but normal babies speak the tongue their mother speaks to
them.) These super-children were bored at their nursery
schools; they chat with adults in a fluent, unconcerned
sort of way which suggests a maturity which usually comes
far later. A vocabulary of 200 words by age 18 months is
common with them: the average child speaks only half a
dozen words at this age.

In the last weeks of pregnancy, the placenta does not
grow any further, and the infant's heart becomes incapable of driving blood through it. Professor Heyns
believes that, in consequence, the brains of most fetuses
fail to develop to their full capacity since the fetus's
oxygen demands outstrip the capacity of the mother to
supply it. The oxygenation of the mother's blood helps to
remedy this deficiency.

Whether these children continue to stay ahead is a
matter to watch with close attention. This could prove one
of the most significant experiments of our generation.

The Baffling Burning Death

Allan W. Eckert

On July 2, 1951, Mrs. P.M. Carpenter, owner of a four-apartment building at 1200 Cherry Street Northeast, St. Petersburg, Florida, had spent a pleasant hour or so the evening before in the one-room apartment of her favorite tenant, Mrs. Mary Hardy Reeser, a rather stout, kindly, 67-year-old widow. Mrs. Reeser had chatted amiably about her beloved Pennsylvania Dutch background with her physician son, his wife, and Mrs. Carpenter. She told her son she had taken a couple of seconal tablets at 8 p.m., as usual, and would probably take two more before going to bed. When the trio left at 9 p.m., she was seated in her armchair facing one of the two open windows, a small wooden end table beside her. She was wearing a rayon nightgown, a cotton housecoat and a pair of comfortable black satin slippers. She was smoking a cigarette.

The next morning, shortly before 8, a Western Union boy knocked at Mrs. Carpenter's door. "Got a telegram here for Mrs. Mary Reeser," he told her. "I knocked on her door but don't get any answer. You take it?"

Mrs. Carpenter said she'd deliver the message, but she was concerned. It wasn't like Mary Reeser, a light sleeper, to miss the sound of a knock. Mrs. Carpenter went to the woman's door and tapped lightly, then harder when there was no answer. Alarmed, she reached to open the door, but jerked her hand back in pain. The brass doorknob was so hot it burned her. She screamed, and two painters working nearby rushed to her aid.

They forced the door and found a macabre scene. Although both windows were open, the room was intolerably hot. In front of one open window was a pile of ashes — the remains of the big armchair, the end table... and Mrs. Reeser.

Firemen arrived at 8:07 a.m., followed by the police. It was instantly apparent that this was no ordinary accident. Only the severely heat-eroded coil springs were left of the chair. There was no trace of the end table. Of Mrs. Reeser, all that remained were a few small pieces of charred backbone, a skull which, strangely, had shrunk uniformly to the size of an orange, and her wholly untouched left foot still wearing its slipper.

The heat necessary for such damage had to be incredible, yet the room was little affected. The ceiling, draperies and walls, from a point exactly four feet above the floor, were coated with smelly, oily soot. Below this four-foot mark there was none. The wall paint adjacent to the chair was faintly browned, but the carpet where the chair had rested was not even burned through. A wall mirror 10 feet away had cracked, probably from heat. On a dressing table 12 feet away, two pink wax candles had puddled, but their wicks lay undamaged in the holders. Plastic wall outlets above the four-foot mark were melted, but the fuses were not blown and the current was on. The baseboard electrical outlets were undamaged. An electric clock plugged into one of the fused fixtures had stopped at precisely 4:20 — less than three hours before — but the same clock ran perfectly when plugged into one of the baseboard outlets.

Newspapers nearby on a table and draperies and linens on the daybed close at hand — all flammable — were not damaged. And though the painters and Mrs. Carpenter had felt a wave of heat when they opened the door, no one had noted smoke or burning odor and there were no embers or flames in the ashes.

Faced with a complete mystery, Police Chief J.R. Reichert quickly asked for FBI assistance. Scrapings from the carpet, metal from the chair, and the ashes and mortal remains of Mrs. Reeser were sent to the FBI laboratory for microanalysis. The first report had clarified nothing, but it contained a blockbuster: Mrs. Reeser had weighed 175 pounds, yet all that remained of her after the fire — including the shriveled head, the whole foot, the bits of spine and a minute section of tissue tentatively identified as liver — weighed *less than 10 pounds!*

Edward Davies, a top-notch arson specialist of the National Board of Underwriters, came in on the case. Hard to fool and quick to detect evidence of deliberate burning, he was stumped. "I can only say," he admitted glumly, "the victim died from fire, with no idea of what caused it."

Then came a lucky break. The famous Dr. (Wilton Marion) Krogman,* was visiting his family just across Tampa Bay at Bradenton, and his presence became known. Told of the pathologist's reputation, Reichert promptly asked for his help. Dr. Krogman agreed to look in on the case.

The doctor quickly checked the findings of the other authorities who had been consulted and began eliminating possibilities. Had lightning struck her? No. No storms, no lightning, no thunder the night of July 1. Having swallowed sedatives, could she have fallen asleep in her chair, dropped her cigarette, ignited the nightgown and chair and burned? Hardly likely, since such a fire couldn't possibly have caused the heat — over 3000 degrees F. — necessary to consume her. Even if an ordinary fire had reached that temperature, the room — or the whole building — would have been heavily damaged. Anyway, though the windows were open, no one saw smoke or smelled any burning odor. Was Mrs. Reeser burned elsewhere and then placed in the room? Residue in the room and other evidence ruled this concept out. Could an electrical induction current have gone through her from faulty wiring? Virtually impossible without blowing a fuse.

---

* Dr. Krogman was incorrectly identified in the original article. He is a physical anthropologist and an anatomist, not a physician (or a member of the AMA) and is not "an outstanding authority on the nature and cause of disease." He states, in a letter to *True,* dated May 1, 1964, "I reject fully and unreservedly the concept of SHC-PC. Any statement direct or implied, that I do accept it is unwarranted and incorrect..." and further, "I have never, by stated or implied word, accepted or even considered as a possibility spontaneous combustion in or of the human body." He states quite simply that he has no explanation for such deaths (see his article in *The General Magazine and Historical Chronicle,* 1964; or, abridged, in *Pageant,* October, 1952).

And no short circuit could have caused such massive destruction.

Eventually, even Dr. Krogman admitted defeat. He told Chief Reichert, "I have posed the problem to myself again and again of why Mrs. Reeser could have been so thoroughly destroyed, even to the bones, and yet leave nearby objects materially unaffected. I always end up rejecting it in theory but facing it in apparent fact."

He was unable to understand how the widow's body could have burned so completely without someone's detecting smoke or, especially, "...the acrid, evil-smelling odor of burning human flesh." Another major point he was unable to comprehend was the shrinking of the head. "In my experience," Dr. Krogman asserted, "the head is not left complete in ordinary burning cases. Certainly it does *not* shrivel or symmetrically reduce to a much smaller size. In presence of heat sufficient to destroy soft tissues, the skull would literally explode in many pieces. I have experimented on this, using cadaver heads, and have never known an exception to this rule. "Never," he concluded, "have I seen a skull so shrunken or a body so completely consumed by heat. This is contrary to normal experience and I regard it as the most amazing thing I've ever seen."

Of the Terrible Doubt of Appearances
Walt Whitman

Of the terrible doubt of appearances,
Of the uncertainty after all, that we may be deluded,
That may-be reliance and hope are but speculations
    after all,
That may-be identity beyond the grave is a beautiful
    fable only,
May-be the things I perceive, the animals, plants, men,
    hills, shinning and flowing waters,
The skies of day and night, colors, densities, forms,
    may-be these are (as doubtless they are) only
    apparitions, and the real something has yet to be
    known,
(How often they dart out of themselves as if to con-
    found me and mock me!
How often I think neither I know, nor any man knows,
    aught of them,)
May-be seeming to me what they are (as doubtless they
    indeed but seem) as from my present point of view,
    and might prove (as of course they would) nought
    of what they appear, or nought anyhow, from
    entirely changed points of view;
To me these and the like of these are curiously answer'd
    by my lovers, my dear friends,
When he whom I love travels with me or sits a long
    while holding me by the hand,
When the subtle air, the impalpable, the sense that
    words and reason hold not, surround us and
    pervade us,
Then I am charged with untold and untellable wisdom, I
    am silent, I require nothing further,
I cannot answer the question of appearances or that of
    identity beyond the grave,
But I walk or sit indifferent, I am satisfied,
He ahold of my hand has completely satisfied me.

The way…to turn over the structure of present physics [is] to consider space, time and mass as illusions in the same way temperature is…a sensory illusion.

David Finkelstein, *Time*, April 23, 1973

…as science has supplanted its predecessors, so it may hereafter be itself superceded by some more perfect hypothesis, perhaps by some totally different way of looking at the phenomena — of registering the shadows on the screen.

Sir James Frazer, *The Golden Bough* (1922)

from **Biological Rhythms in Human And Animal Physiology**
Gay Gaer Luce

Periodically, in mental hospital wards, aggressive patients show intense surges of activity: individuals become hostile, excitable, even violent. Such outbursts occur only sporadically but are striking enough to have invited study. At Douglas Hospital in Montreal, continuous, round-the-clock observation of patients over periods of several months did, indeed, show a picture of such periodic outbursts. Correlations between increased aggression and staff on duty, changes in menu, medication, or visiting days were too weak to explain the group behavior. Barometric pressure, temperature, humidity, and other experimental factors were juxtaposed against the hospital calendar of aggressive behavior. When no explanation could be found, Dr. Heinz Lehman compared his hospital data against data from the U.S. Space Disturbance Forecast Center in Boulder, Colorado. There appeared to be a correlation between solar flare activity (sun spots), geomagnetic disturbances, and excitement on the ward. It seemed unlikely but the study continues. Since sun flares are bursts of gaseous material, high energy particles that influence the ionosphere, causing changes in magnetic fields on earth, a relationship is not impossible. Sun storms sometimes cause a noticeable deflection in a compass needle. Perhaps, since the brain is at least as sensitive as a fine compass, it also responds to large magnetic distrubances.

We know that rats are sensitive to X-rays....The human brain may also respond to such inputs. The possibility of an expanded ''sensory'' range has been raised by studies of biological rhythms.

There was a child went forth everyday,
And the first object he looked upon, that object he
became,
And that object became part of him for the day or a
    certain part of the day,
Or for many years or stretching cycles of years.

Walt Whitman, *Leaves of Grass*

The joy of the child is so complete, so self-delighting, because it is the accompaniment of those primary movements of the imagination by which he discovers and furthers his humanity, and finds and increases his freedom.

William Walsh, *The Use of Imagination* (1959)

Every transformation or creative process comprises stages of possession. To be moved, captivated, spellbound, signify to be possessed by something; and without such a fascination and the emotional tension connected with it, no concentration, no lasting interest, no creative process are possible....The exclusivity and radicality of such "possession" represent both an opportunity and a danger. But no great achievement is possible if one does not accept this risk.

Erich Neumann, *Art and the Creative Unconscious* (1959)

The universe begins to look more and more like a great thought than a great machine.

Dr. J.B. Rhine

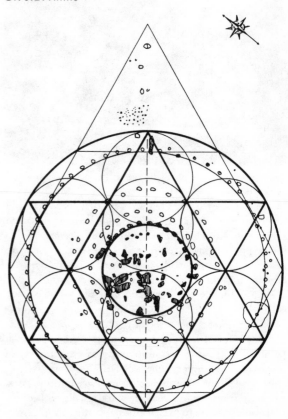

The hidden geometry of Stonehenge: A hexagon of 66600 sq. ft.; Solomon's Seal 66600 sq. ft. in total area; inner circle of 6660 sq. yds.;

John Michell, *A View Over Atlantis*, (1969)

Storm

Jay Macpherson

That strong creature   from before the Flood,
headless, sightless,   without bone or blood,
a wandering voice,   a travelling spirit,
butting to be born,   fierce to inherit
acreage of pity,   the world of love,
the Christian child's kingdom,   and remove
the tall towered gates   where the proud sea lay
crouched on its paws   in the first day —
came chaos again,   that outsider
would ride in,   blind steed, blind rider:
till then wails at windows,   denies relief,
batters the body   in speechless grief,
thuds in the veins,   crumples in the bone,
wrestles in darkness   and alone
for kingdoms cold,   for salt, sand, stone,
forever dispossessed.
                     Who raised this beast,
this faceless angel,   shall give him rest.

The goal is for ever within us; the dream also is within; and the splendour, the meaning, the charm, the witchery, the enchantment, the depth, the height, the distance, are all in a sense within us; for the so-called material universe is only a stage of the soul's advancement in the development of her infinite self.

It is no sea thou seest in the sea,
'Tis but a disguised humanity...
All that interests a man *is* man.

At a higher stage, a higher symbolism, a wider universe, a deeper meaning, an increased joy, an intensified loveliness, till the supreme spirit in the full possession of itself, having achieved its own creation, shall enter the Summer Land of eternal maturity, the New Jerusalem, the beatific vision, the higher consciousness of Nirvana.

Arthur Edward Waite, *Azoth; or, the Star in the East* (1898)

Only giants can save the world
from complete relapse and so
we — we who care for civilization
— have to become giants. We have
to bind a harder, stronger
civilization like steel about
the world.

H.G. Wells, *The Croquet Player from Modern Utopia* (1967)

There are two ways of escaping our...automatized routines of thinking and behaving. The first...is the plunge into...dream-like states, when the codes of rational thinking are suspended. The other way is also an escape — from boredom, stagnation, intellectual predicaments, and emotional frustration — but an escape in the opposite direction; it is signalled by the spontaneous flash of insight which shows a familiar situation or event in a new light, and elicits a new response to it...it makes us "understand what it is to be awake, to be living on several planes at once."

Arthur Koestler, *The Act of Creation* (1964)

Yoke and Star
José Marti

When I was born, my mother said to me:
"My son, Homagno, Flower of my breast,
Reflected sum of me and of the world,
Fish that to bird and horse and man has turned,
See these two signs of life I offer you
With hope and sorrow. Look and make your choice.
This is a yoke. He who accepts it lives.
By it the ox is tamed, and since he gives
Full service to his master, in warm straw
He sleeps and eats good and abundant oats.
But this, O Mystery sprung from my womb
As peaks from lofty mountain range take shape,
This thing that gleams and slays, this is a star!
All sinners flee from one who bears its mark,
And from its spreading light; and so in life,
As though the one who wears it were a beast
Burdened with crimes, he will be shunned by all.
The man who imitates the care-free ox
Becomes himself a dumb, submissive brute
And has to start again the eternal climb.
But he who, confident, shall choose a star
To be his symbol, grows.
                              When for Mankind
The living person freely pours his cup;
When for the bloody human festival
The good man sacrificed his beating heart
Quickly and gravely; when to wandering winds
Of North and South, he gave his sacred words;
The Star, a mantle now, envelops him
And the clear air is bright, as in festive days,
And the living man, who did not fear to live,
Knows he is not alone in dark and death."

"Give me the yoke, O Mother, so that I
Can stamp it under foot, then let the Star
That lights and kills glow brightly on my brow!"

Elijah Browning
Edgar Lee Masters

I was among multitudes of children
Dancing at the foot of a mountain.
A breeze blew out of the east and swept them as leaves,
Driving some up the slopes....All was changed.
Here were flying lights, and mystic moons, and dream-
    music.
A cloud fell upon us. When it lifted all was changed.
I was now amid multitudes who were wrangling.
Then a figure in shimmering gold, and one with a
    trumpet,
And one with a sceptre stood before me.
They mocked me and danced a rigadoon and
    vanished....
All was changed again. Out of a bower of poppies
A woman bared her breasts and lifted her open mouth
    to mine.
I kissed her. The taste of her lips was like salt.
She left blood on my lips. I felt exhausted.
I arose and ascended higher, but a mist as from an
    iceberg
Clouded my steps. I was cold and in pain.
Then the sun streamed on me again,
And I saw the mists below me hiding all below them.
And I, bent over my staff, knew myself
Silhouetted against the snow. And above me
Was the soundless air, pierced by a cone of ice,
Over which hung a solitary star!
A shudder of ecstacy, a shudder of fear
Ran through me. But I could not return to the slopes—
Nay, I wished not to return.
For the spent waves of the symphony of freedom
Lapped the ethereal cliffs about me.
Therefore I climbed to the pinnacle.
I flung away my staff.
I touched that star
With my outstretched hand.
I vanished utterly.
For the mountain delivers to Infinite Truth
Whosoever touches the star!

In moments of a rare penetration, the outer crust of our ordinary personality appears to dissolve for a little, and the radiance of an inner man transfigures the exterior nature. Something within us is attempting to burst through.

Arthur Edward Waite, *Azoth; or, the Star in the East* (1898)

"All confusion is set aside, and serenity alone prevails; even the idea of holiness does not obtain. He does not linger about where the Buddha is, and as to where there is no Buddha he speedily passes by. When there exists no form of dualism, even a thousand-eyed one fails to detect a loophole. Who can ever survey the vastness of heaven?"

THE OX AND THE MAN BOTH GONE OUT OF SIGHT

GODHEAD

"His thatched cottage gate is closed, and even the wisest know him not. No glimpses of his inner life are to be caught; for he goes on his own way without following the steps of the ancient sages. Carrying a gourd (symbol of emptiness) he goes out into the market, leaning against a staff he comes home. (No extra property he has, for he knows that the desire to possess is the curse of human life.) Bare-chested and bare-footed, he comes out into the market-place. There is no need for the miraculous power of the gods, for he touches, and lo! the dead trees are in full bloom."

ENTERING THE CITY, WITH BLISS-BESTOWING HANDS.

Miracles

Walt Whitman

Why, who makes much of a miracle?
As to me I know of nothing else but miracles,
Whether I walk the streets of Manhattan,
Or dart my sight over the roofs of houses toward the
    sky,
Or wade with naked feet along the beach just in the edge
    of the water,
Or stand under trees in the woods,
Or talk by day with anyone I love, or sleep in the bed at
    night with anyone I love,
Or sit at table at dinner with the rest,
Or look at strangers opposite me riding in the car,
Or watch honey-bees busy around the hive of a summer
    forenoon,
Or animals feeding in the fields,
Or birds, or the wonderfulness of insects in the air,
Or the wonderfulness of the sundown, or of stars
    shining so quiet and bright,
Or the exquisite delicate thin curve of the new moon in
    spring;
These with the rest, one and all, are to me miracles,
The whole referring, yet each distinct and in its place.

To me every hour of the light and dark is a miracle,
Every cubic inch of space is a miracle,
Every square yard of the surface of the earth is spread
    with the same,
Every foot of the interior swarms with the same.

To me the sea is a continual miracle,
The fishes that swim—the rocks—the motion of the
    waves—the ships with men in them,
What stranger miracles are there?

from The Doors of Perception

Aldous Huxley

...each one of us is potentially Mind at Large. But insofar as we are animals our business is at all costs to survive. To make biological survival possible, Mind at Large has to be funnelled through the reducing valve of the brain and nervous system. What comes out at the other end is a measly trickle of the kind of consciousness which will help us to stay alive on the surface of this particular planet. To formulate and express the contents of this reduced awareness man has invented and endlessly elaborated those symbol-systems and implicit philosophies that we call languages. Every individual is at once the beneficiary and the victim of the linguistic tradition into which he has been born—the beneficiary inasmuch as language gives access to the accumulated records of other people's experience, the victim insofar as it confirms him in the belief that reduced awareness is the only awareness, and as it bedevils his sense of reality, so that he is all too apt to take his concepts for data, his words for actual things. That which, in the language of religion, is called "this world" is the universe of reduced awareness expressed and, as it were, petrified by language. The various "other worlds" with which human beings erratically make contact are so many elements in the totality of awareness belonging to Mind at Large. Most people most of the time know only what comes through the reducing valve and is consecrated as genuinely real by their local language. Certain persons, however seem to be born with a kind of bypass that circumvents the reducing valve. In others temporary bypasses may be acquired either spontaneously or as the result of deliberate "spiritual exercises" or through hypnosis or by means of drugs. Through these permanent or temporary bypasses there flows, not indeed the perception "of everything that is happening everywhere in the universe"...but something more than, and above all something different from, the carefully selected, utilitarian material our narrow individual minds regard as a complete, or at least sufficient, picture of reality.

120

Cinderella

Sandra McPherson

When she came to the mirror it was to her
Instrument of change, every scene in it
Total background, and her hard looking
Asking only to be plumbed the depth
Of a diamond needle, the broken in her
Still breakable as if new. A red line rose
And fell between images of dawn
And sunset...

           This was the dream room,
That had been lived with and never opened.
Everything in it was imagined, the curtains
The color of Chinese skin, with large printed
Purple blooms like distant ferris wheels
At dusk. At night the stars used themselves
Up on the rug.

           Footsteps sounded
Into many years. Now someone enters
By the window. She turns, quiet.
The temperature drops. On the sill she finds
The alchemical gold ginkgo leaf and it fits
Perfectly the foot that she puts down
Gently on the beginning of autumn.

We and the cosmos are one. The cosmos is a vast living body, of which we are still parts. The sun is a great heart whose tremors run through our smallest veins. The moon is a great gleaming nerve-centre from which we quiver forever. Who knows the power that Saturn has over us or Venus? But it is a vital power, rippling exquisitely through us *all the time*....

D.H. Lawrence, *Apocalypse* (1931)

The earth is covering itself not merely with millions of thinking units, but with a single continuum of thought, and finally forming a functionally single Unit of Thought of planetary dimensions. The plurality of individual thoughts combine...in a single act of unanimous Thought....In the dimension of Thought, like the dimension of Time and Space, can the Universe reach consummation in anything but the Measureless?

Teilhard de Chardin, *The Future of Man* (1959)

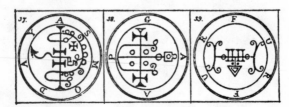

Lirazel Blows Away

Lord Dunsany

And the days went by, the Summer passed over Erl, the sun that had travelled northward fared South again, it was near to the time when the swallows left those eaves, and Lirazel had not learnt anything. She had not prayed to the stars again, or supplicated their images, but she had learned no human customs, and could not see why her love and gratitude must remain unexpressed to the stars. And Alveric did not know that the time must come when some simple trivial thing would divide them utterly.

And then one day, hoping still, he took her with him to the house of the Freer to teach her how to worship his holy things. And gladly the good man brought his candle and bell, and the eagle of brass that held up his book when he read, and a little symbolic bowl that had scented water, and the silver snuffers that put his candle out. And he told her clearly and simply, as he had told her before, the origin, meaning and mystery of all these things, and why the bowl was of brass and the snuffer of silver, and what the symbols were that were carved on the bowl. With fitting courtesy he told her these things, even with kindness; and yet there was something in his voice as he told, a little distant from her; and she knew that he spoke as one that walked safe on shore calling far to a mermaid amid dangerous seas.

As they came back to the castle the swallows were grouped to go, sitting in lines along the battlements. And Lirazel had promised to worship the holy things of the Freer, like the simple bell-fearing folk of the valley of Erl: and a late hope was shining in Alveric's mind that even yet all was well. And for many days she remembered all that the Freer had told her.

And one day walking late from the nursery, past tall windows to her tower, and looking out on the evening, remembering that she must not worship the stars, she called to mind the holy things of the Freer, and tried to remember all she was told of them. It seemed so hard to worship them just as she should. She knew that before many hours the swallows would all be gone; and often when they left her her mood would change; and she feared that she might forget, and never remember more, how she ought to worship the holy things of the Freer.

So she went out into the night again over the grasses to where a thin brook ran, and drew out some great flat pebbles that she knew where to find, turning her face away from the images of the stars. By day the stones shone beautifully in the water, all ruddy and mauve; now they were all dark. She drew them out and laid them in the meadow: she loved these smooth flat stones, for somehow they made her remember the rocks of Elfland.

She laid them all in a row, this for the candlestick, this for the bell, that for the holy bowl. "If I can worship these lovely stones as things ought to be worshipped," she said, "I can worship the things of the Freer."

Then she kneeled down before the big flat stones and prayed to them as though they were Christom things.

And Alveric seeking her in the wide night, wondering what wild fancy had carried her whither, heard her voice in the meadow, crooning such prayers as are offered to holy things.

When he saw the four flat stones to which she prayed, bowed down before them in the grass, he said that no worse than this were the darkest ways of the heathen. And she said "I am learning to worship the holy things of the Freer."

"It is the art of the heathen," he said.

Now of all things that men feared in the valley of Erl they feared most the arts of the heathen, of whom they knew nothing but that their ways were dark. And he spoke with the anger which men always used when they spoke there of the heathen. And his anger went to her heart, for she was but learning to worship his holy things to please him, and yet he had spoken like this.

And Alveric would not speak the words that should have been said, to turn aside anger and soothe her; for no man, he foolishly thought, should compromise in matters touching on heathenesse. So Lirazel went alone all sadly back to her tower. And Alveric stayed to cast the four flat stones afar.

And the swallows left, and unhappy days went by. And one day Alveric bade her worship the holy things of the Freer, and she had quite forgotten how. And he spoke again of the arts of heathenesse. The day was shining and the poplars golden and all the aspens red.

Then Lirazel went to her tower and opened the casket, that shone in the morning with the clear autumnal light, and took in her hand the rune of the King of Elfland, and carried it with her across the high vaulted hall, and came to another tower and climbed its steps to the nursery.

And there all day she stayed and played with her child, with the scroll still tight in her hand: and, merrily though she played at whiles, yet there were strange calms in her eyes, which Ziroonderel watched while she wondered. And when the sun was low and she had put the child to bed she sat beside him all solemn as she told him childish tales. And Ziroonderel, the wise witch, watched; and for all her wisdom only guessed how it would be, and knew not how to make it otherwise.

And before sunset Lirazel kissed the boy and unrolled the Elf King's scroll. It was but a petulance that had made her take it from the coffer in which it lay, and the petulance might have passed and she might not have unrolled the scroll, only that it was there in her hand. Partly petulance, partly wonder, partly whims too idle to name, drew her eyes to the Elf King's words in their coal-black curious characters.

And whatever magic there was in the rune of which I cannot tell (and dreadful magic there was), the rune was written with love that was stronger than magic, till those mystical characters glowed with the love that the Elf King had for his daughter, and there were blended in that mightly rune two powers, magic and love, the greatest power there is beyond the boundary of twilight with the greatest power there is in the fields we know. And if Alveric's love could have held her he should have trusted alone to that love, for the Elf King's rune was mightier than the holy things of the Freer.

No sooner had Lirazel read the rune on the scroll than fancies from Elfland began to pour over the border. Some came that would make a clerk in the City to-day leave his desk at once to dance on the sea-shore; and some would have driven all the men in a bank to leave doors and coffers open and wander away till they came to green open land and the heathery hills; and some would have made a poet of a man, all of a sudden as he sat at his business. They were mighty fancies that the Elf King summoned by the force of his magical rune. And Lirazel sat there with the rune in her hand, helpless amongst this mass of tumultuous fancies from Elfland. And as the fancies raged and sang and called, more and more over the border, all crowding on one poor mind, her body grew lighter and lighter. Her feet half rested half floated, upon the floor; Earth scarcely held her down, so fast was she becoming a thing of dreams. No love of hers for Earth, or of the children of Earth for her, had any longer power to hold her there.

And now came memories of her ageless childhood beside the tarns of Elfland, by the deep forest's border, by those delirious lawns, or in the palace that may not be told of except only in song. She saw those things as clearly as we see small shells in water, looking through clear ice down to the floor of some sleeping lake, a little dimmed in that other region across the barrier of ice; so too her memories shone a little dimly from across the frontier of Elfland. Little queer sounds of elfin creatures came to her, scents swam from those miraculous flowers that glowed by the lawns she knew, faint sounds of enchanted songs blew over the border and reached her seated there, voices and melodies and memories came floating through the twilight, all Elfland was calling. Then measured and resonant, and strangely near, she heard her father's voice.

She rose at once, and now Earth had lost on her the grip that it only has on material things, and a thing of dreams and fancy and fable and phantasy she drifted from the room; and Ziroonderel had no power to hold her with any spell, nor had she herself the power even to turn, even to look at her boy as she drifted away.

And at that moment a wind came out of the northwest, and entered the woods and bared the golden branches, and danced on over the downs, and led a company of scarlet and golden leaves, that had dreaded this day but danced now it had come; and away with a riot of dancing and glory of colour, high in the light of the sun that had set from the sight of the fields, went wind and leaves together. With them went Lirazel.

The Heavy Bear Who Goes With Me
Delmore Schwartz

The heavy bear who goes with me,
A manifold honey to smear his face,
Clumsy and lumbering here and there,
The central ton of every place,
The hungry beating brutish one
In love with candy, anger, and sleep,
Crazy factotum, dishevelling all,
Climbs the building, kicks the football,
Boxes his brother in the hate-ridden city.
Breathing at my side, that heavy animal,
That heavy bear who sleeps with me,
Howls in his sleep for a world of sugar,
A sweetness intimate as the water's clasp,
Howls in his sleep because the tight-rope
Trembles and shows the darkness beneath.
—The strutting show-off is terrified,
Dressed in his dress-suit, bulging his pants,
Trembles to think that his quivering meat
Must finally wince to nothing at all.

That inescapable animal walks with me,
Has followed me since the black womb held,
Moves where I move, distorting my gesture,
A caricature, a swollen shadow,
A stupid clown of the spirit's motive,
Perplexes and affronts with his own darkness.
The secret life of belly and bone,
Opaque, too near, my private, yet unknown,
Stretches to embrace the very dear
With whom I would walk without him near,
Touches her grossly, although a word
Would bare my heart and make me clear,
Stumbles, flounders, and strives to be fed
Dragging me with him in his mouthing care,
Amid the hundred million of his kind,
The scrimmage of appetite everywhere.

The Inward Angel
Jay Macpherson

A diamond self, more clear and hard
Than breath can cloud or touch can stain,
About my wall keeps mounted guard,
Maintaining an impervious reign.

But planted as an inward eye
And nourishing my patient mold,
He's soft with sense, and round him I
Ingather sun where all was cold.

Look, inward Angel, cast your light:
My dark is crystal in your sight.

Tattoo
Wallace Stevens

The light is like a spider.
It crawls over the water.
It crawls over the edges of the snow.
It crawls under your eyelids
And spreads its webs there—
Its two webs.

The webs of your eyes
Are fastened
To the flesh and bones of you
As to rafters or grass.

There are filaments of your eyes
On the surface of the water
And in the edges of the snow.

from The Doors of Perception
Aldous Huxley

I was sitting on the seashore, half listening to a friend
arguing violently about something which merely bored
me. Unconsciously to myself, I looked at a film of sand I
had picked up on my hand, when I suddenly saw the
exquisite beauty of every little grain of it; instead of being
dull, I saw that each particle was made up on a perfect
geometrical pattern, with sharp angles, from each of which
a brilliant shaft of light was reflected, while each tiny
crystal shone like a rainbow....The rays crossed and
recrossed, making exquisite patterns of such beauty that
they left me breathless....Then suddenly, my consciousness was lighted up from within and I saw in a vivid
way how the whole universe was made up of particles of
material which, no matter how dull and lifeless they might
seem, were nevertheless filled with this intense and vital
beauty. For a second or two the whole world appeared as a
blaze of glory. When it died down, it left me with
something I have never forgotten and which constantly
reminds me of the beauty locked up in every minute speck
of material around us.

Without beginning, without end,
Without past, without future.
A halo of light surrounds the world of the law.
We forget one another, quiet and pure, altogether
powerful and empty.
The emptiness is irradiated by the light of the heart
and of heaven.
The water of the sea is smooth and mirrors the moon
in its surface.
The clouds disappear in blue space; the mountains
shine clear.
Consciousness reverts to contemplation; the moon
disk rests alone.

Lin Hua-Yong, *Hui Ming Ching* (1794)
tr., Richard Wilhelm

from Psychological Aspects of the Mother Archetype
C.G. Jung

From a low hill in the Athi plains of East Africa I on
watched the vast herds of wild animals grazing in soun
less stillness, as they had done from time immemoria
touched only by the breath of a primeval world. I felt th
as if I were the first man, the first creature, to know that
this *is*. The entire world round me was still in its prime
state; it did not know that it *was*. And then, in that
moment in which I came to know, the world sprang in
being; without that moment it would never have bee
All Nature seeks this goal and finds it fulfilled in man, b
only in the most highly developed and most fully co
scious man. Every advance, even the smallest, along t
path of conscious realization adds that much to the world

And I do think that man is related to the universe
some 'religious' way even prior to his relations to h
fellow men. And I do think that the only way of tr
relationship between men is to meet in some comme
'belief', but physical not mental....There is a princip
in the universe towards which man turns religiously—
life of the universe itself. And the hero is he wh
touches and transmits the life of the universe....

D.H. Lawrence, *Collected Letters of D.H. Lawren*
(1955)

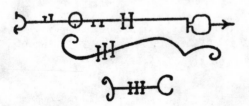

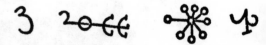

from The Transformation

George B. Leonard

It is midnight of the first full moon after the autumnal equinox. An old man stands on a rocky prominence near the east peak of the sacred mountain. He is dressed in battered work shoes, faded khakis and a shabby parka. Above his head he holds a crystal about the size of a soccer ball. His head is flung back so that his eyes and the crystal and the moon are perfectly aligned.

Earlier in the evening this man, the last shaman of the tribe of Indians that once lived on the mountain's slopes, drove south to the mountain from the little town where he makes a living doing odd jobs in the white man's world. He parked his old pickup truck at the end of a dirt road that runs about halfway up the mountain, took out a shovel, and climbed to the crystal's hiding place. He followed no trail, only his sure sense of where it would have to be.

The shaman dug the crystal from the ground, placed it in a gunnysack, and returned to the truck. He drove then to the ocean on the other side of the mountain. He parked near a lonely stretch of beach. He unbuttoned two buttons of his parka and slipped the crystal inside. Cradling it there, he walked out into the moonlit water where it ebbed and flowed among rugged rocks.

He washed the crystal thoroughly, then, holding it carefully in both hands, approached one of the projecting rocks. Chanting softly, he struck the crystal on the rock four times, each time with increasing force. It was a perilous operation. The shaman knew he had to strike hard enough to jar loose any demon that might be clinging to the crystal. But if he struck too hard the crystal would

break, which would bring the world to an end. He was not absolutely sure that would happen. He did know, however, that if the crystal broke he would die in an instant....

The shaman drove back to the mountain and climbed to the prominence. He waited there for the moon to mount to the zenith, then raised the crystal above his head. A faint pulse from the sun, reflecting off the moon, resonated at the precise frequency of the crystal and entered the shaman's very being. He fell into a trance and was transported to the circumference of that sphere where physical distance yields its domain, where past, present and future touch....

At the same time three other men, also shamans of near-extinct tribes, raised their crystals to the moon. They too were standing on sacred mountains. The mountains were many miles apart, the four corners of a great square on this earth. In an instant the four men were joined into a single being.

The shaman was so filled that there was no space left for regret or exaltation. He had seen it before. Those who came before him had seen it. He was an old man. He would probably not see it again on this plane of existence. But that was all right, for it *is:* The passing away of his people's way of life. The coming of the white men. The passing away of their way of life. The coming of something different, long awaited. Was it a way his people might have hoped for? He was not sure. But that is not a question he would ask, for the end may precede the beginning, and beneath every conceivable sky it is always now.

The shaman stands there in my memory, a moonlit statue against the cloudless night.

...For this darkness, though of deepest obscurity, is yet radiantly clear; and, though beyond touch and sight, it more than fills our unseeing minds with splendours of transcendent beauty....We long exceedingly to dwell in this translucent darkness and, through not seeing and not knowing, to see Him who is beyond both vision and knowledge—by the very fact of neither seeing Him nor knowing Him. For this is truly to see and to know and, through the abandonment of all things, to praise Him who is beyond and above all things. For this is not unlike the art of those who carve a life-like image from stone; removing from around it all that impedes clear vision of the latent form, revealing its hidden beauty solely by taking away. For it is, as I believe, more fitting to praise Him by taking away than by ascription; for we ascribe attributes to Him, when we start from universals and come down through the intermediate to the particulars. But here we take away all things from Him going up from particulars to universals, that we may know openly the unknowable, which is hidden in and under all things that may be known. And we behold that darkness beyond being, concealed under all natural light.

Dionysius the Areopagite

...man is in some way a sharer in the divine life. He therefore longs to return to that from which he feels he has come....He feels himself to be a pilgrim of eternity, a creature in time but a citizen of a timeless world.

...The mysticism of love and union can be described not only in terms of man's search for God but also in terms of God's search for man.

Frank C. Happold, *Mysticism* (1962)

Why hast thou enticed thyself
Into the old serpent's Paradise?
Why hast thou stolen
Into thyself, thyself?...
Encaved within thyself,
Burrowing into thyself...
Piled with a hundred burdens...
A knower!
Self-knower!
You sought the heaviest burden
And found yourself.

Nietzsche

The Funnel of God

Robert Bloch

When Harvey Wolf was seven, he met the Black Skelm.

Now "skelm" means rascal, and at his age, Harvey knew nothing of duplicity and the ways of men, so he was not afraid. Nor did the man's skin repel him, for Harvey was ignorant of *apartheid*.

The Basutos on his father's place called him *baas*, but he did not feel that he was their master. Even Jong Kurt, his father's foreman, treated the men of color without contempt. Harvey came to know the Bechuanas, the Kaffirs, the Fingos and the Swazis far better than the *Roinecks*, which was their name for Englishmen.

Harvey knew his own father was a *Roineck*, who owned this place, but that was virtually the extent of his knowledge. His father never visited him; he spent all his time at the Cape, and had ever since Harvey's mother died when he was born, Harvey had been left in care of Jong Kurt and of his wife, whom Harvey learned to call Mama.

"Poor little one," Mama said. "But you are free and happy with us, so *gued geroeg.*"

And Harvey was happy. Mama made him *veldschoen* of rawhide, and he roamed at will over the *karroo* beyond the drift where the *fontein* gushed. As he grew older, he sought the *krantz* above the valley where he made his home, and soon he was climbing the great *berg* which towered over all.

Here he found the wild orchids of the upland plateaus, plucked as he wriggled his way through the mimosa, the thornbush and the hartekoal trees where the *aasvogel* perched and preened and peered for prey.

Harvey came to know the beasts of the mountain and the plain—the aard-wolf and the inyala, the oribi and the duiker, the springbok and the kudu. He watched the tall secretary-bird and the waddling kori bustard, and traced the flight of bats from out of the hidden caves on the *berg* above. From time to time he encountered snakes; the *cobra di capello,* the puff adder, and the dreaded mamba.

But nothing that loped or trotted or flew or crawled ever harmed him. He grew bolder and started to explore the caves high upon the faraway *berg*.

That was when Mama warned him about the Black Skelm.

"He is an evil man who eats children," Mama said. "The caves are full of their bones, for on such a diet one lives forever. You are to stay away from the *berg*."

"But Kassie goes to the *berg* at night," Harvey protested. "And Jorl, and Swarte."

"They are black and ignorant," Mama told him. "They seek the Black Skelm for charms and potions. The wicked old man should be in prison. I have told Jong Kurt time and again to take the dogs to the *berg* and hunt him out. But he is too slim, that one, to be easily captured. They say he sleeps in the caves with the bats, who warn him when strangers approach."

"I would like to see such a man," Harvey decided.

"You are to stay away from the *berg*, mind?"

And Mama shook him, and he promised, but Harvey did not mind.

One hot morning he toiled across the *karroo,* slipping out unobserved from the deserted, heat-baked house, and made his way painfully up the *krantz.* The *aasvogels* drooped limply in the trees, their eyes lidded, for nothing moved in the plain below. Even the orchids were wilting.

It was no cooler on the *krantz,* and when Harvey found the winding *pad* which circled the *berg,* he paused, parched and faint, and considered turning back. But the trip would be long, and perhaps he could find a *fontein* up here. There were *pads* he had not yet explored—

He started off at random, and thus it was that he came to the cave of the Black Skelm.

The Black Skelm was a gnarled little monkey-man with a white scraggle of beard wisping from his sunken cheeks. He sat at the mouth of the cave, naked and crosslegged, staring out at the veldt below with immobile eyes.

Harvey recognized him at once and put his knuckles to his mouth. He started to edge back, hoping that the old man hadn't observed him, but suddenly the scrawny neck corded and swivelled.

"Greetings, *baas.*"

The voice was thin and piping, yet oddly penetrating. It gained resonance from an echo in the cave behind.

"G-greetings," Harvey murmured. He continued to edge away.

"You fear me, boy?"

"You are the Black Skelm. You—"

"Eat children?" The old man cackled abruptly. "Yes, I know the tale. It is nonsense, meant only to deceive fools. But you are not a fool, Harvey Wolf."

"You know my name?"

"Of course. An old man learns many things."

"Then you've come down to the plains?"

"Not for long years. But the bats bear tidings. They are my brothers of the nights, just as the *aasvogels* are my brothers by day." The Black Skelm smiled and gestured. "Sit down. I would invite you inside the cave, but my brothers are sleeping now."

Harvey hesitated, eyeing the little old man. But the man *was* little, and so very old; Harvey couldn't imagine him to be dangerous. He sat down at a discreet distance.

"The bats told you my name?" he ventured.

The wrinkled black man shrugged. "I have learned much of you. I know you seek the *berg* because it is your wish to see what is on the other side."

"But I've never told anyone that."

"It is not necessary. I look into your heart, Harvey Wolf, and it is the heart of a seeker. You think to gaze upon the lands beyond this mountain; to see the *olifant*, the *kameel*, the great black brothers of the rhenoster birds. But to no purpose, my son. The elephant, the giraffe, the rhinoceros are long gone. They have vanished, with my own people."

"Your people?"

"Those you call the Zulus." The old man sighed. "Once, when I was a *jong*, the plains beyond the *berg* were black with game. And beyond the plains the *leegtes* were black with the *kraals* of my people. This was our world."

And the Black Skelm told Harvey about his world; the Zulu empire that existed long before the coming of the *Roinecks* and the Boers. He spoke of Chaka and the other great *indunas* who commanded armies in royal splendor, wearing the leopardskin *kaross* and lifting the knobkerrie of kingly authority to command the *impis*—the regiments of grotesquely painted warriors in kilts of wildcat tails. They would parade by torchlight, the ostrich plumes bobbing like the wild sea, and their voices rose more loudly than the wind in the cry of *"Bayete!"* which was the regal salute. And in return the *induna* chanted but a single response: *"Kill!"* Casting his spear to the north, the south, the east, or the west, he sent the regiments forth. And the *impis* killed. They conquered, or never returned. That was the way of it, in the old days.

Until, finally, none were left to return.

None but the Black Skelm, who sought the caves of the bats and the vultures, to live like a scavenger in a world of death.

"But my people are down there," Harvey protested. "They are not dead. They tell me Cape Town is a great city, and beyond that—"

"Cape Town is a cesspool of civilization," said the Black Skelm. "And beyond that are greater sewers in which men struggle and claw at one another, even as they drown. It is a sickening spectacle, this. The world will soon end, and I would that I could die with it. But, of course, I shall never die."

Harvey's head hurt: the sun was very hot. He wondered if he had heard aright.

"You can't die?"

"It is true, *baas*. Soon, of course, I must decide upon my next move, for this body of mine is no longer suitable. But—"

Harvey rose, reeling a bit, and backed away.

"Don't eat me!" he cried.

The old man cackled again. "Nonsense!" he said. "Sheer, superstitious nonsense. I do not eat children. My brothers feed me." He stretched forth his hand. "Look!"

And the air was filled with the odor of carrion, as the *aasvogels* gathered, fluttering frantically up the face of the sheer cliff and clustering about the bony body of the wizened black. In their beaks they carried bits of rancid flesh, dropping their tribute into the Black Skelm's fingers.

Then Harvey knew that he was very sick indeed; the sun had played tricks. He ran into the cave, and it was dark and musty, and from the twisted caverns beyond welled a terrible odor of decay. The bats hung head downwards, hung in mute millions, and the floor of the cave was not covered with bones but with whitish droppings. On the walls great eyes winked—eyes that had been painted by hands long dead. The eyes whirled and Harvey felt his kneecaps turn to water. He would have fallen, but the Black Skelm came up behind him and caught him.

The old man's grip was surprisingly strong.

"Do not fear," he whispered. "Drink this." And he held out the hollowed skull. The liquid was warm and red.

"Blood," Harvey quavered.

"Of cattle. It is pure and fresh."

"But you are a wizard—"

"What is a wizard? Merely a seeker, like yourself. A seeker who has perhaps peered further than the land beyond the mountain."

The black Skelm led him back to the mouth of the cave, and bade him sit in the shadows there. Harvey was suddenly very tired. He closed his eyes, scarcely listening, as the Black Skelm droned on.

"All men are seekers, but each chooses a different path in his search for understanding. There is the path of Columbus who sought to encompass the earth and the path of Galileo who sought to search the heavens; the sevenfold path of Buddha which led, he hoped, to Nirvana, and the path of Apollonius which is an inward spiral with oblivion at its core. There is Einstein and—"

Harvey opened his eyes. He was, he knew, quite delirious. The black man sitting beside him, chanting strange names, eating out of the beaks of vultures, talking of Zulu *kraals* which had vanished a hundred years ago—this was a feverdream. He could hear only bits and snatches.

"You will be a seeker, too, Harvey Wolf. You will go

out into the world to look for knowledge. Eventually you will sicken of knowledge and try to find truth. Perhaps we can discover it together—''

Harvey's head throbbed. The sun was blazing off in the west, sinking beneath the purple lower lid of a gigantic cloud. And a voice was echoing along the *berg,* calling, ''Harvey—Harvey, where are you?''

''Jong Kurt!'' Harvey rose.

The Black Skelm was already on his feet, scuttling into the shadows of the cave.

''No, wait—come back!'' Harvey called, groping after the old man and nearly falling as his fevered body convulsed in a sudden chill.

But the old man retreated into the cave.

And then Jong Kurt was looming on the pathway, his face grave and his forehead seamed with apprehension. He caught the reeling boy in his arms.

Suddenly the blackness blossomed and burst forth from the cave, a blinding billowing of squeaking, stenchful shadows—shadows that flapped and fluttered and stared with millions of little red eyes.

Jong Kurt fled down the mountain, carrying Harvey Wolf. But the eyes followed, haunting Harvey's delirium in dreams....

They sent him away, then. Harvey wasn't conscious when the decision was made, though he did see his father once, afterwards, at the dock in Cape Town. His father introduced him to his Uncle Frank, from America, and gave him strict orders about minding his manners and following instructions. There was talk about a New Life and a Good School and the Unhealthy Outlook that comes from being alone.

Harvey tried to tell his father about the Black Skelm, but his father wouldn't listen; not even Mama or Jong Kurt had listened. They all said Harvey had suffered from sunstroke, and in the end he came to believe it himself. It had all been heat and hallucination and nothing was real now but the great ocean and the great city.

In New York his Uncle Frank and his Aunt Lorraine were very kind. They took vicarious pleasure in his amazement at the sight of the city, and conducted him to his first motion picture.

That seemed to be a mistake, and after they dragged the frightened, hysterical child out of the theater he suffered what the doctor called a ''relapse.'' Afterwards, he forgot the whole incident, and it wasn't until years later—

But meanwhile, Harvey grew up. He went to school and he managed to endure the tight, idiotic abominations called ''Health Shoes.'' Gradually he accumulated the fund of knowledge necessary for a child to flourish in our society—that is to say, he could identify the various makes and models of automobiles in the streets, he learned the names of ''baseball stars,'' and the meanings behind the four-letter words and the slang-phrases of the day.

Also, he learned to insulate his interior existence from other eyes; he found that seekers are not popular with their fellows, so he concealed his interests from his playmates. His teachers, however, were not unaware of his intelligence; at their advice he went on to private schools and from there to an Ivy League college.

He was still there when Uncle Frank and Aunt Lorraine went over to Cape Town to bring his father back for a reunion; he was there when the news came to him that the private plane had crashed on the return flight.

After the funeral he visited the attorneys.

They told him he had inherited the entire estate. Once liquidated, with all taxes paid, he could count on an accumulation of better than three million dollars. It would be ready for him by the time he reached his twenty-first birthday.

Right then and there he made a sensible decision; he decided it was time to retire.

It was not just the caprice of a spoiled brat or a rich man's heir. At twenty-one, Harvey Wolf was a fairly presentable young man—many girls even found him handsome, for three million reasons—and he possessed an alert intellect.

He turned his back on the world only because he was fed up with hypocrisy and liars.

Harvey's first move was to leave the college. He said farewell forever to its small Humanities Department and its huge football stadium.

Next he departed from a church whose spiritual representatives appeared at launching ceremonies to bless aircraft carriers and destroyers.

At the same time he walked out on most of the phenomena and beliefs held dear by his peers; on chauvinism, on racial prejudice, on the feudal caste-system glorified by the armed forces of our democracy.

He briefly considered going into business, until he found he couldn't subscribe to the widespread doctrine that there is some mystically ennobling value attached to ''competition'' and that somehow everybody benefits under a system where one man is dedicated to outsmarting another.

Harvey turned his back on the life of a wealthy idler because he could not tolerate the common amusements. He did not believe that animal-killers were ''sportsmen,'' whether they dressed in red coats and drank champagne before chasing a fox or wore dirty dungarees and guzzled beer out of the bottle before shooting at an unsuspecting duck. He did not think that baseball players or boxers or even bullfighters were as much heroic as they were overpaid. He squinted but saw nothing in abstract art; he listened, but heard nothing in its credos and critiques.

Harvey Wolf turned his back on Mother's Day, Valentine's Day, Christmas, and all the other holidays heralded by the joyous tinkle of cash-registers on high. He deplored the phony virility of the men's magazines, the fake coyness of the women's magazines, and the artificial social values which emotionally warped young people into ''manliness'' or ''femininity.''

Taking stock of himself, Harvey found he did not worship sportscars or subscribe to the ''theory of obsolescence'' dearly beloved by manufacturers and dearly paid for by consumers. He abhorred drum-majorettes, bathing beauty contests, and the publicity given "Miss Canned Goods" or the "Oklahoma Cucumber Queen." He took a dim, pained view of billboards, and disliked the transformation of natural parks and beauty spots into commercialized locales for hot-dog stands and souvenir concessions which sold little wooden outhouses.

He held opinions which would automatically antagonize all fraternity-members, morticians, professional evangelists, Texans, and the marchers in St. Patrick's Day parades. He did not believe in *caveat emptor:* card players who slam each trick down on the table and bellow at the top of their lungs; fake "frontier days" held by rough, tough pioneer towns in the wilds of New Jersey; sound engineers who "ride the gain" on TV commercials; professional fund-raisers who take 40% off the top in charity drives, or people who take pride in announcing that they are "quick-tempered," as though this statement entitled them to special privileges.

Harvey held a bias against practical jokers, and people who obscure driving visibility by decorating their car-windows with dangling dolls, oversize dice, baby shoes, and imitation shrunken heads. He saw no sense to endurance-contests, had no patience with litter-bugs, failed to believe in Beggar's Night or politicians who "compromise" after election at the expense of repudiating their campaign pledges. He had a contempt for Muscle Beach exhibitionists and he objected to the rewriting of history under the guise of "patriotism." He—but the list is endless, and of interest only to psychiatrists; *they* get $50 an hour for listening.

The aim of the extraverted type of hero is action: he is the founder, leader, and liberator whose deeds change the face of the world. The introverted type is the culture-bringer, the redeemer and savior who discovers the inner values, exalting them as knowledge and wisdom, as a law and a faith, a work to be accomplished and an example to be followed. The creative act of raising the buried treasure is common to both types of hero, and the prerequisite for this is union with the liberated captive.

Erich Neumann, *Origins & History of Consciousness* (1954)

Harvey Wolf didn't go to the psychiatrists—not yet, at any rate, including the $50-an-hour one.

He thought he was searching for something to believe in and that perhaps he could find it in good, hard, scientific logic.

So he sailed for Europe, to study at the source.

In Edinburgh, Harvey encountered a Brilliant Doctor who prided himself on complete objectivity.

"Nothing," said the Brilliant Doctor, in one of his famed private seminars, "is ever finally 'proved' and everything remains possible in theory.

"For example, granted the loose molecular structure of both a human body and a brick wall, it is only logical to concede that, with the exact proper alignment of every single molecule in the given body with every single molecule in the given wall, at a given instant it would be possible for said body to walk through said wall and emerge unscathed on the other side.

"The chances are almost inconceivably infinitesimal, but the *possibility* must be granted."

Harvey Wolf thereupon asked the Brilliant Doctor, in the light of this opinion, what he thought of allied phenomena. What of his late countryman, the Scottish medium, D.D. Home, who practiced levitation? He rose, resting on his back in mid-air, then floated out of one second-story window and back into the room through another, in full view and broad daylight.

"Nonsense!" said the Brilliant Doctor.

Harvey Wolf blinked. "But no less an observer than the distinguished scientist, Sir William Crookes, testified he had witnessed this feat with his own eyes," Harvey replied.

"Impossible!" said the Brilliant Doctor....

At Oxford, Harvey Wolf was enthralled by a Learned

Scholar who spoke of the biological basis of Life and the almost metaphysical borderland between Being and Nothingness.

"The electromagnetic principles governing sentience and consciousness are still indefinable," he announced. "No man has yet isolated the Life Force or truly defined death or nonexistence except in terms of its absence."

Harvey Wolf was interested. What, he asked, did the Learned Scholar think of Pierre and Eve Curie's signed testimony that they had seen genuine evidence of psychic phenomena demonstrated by a medium? What about Thomas Edison's similar convictions, and his final experiments in communication with the spirit world?

"There is no objective validity offered in evidence here," said the Learned Scholar.

"But we ignored electricity for thousands of years," Harvey protested. "Its omnipresent existence was unknown to us except in lightning until we found a means of harnessing this force. Surely, if the borderline between existence and nonexistence, consciousness and unconsciousness, cannot be exactly defined, and yet is apparently subject to certain definite principles—"

"Utter rot!" said the Learned Scholar....

In Heidelberg, Harvey Wolf studied under a famous Herr Doktor-Professor whose technical mastery of neuropathology was exceeded only by his interest in psychosomatic medicine. The Herr Doktor-Professor was extremely liberal in his outlook, and even admitted prodromosis as a basis for diagnosis.

"I knew a surgeon who was in charge of an army hospital during the war," Harvey said. "One of his patients was completely paralyzed from the waist down—the spinal cord had been entirely severed and there was no nervous response. He lay in bed, wasting away, and was informed he'd never move his legs again. He refused to accept the verdict. Each day he pulled himself up in bed, lifted his legs over the side, tried to stand. The surgeon gave strict orders to restrain him, but he persisted. After two gruelling months, he stood. A month later he took his first step. All tests showed it was physically impossible for him to exercise any control over his legs, but he walked—"

"Impossible!" muttered the Herr Doktor-Professor.

"Yet what about Edgar Cayce and his clinically-verified healings of organic disorders with no possible basis in hysteria? What about—"

"*Dummkopf!*" opined the Herr-Doktor-Professor....

In the Sorbonne faculty, Harvey met a Celebrated Savant with unorthodox views; a man who dared to side with Charles Fort in his questioning of organized science. He once stated that if we accepted the theory of evolution from a non-anthropomorphic viewpoint, it was quite possible to believe that man's function on earth was merely to act as host for cancer cells which would eventually learn to survive the death of the human body and emerge as the next, higher life-form. He was even fond of quoting Mark Twain and others to the effect that the stars and planets of our universe might be merely the equivalent of tiny corpuscles moving through the bloodstream of some incalculably huge monster. And that this monster, in turn, might walk the surface of another world in another universe which in turn might be composed of similar corpuscles—*ad infinitum to the nth* power.

"It is a humbling thought," the Celebrated Savant observed, and Harvey Wolf agreed.

"A far remove from petty human concepts," Harvey mused. "There is no need to concern oneself with trivia in the face of it now, is there?"

But the Celebrated Savant wasn't listening; he was reading the newspaper and scowling.

"Those pigs of Algerians!" he muttered to himself. "Yes, and those lousy *colons,* bidding for power and setting up education for all. It is a disaster!"

Harvey shrugged. "The world is only a corpuscle," he said. "Or perhaps it's just a virus-cell in the bloodstream of the Infinite. What does it matter?"

"*Cochon!* The purity of the State depends upon maintaining our autonomy. And furthermore, young man—"

Harvey Wolf found himself walking out once more. But this time he was walking out into Paris.

Paris, of course, is what you make it. To cutpurse Villon, living from hand to mouth and from the *Small* to the *Grand Testament,* it was a city of cold cobblestones where every twisted alley led only to the inevitable gibbet. To Bonaparte it was the site of a triumphal arch through which he marched to celebrate victory—or furtively avoided, in a solitary coach, as he whipped his horses from the field of Moscow or Waterloo. Toulouse-Lautrec clattered across Paris leaning upon two sticks, and his city was a gaslight inferno. There is the *Sec* and *Brut* Paris of poutlipped Chevalier, the cerebral city of Proust and Gide and Sartre, the Paris of the GI on leave for *couchez-vous* carnival. There is the Paris of the tourist—the Louvre's legweary legacy, the giddy gaping from the Eiffel Tower, the hasty concealment of the paperbound *Tropic of Cancer* at the bottom of the suitcase. There is a Paris as gay as Colette, as tough as Louis-Ferdinand Céline, as weird as

Huysmans. You pay your money and you take your choice.

And when you have three million dollars—

Harvey Wolf brooded about it in a Montmartre *bistro*. A bearded man stared at him with yellow cat-eyes and said, "Welcome, Pontius Pilate."

"Pilate?" echoed Harvey Wolf.

"I recognize the mood," said the bearded man. "You are asking yourself Pilate's age-old question—*what is Truth?*"

"And the answer?"

"Truth is sensation," the bearded man told him.

"Sensation alone is reality. All else is illusion."

"Hedonism, eh? I don't know—"

"You can learn. Experience is the great teacher."

Harvey was sated with civilization, sick of science. He spent six months with the bearded man and the bearded man's friends. He rented a villa near Antibes, and many guests came.

There was the dwarf girl and the giantess and the woman with the filed and pointed teeth; the lady who slept only in a coffin and never alone; the girl whose luggage consisted solely of a custom-made traveling case

filled entirely with whips. There was a rather unusual troupe of artists whose specialty consisted of a pantomime dramatization of the *Kama Sutra.*

Long before the six months were up, Harvey realized that his meeting with the bearded man had not been accidental. Behind the beard was neither Jesus, D.H. Lawrence or even a genuine Gilles de Rais—merely a weak-chinned, loose-lipped voluptuary adventurer who had visions of sugarplum splendor in the form of a billion-*franc* blackmail scheme.

Harvey got rid of him, at last, for considerably less, and he did not begrudge the price he finally paid. For he had learned that the senses are shallow and the orgasmic is not the ultimate peak of perceptivity.

Harvey went to Italy and immersed himself in Renaissance art. He journeyed to Spain and somehow he found he'd started to drink. A girl he met introduced him to some little capsules her friends smuggled in from Portugal. At the end of another six months he was picked up in the streets of Seville and shipped back home through the kindly offices of the American consulate.

They put him in Bellevue and then in a private san upstate. Harvey kicked the habit and emerged after a loss of four months and forty pounds.

He ended up, as do most seekers after Truth, on the confessional couch of a private psychiatrist.

The psychiatrist decided that perhaps Walt Disney was to blame for it all.

Harvey admitted the man had an interesting argument. He was able, after many sessions, to recall his first visit to the movies when he'd come to America. Uncle Frank and Aunt Lorraine had taken him to see what was perhaps the most famous short cartoon of the Depression era—*The Three Pigs.*

He could recreate quite vividly, without the aid of narcohypnosis, the strong fear-reaction engendered by the sight of the Big Bad Wolf stalking the helpless pigs. He remembered how the Wolf huffed and puffed and blew the straw house in. What happened immediately thereafter he did not know, because it was then that he had been carried, screaming, from the theater.

It was, the psychiatrist averred, a "traumatic incident." And now, as an adult, Harvey had read a great deal about animated cartoons and their possible effect on children. Following the success of *The Three Little Pigs* it seemed as if the entire concept of cartoon-making underwent a drastic change. In place of playful Pluto and droll Donald Duck came a horde of ferocious bulldogs, gigantic cats with slavering fangs; huge animal menaces who tormented smaller creatures and sought to devour them in their great red maws.

But, if anything, their little intended victims were worse; they always outwitted the hulking pursuers and seemed to take fiendish delight in sadistic revenge. One animal was always crushing another under a truck or a steamroller; pushing his enemy off a steep cliff, blasting his head open with a shotgun, blowing him up with dynamite, dragging his body across the teeth of a great circular saw. During the years, the so-called "kiddy matinee" became a horror-show, a *Grand Guignol* of the animal kingdom in which atrocious crimes and still more atrocious punishments flashed in fantastic fashion across the screen in lurid color, to the accompaniment of startlingly realistic shrieks, groans, screams of agony, and cruel laughter.

Parents who carefully and conscientiously shielded their supposedly innocent youngsters from the psychological pitfalls of the dreaded comic-books were quite content to listen to the same moppets shriek uncontrollably at the sight of a twenty-foot-high animated hyena being burned to death while the happy little rabbit squealed in ecstatic glee.

Harvey had read about this and he listened when the psychiatrist told him there was probably no harm in such fantasies—to the average child it was merely a vicarious outlet for aggression. Such a child unconsciously identified with the small animal who destroyed the larger tormenter; the bigger creature symbolized Daddy or Mama or some authority-figure, and it was satisfying to witness their defeat. The weapons employed were direct concepts and representations of adult civilization and its artifacts. Most children were exposed to such films from infancy on and grew up without psychic damage. As normal adult human beings they were able to go out into the world and fight its battles. Indeed, it was the avowed purpose of many psychiatrists to keep them "mentally fit" during real battles, so that they could continue to spray liquid fire from flame-throwers upon enemy soldiers cowering in tanks, or drop bombs on unseen thousands of women and children.

It was merely unfortunate, said the psychiatrist (at $50 an hour) that Harvey had been brought up away from the influences of normal society and abruptly exposed to the symbolism of the cartoon. And there were, of course, other factors.

The fact that Harvey's last name happened to be Wolf—so that his little American playmates insisted on calling him "The Big Bad Wolf" when they innocently ganged up on him at recess and tried to emulate the punishments inflicted by the heroic little pigs in the film.

The fact that Harvey, instead of acting like any normal, redblooded American boy and fighting back against the six or eight older bullies who came after him with planks and stones, chose to cry and bleed instead.

The fact that Harvey soon underwent another traumatic cinematic experience when he saw a picture called *The Wolf Man* and its sequels, and gradually came to accept and identify with the role symbolized by his last name.

The fact that Harvey seemed to have totally misinterpreted the message; to him it wasn't important that the Wolf was destroyed, but that he was revived again in the sequels.

Regrettably, said the psychiatrist (at great and expensive length) he seemed to have equated acceptance of his Wolf role with survival. As an adult, he had become a Lone Wolf, moving away from the pack. And his self-styled search for Truth was merely a search for the Father-Image, denied him in childhood.

Harvey attempted, at one point in his analysis, to talk about the Black Skelm and that fantastic fever-dream atop the *berg*. The psychiatrist listened, made notes, nodded gravely, inquired into the duration of his subsequent illness, and went back to his theory about the traumatic effect of the films. What had Harvey thought when the Wolf Man was beaten to death with a cane by his father in the movie? Did Claude Rains, as the father, remind Harvey of his own parent? Did he perceive the phallic symbolism of the silver cane used as an instrument of punishment? And so on, blah, blah, blah—until Harvey Wolf got up from the couch and walked out again.

Where Darkness and Light 'stand not distant from one another, but together in one another' (there are) the single track and 'strait way' that penetrate the cardinal 'point' on which the contraries turn; their unity is only to be reached by entering in there where they coincide: That is, in the last analysis, not any where or when, but within you; 'World's End is not to be found *by walking*. It is within this very fathom-long body that the pilgrimage must be made.'

Ananda K. Coomaraswamy

Psychotherapy had its own truths, but its methodology was still magic. One had to believe in certain *formulae,* in spells and incantations designed to cast out demons. At the same time there was this pitiful insistence upon a "realistic" interpretation; an attempt to reconcile frankly magical methodology with the so-called "normal" world.

Perhaps it was silly to compromise. The therapy sessions had caused Harvey to think about the Black Skelm once more, for the first time in twenty years. He remembered how the little shriveled savage had spoken of Einstein, and of Apollonius of Tyana. He had sat all alone in a bat-cave atop a mountain, drinking warm blood from a skull, but he *knew*. He had a surety which science and philosophy and art only adumbrated, and the source of his knowledge must be magical insight.

Harvey moved down into the Village and began to fill his ramshackle apartment with books on occultism and theosophy. He avoided the local Beat types, but inevitably the word leaked out. The crackpots came to call, and eventually he met a girl named Gilda who claimed to be one of the innumerable illegitimate offspring of the late Aleister Crowley.

Soon he found himself standing in a darkened room, facing the East, with a steel dagger in his right hand. He touched his forehead saying, in the Hebrew tongue, *Ateh;* touched his breast and murmured *Malkuth;* touched his right shoulder as he intoned *Ve-Geburah* and his left as he muttered *Ve-Gedullah.* Clasping his hands upon the breast, with dagger pointed upwards, he shouted *Le-Olahm, Aum.*

Nothing happened.

Gilda's further experiments in sex-magic were equally (and fortunately) nonproductive. She attempted to interest him in a Black Mass, but before details could be arranged she ran off with a young man who yapped obscene ballads in public places but was granted the protection the law affords a folksinger.

Harvey Wolf decided that he would continue his search alone.

During the year that followed he made many contacts and experiments. Undoubtedly he met with followers of Gerrald Heard and Aldous Huxley. Quite certainly he investigated the effects of lysergic acid and peyote.

Both produced the same trance phenomena. Harvey found himself regressing, the film of his life running backwards, until he reached the point where he was enveloped in the billowing black bat-cloud from the *berg.* The little red eyes swirled fire-fly fashion all round him, then vanished into a greater darkness. He stood alone on the mountain.

Yet not quite alone, because the Black Skelm was there, pointing to the path and whispering, "I have waited long, *baas.* The time has come when we must journey together."

The message was manifest; Harvey Wolf knew he would go back to Africa.

Another Wolfe had said *You Can't Go Home Again,* and in his more objective moments Harvey knew this was right. Twenty years had passed and nothing was left of the Africa he'd known. The world kept changing.

There were new governments with slogans, new reasons to hate their neighbors, and new weapons poised to punish them. A new spurt of population, subject to new mutations of disease, sought new areas of conquest. Missiles had reached the moon and Man would follow, then go on to the stars with his civilized cargo of bombs, chewing gum, carbon monoxide and laxatives. Eventually the millennium would come; a Soviet Federated Socialist Republic of the Solar System or a United Interplanetary States. If the former prevailed, Saturn would be set up as the new Siberia; if democracy triumphed, special facilities for certain groups would be set up on Pluto—separate, but equal, of course.

Harvey Wolf made one last effort to escape such cynical considerations and their consequences. He became an ascetic; a disciple of Raja, Brahma and Hatha Yoga. He took a cabin in the Arizona desert and here he meditated, fasted, and grew faint.

And the Black Skelm came into his dreams and chanted,

"This is not the path. Come to me. I have found the way."

So, in the end, Harvey returned to the dark womb—to the Africa of his birth.

He found a new spirit at the Cape; *apartheid* had arisen, sanctioned by the sanctimonious and condoned by the cartel of dedicated men whose mission it was to artificially inflate the price of diamonds with which the wealthy bedeck their wives and their whores.

At first they would not even give Harvey permission to journey upcountry, but his father's name—and a distribution of his father's money—helped.

This time Harvey made the trip in a chartered plane, which set him down on the flat *veldt* near the old place and (in accordance with orders) left him there.

The old place had changed, of course. Kassie, Jorl, Swarte and others were gone, and no herds of humpbacked cattle roamed over the plain. The great house was deserted, or almost so; Harvey prowled the ruins for ten minutes before the elderly man with the rifle ventured forth from an outbuilding and leveled his weapon at him in silent menace.

"Jong Kurt!" Harvey cried. And the old man blinked, not recognizing him at first—just as Harvey didn't recognize a Kurt whom the years had robbed of any right to retain his nickname.

Kurt lowered his rifle and wept. He wept for the passing of the old place, for the death of Mama, for the changes which had come to both of them. Did the *baas* remember the way it had been? Did he remember the night Kurt had carried him, faint with delirium, down the mountainside?

"Yes, I remember," Harvey murmured. "I remember it very well."

"When you left, your father sold the cattle. The boys went into the mines, everybody left. Only Mama and I stayed on alone. Now she is gone, too." Kurt knuckled his eyes.

"And the Black Skelm?" Harvey said. "What happened to him?"

"He is dead," Kurt answered, shaking his head solemnly.

"Dead?" Harvey stiffened in the suddenness of the thought. "Do you mean that you—"

Kurt nodded. "Your father gave orders. The day after you went to the Cape, I took the dogs up to the *berg*. I meant to hunt him down, the *verdamte* scoundrel."

"You found him there?"

The old man shrugged. "Only the bones. Picked clean, they were, on the side of the ledge near the mouth of the cave. The carrion had fed his vultures for the last time."

Kurt wheezed and slapped his thigh, and he did not see the pain in Harvey's eyes.

"But why do we stand here, *baas?* You will stay the night with me, eh? Your plane does not return before tomorrow?"

Harvey murmured an acceptance of the invitation. It

was true, his plane would not return until the next day. He'd thought to spend the interval in ascending the *berg,* but there was no need now. The Black Skelm was dead. *You Can't Go Home Again.*

Kurt had comfortable quarters in one of the smaller outbuildings. Game was scarce, but there was eland steak for dinner. The old man had learned to brew beer in the traditional Kaffir fashion, and after the meal he sat reminiscing with the young *baas* and drinking toasts to the past. Finally he succumbed to stuporous lumber.

Harvey stretched out on a bunk and tried to sleep. Eventually he succeeded. Then the bat came.

It flew in through the open window and nuzzled at his chest, brushing its leathery wings against his face and nuzzling him with tiny teeth that grazed but did not bite. It chittered faintly.

Harvey awoke to a moment of horror; horror which subsided when the bat withdrew to a corner of the room. Kurt snored on, stentoriously, and Harvey sat up, brushing at the black, winged creature in an effort to drive it back out through the window.

Truth exists only as the individual himself produces it in action.

Søren Kierkegaard

The bat wheeled about his head, squeaking furiously. Harvey rose, flailing his arms. He opened the door. The bat hung in the doorway. Harvey beat at it. It whirled just out of arm's reach. Then it hung suspended in midair and waited.

Harvey advanced. He stood gazing across the moonlit emptiness of the *veldt*—a lake of shimmering silver beyond which towered the black hulk of the *berg*.

The bat cheeped and flapped its wings before him. Suddenly Harvey conceived the odd notion that the wings were *beckoning*. The bat wanted to him to *follow*.

Then he knew. The Black Skelm wasn't dead. He was waiting for Harvey, there on the mountain. He had sent a messenger, a guide.

Harvey didn't hesitate. He went out into the moonlit plain and it was like the first time. Now he was a grown man in boots instead of a child in rawhide *veldschoen*, and it was night instead of day, but nothing had changed. Even the odd delirium rose to envelop him once again; not the fever born of the hot sun but the chill of the cold moon. He trudged across the silver silence of the sand and the bat swooped in sinister silhouette before him. When Harvey reached the *krantz* he almost decided to turn back; this was no mysterious midnight mission, only the tipsy *fugue* of an over-imaginative man unused to the potency of Kaffir beer.

But they were waiting for him there in the shadows;

huddled in teeming thousands, their tiny red eyes winking a greeting. And now they all rose about him, covering him in a living cloak. He glanced back and found they had closed in solidly, forming a living barrier against retreat. The acrid stench was in itself a wall through which he dared not pass, so he went forward, up to the winding *pad* which took him, toiling, to the top of the *berg*.

He saw the mouth of the cave looming before him, and then all vision faded as the moon was blotted out by a cloud—a cloud of wavering wings. The bats flew off and he stood alone on the mountain-top.

The Black Skelm came out of the cave.

"You *are* alive," whispered Harvey. "I knew it. But Kurt spoke of finding bones—"

"I placed them there for that purpose." The Black Skelm wove his wrinkles into a smile. "I did not wish to be disturbed until you returned. I have waited a long time, *baas*."

"Why didn't you summon me sooner?"

"There were things you had to learn for yourself. Now you are ready, having seen the world. Is it not as I described?"

"Yes." Harvey nodded at the gnarled little black man. "But how could you know these things? I mean—"

He hesitated, but the Black Skelm grinned. "You mean

I am an ignorant old savage, a witch-doctor who believes in animism and amulets." He scratched his grisly chest. "Whereas you are a man of worldly wisdom. Tell me—what is Jack Paar *really* like?"

Harvey blinked, and the old man chuckled. "You are so naive in your sophistication! *Baas*, I have seen far more than you in your brief lifetime. Although my base body sat shriveled in this cave, my spirit ventured afar. I have been with you throughout your wanderings. I was in the theater when you screamed; I sat with you in seminars; I felt the caress of the woman with the silver-tipped whips; I was one with you when you raised the dagger to invoke the All-Being. There are ways of transcending space and time."

"But that's impossible!" Harvey muttered. "I can't think—"

"Don't try to think." The Black Skelm rose, slowly and stiffly. "One does not learn through processes of organized logic, for the world is not a logical place. Indeed, it is not a place at all—merely an abstract point in infinity. True knowledge is institutional; an impressionary process which might be labelled as heuristics."

Harvey shook his head. "You drink cattle-blood and summon bats, and you speak of heuristics—unbelievable."

"Yet you believe."

"I believe. But I don't understand. You have these powers. Why live like an animal in a cave when you might have gone forth to rule the world?"

"The world?" the old man put his hand on Harvey's shoulder; the weight was as slight as a sere and blackened leaf. "Look down there."

Together they stared at the silvery *veldt*.

"The world is a plain," said the Black Skelm. "And beyond, as we know, are the cities of the plain. Do you remember what happened to those cities? *Then the Lord rained on Sodom and Gomorrah brimstone and fire from the Lord out of heaven, and he overthrew those cities and all the valley and all the inhabitants of the cities, and what grew on the ground.* Remember?"

"Yes. You're trying to tell me that the world will soon come to an end."

"Can you doubt it, after what you've seen?"

"No."

"The Lord remembered Abraham and brought him to the safety of the hills." The black man smiled, but Harvey stared at him.

"Is that why you sent for me? Because you're—"

"God?" The black man shook his head. "Not yet. I have not chosen. That is why I waited for you. Perhaps you can help me choose."

"I don't understand—"

"Every man is God, or contains within him the seed of godhead. Look." The Black Skelm fumbled with a little leather pouch at his waist and drew forth a dark, shrivelled object.

"This is a nut, encased in an outer shell. Within is the

seed, the kernel. The hard shell is our human consciousness. Once broken, the kernel can be reached, the seed liberated to sprout and grow, to spread through space and thrust beyond the stars.''

The Black Skelm twirled the spheroid in his wrinkled palm. ''Shall we open the shell and partake?'' he murmured. ''No, it isn't like peyote, or your lysergic acid, either. I spent years searching for the seed, which indeed comes from the Tree of Knowledge. Once eaten, it will do more than merely expand and extend consciousness. Consciousness will be discarded, like the empty husk it is, and the soul will flourish. Flourish and soar beyond all being.''

He cracked the shell and dug within.

''Here, will you share with me?''

''But—why?''

The Black Skelm sighed. ''Because the human part of me is old, and afraid. It may be that I will not enjoy being God. It must, I think, be a lonely estate. When you came to me as a child I recognized a fellow-seeker, and I knew that I would wait for you to join me on the quest.''

Harvey stared. ''This isn't just part of some crazy dream?''

''It's all a crazy dream, you know that,'' said the Black Skelm, softly.

''And if it works—suppose I want to turn back?''

''There is no turning back, as you have learned. One can only go forward, through the mist called life and into the mist called death. Or one who dares can go beyond. It is your choice.''

''But why now?''

''Why not? Does life, as you have seen it, appeal to you?''

''No.''

''Do you look forward to death?''

''No.''

''Then let us move on.''

The Black Skelm carefully broke the dried kernel in half and extended a portion to Harvey.

''Place it on your tongue,'' he said. ''Then swallow slowly.''

Harvey knew now that he was dreaming. He knew he was back in the bunk at Kurt's place, and there was nothing to fear—in a moment he'd awake. Meanwhile there was no harm in putting the insignificant morsel on his tongue, no harm in gripping the black man's shrivelled hand as the waves of sensation coursed through him.

Because he was back at Kurt's place now, and as he swallowed *that* too was a dream and he was back in America in Arizona, he was back with Gilda, he was back with the bearded man in France, he was back at the universities, back at the theater watching that preposterous cartoon, back here again on the mountain-top meeting the Black Skelm for the first time. No, he was further back than *that*, he was a little boy in Mama's arms, he was crawling, he couldn't even crawl, he was kicking inside a warm darkness, he was only a speck of liquified life, he was nothing, he was—

Instantly he leaped forward and upward. The plain faded away beneath him, faded out of focus. He had no eyes to see it with, but he needed no eyes. He was one with immensity and perceived everything. He knew he was still standing—somewhere—and still grasping the black man's hand with his own. But the hand was huge enough to balance a sun on its palm, yet insubstantial enough to feel no pain from its molten mass.

Far below (*yes, it was below, there was still space and dimension, immeasurably transfigured as his body had been transfigured*) the wheeling planets moved in inexorable orbit.

A voice that was not a voice, a mere beat observed in soundlessness, impinged upon his expanded awareness.

He who would not sacrifice his own soul to save the whole world, is, as it seems to me, illogical in all his inferences, collectively.

Charles Peirce

"Behold the earth," it said. "A speck, a mite, an errant, inconsequential atom."

Harvey—or that part which remembered Harvey—had a momentary awareness of the old theory of the world as a single cell in the bloodstream of a cosmic monster. But it was not a cell, he perceived, any more than he was now a monster. It was just a speck, as the voice had said.

"Is this what God sees?" he asked.

"I do not know, for I am not yet God. To be God is to act. And I cannot decide. Shall I become God through action?"

"What action is possible?"

"Only one. To destroy this earth. To rearrange the cosmic pattern by removing the atom from being."

"Destroy? Why not save mankind?"

"God cannot save mankind. This I now know. God is great and Man is small. If left alone, Man will destroy himself. We alone can be saved—by becoming one with God."

"I dare not."

"Why? Do you so love the race of Man after what you've seen? Do you love the cesspool in which he wallows, the devices with which he brings about the destruction of others and of himself?"

"But I am a man."

"No longer. You are in Limbo now. Not God, not human. There is no turning back. One must go forward."

"I cannot." Harvey—or the greater being that stood between the stars—turned and faced the black, brooding face—an image of immensity, intangible yet limned and luminous in space.

"Perhaps your life on earth was a sweeter one than mine. You did not see your people perish, and the old ways of nature vanish from the world. You did not skulk in a cave on a mountain-top for endless years, companioned by scavengers—nor feed, like them, on carrion corruption. Your skin was not black."

"You hate the world."

"I am above hate. And above love."

"Pity, then? Compassion?"

"For what? This insignificant speck, crawling with midges that will soon destroy it if left to their own devices?" The soundless voice thundered. "If there is pity, if there is compassion, let it be for one's self. I shall survive, in eternity. There will be other earths—"

"No!"

But the black, brooding face stared down and pursed its lips. Suddenly it blew, and spat. A cloud of ichor issued from the titanic, toothless maw. It spiralled, gathering speed and form as it fell, twisting into a tunneling black cloud.

The cloud encompassed the earth. The earth seemed to be sucked into the spiralling mass; its shell cracked and fire flared forth fitfully. But only for an instant. Then the spittle evaporated into nothingness and what it had encompassed was gone.

Gone? It had never existed.

Harvey—that which was Harvey now—turned and glanced into the great glowing face in the heavens beside him. But it too was gone. Not gone, but growing—growing to such size and at such a speed that it was impossible to perceive even a portion of its features. It was becoming space itself. The Black Skelm was God and had destroyed the earth—

Harvey's mouth opened, swallowing the universe in a soundless scream.

He could not follow the Black Skelm, grow into godhead. He could not go back to an earth which no longer existed, had never existed.

He could only scream, and merge into a swirling nothingness, a funnel that engulfed him without end....

To know that what is impenetrable to us really exists, manifesting itself as the highest wisdom and the most radiant beauty.

Albert Einstein

You are your own creator; you appear In the splendor of your own. Heaven and earth are made light by you

Pyramid Text

Somewhere in the eternities a crash might end me. Forever? What if my disrupted being should float together in cycles measurelessly on? Reunited, I should wander once more a godless wretch!

From horizon to horizon there flashed a quick glory; heaven rang through all its dome with a multitude of tremendous bands, and a sound of chanting joined in the symphony. "Ah! what is this?" I said, and started up. "I hear a harmony, and Fate knows only discords."

Again the aerial voice responded, but now in a triumphant song, "After all, there is a Supreme; he rules whose right it is; there is no destiny but God, and he is over all forever." I leaped into the air—I shouted for joy. The hope of the ages was sure—there was a God!

Fitz Hugh Ludlow, *The Hashish Eater* (1857)

I sought for God for thirty years, I thought it was I who desired Him, but, no, it was He who desired me.

Abu Yazid

Man is made by his belief. As he believes, so he is.

Bhagavad Gita

Good Friday, 1613. Riding Westward

John Donne

Let man's soul be a sphere, and then, in this,
The intelligence that moves, devotion is,
And as the other spheres, by being grown
Subject to foreign motions, lose their own,
And being by others hurried every day,
Scarce in a year their natural form obey;
Pleasure or business, so, our souls admit
For their first mover, and are whirled by it.
Hence is't, that I am carried towards the West
This day, when my soul's form bends towards the East.
There I should see a Sun, by rising, set,
And by that setting endless day beget:
But that Christ on this cross did rise and fall,
Sin had eternally benighted all.
Yet dare I almost be glad I do not see
That spectacle, of too much weight for me.
Who sees God's face, that is self-life, must die;
What a death were it then to see God die?
It made his own lieutenant, Nature, shrink;
It made his footstool crack, and the sun wink.
Could I behold those hands which span the poles,
And tune all spheres at once, pierced with those holes?
Could I behold that endless height which is
Zenith to us, and our antipodes,
Humbled below us? Or that blood which is
The seat of all our souls, if not of His,
Make dirt of dust, or that flesh which was worn
By God, for his apparel, ragg'd and torn?
If on these things I durst not look, durst I
Upon his miserable mother cast mine eye,
Who was God's partner here, and furnished thus
Half of that sacrifice which ransomed us?
Though these things, as I ride, be from mine eye,
They are present yet unto my memory,
For that looks towards them; and Thou look'st towards
me;
O Saviour, as Thou hang'st upon the tree.
I turn my back to Thee but to receive
Corrections, till Thy mercies bid Thee leave.
O think me worth Thine anger; punish me;
Burn off my rusts and my deformity;
Restore Thine image so much, by Thy grace,
That Thou may'st know me, and I'll turn my face.

**God forces no one, for love cannot compel, and God's
service, therefore, is a thing of perfect freedom.**

Proverbial Hebraic saying

Evensong

Lester del Rey

By the time he reached the surface of the little planet, even
the dregs of his power were drained. Now he rested,
drawing reluctant strength slowly from the yellow sun that
shone on the greensward around him. His senses were dim
with an ultimate fatigue, but the fear he had learned from
the Usurpers drove them outward, seeking a further hint
of sanctuary.

It was a peaceful world, he realized, and the fear
thickened in him at the discovery. In his younger days, he
had cherished a multitude of worlds where the game of
life's ebb and flow could be played to the hilt. It had been
a lusty universe to roam then. But the Usurpers could
brook no rivals to their own outreaching lust. The very
peace and order here meant that this world had once been
theirs.

He tested for them gingerly while the merest whisper of
strength poured into him. None were here now. He could
have sensed the pressure of their close presence at once,
and there was no trace of that. The even grassland swept in
rolling meadows and swales to the distant hills. There were
marble structures in the distance, sparkling whitely in the
late sunlight, but they were empty, their unknown
purpose altered to no more than decoration now upon this
abandoned planet. His attention swept back, across a
stream to the other side of the wide valley.

There he found the garden. Within low walls, its miles of expanse were a tree-crowded and apparently untended preserve. He could sense the stirring of larger animal life among the branches and along the winding paths. The brawling vigor of all proper life was missing, but its abundance might be enough to mask his own vestige of living force from more than careful search.

It was at least a better refuge than this open greensward and he longed toward it, but the danger of betraying motion held him still where he was. He had thought his previous escape to be assured, but he was learning that even he could err. Now he waited while he tested once more for evidence of Usurper trap.

He had mastered patience in the confinement the Usurpers had designed at the center of the galaxy. He had gathered his power furtively while he designed escape around their reluctance to make final disposition. Then he had burst outward in a drive that should have thrust him far beyond the limits of their hold on the universe. And he had found failure before he could span even the distance to the end of this spiral arm of one galactic fastness.

Their webs of detection were everywhere, seemingly. Their great power-robbing lines made a net too fine to pass. Stars and worlds were linked, until only a series of miracles had carried him this far. And now the waste of power for such miracles was no longer within his reach. Since their near failure in entrapping and sequestering him, they had learned too much.

Now he searched delicately, afraid to trip some alarm, but more afraid to miss its existence. From space, this world had offered the only hope in its seeming freedom from their webs. But only microseconds had been available to him for his testing then.

At last he drew his perceptions back. He could find no slightest evidence of their lures and detectors here. He had begun to suspect that even his best efforts might not be enough now, but he could do no more. Slowly at first, and then in a sudden rush, he hurled himself into the maze of the garden.

Nothing struck from the skies. Nothing leaped upwards from the planet core to halt him. There was no interruption in the rustling of the leaves and the chirping bird songs. The animal sounds went on unhindered. Nothing seemed aware of his presence in the garden. Once that would have been unthinkable in itself, but now he drew comfort from it. He must be only a shadow self now, unknown and unknowable in his passing.

Something came down the path where he rested, pattering along on hoofs that touched lightly on the spoilage of fallen leaves. Something else leaped quickly through the light underbrush beside the path.

He let his attention rest on them as they both emerged onto the near pathway at once. And cold horror curled thickly around him.

One was a rabbit, nibbling now at the leaves of clover and twitching long ears as its pink nose stretched out for more. The other was a young deer, still bearing the spots of its fawnhood. Either or both might seemingly have been found on any of a thousand worlds. But neither would have been precisely of the type before him.

This was the Meeting World—the planet where he had first found the ancestors of the Usurpers. Of all worlds in the pested galaxy, it had to be *this* world he sought for refuge!

They were savages back in the days of his full glory, confined to this single world, rutting and driving their way to the lawful self-destruction of all such savages. And yet there had been something odd about them, something that then drew his attention and even his vagrant pity.

Out of that pity, he had taught a few of them, and led them upwards. He had even nursed poetic fancies of making them his companions and his equals as the life span of their sun should near its ending. He had answered their cries for help and given them at least some of what they needed to set their steps toward power over even space and energy. And they had rewarded him by overweening pride that denied even a trace of gratitude. He had abandoned them finally to their own savage ends and gone on to other worlds, to play out the purposes of a wider range.

It was his second folly. They were too far along the path toward unlocking the laws behind the universe. Somehow, they even avoided their own destruction from themselves. They took the worlds of their sun and drove outwards, until they could even vie with him for the worlds he had made particularly his own. And now they owned them all, and he had only a tiny spot here on their world—for a time at least.

The horror of the realization that this was the Meeting World abated a little as he remembered now how readily their spawning hordes possessed and abandoned worlds without seeming end. And again the tests he could make showed no evidence of them here. He began to relax again, feeling a sudden hope from what had been temporary despair. Surely they might also believe this was the one planet where he would never seek sanctuary.

Now he set his fears aside and began to force his thoughts toward the only pattern that could offer hope. He needed power, and power was available in any area untouched by the webs of the Usurpers. It had drained into space itself throughout the aeons, a waste of energy that could blast suns or build them in legions. It was power to escape, perhaps even to prepare himself eventually to meet them with at least a chance to force truce, if not victory. Given even a few hours free of their notice, he could draw and hold that power for his needs.

He was just reaching for it when the sky thundered and the sun seemed to darken for a moment!

The fear in him gibbered to the surface and sent him huddling from sight of the sky before he could control it. But for a brief moment there was still a trace of hope in him. It could have been a phenomenon caused by his own need for power; he might have begun drawing too heavily, too eager for strength.

Then the earth shook, and he knew.

The Usurpers were not fooled. They knew he was here—had never lost him. And now they had followed in all their massive lack of subtlety. One of their scout ships had landed, and the scout would come seeking him.

He fought for control of himself, and found it long enough to drive his fear back down within himself. Now, with a care that disturbed not even a blade of grass or leaf on a twig, he began retreating, seeking the denser undergrowth at the center of the garden where all life was thickest. With that to screen him, he might at least draw a faint trickle of power, a strength to build a subtle brute aura around himself and let him hide among the beasts. Some Usurper scouts were young and immature. Such a one might be fooled into leaving. Then, before his report could be acted on by others, there might be a chance....

He knew the thought was only a wish, not a plan, but he clung to it as he huddled in the thicket at the center of the garden. And then even the fantasy was stripped from him.

The sound of footsteps was firm and sure. Branches broke as the steps came forward, not deviating from a straight line. Inexorably, each firm stride brought the Usurper nearer to his huddling place. Now there was a faint glow in the air, and the animals were scampering away in terror.

He felt the eyes of the Usurper on him, and he forced himself away from that awareness. And, like fear, he found that he had learned prayer from the Usurpers; he prayed now desperately to a nothingness he knew, and there was no answer.

"Come forth! This earth is a holy place and you cannot remain upon it. Our judgment is done and a place is prepared for you. Come forth and let me take you there!" The voice was soft, but it carried a power that stilled even the rustling of the leaves.

He let the gaze of the Usurper reach him now, and the prayer in him was mute and directed outward—and hopeless, as he knew it must be.

"But—" Words were useless, but the bitterness inside him forced the words to come from him. "But why? I am God!"

For a moment, something akin to sadness and pity was in the eyes of the Usurper. Then it passed as the answer came. "I know. But I am Man. Come!"

He bowed at last, silently, and followed slowly as the yellow sun sank behind the walls of the garden.

And the evening and the morning were the eighth day.

"Unless you make yourself equal to God, you cannot understand God: for the like is not intelligible save to the like. Make yourself grow to a greatness beyond measure, by a bound free yourself from the body; raise yourself above all time, become Eternity; then you will understand God. Believe that nothing is impossible for you, think yourself immortal and capable of understanding all, all arts, all sciences, the nature of every living being. Mount higher than the highest height; descend lower than the lowest depth. Draw into yourself all sensations of everything created, fire and water, dry and moist, imagining that you are everywhere, on earth, in the sea, in the sky, that you are not yet born, in the maternal womb, adolescent, old, dead, beyond death. If you embrace in your thought all things at once, times, places, substances, qualities, quantities, you may understand God."
Giordano Bruno

Frances A. Yates, *Giordano Bruno and the Hermetic Tradition* (1964)

Vestigia
Bliss Carman

I took a day to search for God,
And found Him not. But as I trod
By rocky ledge, through woods untamed,
Just where one scarlet lily flamed,
I saw His footprint in the sod.

Then suddenly, all unaware,
Far off in the deep shadows, where
A solitary hermit thrush
Sang through the holy twilight hush—
I heard His voice upon the air.

And even as I marvelled how
God gives us Heaven here and now,
In a stir of wind that hardly shook
The poplar leaves beside the brook—
His hand was light upon my brow.

At last with evening as I turned
Homeward, and thought what I had learned
And all that there was still to probe—
I caught the glory of His robe
Where the last fires of sunset burned.

Back to the world with quickening start
I looked and longed for any part
In making saving Beauty be—
And from that kindling ecstasy
I knew God dwelt within my heart.

from **Passage to Magonia**

Jacques Vallee

On June 15, 1952, in the jungles of Yucatan, an archaeological expedition led by Alberto Ruz Lhuillier and three companions made a remarkable discovery. The team was investigating the impressive Palenque monuments, located in the state of Chiapas, on the site of a well-known Mayan city that scientists were busy restoring and mapping in systematic fashion. Yucatan is a region of constant humidity and high temperature, and the tropical vegetation had caused considerable damage to the temples and pyramids erected by the Mayas, whose civilization was marked by the genius of its architects and is thought to have declined in the first centuries of our era, disappearing almost completely about the ninth century—that is, at the time of the Charlemagne Empire in Europe.

One of the most impressive constructions on the Palenque site is the "Pyramid of Inscriptions," an enormous truncated pyramid with a long stairway in front. The pyramid is of a somewhat unusual design, for on the top is a large temple. The purpose of the monument was unknown until Lhuillier and his companions suggested that it might have been built as a tomb for some exceptional king or illustrious priest. Led by this idea, they began to search the temple at the top of the pyramid for some passage or stairway leading directly into the monument. And on June 15, 1952, they discovered a long flight of stairs going down through the enormous mass and actually under ground level.

The passage was built after the traditional Mayan fashion, the inclined walls giving the enclosure a high, conical shape ending with a narrow ceiling. Some Indian huts in Yucatan are still built this way, a most efficient design in the tropical climate since it allows hot air to rise, thereby providing a relatively comfortable temperature inside the hut. At the bottom of the temple passage

stairway was a splendid crypt, and in the crypt was a sarcophagus covered with a single carved stone measuring twelve feet by seven. Ten inches thick, the slab weighed about six tons. The fantastic scene depicted by the artists had not suffered; it came to light in every detail; and archaeologists are completely at a loss to interpret its meaning.

The Mayans are supposed to have vanished without having invented even the rudiments of a technology. Some archaeologists doubt that they knew the wheel, and yet the design on the Palenque sarcophagus appears to show a very complex and sophisticated device, with a man at the controls of an intricate piece of machinery. Noting that the man is depicted with his knees brought up toward his chest and his back to a complicated mechanism, from which flames are seen to flow, several people, among them Soviet science writer Alexander Kazantsev, have speculated that the Mayans had actually been in contact with visitors from a superior civilization—visitors who used spaceships. Kazantsev's interpretation is difficult to prove. However, the only object we know today closely resembling the Mayan design is the space capsule.

The demigod for whom sarcophagus, crypt, and pyramid were built with such splendid craftsmanship by the Mayan artists is something of a puzzle, too. The body is radically different from the morphology of the Mayans, as we imagine them: the corpse is that of a man nearly six feet tall, about eight inches taller than the average Mayan. According to Pierre Honore, the sarcophagus was made for the "Great White God," Kulkulkan, but no final clue to the mystery has yet been found, and the tropical jungles of Central America where dozens of temples and pyramids are still buried under the exuberant vegetation have not yet yielded the secret of the Palenque sarcophagus.

The chariots of God are twenty thousand, even thousands of angels: the Lord is among them...

Psalms 68:17

...the UFO may represent the prenatal care of the Earthman by a...superbeing in preparation for the forthcoming linkage of the human species and the birth of another...superbeing.

Brad Steiger, *Gods of Aquarius* (1976)

Within The Pyramid *

R. De Witt Miller

Garvin Matthews, of the International Anthropological Society, stared unbelievingly at the giant white pyramid poised on top of the sheer ridge. It seemed utterly unreal. The fading sunlight gleamed on the pure-white sandstone of its sides, making it stand out in sharp contrast to the dark green of the Yucatan jungle which struggled for a foothold on the sides of the ridge.

Somehow Matthews couldn't force himself to believe that it was man-made. But those sure, straight lines were not the chance of nature. It must have been built by human beings. But how—and why?

Black clouds, forerunners of a storm, drifted slowly behind the apex of the pyramid. The daylight was dying rapidly. He shook himself free from the spell of unreality and turned to the old man beside him.

"This will be the greatest scientific discovery of the century," he said. "When I make my report the society will immediately equip an expedition to make a thorough exploration."

Professor Phinias Hexter shifted uneasily.

"It's really not so large," he declared. "It's the first impression that makes it seem huge."

"Don't be foolish," Matthews replied. "I've done some work in Egypt. This thing makes the Great Pyramid of Cheops seem like a dwarf."

Hexter glanced at the tenuous arms of the black clouds which were gradually blending into a single dark curtain.

"It will storm in a few minutes," he said. "Don't you think we'd better wait until to-morrow to get a closer view?"

* Within the Pyramid was first published in 1937–ed.

"Not on your life. I'm going to get inside that thing to-night—that is, if there's an entrance."

"Yes," Hexter replied slowly, "there is. But it's on the other side. It will be dark by the time we reach it."

Matthews glanced at him sharply.

"What's wrong with you? You act as if you're afraid of the thing."

"No," Hexter muttered, "not afraid. I've seen that pyramid too long to be afraid of it. It's what it stands for that has——"

His voice dropped into silence.

"I think you'd better do all you can to aid my expedition," Matthews said meaningly. "Remember, I don't have to tell the world what you've done—if I don't want to."

"Whether you tell them or not is of no consequence to me."

Matthews looked wonderingly at the gaunt, sun-bitten old professor.

"Why did you keep quiet?" he asked suddenly. "You've known of the existence of this pyramid for years—and you've told no one. This is the toughest place to get to on the American continents. There isn't a chance of seeing the thing unless you get into this valley. It's only visible from above. Do you realize that if I hadn't happened to stumble on it, it might have been centuries before it was found?"

"One century more will be long enough."

"I don't know what you're talking about—and I don't much care. What I want to know is why you didn't tell the world of your discovery—and what you're doing camping here alone?"

"As to the first question," Hexter said quietly, "I don't care to answer it now. As to the second, I am here to make explorations, just as you are."

"But you are connected with no society?"

"Does a man have to be connected with a society to be a scientist? I had an idea when I first saw this pyramid. It's an idea that's been in the back of my mind ever since I started archaeology thirty years ago. On my first exploration here I found enough evidence to indicate that I might be right. It has taken ten years and five trips to prove it."

"What is your theory?"

"I think facts will be more potent than my arguments."

"Then let's get on. What's the best way to reach it?"

"You're determined to go to-night?"

"Cetainly. What did you expect me to do?"

"Yes," Hexter said half to himself. "I suppose I would have done the same thing at your age. Have you a carbide lamp?"

"Two of them."

"Good. If you'll follow me, I'll bring you to the entrance in fifteen minutes."

When they came close to the side of the pyramid, Matthews was stunned by the sheer immensity of the thing. As they walked parallel to the wall he studied the construction. It was unbelievable. The blocks fitted with the precision of the finest Egyptian workmanship. Only these blocks made those of the Egyptian pyramids seem puny.

Halfway along the farther side, Hexter stopped and pointed to a barely discernible set of steps in the stonework.

"These lead to the entrance of the tunnel," he said.

They climbed steadily for perhaps a hundred feet. Here the steps widened out into a broad ledge. In front of them was the entrance of a passage, slightly higher and wider than a man, which led into the heart of the pyramid.

"Something similar to the Egyptian pyramids," Matthews murmured.

"They were little copies," Hexter said. "The idea was handed down from this one, an almost universal legend of the days when they were alive."

"Who do you mean by 'they'?"

"Later," Hexter muttered, "later. First we will go to the conventional burial chamber."

Taking one of the carbide lamps, he led the way into the passage. Matthews lighted the second lamp and followed.

The passage ran level for a distance; then it slanted sharply upward. There was a damp, musty smell, the stale odor of things long forgotten and unused.

Suddenly the dark walls about them receded. Matthews realized that they had entered a small room. He held his light above his head. The room was perhaps twenty feet square. It was lined with hard, pink sandstone blocks, so beautifully fitted together that his eyes could scarcely make out the joints.

In the center, on a raised dais, were four elaborately carved sarcophagi.

With a sudden cry, Matthews stepped forward and struggled to lift the lid of the nearest sarcophagus.

"You will be disappointed," Hexter said. But he helped wrench off the massive stone slab.

The blue-white flame of the lamp cast long shadows into the open sarcophagus. By looking closely, Matthews could make out a few bits of what might once have worn human form. Some whitened pieces of bones, several odd bits of metal, and something resembling fabric, which fell to dust at his touch.

With a curse of disappointment he turned away.

"The others are the same," Hexter said. "That was their masterpiece. No one would ever look farther than this room. It is all so perfectly obvious. It was the legend of the gigantic burial place which was carried over into Egypt."

"Hexter," Matthews said harshly, "are you going to quit talking nonsense and help me get the lids off the rest of these boxes? Or am I going to have to wring whatever you know about this place out of that scrawny neck of yours?"

For a moment the old man did not answer. His lamp, held below his face, made his features seem grotesque.

Finally he shrugged wearily.

"You are determined to report this find?" he asked.

"Of course."

"Then a great expedition will be sent. This whole place will be gone over almost with a microscope, in hopes of finding secret passageways. Finally the tourists will come."

"And why not? What are you afraid of? Are you a scientist or an old woman?"

Again Hexter did not answer for a moment. At last he seemed to reach a decision.

"I'm trusting you," he said slowly. "After all, you are a man of science. You have a good brain. If, after I am through, you decide to go on with your original plan, there is no way I can stop you."

"Well, if you are going to show me something, get at it."

"Not yet." Hexter sat down on one of the unopened sarcophagi. "I would like to ask you a few questions."

"What is this? A game?" Matthews said sarcastically.

"Perhaps—but it is my game. And in the end I promise to show you something that will change your whole conception of the history of the Earth."

Matthews sat down on another sarcophagus.

"All right," he said, "but don't be too long."

"You're an Egyptologist," Hexter began slowly. "Didn't you ever wonder what was back of the old civilization, and what it was that we keep seeing dimly in the legends and folklore of all people?"

"No."

"Well, I suppose you wouldn't. One has to blast his mind out of its conventional ideas before he can ever conceive the truth. But when you get the key, it all fits together. First, let's suppose that thousands of years ago, when man was still only half civilized, the Earth was visited by creatures from another world."

"Shall we tell ghost stories now?"

Hexter ignored the remark.

"I am merely making a hypothesis," he said, "just part of my little game. But to continue—say that some astral body similar to the Earth chanced to pass near our planet. That would account for the floods in all legends, and for the seven days of darkness in Egyptian and Jewish writings?"

"It might."

"It's more than guesswork," Hexter declared. "You must have heard of Kobal's theory, based on the eccentricities in the orbits of Neptune and Pluto, that there is a body with about the specific gravity of the Earth which pursues an orbit similar to a comet."

"I've read something about it."

"Very well. Say further that intelligent beings on this astral body sent an expedition to the Earth. Perhaps their world was running out of natural resources, or it was overcrowded. Whatever the reason, certain brave members of their race decided to make the attempt to establish a new home."

146

"I wish you'd get to the point," Matthews said wearily. Hexter paid no attention.

"Perhaps," he continued, "after the expedition reached the Earth, they discovered that its climate was incompatible with their type of life. They took a gamble, and they lost. Some essential element—perhaps a gas in the atmosphere or a necessary part of their food—was lacking. Even spectroscope analysis leaves you pretty much in the dark as to the true conditions on another planet. Say, for argument, that such a state of affairs occurred and you, Matthews, were a member of the expedition, what would you do?"

Matthews looked away at an inscription in Mayan on the wall of the room, but he seemed slightly more interested in the conversation.

"Die," he said after a moment. "What else would there be to do?"

"Nothing—unless. Even our crude science has practically succeeded in producing artificially suspended animation. A more advanced science should be able to do that, shouldn't it?"

"It's possible."

"I'm glad you admit that much. At least, you must grant that it's an interesting hypothesis. Let us follow it through for a moment. Say you could suspend your life—by the use of some anesthetic—indefinitely, what would you do then?"

"I'd suspend it and wait. At least it would be better than simply dying."

"Not only that. It may be that my hypothetical expedition had some definite reason to hope that if they could suspend their lives long enough, there would be a chance to escape. But passing over that possibility—before you suspended your life, what would you do?"

"I'd arrange to protect my body so it would be still in existence if a chance ever occurred for me to resume normal life."

"Then if you had access to super-science by which you could build a greater structure than any which puny man can create, you would construct a giant edifice that would protect your body during the dormant period."

"It at least sounds logical—which is more than I can say for most of your ideas."

"All right—there is only one more step. If you still had hope that the people of your world might send another expedition after you, it would be necessary to make sure that they knew you had been successful in living for at least a time on Earth. Remember, the inhabitants of this other world probably wouldn't believe there was any intelligent life on Earth. At the time their expedition landed, man hadn't yet built anything large enough to be seen far out in space. Therefore it would be necessary to prove that your expedition hadn't perished immediately."

"I suppose so."

"I know so. There is one thing nature does not create: a straight line. A gigantic pyramid, placed on a bare ridge,

from The Outer Space Connection
Alan and Sally Landsburg

I started to fight my way along an overgrown path leading away from the settlement. I was headed for the remains of a structure that is usually bypassed. I had missed it on my first visit, content with the guide's opinion that there wasn't much to see. On the map of Uxmal the ruin is called the House of Death. In fact, there was almost nothing left of the building. A fragment of one wall still stood but I had to strip away a mass of vines to examine it. At that moment I understood why the name House of Death had been applied to the small temple: a skull and two crossed bones had been carved at the base of the wall. Then I stopped short. Sure, a skull and crossed bones had become our modern symbol for poison, but Mayan symbols and language glyphs originated in the distant past. The mistake that had been made, I felt, was applying modern logic to the interpretation of an ancient sign.

I looked at the carving again. It did not have the traditional character of the figures engraved on other Mayan temples. What little is known of the Mayan language was drawn from interpretation of symbols used repeatedly in all the surviving artifacts. Each pictograph is highly stylized, and the exact same figures appear in calendars and mathematical computations, making it easy to sort out a possible meaning for each sign. Nowhere had I seen a graphic representation equal to the skull and crossed bones of Uxmal's House of Death.

What if the symbol meant *life*, not death? What if the Mayas possessed a method of preserving life through some form of surgical transplant? What if the House of Death was the storehouse of parts or...?

New York—Sir Martin Ryle, Nobel laureate in physics and Britain's astronomer royal, is trying to persuade the radio astronomers of the world to refrain from making known the existence of intelligent life on this planet, lest the earth be invaded by hostile beings.

New York Times Service Nov. 8, 1976

All the same, the mystery of the pyramids of Egypt cannot be explained except by the study of the pyramids of France, Ireland, Peru and China and by investigating the use of cryogen. The actual freezing of the dead in nitrogen liquid at 169 degrees, to permit eventual resurrection into the future, is the explanation of the immortal chambers which are the pyramids of Gizeh, where the mummy had to remain intact while waiting for resurrection by the grace of Osiris.

Robert Charroux, *The Mysterious Past* (1973)

would stand out as an eternal proof of the existence of intelligent beings. No other form of architecture so completely demonstrates the existence of a guiding mind. A pyramid is all straight lines.''

''A most interesting theory,'' Matthews said with a short laugh, ''but how about the facts?''

''That,'' Hexter declared, ''is the next step.''

He crossed the room, made a swift computation, and selected one of the giant stone blocks. He threw his weight against it. Noiselessly it slipped inward.

''A piece of balance that our science cannot duplicate,'' he said simply. ''The concealment is marvelous, too. It took me months to find it.''

The block had completely vanished now. The passage it revealed was smaller than the one by which they had entered the pyramid.

Again Hexter led the way. The passage descended endlessly. Matthews calculated that they must have reached a point below the surface of the ground when the passage broadened into a room. It was slightly larger than the burial chamber, but there was none of the ornamentation. There were no inscriptions on the walls.

In the center of the room were four caskets. They gleamed dully in the flickering light. Apparently they were composed of some metal, but it was not one with which Matthews was familiar.

''You see there are the same number as in the room above,'' Hexter said. ''That was their great deception. Several beings existed for a short while on Earth. While they were alive they built a giant burial chamber.

''Then these four other-world people apparently died. One or two must have remained active to arrange the thing. Anyway, four bodies were solemnly buried in the upper chamber. But they were really human beings, killed, and disguised to resemble the other race. After a few years in this climate no one could tell the difference anyway. They would look no further than that upper burial chamber. The whole thing became a religion. It was a burial cult when it reached Egypt.''

But Garvin Matthews did not hear. He was staring into one of the caskets. His mind was struggling with the thing that he saw. It didn't square with reason. It was utterly alien to every conception he had ever known—and yet it was there.

The casket was covered by a transparent material resembling glass—and yet not glass. Lying within the cushioned interior was the nude body of a young woman.

But the ghostly calm of death was not on the chiseled, aquiline features.

She was merely sleeping there. Death seemed completely apart from this lovely creature.

Slowly another idea was fighting its way into his mind. That strange pastel tint which suffused her skin! It was a light, delicate green—not the ghastly hue of death. Somehow it seemed natural to her, as natural as the pink flush of human skin.

''Notice the hands,'' Hexter said softly.

Again Matthew's mind refused at first to admit the idea. Finally it broke through.

Each of the slim, delicate hands had six fingers!

''You see,'' Hexter said softly, ''not of this world——''

And suddenly Matthews came to life. There was a way to end this mystery. It was the way of science. He jerked loose the heavy geologist hammer that swung from his belt, raised it above his head.

With a quick movement Hexter grasped his upraised arm. There was a remarkable strength in the frail body of the old professor.

''Not yet,'' he said. ''There is one thing more to show you. After that, if you wish to break open the caskets, it is your affair.''

Slowly Matthews lowered the hammer.

''What difference will it make?'' he asked.

''Those caskets were sealed for a purpose. They were meant to be opened only by scientists of their own race. Before you decide to do anything, let's go back to the upper chamber.''

''How do I know you will show me the secret of the sliding block?'' he asked.

''I will leave the stone displaced,'' Hexter said quietly. ''But first look in the other caskets.''

Matthews went slowly to each of the three metal coffins. Each contained a body—sleeping—but not the sleep of death. There was another young woman and two young men.

When Matthews had finished his observations, Hexter led the way back through the passageway to the outer room. He pointed to the Mayan inscription.

''You can skim over it,'' he said, ''except the last line. Of course, they wrote in the language of the country.''

Matthews deciphered it quickly, keeping an eye on the open passageway to the inner chamber. The inscription was a conventional curse, calling down the wrath of the gods on whoever should desecrate the tomb.

''The last line,'' Hexter repeated.

Matthews read the line, read it again, a queer look on his face.

''But there's something wrong,'' he said. ''The old boys must have made some mistake. There's a date in this last line—but it is still in the future. It seems to be the date when the curse ends. According to our calendar, it would be 2040.''

Hexter spoke with slow emphasis, each syllable distinct.

''If this astral body or planet does pursue some sort of elongated orbit about the Sun, it will come back some time—say in 2040.''

''What do you mean?''

There was a queer, soft note in Hexter's voice.

''Don't you have any admiration for these people? Think of them refusing to accept fate, struggling against the cosmos for a chance to live. It took supreme intelligence to figure it all out—and it took faith to lie down quietly in those caskets, in the forlorn hope that they would be safe through thousands of years. How about the ones that stayed outside to seal the caskets, and tend to the burial? They died calmly that others might live. Do you want to wreck it all now—less than a hundred years from the date they are waiting for?''

Matthews did not look at Hexter. He stared at the Mayan inscription—but he did not see it.

Hexter spoke again, but this time his voice was hard, driving.

''What if the creatures who built this pyramid, that makes our modern buildings seem like doll houses, should come back and find those caskets broken open, and the members of their ill-fated expedition dead and in our museums? It would not be well for man and his civilization in that hour.''

There was silence in that room of the dummy dead. The dank smell of age-old things seemed a tangible presence. Faintly from outside came the roar of the storm which had broken over the Yucatan jungle.

Matthews' face was hard, like old, weather-stained ivory. His breath was short, gasping. At last he said, ''I shall report, but—I will omit the pyramid.''

They come from a far country, from the end of heaven, even the Lord, and the weapons of his indignation, to destroy the whole land.

Isaiah 13:5

from St. Jerome: Life of Paulus the first Hermit
tr. *W.H. Freemantle*

In the desert, St. Anthony met with a strange being of small stature, who fled after a brief conversation with him:

Before long in a small rocky valley shut in on all sides he sees a mannikin with hooted snout, horned forehead, and extremities like goat's feet. When he saw this, Anthony like a good soldier seized the shield of faith and the helmet of hope: the creature none the less began to offer him the fruit of the palm tree to support him on his journey and as it were pledges of peace. Anthony perceiving this stopped and asked who he was. The answer he received from him was this:

''I am a mortal being and one of the inhabitants of the Desert whom the Gentiles deluded by various forms of error worship under the names of Fauns, Satyrs and Incubi. I am sent to represent my tribe. We pray you in our behalf to entreat the favour of your Lord, and ours, who, we have learnt, came once to save the world, and 'whose sound has gone forth into all the earth.' ''

As he uttered such words as these, the aged traveller's cheeks streamed with tears, the marks of his deep feeling, which he shed in the fullness of his joy. He rejoiced over the Glory of Christ and the destruction of Satan, and marvelling all the while that he could understand the Satyr's language, and striking the ground with his staff, he said,

''Woe to thee, Alexandria, who instead of God worshippest monsters! Woe to thee, harlot city, into which have flowed together the demons of the whole world! What will you say now? Beasts speak of Christ, and you instead of God worship monsters.''

He had not finished speaking when, as if on wings, the wild creature fled away.

Let no one scruple to believe this incident; its truth is supported by what took place when Constantine was on the throne, a matter of which the whole world was witness. For a man of that kind was brought alive to Alexandria and shewn as a wonderful sight to the people. Afterwards his lifeless body, to prevent its decay through the summer heat, was preserved in salt and brought to Antioch that the Emperor might see it.

All creatures have existed eternally in the divine essence, as in their exemplar. So far as they conform to the divine idea, all beings were, before their creation, one thing with the essence of God. (God creates into time what was and is in eternity.) Eternally, all creatures are God in God.... So far as they are in God, they are the same life, the same essence, the same power, the same One, and nothing less.

Suso

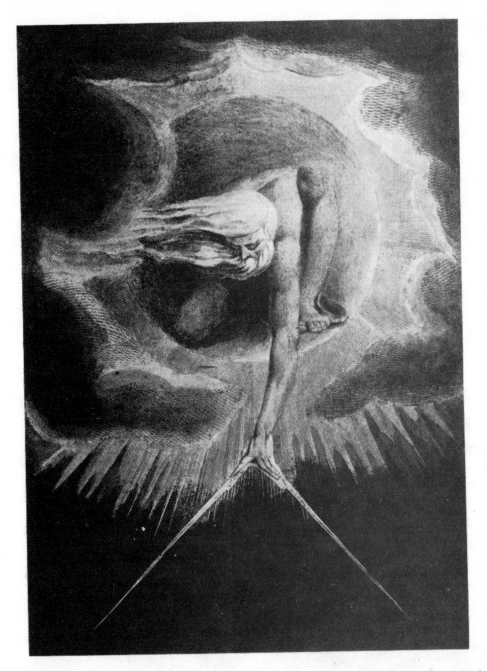

...only twenty-five years to the millennium. Will the space beings—once similar to us, but now gods —return then? Will they be emissaries of the powers of light, or will they be, as it were, the avenging angels on the side of the forces of darkness? Mankind must pray that they will be the former. For only from them might he learn the secrets that are essential for his salvation. The power of cosmic projection—of existence that transcends time, space, and matter—is the only solution; one that will, hopefully, enable him to walk with the gods throughout all eternity.

Between now and then, he must prepare himself in every way he can. Science must push back its frontiers and break down the barriers that separate it from unknown areas of thought. Religion must reexamine its message and question its very substance. Science and religion must reconcile their differences. The human race must put itself in order, both materially and spiritually.

For the next twenty-five years could perhaps mean the Beginning or...the End.

Zarkon; *The Zarkon Principle* (1975)

"The man watches the growth of things, while himself abiding in immovable serenity. Sitting alone, he observes things undergoing changes. To return to the Origin, to be back at the Source — already a false step this! Far better it is to stay at home, blind and deaf, and without much ado; sitting in the hut, he takes no cognisance of things outside, behold the streams flowing — whither nobody knows; and the flowers vividly red — for whom are they?"

RETURNING TO THE ORIGIN, BACK TO THE SOURCE.

The Caterpillar and Alice looked at each other for some time in silence: at last the Caterpillar took the hookah out of his mouth, and addressed her in a languid, sleepy voice.

"Who are *you*?" said the Caterpillar.

This was not an encouraging opening for a conversation. Alice replied, rather shyly, "I—I hardly know, Sir, just at present—at least I know who I was...

Lewis Carroll, *Alice's Adventures in Wonderland* (1865)

Illustration credits.

Virgil Finlay: 5,10,25,26,44,46,54,69,75,88,91,93,95,97,
99, 101,105,115,123,132,136,137,139.
Lynd Ward: 16,17,18,19,20,21,23.
Stephen Fabian: 30,121,130,131.
Hannes Bok: 15,43,127.
Edd Cartier: 62,63.
Kelly Freas: 39.
Robert Zebic: 36,58,83.
Ken Stampnick: 31,50,51,87.
Saul Jaskus: 33,74.
Rene Zamic: 79,80.
Helen Fox: 67.
William Fox: 27,28,29.
Emma Hesse: 125.
David Simmons: 13.

I am that I am, the flame
Hidden in the sacred ark.
I am the unspoken name,
I the unbegotten spark.
I am he that lifteth up
Life, and flingeth it afar;
I have filled the crystal cup;
I have sealed the crystal star.
I the wingless god that flieth
Through my firmamental fane,
I am he that daily dieth
And is daily born again.

Aleister Crowley

Acknowledgements:

This page constitutes an extension of the copyright page. Every reasonable care has been taken to trace ownership of copyright material. Information will be welcome which will enable the publisher to rectify any reference or credit.

The Circular Ruins: from Jorge Luis Borges, *Labyrinths*, Copyright (c) 1962 by New Directions Publishing Corporation. Reprinted by permission of New Directions Publishing Corporation, New York.

The Awakening: by Arthur C. Clarke. Copyright (c) 1951 by Columbia Publications Inc. Reprinted by permission of the author and the author's agents, Scott Meredith Literary Agency, Inc., 845 Third Avenue, New York, N.Y. 10022.

Vestigia: by Bliss Carman, from *Poems*. Reprinted by permission of DODD, MEAD & COMPANY INC.

Lizarel Blows Away: by Lord Dunsany, from *The King of Elfland's Daughter*, published by Ballantine Books, New York, reprinted by permission of John Cushman Associates.

Evensong: by Lester del Rey, reprinted by permission of the author and the author's agents, Scott Meredith Literary Agency, Inc., 845 Third Avenue, New York, N.Y. 10022.

The Whimper of Whipped Dogs: by Harlan Ellison, reprinted by kind permission of the author.

Design: by Robert Frost, from *The Poetry of Robert Frost*, ed. Edward Connery, published by Holt, Rinehart and Winston, 1969. Reprinted by permission of Holt, Rinehart and Winston.

The Bride of Frankenstein: by Edward Field, from *Variety Photoplays*. Reprinted by permission of Grove Press, Inc. Copyright (c) 1967 by Edward Field.

Hush!: by Zenna Henderson, from *Beyond Fantasy Fiction*, published by Galaxy Publishing Corp., New York. Reprinted by permission of Curtis Brown.

Flower Arranger, Dwarf Trees, Waiting, all the trees coloured were: by Joy Kogawa, reprinted from *A Choice of Dreams* by permission of McClelland and Stewart Ltd.

The Outsider: by H.P. Lovecraft from *Dunwich Horror and Others*. Reprinted by permission of the author's Estate and Scott Meredith Literary Agency, Inc., 845 Third Avenue, New York, N.Y. 10022.

On Seeing: by Dorothy Livesay, from *Collected Poems, The Two Seasons* by Dorothy Livesay, Copyright (c) Dorothy Livesay 1972. Reprinted by permission of McGraw-Hill Ryerson Ltd.

The Hounds of Tindalos: by Frank Belknap Long. Reprinted by permission of Arkham House Publishers, Inc.

Nine Lives: by Ursula K. Le Guin. Copyright (c) 1969, 1974 by Ursula K. Le Guin. Originally appeared in *Playboy* Magazine; reprinted by permission of the author and her agent, Virginia Kidd.

The Man Who Was Put In A Cage: by Rollo May, from *Man's Search For Himself*. Reprinted by permission of W.W. Norton & Company Inc. Copyright 1953 by W.W. Norton & Company Inc.

Storm, The Inward Angel: from Jay Macpherson, *The Boatman*, by permission of Oxford University Press.

Elijah Browning: by Edgar Lee Masters, from *Spoon River Anthology*, published by the Macmillan Publishing Co. Ltd., London. Preprinted by permission of Mrs. Ellen C. Masters.

Cinderella: Copyright (c) 1973 by Sandra McPherson. From *Radiation*, published by The Ecco Press.

Paranoid: by P.K. Page, from *Poems Selected and New*, 1974, House of Anansi Press Limited, Toronto.

Yoke and Star: by Jose Marti & The Street: by Octavio Paz, translated by Willis Knapp Jones, from *Spanish-American Literature in Translation. A Selection of Poetry, Fiction and Drama since 1888*, edited by Willis Knapp Jones. Copyright (c) 1963 by Frederick Ungar Publishing Co., Inc.

Minotaur: by Michael Ayrton, *A Chamber of Horrors*, ed. John Hadfield, published by Studio Vista Ltd., Highgate Hill, London.

In a Dark Time: by Theodore Roethke, form *Collected Poems* by Theodore Roethke. Copyright (c) 1960 by Beatrice Roethke administratrix of the Estate of Theodore Roethke. Reprinted by permission of Doubleday & Co., Inc.

Anti-Christ as a Child: Reprinted by permission of the author and his agent, Sybil Hutchinson.

The Tale of the Sands, When the Waters Were Changed: from *Tales of the Dervishes* by Idries Shah. Reprinted by permission of the author and Jonathan Cape Ltd., London.

The Trap: from *The Apple Barrel: Selected Poems 1956-1963* by John Stallworthy. Reprinted by permission of the author and Oxford University Press.

The Shell: by James Stephens, from *Collected Poems*. Copyright 1916 by Macmillan Publishing Co., Inc. Renewed 1944 by James Stephens.

Tattoo: by Wallace Stevens. Copyright 1923 and renewed 1951 by Wallace Stevens. Reprinted from *The Collected Poems of Wallace Stevens*, by permission of Alfred A. Knopf, Inc.

Not Ideas About the Thing but the Thing Itself: by Wallace Stevens. Copyright 1954 by Wallace Stevens. Reprinted from *The Collected Poems of Wallace Stevens* by permission of Alfred A. Knopf, Inc.

Reality is an Activity of the Most August Imagination: from *Opus Posthumous* by Wallace Stevens. Copyright (c) 1957 by Elsie Stevens and Holly Stevens. Reprinted by permission of Alfred A. Knopf, Inc.

Connoisseur of Chaos: copyright 1942 and renewed 1970 by Holly Stevens. Reprinted from *The Collected Poems of Wallace Stevens* by permission of Alfred A. Knopf, Inc.

Applelore: by Judy Stonehill, appeared in Analecta Magazine, (Winter 1968)

Noise: reprinted from *Eight Fantasms and Magics* by Jack Vance. Copyright Jack Vance. Reprinted by permission of the author and his agents, Scott Meredith Literary Agency, 845 Third Avenue, New York, N.Y. 10022.

The Door: from *The Second Tree From the Corner* by E.B. White. Copyright 1939 by E.B. White. Originally appeared in *The New Yorker* and reprinted by permission of Harper & Row, Publishers, Inc.

The Man Who Loved the Faioli: from *The Doors of His Face, The Lamps of His Mouth* by Roger Zelazny, published by Doubleday & Company.

The Second Coming: by William Butler Yeats. Reprinted with permission of Macmillan Publishing Co., Inc. from *Collected Poems*. Copyright 1924 by Macmillan Publishing Co., Inc. Renewed 1952 by Bertha Georgie Yeats.

The Funnel of God: by Robert Bloch. Copyright 1959 by Ziff-Davis Publishing Co. Reprinted by arrangement with Universal-Award House, Inc.

The Hounds of Tindalos: by Frank Belknap Long. Reprinted by permission of Arkham House Publishers, Inc.

Within The Pyramid: by R. de Witt Miller, from *Famous Science Fiction Stories: Adventures in Time and Space*, edited by Raymond J. Healy and J. Francis McComas, Random House 1946.

The Weed of Time: by Norman Spinrad, from *No Direction Home*, Pocket Books 1975.

The Doors of Perception: by Aldous Huxley. Copyright 1954 by Aldous Huxley. Reprinted by kind permission of Harper & Row, Puplishers, Inc.

The Fear: by Andrew Young, from *Complete Poems*, by Andrew Young, edited by Leonard Clark, published by Martin Secker & Warburg Limited, London. Reprinted by permission of Martin Secker & Warburg.

A Recognition: by Mark Rudman. First appeared in Harper's Magazine, January 1970, Vol. 240, No. 1436.

The Heavy Bear Who Goes With Me: by Delmore Schwartz, from *Selected Poems: Summer Knowledge*. Copyright 1938 by New Directions Publishing Corporation. Reprinted by permission of New Directions Publishing Corporation, New York.